NIGHT
ROUNDS

Also by Helene Tursten

Detective Inspector Huss
The Torso
The Glass Devil
The Golden Calf

NIGHT
ROUNDS

HELENE
TURSTEN

Translation by Laura A. Wideburg

Originally published, in Swedish, as *Nattrond*, in 1999.

Copyright © 1999 by Helene Tursten
English translation copyright © 2012 by Laura A. Wideburg

Published in agreement with H. Samuelsson-Tursten AB, Sunne,
and Leonhardt & Hoier Literary Agency, Copenhagen

First English translation published in 2012 by
Soho Press
853 Broadway
New York, NY 10003

Library of Congress Cataloging-in-Publication Data

Tursten, Helene, 1954–
[Nattrond. English]
Night rounds / Helene Tursten ; [translation by Laura A. Wideburg].
p. cm.
ISBN 978-1-61695-208-2
eISBN 978-1-61695-007-1
1. Women detectives—Sweden—Fiction. 2. Nurses—Crimes
against—Fiction. 3. Murder—Investigation—Sweden—Fiction. I.
Wideburg, Laura A. II. Title.
PT9876.3.U55N3813 2012
839.73'8—dc23
2011034073

Printed in the United States of America

10 9 8 7 6 5 4 3 2 1

NIGHT
ROUNDS

"YOU'RE ABSOLUTELY CERTAIN this was the nurse you saw last night?" Superintendent Sven Andersson frowned down at the thin woman sitting at the desk. Her lips were pressed tight shut, and she'd shrunk back into her loose-knit poncho.

"Yes, I am!"

With a resigned sigh, the superintendent turned back into the hallway. Holding a yellowed black-and-white photograph between his right thumb and index finger, he paced the room, pausing deliberately before each window. Finally he stopped in front of a particular one, checking the view against the photo. The foggy gray February morning had softened the edges of everything outside, but he could tell that the photo had been taken from this very spot.

A newly planted birch was barely visible on the left-hand side of the photo. As he peered through the transom window, he found himself looking directly into the crown of a full-grown tree.

He walked ponderously back to the woman at her desk. He hesitated, then loudly cleared his throat. "Well, Nurse Siv, you can certainly understand my difficulty here."

Her ash-gray face turned toward him. "It was that nurse I saw."

"Oh, for . . . !" He swallowed the curse. "The woman in this photo has been dead for fifty years!"

"I know. But it was her!"

Chapter 1

THE NIGHT NURSE, Siv Persson, had just stepped into the hallway when the lights went out. The street lamps outside spread a weak glow through the tall windows, but not enough to light up the hall. It appeared that only the hospital had lost power.

The nurse stopped short and spoke aloud into the darkness. "My flashlight!"

Hesitantly, she returned to the nurses' station. With help from the streetlamps, she fumbled for the desk chair and sank down into it. She jumped, startled, when the respirator alarm went off in the small intensive-care unit. The sound was dampened by the solid double doors that isolated the unit, but the alarm still pierced the silence.

From her station she cast a practiced glance along the hallway and screamed. A dark shadow loomed in the door.

"It's only me," came the doctor's exasperated voice. Nurse Persson jumped up from her chair. Without another word, the doctor rushed down the hallway to the ICU; the nurse followed him, using his fluttering white coat like a beacon in the dark.

Inside the ICU the sound was deafening.

"Marianne! Turn off the alarm!" the doctor shouted.

There was no answer from the ICU nurse who was supposed to be on duty.

"Siv. Find a flashlight."

Nurse Siv said weakly, "I . . . forgot my flashlight when I was here helping Marianne turn Mr. Peterzén. It must be underneath the examination cart."

"Go get it!"

She fumbled her way back toward the door. Her fingers rooted around in the darkness until they knocked against a hard plastic case. She pulled the case out and headed back in the direction of the doctor.

"Where are you?" she asked.

His hand on her arm made her jump. He grabbed the case from her.

"What's this? The emergency kit? How can we use that when we can't see?"

"Look inside. The bag-valve mask and a laryngoscope are in there," she answered. "The laryngoscope is powered up, and you can use its light."

The doctor muttered to himself as he opened the case. After some searching he found the lamp for guiding a breathing tube into the pharynx of anesthetized or unconscious patients. He clicked it open and shone the narrow beam of bright light toward the old man lying in the bed.

Now that they could orient themselves, Nurse Siv stepped toward the respirator by the bed and shut off the alarm. The silence echoed in their heads. They heard the sound of their own breathing.

"His heart's stopped. Where is Marianne? Marianne!" the doctor shouted. He placed the ventilator mask over the patient's nose and mouth. "Take care of his breathing while I do CPR," he hissed through tight lips.

Siv began to pump air into the unmoving lungs. The doctor pressed down on the man's breastbone, his palms rhythmically trying to stimulate the silent heart. They did not speak while they worked. The doctor took a minute to inject epinephrine directly into the heart muscle. It was no use. The heart would not resume beating. Finally they were forced to give up.

"It didn't work, damn it. Where is Marianne? And why hasn't the backup generator turned on?"

When the doctor flashed the light of the laryngoscope around the room, Nurse Siv glimpsed the examination cart. She stepped carefully toward it, her arm out stiffly, hip high. She moved her right hand along the top of the cart, over the examination instruments and plastic gloves. Finally she found the barrel of her flashlight and turned it on.

The beam of light struck the doctor right between the eyes, and he threw up his hands with a muffled curse.

"Uh . . . sorry," Siv stammered. "I didn't realize where you were."

"Okay, okay. I'm just glad you found a working flashlight. Check out the floor. See if she's here. Maybe she's fainted."

But the ICU nurse was not to be found anywhere in the small ICU.

The beam of the flashlight caught a phone, and the doctor strode to it and lifted the receiver. "Dead as a doornail." After thinking a moment, he said, "My cell phone is in the on-call apartment. Let me take the flashlight up there to call emergency services. Then I'll start searching for Marianne. You didn't see her go past your station, did you?"

"No. I haven't seen her since eleven this evening, when we were in here turning Mr. Peterzén."

"So she must have gone out the back door. I'll go that way to the on-call apartment and walk upstairs through the operating rooms. That's the closest."

The doctor swung the beam toward the door. Beyond it were the stairs and the elevator to surgery, one floor up. One floor down, on the ground floor, were the polyclinic and physical therapy rooms; one floor below that was the basement, where the X-ray suite, employee changing rooms, and building machinery were located. The hospital was a large area to search, but Surgical Chief of Medicine Dr. Löwander was the person who knew its layout the best.

Nurse Siv was left alone in the dark. Her legs trembled slightly as she made her way back down the hall to the nurses' station. Out of habit she glanced through the ward door's window. A bone-white moon augmented the mild glow from the street lamps outside. In the cold light from the windows, she could see a woman moving in the stairwell, her back to the nurses' station. The woman's white collar glowed against the dark fabric of her calf-length dress. Her blond hair was pinned back severely, and above it she wore a starched nurse's cap.

Chapter 2

DR. SVERKER LÖWANDER paused on the other side of the ICU door. He let the beam of his flashlight play over the stairwell. Nothing. Rapidly, he climbed the stairs to the top floor and stopped again up there to shine his beam around the landing outside surgery. Everything appeared normal. Two rolling beds were parked next to the closet to his left. He went to the elevator shaft and shone his light through the window. As he aimed the beam down, he could see the top of the elevator just below him. He pulled out his key chain, which jingled as he searched for the master key.

Beyond the door to surgery, everything was still. The smell of disinfectant stung his nose. The doctor made a quick pass through the two anterooms and decided that all was as it should be.

He hurried through the surgery ward and opened the door to the other, somewhat smaller, stairwell. At the administration offices on the other side of the stairs, Dr. Löwander tested the doors to the house mother's station, the doctors' assistants' offices, and his own office. He felt relief to find them all locked. The last door in the hallway belonged to the on-call apartment.

He rushed inside, snatched his cell phone from his briefcase, and tapped 112, his hands shaking slightly. The emergency-services operator promised to send a police car as soon as possible. They would also contact the emergency electric service but made no promises about when an electrician could get there.

Dr. Löwander held the flashlight in his teeth to search through the phone book, which, luckily, was on his desktop. He flipped through the Bengtssons of Göteborg until he got to Folke Bengtsson, security guard, Solrosgatan 45. He had to describe the situation first to the newly awakened Mrs. Bengtsson and then again to Folke Bengtsson himself. Folke promised to jump into his car right away. As Dr. Löwander pressed end, he found he was covered in sweat. He took a few deep breaths before heading back out into the hallway and down the steps as quickly as he dared. He slowed as he got to the ward and carefully opened the door to the darkened room.

Nurse Siv was sitting on the floor outside the nurses' station, crying softly. She'd wrapped her arms tightly across her body, and she was rocking back and forth. When she saw the doctor, she began to wail.

"I saw her! I saw her!"

"Who?" the doctor asked, more sharply than he'd intended.

"The ghost! Nurse Tekla!"

Confused, Dr Löwander gaped at the nurse, who continued rocking and shut her eyes against the bright glare of the flashlight. Tears ran down her face. He pondered what to do. Finally he said, "Here. Take the flashlight. Sit here at the station. I'll come back with the police. We'll find out what's at the bottom of all this."

He helped the shaking woman to her feet, pushed the flashlight into her hand, and led her back to the nurses' station and to her desk. Unresisting, she let him push her into her chair.

Now that the moonlight was stronger, Dr. Löwander was able to find his way much more easily down the stairs to the ground floor. Once he reached the foyer, he had to slow his pace. The darkness among the pillars of the art nouveau arches was impenetrable. As he got to the main door, a chill went down his spine. He was certain that someone was watching him. He felt as if a person were standing amid the pillars observing his every move. His fingers fumbled with the key. He almost yelled with relief as the heavy door swung open. The chill of the night swept across his sweaty forehead, and he took a deep breath.

"I'VE SEARCHED THE entire upper floor, and there's no trace of Marianne." Dr. Löwander filled the police in, trying to speed their search for the nurse. "She's not on the middle floor either. That's where the care wards and ICU are located. Probably she's here on the ground floor or even in the basement. If she hasn't gone outside into the park, that is."

Security guard Bengtsson had brought his own flashlight. Dr. Löwander had already sent him to the basement to check on what had happened with the electricity and the backup generator.

The three policemen had brought strong flashlights as well. The oldest, who had introduced himself as Sergeant Kent Karlsson, swung the beam of his around the large, dark foyer. Dr. Löwander felt slightly irritated with himself; there was clearly no one hiding among the pillars.

"If you loan us your keys, Jonsson and I could make a round through this floor and—"

"Hey there! Help! I found her!"

A call from the basement interrupted the sergeant. They could see the wavering glow of his flashlight before the full beam blinded them and obscured the guard. Nevertheless, his excited words were clear: "I've found Nurse Marianne!"

"Where?" Dr. Löwander asked sharply.

"In the main electrical room. I believe . . . I believe she's . . . dead." Bengtsson's voice was failing, and the word "dead" was nothing more than a hoarse whisper echoing among the pillars.

"Show us where you found her," Sergeant Karlsson ordered.

• • •

HER BODY WAS stretched facedown across the backup generator. The men standing in the doorway could just see the backs of her legs and her rear, encased in long pants. Her head and arms were out of sight over the other side. Dr. Löwander registered that she was missing a shoe. He walked around the generator, bent down, and dutifully checked the pulse at her neck, but he could feel that the chill of death had already set in. Her thick, dark braid brushed the floor. A sharp bluish red mark ran across her throat.

"She's dead," he said quietly.

Sergeant Karlsson took charge. "We're leaving the room now. Do not touch anything. I have to call for reinforcements."

Dr. Löwander nodded and obediently left with the others. "We've got to get back to Nurse Siv. She's all alone," he said.

Sergeant Karlsson looked at him with surprise. "Night nurses are used to being alone."

"True enough, but not under these circumstances. She's in shock."

"Why?"

"She believes she saw a ghost." Dr. Löwander said this lightly, hoping that the police would not pay too much attention to it. He quickly turned to Bengtsson and said, "Come with me. Let's check on Siv."

He took Bengtsson's flashlight and led the way to the stairs. Folke Bengtsson followed him with relief.

AT SEVEN O'CLOCK, Superintendent Sven Andersson and Detective Inspector Irene Huss arrived at Löwander Hospital.

The investigators climbed out of their blue Volvo, which the superintendent had parked by the main entrance. They paused for a moment and looked up at the impressive building. The hospital was built of brownish red brick. The entrance led to a grand stairway right at the center of the structure. The main entrance was covered with stucco decorations. Two carved marble Greek gods kept watch on each side.

They pushed open the heavy door. Detective Fredrik Stridh · was sitting in a chair by the entrance, waiting for them. They knew he was not sitting to rest tired legs but was taking the opportunity to write up his notes. When he saw them, he leaped to his feet and came to meet them.

"Good morning," Superintendent Andersson said to his youngest detective.

"Morning, sir!" Stridh eagerly launched into his report. "The crime scene was secured by the patrol, and the technicians were already hard at work when I arrived at three-thirty A.M. Malm is here from Forensics, and he says it appears the girl was strangled."

The superintendent nodded. "Why weren't you here before three-thirty?" he asked.

"I'd swung by Hammarkullen to look at a guy who flew out of a ninth-floor window just before midnight. There were quite a few people in the apartment, and the party was still going strong. Either they'd all worked together to throw him out or he'd decided to jump on his own. We'll have to see what the chief forensics officer has to say. Speak of the devil, here she comes now."

They looked out the thick panes of the window as a white Ford Escort shot in through the gate and stopped sideways behind the superintendent's car. The driver-side door opened, and flaming red hair popped up over the roof.

"Yvonne Stridner!" moaned Superintendent Andersson.

Criminal Inspector Irene Huss was irritated by the tone of her boss's voice, but she hoped he'd control his temper long enough to profit from Stridner's invaluable information. Stridner was incredibly capable, according to many people working in the department, and Irene agreed with them. The superintendent was probably thinking along the same lines, since he lumbered forward and held the door open for Professor Yvonne Stridner. She nodded condescendingly.

"Good morning, Andersson. I see that the Violent Crime Division has put in an appearance."

The superintendent mumbled that this was indeed the case.

"Where's the body?" Professor Stridner wondered aloud in her typical businesslike tone.

Fredrik Stridh showed them the way down the stairs to the basement.

"THE VICTIM HAS been identified as Marianne Svärd. A nurse. Twenty-eight years old. Just below medium height, slim build. Lying on her stomach across a motor . . . rather, the hospital's backup generator. Her clothes are in order. Missing a shoe from her right foot. Judging by rigor mortis, she has been dead approximately six hours, probably slightly longer. Livor mortis on the body parts closest to the ground corroborates this. I am measuring the body temperature now at the scene. The room temperature according to a thermometer on the wall is nineteen degrees Celsius."

Yvonne Stridner turned off her tiny pocket recorder and began to examine the corpse. Police technician Svante Malm was careful to stay out of her way. Superintendent Andersson pulled his two inspectors out into the hall and whispered, "While Stridner sucks all the oxygen out of the room, what have you learned so far?"

He looked at Fredrik Stridh, who took his notebook from his pocket, licked his thumb, and began to flip through the pages. "The alarm came in at twelve forty-seven A.M. Dr. Sverker Löwander called from his cell phone to report that Löwander Hospital had a power failure. The backup generator also did not start. At the same time, a nurse had gone missing. The patrol arrived at one-ten A.M., the same time as security guard Folke Bengtsson. Dr. Löwander met them at the entrance. Since Bengtsson had a flashlight, Dr. Löwander asked him to go and check what was wrong with the backup generator. The guard was the one who found the body in the room where the main electrical-distribution panel and the backup generator are located."

Fredrik Stridh had to stop and take a breath at that point. The superintendent quickly put in a question. "What was wrong with the lights? They're working fine now." He gestured at the fluorescent ceiling fixtures.

"Bengtsson took a look at the panel and saw that the main circuit breaker had been disconnected. All he had to do was reset it."

"And what about the backup generator?"

"Someone had cut all the cables to and from the unit. Not a chance that it would work."

Andersson's eyebrows rose to his nonexistent hairline. "Anything else of interest?"

"The victim's shoe was found in the elevator. By me. A hefty sandal. Scholl brand."

"The victim. What do you know about her?"

"Dr. Löwander identified her as Marianne Svärd. One of the night nurses employed at Löwander Hospital."

"So you've talked to the doctor."

"Yes. It appears he was spending the night at the hospital to keep an eye on a patient who was on a respirator. An elderly man, who'd been operated on earlier that day. By the way, the patient died while the power was out."

The chief inspector took a quick, deep, audible breath. "So another person died, too?"

Detective Stridh lost his train of thought and said, slightly confused, "Yes . . . well . . . the respirator stopped working. He couldn't breathe. He was in the ICU. Dr. Löwander and the old nurse who was making night rounds on that ward tried to revive him. But they couldn't. It was then they realized that the victim—Nurse Marianne—had gone missing."

Irene Huss looked thoughtfully at her colleague. "It seems that she was not at her station right before the power outage," she pointed out.

Fredrik Stridh shrugged. "So it seems."

Superintendent Andersson looked grim. "So. We have two people who died here at the hospital last night."

"What did the other nurse have to say?" wondered Irene.

Fredrik Stridh snorted. "When I arrived, she appeared calm, but as soon as I started to question her about last night, she began to wail. By the way, her name's Siv Persson. She insists that she saw a ghost walking through the hospital and that that's who murdered Nurse Marianne. She even went to find an old photograph from some cupboard or other to show me."

Fredrik Stridh was interrupted by the pathologist, who came out into the hallway. "You can move her now. The technician is almost finished," Stridner said. Svante Malm was taping broad strips onto Marianne Svärd's body to prevent anything important from falling off it as well as protect it from any outside contamination.

The pathologist glanced sharply at Andersson, who'd unknowingly hunched his shoulders in defense. "An extraordinary case, Andersson," she said. "That's why I wanted to be here at the crime scene myself. Sometimes it reveals a great deal."

"So what does this crime scene show you? How did Marianne Svärd die?" Irene hurried to ask.

Yvonne Stridner looked at Irene with surprise, as if she'd just now noticed that she and the superintendent were not alone in the basement hallway. She raised her eyebrows slightly before she replied.

"She was strangled by a noose, and probably not in the room in which she was found. The traces of dirt on her heels indicate that she was dragged here. It appears that the murderer just opened the door and threw her inside, which is why she landed on the generator. She died sometime around midnight."

The hallway was quiet as the police officers digested the information. Finally Irene asked, "Is the noose still around her throat?"

"No, but it's left a deep mark. The murderer has strong arms. Now I must head off to the pathology lab. I'll do an autopsy after lunch."

Yvonne Stridner swept up the stairs, leaving behind her the scent of her perfume and the sound of her high heels clicking. Irene wondered what her boss would say if she informed him that Yvonne's perfume was named Joy.

The police trio were lost in their thoughts until Andersson broke the silence.

"Marianne Svärd apparently was murdered during the night, and there were only two people on the night shift in the entire hospital: Dr. Löwander and that nurse . . . Siv Persson. Am I right, Fredrik?"

"Yes, but they were not alone. There were six patients who'd been admitted into the care ward, not to mention the old guy on the respirator."

"Irene and I will have a little chat with the doctor and Nurse Siv. Fredrik, go back to the station and get two or three people to canvass the neighborhood. Have them interview the other patients, too. Then go home and go to bed."

"But I'm not tired!"

"Don't backtalk. The directive coming down from the powers-that-be stipulates no expensive overtime."

The inspector waved his finger under Stridh's nose. Stridh loped away without a reply.

• • •

DR. SVERKER LÖWANDER looked worn to the bone. Lack of sleep carved deep lines around his eyes. He seemed to have no shirt on beneath his doctor's coat, and the coat itself had been buttoned wrong. He had sunk deep into his armchair, his eyes closed, the small muscles on his face twitching sporadically. Superintendent Andersson and Inspector Huss stood quietly in the doorway watching until the superintendent cleared his throat loudly. The doctor startled and opened his eyes. He quickly ran his fingers through his thick hair, but it hardly made a difference in his appearance.

"Excuse me if I woke you up. Let me introduce myself. I am Superintendent Sven Andersson, and this is Detective Inspector Irene Huss.

"Yes, of course . . . What time is it?"

"Quarter past eight."

"Thanks. I have my first patient in fifteen minutes."

"Will you be up to performing surgery this morning?"

"I have to be. The patients come first. Thank God there's nothing major today."

"But after a night like this?"

Sverker Löwander gave him a tired look as he rubbed one of his eyes. "I have to. We don't have many people on staff right now. And the patients can't wait. They don't seem to understand there could be anything else going on in their doctors' lives."

The two officers contemplated Löwander for a moment in silence. Finally the superintendent pulled a notebook from his jacket pocket and began to pat the other pockets fruitlessly. Sverker Löwander understood and handed him his own pen from his jacket pocket. In gold lettering the pen advertised, LÖWANDER HOSPITAL YOU'RE IN SAFE HANDS.

"Are you able to answer some questions for us?"

"Sure, as long as you're quick about it. Or we could schedule an appointment for this afternoon, when I'm not so short on time. Why don't you come back at four-thirty?"

"All right, but let me ask one short question right now: Why aren't you wearing anything underneath your coat?"

Sverker Löwander started and stared down at his misbuttoned doctor's coat. "Thanks for pointing that out. I'd forgotten. I'll have to put something on before I leave." He moved as if to get up from the armchair but then sank back down again. He continued, "Yesterday I took a shower and went to lie down in bed to read. It was a tough day, with several difficult operations. Not to mention the complications that set in with Nils Peterzén. Just as I was about to turn off the light, the power went out. My first thought was for the respirator. I wasn't really worried, though, because Marianne Svärd is . . . was an extremely competent ICU nurse."

He stopped speaking for a moment and sighed. The superintendent had the chance to slip in another question. "Were you lying down with your clothes on?"

"No. I was intending to sleep for a little bit. Peterzén's condition was stable. . . . Where was I? Yes, the power went out. I stayed put, waiting for the backup generator to kick in, but it didn't. When I heard the respirator alarm, I threw on my pants and coat as I rushed out. The rest of the night was just as hectic. I haven't had the chance to think about how I look."

Now Löwander did get up from the armchair and knelt to look under the furniture. He found a T-shirt beneath the bed. "Sorry. I've got to run. Come back at four-thirty and we can talk more."

The doctor held the door open for the police officers.

IRENE DECIDED TO plant herself on a wooden chair just inside the door to listen to the superintendent's first round of questioning the night nurse Siv Persson.

"Nurse Siv, you must understand our difficulties believing that a ghost was the murderer," Andersson began carefully.

Siv Persson pursed her mouth but did not answer. The

superintendent spent a moment considering the photograph that Siv Persson still held in her hand.

"Would you be so kind as to describe this ghost?" he continued.

"You and I are probably the same age, so don't be so polite," Nurse Siv snapped.

"Fine." He looked down at the old picture again. "Did she look the same as she does in this photo?"

"Yes, she looked exactly like this."

The photograph had been taken from overhead and from a distance. The superintendent remembered the window he'd checked not that long ago. Farthest to the right side, there was a black car. A tall, muscular man was opening the door to the passenger's seat for a much shorter woman. She was holding her hat in the gusty wind so that her coat sleeve blocked her face. The man's light-colored coat was fluttering, and the tiny birch sapling's branches were bending to the left.

Between the tree and the people next to the car stood a nurse. She was in profile. In spite of the camera angle, it was easy to see that she was tall. The lens was sharply focused on her. She wore a nurse's uniform: white hat with a curly brim and black ribbon, white collar, white cuffs, calf-length black dress, and black shoes with stout heels. It was apparent that she had blond hair, which had been pinned up under her hat. She carried a suitcase in each hand.

Slowly, the chief inspector turned over the photo and read the caption written in black ink. The handwriting was elegant but gave only the date: May 2, 1946.

"Where did you find this picture?" Andersson asked.

"It's always been here in the ward. Nurse Gertrud showed it to me."

"Is Nurse Gertrud still working here?"

"No, she died last year. She was exactly ninety years old." Nurse Siv looked directly into the superintendent's face, with eyes that seemed unnaturally large behind the thick lenses of her old-fashioned glasses. She hesitated before she continued. "Nurse Gertrud came here in 1946, in the fall. She took Nurse Tekla's place as the head nurse of the ward and house mother. Gertrud never met Tekla in person. She only met her, so to speak, after she died."

Siv Persson reached for the photograph, and Andersson let her take it. Nurse Siv contemplated the picture for a moment. "Of course, Gertrud had heard a great many rumors concerning her. Nurse Tekla was an extremely fashionable woman." Nurse Siv fell silent. When she picked up her story again, she seemed even more troubled.

"Now, I've only heard this thirdhand, but . . . they say there'd been a love affair between Nurse Tekla and Dr. Löwander."

Superintendent Andersson stirred suddenly. "Wait a minute! I've just met Löwander. He wasn't even born when Nurse Tekla worked here!"

Nurse Siv snorted. "Of course not! I'm talking about the old Dr. Löwander, Hilding Löwander. Sverker Löwander's father."

Naturally. Irene knew that Superintendent Andersson was probably feeling just as sheepish as he looked. The hospital had been named Löwander Hospital after the deceased doctor.

"Apparently his wife found out about the affair and demanded that Tekla be fired. The hospital belonged to the family of Mrs. Löwander, after all. She'd inherited it from her father."

"So Sverker Löwander's mother was wealthy?"

"Yes."

"Tell me about his father . . . Hilding?"

"I remember Hilding Löwander very well. He was a doctor from the old school. No one dared talk back to him. He performed surgery until he was seventy-five years old."

"What happened to Nurse Tekla?"

"Gertrud told me all about this love affair. Nurse Tekla had just turned thirty, and he was twenty years her senior. What's remarkable is that, according to rumor, Mrs. Löwander didn't mind at first. All three of them even went on vacation together. According to Gertrud, this photograph was taken secretly as they left for one such vacation."

Andersson took the photo back and peered at it with renewed interest while Siv Persson continued.

"The Löwanders had been married for many years when Mrs. Löwander unexpectedly became pregnant. She'd already turned forty. It was then she decided that Nurse Tekla had to go. Somehow Nurse Tekla found a job in Stockholm and moved there early in the fall of 1946. No one heard anything from her until March 1947. It turned out she was found in the attic of this building at that time. She'd committed suicide. Hanged herself."

The room was quiet. Irene realized that the superintendent had no idea how to interpret Nurse Siv's story. She looked as if she truly believed she'd seen the long-dead Nurse Tekla during the night. In order to break the silence, Irene asked, "How did you find this photograph?"

"Gertrud found it. The old medicine cabinets were going to be discarded, and she and a colleague were supposed to clean out all the expired medicine. She found the picture stuffed behind an extra shelf at the bottom of one cabinet. They had no idea what to do with it, so they put it back when the renovation was over. It became one of the nurses' secrets. The picture has been there all these years, and every new nurse gets to see it when she starts working here. Naturally, everybody has heard of the hospital ghost. And whenever it's discussed, we take out this old photo."

"Why? To prove that the stories are true?"

"The stories are absolutely true! Nurse Gertrud was the person who cut Tekla down. She'd been hanging in the attic for a few days before someone noticed the smell."

"And you really believe she haunts this place?"

"Lots of folks have seen her over the years," Siv protested. "I've heard her before, but I've never seen her. Until last night."

She glanced at the superintendent, and Irene hurried to ask, "What do you mean when you said you heard her?"

Nurse Siv answered slowly. "Sometimes there are rustling noises by the sinks in the disinfection room, even though nobody is there. Sometimes you hear her skirts swish in the hallway. Once I felt an ice-cold breeze pass right next to me. Most people here avoid this hallway between midnight and one in the morning."

"What about you? What do you do at that hour?"

"We usually go to my office and have a cup of coffee and something to eat."

"You and the ICU nurse?"

"That's right."

"Are you the only two people working here at that time?"

"Yes, we are."

"But after twelve A.M. you could be joined by Nurse Tekla, you say?"

"Between twelve and one. She never appears after one."

Andersson said, "So she's a classic ghost who observes the witching hour. In that case what happens during the summer when it's still light? Does she come between one and two then?"

Nurse Siv realized he was making fun of her and clamped her mouth shut.

To steer the interview in another direction, Irene asked, "How long had Marianne Svärd worked at this hospital?"

At first it seemed that Nurse Siv would not answer, but after a moment she blew her nose with a tissue she'd been holding in her hand and said, "Just about two years."

"What did you think of her?"

Nurse Siv took her time answering. "She was extremely

good at her job. She was able to deal with all these new machines. I'm not, but I'm going to retire soon. "

"How was she as a person?"

"She was sweet and pleasant. Helpful."

"Did you two get to know each other well?"

The nurse shook her head. "No, but she was easy to talk to. Just when we got on something personal, like family and such, she didn't share anything."

"Was she married?"

"No, divorced."

"Did she have children?"

"No."

Irene couldn't think of any more questions. The tiny gray nurse appeared to sink deeper into her poncho, her face tired and stressed. Even the chief inspector noticed this and started to feel sympathy.

"Shall I ask someone to drive you home?" he asked in his friendliest voice.

"No, thanks. I live just around the corner."

Chapter 3

IT BECAME CLEAR to Irene Huss rather quickly that none of the hospital patients could have committed any crime. All four of the female patients had been awakened by the respirator alarm. Woozy from pain and sleep medications, they'd fallen asleep again right away. Two of the women had bandaged chests. The other two had large bandages wrapped around their heads; small, see-through corrugated plastic tubes full of blood threaded through their dressings.

The two male patients had not awakened at all that night.

The day nurse, Ellen Karlsson, was a steady, friendly middle-aged woman. Her salt-and-pepper hair was cut into a pageboy, with bangs over her brown eyes. "How horrible. Poor little Marianne . . . unbelievable. Who in the world would ever want to kill her?" she exclaimed, holding back tears.

Irene Huss was ready to cut in with a question. "That's exactly what we're trying to figure out. Do you have any idea who might have done it?"

"None at all. She always seemed so pleasant, though I can't say I knew her really well, since we're on different shifts. I'm on days, and she worked nights. And of course we're in different departments. Maybe you could ask Anna-Karin. She's the ICU nurse on the day shift. They know . . . they knew each other a bit better."

The two women stood up and left the office together. Irene was struck by how quiet the hospital hallway was, unlike any hospital she'd ever been in. She asked, "Why are there so few patients here?"

"Today most operations are done at the polyclinic. Mostly to save on expenses. This hospital is completely private, as you know. When I started working here twenty-three years ago, we had two care wards and four surgeons. In those days the wards and the ICU were always full, and we worked through the weekends as well. Nowadays the hospital is closed on the weekends, and there are just two nurses on the day shift and two at night to cover both the ward and the ICU. Even the staff in surgery and receiving is down to half the previous number."

"Why so many layoffs?" Irene asked, surprised.

"To save money. We do the complicated surgeries at the beginning of the week. Wednesdays and Thursdays we just do polyclinic operations. On Fridays we run only the reception desk and follow-up visits."

"How many patients can you handle at a time?"

"Twenty in the ward and two in the ICU, with ten of the beds dedicated to day patients. The ward closest to ICU is a recovery ward for the polyclinic patients."

"So the patients wake up there and rest a few hours before they're sent home?"

"Exactly."

"What do you do if something comes up and the patient can't go home before the weekend?"

"We have an agreement with one of the private hospitals downtown. Källberg Hospital. We send our patients there if we have to."

"So Löwander Hospital is never open during the weekends?"

"That's correct."

They'd reached the large double doors between the departments. Nurse Ellen pulled one door open, and they went into the next area.

Two beds flanked the minimal reception desk. In one lay the body of Mr. Peterzén. On the nightstand next to it, a candle had been lit, and its flame smoothed a gentle light across his peaceful face. His hands were crossed over his chest, and his jaw had been closed with an elastic bandage. A middle-aged woman was looking down at him, and she jumped when Irene and Nurse Ellen came in.

"Please excuse us for disturbing you," Nurse Ellen apologized. "We were just looking for Nurse Anna-Karin."

"She'll be back in a moment. She had some paperwork she needed to finish." It was obvious the woman had been crying, but she appeared composed.

"My sympathies. Let me introduce myself. I'm Inspector Irene Huss from the police."

"Inspector?" The woman started. "Criminal inspector? Why are you here?"

"Are you aware of what happened last night here in the hospital?"

The woman's expression was filled with shock. "Something connected to Nils's death?"

It was clear she had not been told anything about the interruption of electric service or the ICU nurse's murder. All the details would be splashed across the evening papers anyway, so Irene Huss continued. "I'm sorry, but the fact that Nils Peterzén died is a direct result of these events. May I ask you for your name?

"Doris Peterzén. Nils is my husband." Only a slight tremble in her voice betrayed her feelings.

Irene observed this self-possessed woman. She and Doris were about the same height, slightly less than six feet, unusually tall. She was around fifty and was dressed very fashionably. She was definitely beautiful even with no makeup and after much crying. Her hair was a discreet platinum, probably the work of a skillful stylist, and it surrounded a perfectly formed face without a wrinkle or blemish. She had grayish blue eyes and dark lashes. Irene vaguely recognized her face but couldn't place it. She wore a blue coat with a black fur collar and a matching fur hat.

"Your husband was put on a respirator yesterday after his operation," Irene began.

"I know. Dr. Löwander called and told me himself. Nils was aware that might happen. He'd quit smoking ten years ago, but after the fifty years before. . . . His lungs. . . . We. . . . Dr. Löwander believed that he'd survive the operation. It was absolutely necessary, because the arterial hernia was large."

"How old was your husband?"

"Eighty-three."

Doris Peterzén returned to the foot of the bed where her husband lay. She bowed her head and began to weep softly again.

At that moment the door burst open and a young nurse, her face flushed red with hurry, rushed in. A shock of short blond hair stood up on her head.

"Have they come yet?" she asked Nurse Ellen in an agitated voice.

A frown appeared on the older nurse's brow. "No," she answered severely.

Irene wondered who "they" might be, but her unasked question was answered immediately as two men in matching black suits came through the doorway right behind the blond nurse. They pushed a gurney between them, a dark gray bag with a zipper draped over the top.

Nurse Ellen said softly to Doris Peterzén, "The men from the funeral home are here."

When Doris caught sight of the men, her weeping intensified. Nurse Ellen put an arm around her and led her out through the double doors. She was probably taking the recent widow into her office, Irene thought, but she stayed put to talk further with the young ICU nurse.

Nils Peterzén's body was lifted onto the bag spread over the rolling table and zipped into it, and the men disappeared again through the doors as quickly as they'd come.

Irene walked over to one of the two windows in the ICU unit overlooking the large park and parking lot. She rested her forehead on the cool windowpane and watched as the gurney was rolled out through the back entrance toward the funeral home's dark gray station wagon. The entire process took less than a blink of the eye, a journey no one would have noticed.

Irene decided to look through the same door the undertakers had just used. The red exit box over it was brightly lit. The door itself was heavy and steel-coated, with automatic door openers on each side. Irene could see that this area was part of a later addition to the hospital. Here there were no fancy art nouveau embellishments. The stairs were wide and made from common stone. An ordinary iron handrail was fastened to one of the cream-colored walls. The stairway curved around an elevator shaft whose gray metal door was marked bed elevator in black letters.

Irene closed the door again. Nurse Anna-Karin, whose flushed cheeks had had no time to fade, was frenetically stripping the bed Nils Peterzén's body had occupied only three minutes earlier. She started to stuff the bedclothes into a laundry bag.

Irene cleared her throat. "Anna-Karin, do you have a moment?" she asked. "I need to talk to you. My name is Irene Huss. I'm a criminal inspector, and this is about the murder of your colleague, Marianne Svärd."

The nurse stiffened and whirled around to face Irene. "I don't have time. The first polys are coming soon."

"Polys? What's that?"

"Oh, the patients from the polyclinic who've just had their operations. Today two colons and one gastro. And later today a rhino. It's crazy to do a rhino on a day like this."

Irene puzzled through the jargon. The young nurse was stressed and scattered. Not so strange considering that her colleague had been murdered the night before. Probably a bit of shock as well. Irene went to the nurse and put a hand on her shoulder.

"I still have to talk to you for a moment. For Marianne's sake," she said calmly.

Nurse Anna-Karin stood still, and her shoulders dropped. She nodded in resignation. "All right. Let's go sit down at the registration desk."

At the desk Anna-Karin gestured for Irene to take the chair while she herself sat on the stainless-steel stool.

Irene began, "I know that your first name is Anna-Karin. Could you please tell me your last name and your age?"

"My whole name is Anna-Karin Arvidsson. I'm twenty-five."

"How long have you worked at Löwander Hospital?"

"About a year and a half."

"So you're about as old as Marianne and you've been here about the same length of time. Did you hang out together after work?"

Anna-Karin looked surprised. "Not at all."

"Never?"

"No. Well, once we went out dancing. Marianne, Linda, and me."

"When was this?"

"About a year ago."

"And you never were out together with her again?"

"No, except for the holiday party. The entire staff is invited to a Christmas smorgasbord right before we close for the holidays."

"Did you know Marianne well?"

"No."

"What did you think of her?"

"Nice. A little shy."

"Do you know anything about her personal life?"

The nurse needed a moment to think. "Not much. I knew she was divorced. They separated right before she started working here."

"Do you know anything about her ex-husband?"

"No. Except he's a lawyer."

"Did she have children?"

"No."

"Where did she work before she came to Löwander Hospital?"

"Östra Hospital. Also in their ICU."

"Do you know why she changed jobs after her divorce?"

Anna-Karin thought about this. She dragged her fingers through her blond stubble a number of times. "She never said, but I got the feeling she was trying to stay away from some guy."

"Who?"

"No idea. But that one time when we all went out dancing, we met at my place first for a bite to eat and a little wine. I asked Marianne why she'd quit her job at Östra, and she said, 'I couldn't stand meeting him every day and pretending there was nothing wrong.' But she didn't want to talk about it any longer."

"Did Marianne spend more time with Linda?"

"No. Linda and I hang out together all the time."

"Does Linda also work ICU?"

"No, she's in the care ward."

"But not right now."

"No, Ellen works here for the morning shift."

"Do you know when Linda will be coming in to work?"

"She starts the evening shift, at two o'clock."

They were interrupted when the steel-plated door opened and a rolling bed with a still-slightly-groggy patient was wheeled in. An operating-room nurse wearing a green uniform, a paper cap, and a mask said mechanically, "First colon. The gastro will be here soon."

Nurse Anna-Karin flew from the stool. Both nurses flipped busily through the paperwork, mumbling to each other over the drowsy patient.

Irene decided it was time to find Nurse Ellen and Doris Peterzén.

IRENE FOUND THE recent widow in the empty nurses' office. Doris Peterzén sat ramrod straight, her fingers laced in her lap. She'd taken off her hat and placed it on the desk but kept on her elegant coat. Irene paused in the doorway for a moment, considering whether she should question Doris Peterzén now or wait awhile. Perhaps it was too soon. On the other hand, Irene felt that Doris had the right to know about the events of the night before.

The widow turned her beautiful face toward Irene and said tiredly, "Nurse Ellen had to release a patient or something like that. She'll be right back."

"That's good. I have to speak with her, but you need to know what happened here at the hospital last night."

Irene tried to be tactful, but when Doris Peterzén heard about the murder, she lost her composure and began to cry. Irene did not know how to comfort her. She got up to close the door in order not to disturb the other patients and then sat down next to the weeping woman. Tentatively, she rested her hand on Doris's shoulder. It didn't seem to help.

When Nurse Ellen returned to the office, she took only one glance at Doris and said, "She needs a taxi home. I'll call for one."

Irene nodded. She bent closer to Doris and asked, "Should I contact your family? Anyone in particular? Your children?"

Doris could hardly speak but managed to say, "Gör— Göran. He's . . . not home. London . . . He's in London."

Chapter 4

FOR THE REST of the morning, the police interviewed the day-shift staff, one by one. Then there was a break for the officers to grab a quick lunch. It wouldn't be until two o'clock in the afternoon when the evening shift arrived.

Superintendent Andersson and Irene found a pizza place on Virginsgatan. They sat at a tiny table at the back, grateful that they didn't have to eat their pizza and near beer in the car. In low voices they went over what they'd gotten from that morning's work. Obviously Nurse Siv's tale of a ghost nurse was more than odd. Irene had no idea whom or what the nurse had actually seen, but she hypothesized that the "ghost" had really been the murderer. Perhaps, in the old nurse's frightened state and overactive imagination, the figure she'd seen had been coupled with the ghost story. That seemed the most likely.

Irene's boss nodded and grunted, his mouth full. He attacked his pizza vigorously, snapping the flimsy plastic fork in half. He turned around to ask the pizza baker behind the counter for another and realized that the man had been leaning over the counter and listening, enthralled, to their conversation. The superintendent swallowed his rage and his opinions of eavesdroppers. It had been his own fault; the pizza parlor was much too small for this type of discussion. "Let's go!" Andersson barked, his face flaming red as he stared into the pizza baker's friendly smile. But he stopped halfway in his march out to turn back and snatch up the rest of his pizza.

• • •

THEY DROVE TO Härlanda Lake. Irene hoped that a dose of fresh air would clear their thoughts and a nice walk would settle the pizza in their stomachs.

They parked the car and walked into a nature scene covered with ice crystals. Irene stomped on the rock-hard ground. "This cold snap gives us a big problem. It was thirty below last night. The ground around the hospital is frozen solid and won't leave any footprints or traces. And there's no snow either."

"True. I wonder if Malm has found anything inside the building. He's due in tomorrow morning at roll call."

"Perhaps Stridner will find something in the autopsy this afternoon."

Andersson's face darkened reflexively. He was unaware, as always, that this happened whenever Yvonne Stridner's name was mentioned.

"I'll call her. No rest for the wicked." He sighed.

They walked in silence along the perimeter of the iced-over lake. A weak sun managed to get a few meager rays through the thin clouds, sending a cascade of glitter across the icy surface. The chill bit at their noses and cheeks. Irene took a deep breath. For a moment she imagined that the crisp, sharp air she drew into her lungs was totally pure and clean, like the air near her parents-in-laws' summer cabin deep in the forests of Värmland. But she was jolted away from her daydream by the superintendent's voice.

"Time to go back. The evening shift will be in soon."

THE EVENING SHIFT worked the care ward and the ICU only until nine-thirty, when the night shift took over.

"Will Siv Persson be working tonight?" the superintendent asked.

"No," Nurse Ellen said. "Before she went home today, she asked for time off. We've found a substitute. But it looks like there's no one to take over from me." Her voice was tired and worried.

"What about Linda?" asked Irene.

"Yes, she was supposed to come in at two. Now it's almost two-thirty. I've just called her place, but no one's picking up."

"What's Linda's last name?"

"Svensson."

"Does she have a family?"

"She lives with a guy, but he doesn't seem to be home. I just hope there hasn't been some kind of accident. Linda always bikes to work."

"Even at thirty below?"

"Oh, yes."

"I see. I guess we will just have to wait until she comes in. We can probably talk to the nurse on duty at the ICU for now," Irene suggested to her boss.

"You go do that," was the chief inspector's immediate reply. "I'll wait for Linda here. And I also want another chat with Nurse Ellen. If that's all right with you, Nurse Ellen?"

"Well . . . sure. It'll be no trouble at all if Linda shows up. But right now I'm the only one on the care ward and there's a lot to do."

"Are there any other doctors at this hospital, or is Löwander the only one?"

Nurse Ellen had stood up to unlock the medicine cabinet. She drew some fluid into a syringe and tapped it with her fingernail to clear the air bubbles. "We have an internist at the polyclinic who serves also as a consultant on more complicated surgery," she answered. Then there's a consulting X-ray specialist as well as a full-time anesthesiologist. You know, the doctor who puts you under before an operation. His name is Konrad Henriksson. And of course we have Dr. Bünzler, who is our plastic surgeon. He's very good."

"Isn't Dr. Löwander a plastic surgeon?"

Nurse Ellen looked at the superintendent with her bright brown eyes. Irene noticed that her boss began to blush.

"No, he's a general surgeon. But since there is less call for general surgery, he's started to do some minor plastic procedures as well." Nurse Ellen held the needle up to the light to inspect for any remaining air bubbles.

Masking a grin, Irene followed up, "So he doesn't do rhinoplasty?"

Nurse Ellen glanced at Irene. She said with a slight smile, "No. If you'll excuse me?"

The nurse swept out of the room brandishing the syringe. The chief inspector frowned. "What the hell? Rhino what?"

"Rhinoplasty," Irene said.

"What's that?"

"Something that should not be done on a day like this," recited Irene in a singsong voice. "According to Anna-Karin at the ICU."

Andersson took a deep breath. "And weren't you supposed to be there already?"

Irene gave a flip salute. "Aye-aye! But there's one more thing first."

She went to the bookshelf mounted on brackets above the desk. She'd seen the title Medical Terminology in faded gold letters on a green linen spine. She pulled down the book and searched under rh. "Aha! Rhinoplasty is a nose job!" She shut the book with a bang, turned on her heel, and marched through the office door.

Sighing, the superintendent looked at his watch, which showed 2:47. Nurse Linda was long overdue.

THE ICU WAS chaotic. Nurse Anna-Karin was arguing with someone on the phone. "If there's no more O-positive, you have to send O-negative! The patient is hemorrhaging! Last hemo was eighty-three!"

Her cheeks were bright red from urgency. Her short hair stuck out in all directions. The fact that she kept running her fingers through it wasn't helping.

"All right, then! Send it by taxi!"

The receiver banged down. Irene could hear Anna-Karin's quick breaths. The nurse lifted her head and spied Irene. She jerked up her palm and said, "Stop! We don't have time for questions! The rhino's turned into an emergency!"

Irene glanced at the same bed where Nils Peterzén's body had rested a short time before. A man in green scrubs and a middle-aged nurse were bent over the patient who now occupied the bed. Irene assumed that the man in scrubs was a doctor, but he wasn't Dr. Löwander. Irene walked to Anna-Karin and said in a low voice, "Linda hasn't come in for her evening shift. Do you know where she might be?"

It took a second for Anna-Karin to realize the implication of the inspector's words. She showed real surprise. "She's not here?"

"No. And there's no answer at her place."

The nurse's surprise turned to worry. "That's strange! Linda's never late. Maybe she had a bike accident? Maybe she's hurt?"

"We don't know, but we'll have to find out. Do you know where we can find her partner?"

Anne-Karin stiffened and pressed her lips together. What a perfect witness, Irene thought. This girl can't hide anything. Since it looked like she wasn't going to answer, Irene pressed on more firmly. "It would save time if you tell us now. We'll find out anyway. And after what happened here last night, it looks strange that you're not helping us."

The nurse shrugged. "They broke up. He moved out last Saturday."

"They separated?"

"Yep."

Irene felt a real sense of worry regarding the nurse's whereabouts. It had hardly been twenty-four hours since her colleague had been murdered.

"What's the guy's name, and where does he live now?"

"Pontus . . . Pontus Olofsson. I have no idea where he's living now. I haven't had a chance to talk to Linda much since they broke up."

"Anna-Karin! More cyclosporine! Same dose!"

The doctor's command cut their conversation short. Anna-Karin hurried to the medicine cabinet. At the same moment, the older nurse looked up from the bed and ordered, Call surgery and have them send Bünzler down here at once!

Now was not the time to question Anna-Karin further, Irene realized. She'd have to come back later.

OUT ON THE floor, there was palpable worry in the air. Nurse Ellen spoke for everyone: "I wouldn't normally be worried, but after last night . . . and Linda's never late to work. There must be some explanation for all this!"

She's right, Irene thought. We have to find Linda Svensson. "Where does Linda live?" she asked.

"Let me think. . . . Kärralundsgatan. The building number is in the department address book."

The nurse pulled open the top drawer of the desk. She shuffled through a few papers until she found a black address book, paged through it, and then wrote down an address on a slip of paper. "Are you going right over? I mean, maybe she's sick or something."

Irene nodded.

Superintendent Andersson cleared his throat. "Yes, you go check on her. I'll remain here in case she shows up. And all emergency rooms should be contacted." He looked at the nurse.

Nurse Ellen smiled gently at the superintendent. "Then I

hope that you can make those calls yourself. I have a mountain of extra paperwork."

Before Andersson had a chance to reply, Nurse Ellen whisked out the door. Irene grinned slyly as she, too, waved good-bye and headed off.

Chapter 5

IRENE HEARD THE doorbell echo through the apartment, but no one came to the door. She hadn't expected that anyone would. She bent down and looked through the mail slot. Her eyes met another pair of eyes, turquoise blue and wide open. She heard a sharp intake of breath and jumped back as the lid of the mail slot banged shut.

Meeeow . . . hiss, came from behind the closed door.

Irene giggled quietly. She looked around to make sure that no one on the floor had witnessed her smooth move. The public wouldn't understand a police officer having a heart attack during a confrontation with a Siamese cat.

But the cat gave her an idea. There were two more doors on the ground floor of the apartment building. No one answered when she rang the bell on the door to the right. Undeterred, Irene rang the bell to the door on the left. The nameplate on it said R. BERG. Irene could hear a rustling sound on the other side before the brittle voice of an old woman called, "Who is it?"

Irene did her best to sound friendly. "I'm Inspector Irene Huss from the police." She held her ID to the door's peephole. Apparently the elderly lady inside was convinced, because Irene heard the rattling sound of a safety chain being pulled back and then the thud of a dead bolt. The door opened an inch. Irene leaned forward and tried to appear harmless.

"Good afternoon, Mrs. Berg—"

"Miss. Miss Berg."

"Excuse me. Miss Berg. We've received a call at the station about a cat howling incessantly in the apartment next door."

The door opened, and Irene could get a better view of the apartment's inhabitant. There wasn't much to see. The elderly lady was less than five feet tall. Her scanty white hair was pulled together at the back into what looked like a rat's tail. She was bent and so thin that she seemed almost transparent. Her frail hand with its blue veins quivered on the door handle, a movement that traveled through her entire body.

"It wasn't me that called. But I've certainly heard that cat. It's been going on since early this morning. Doesn't bother me, though. I hardly ever sleep these days."

The elderly woman's voice was surprisingly steady and clear, but she seemed barely able to stand. Irene felt she had to hurry her questions. "What about its owner? Have you seen or heard her?"

"No. Miss Svensson is a nurse at Löwander Hospital, and I never know what her hours are," the old lady said.

"I see. When was she home last?"

The wrinkles on the small face puckered in thought. Then she smiled, such a large smile that her dentures slipped.

"Last night." Miss Berg paused for a minute to suck her teeth back into place. "She was home late last night. She always plays her music too loud. I've argued with them. The young man has just moved out, but I used to argue with him, too. We have a rule. After ten they're supposed to turn down the music. They usually keep to the agreement."

"Did Linda do that last night?"

"Yes, two minutes past ten, she turned the music down. Then she turned it off and left."

"When was that?"

"About eleven-thirty."

Irene felt worry harden in her chest, but she worked to hide it so she wouldn't upset the old woman. "Does Linda usually go out so late?"

"Sometimes she goes out with Belker."

"Who's Belker?"

"The cat."

Of course the cat.

"She takes him out in a little harness," Miss Berg explained.

"Did she return very late last night?"

"Come to think of it, I didn't hear her come home at all. The first thing she does when she comes through the door is to turn on the music, no matter what time it is. Sometimes the TV, too. At the same time." Miss Berg snorted to emphasize her opinion about this noise pollution.

Irene thought about her own fourteen-year-old twin girls. She said nothing at all.

The old woman continued. "I haven't heard any more music or anything else coming from there since she went out last night. And I didn't hear her arrive home. I usually do."

Irene didn't doubt that for a minute. She was certain that something was wrong. "So nothing at all from next door."

"No. Just the cat meowing and meowing. He's probably hungry. Poor thing."

Irene tactfully explained the situation to the old woman. "It's a little worrying that Linda has not come home. I'll have a locksmith pay a visit. We need to get inside and see to poor . . . Belker."

Miss Berg nodded with enthusiasm. "You do that. Belker is a wonderful cat. He's one of a kind, like all Siamese."

"I'll phone right away for the locksmith," Irene said pleasantly as she tapped in the numbers for the emergency dispatcher.

"Dispatch. Detective Rolandsson."

"Hi, Inspector Irene Huss here. We've gotten a complaint from a neighbor that a cat has been howling all day. The owner hasn't been seen since late last night, and she also has not shown up at work today. I need to get in to check on her. Can you send a locksmith?"

"All right. Who is making the complaint?"

Irene took her phone away from her ear and whispered to Miss Berg.

"What's your first name?"

"Ruth," Miss Berg said hesitantly.

"Ruth Berg," Irene spoke into the phone. She gave Rolandsson the address and clicked off.

"But I didn't make a complaint!" Ruth Berg looked somewhat resentful.

"I know. It's just procedure. Now everything will go faster. For Belker's sake," Irene added.

The old woman's face softened at the mention of the cat's name. "I see. Something must have happened, but don't ask me to go on any witness stand."

Irene reassured her that that would be highly unlikely. She jerked her thumb toward the door of Linda Svensson's other neighbor. "Who lives there?"

"Nobody," Ruth Berg sniffed. "Not right now. An old man lived there until he couldn't take care of himself any longer. Finally, right after Christmas, they had to put him in a nursing home. He got filthy. Did his business anywhere he pleased, not in a toilet like normal people. Now they'll have to renovate the whole place before they can rent it out again."

Irene was reluctant to ask her next question. "Miss Berg, may I have your age, please?"

At first it seemed as if Ruth Berg did not intend to answer. Eventually, though, she shrugged and sighed. "Ninety-one next month. But no one's coming here to celebrate it. I live all alone. Everyone else has passed on. Sometimes I believe that our Lord has forgotten me." Miss Berg fell silent. Then she said, "I really can't stand up and answer questions any longer. If you need anything else, please ring the bell again."

Miss Berg closed her door. Irene could hear the rattling of the chain and then the thud of the bolt.

WHILE SHE WAITED for the locksmith, Irene called Löwander Hospital to check in with the superintendent. Linda Svensson still had not shown up at work. She also had not been admitted to any emergency room, Chief Inspector Andersson reassured Irene, mentioning that he'd placed those calls himself. The fact that Linda hadn't been seen since last night worried him also.

"Please don't tell me that another nurse has become a victim!" he said.

THE LOCKSMITH ARRIVED and easily unlocked the door, letting Irene inside. She carefully shut the door behind her so Belker couldn't get out, then switched on the ceiling lamp in the small entry hall. The cat was nowhere to be seen. He'd obviously gone into hiding. On the right there was a tiny bathroom, directly ahead a small kitchen, and to the left of the kitchen was the entrance to a large living room with a sleeping alcove. All the rooms were tidy. The furniture was mostly from IKEA, and splashy movie and theater posters had been framed and hung on the walls. The whole impression was functional, youthful, and pleasant.

There was no trace of Linda. Irene called the chief inspector again to let him know. His only response was a deep sigh.

Irene found the litter box next to the shower stall, and it reeked. She had no idea how to take care of a cat, since she'd owned only dogs, but she expected that the sand in the box had to be changed and the cat was certain to need some food.

Resolutely, Irene searched the kitchen cabinets until she found cans of cat food. She washed the two ceramic bowls she saw on the floor and filled one with water and the other with the food. Now only the guest of honor had to be found.

"Here, kitty, kitty, kitty. Food! Belker! Come and get your food!" she called.

Her dog would have responded immediately. Before she'd finished the final syllable, Sammie would be standing right next to his bowl. The area rugs in the hallway would be scrunched together like the bellows of an accordion after his sprint to the kitchen.

Apparently cats didn't work like dogs. Or perhaps Siamese cats didn't let themselves be commanded. Belker did not show up. Irene decided to search the apartment, both for Belker and for any clues to Linda's disappearance.

She searched the kitchen thoroughly. Either Linda Svensson was anorexic or she never ate at home. All Irene found was one almost-finished bag of muesli, one unopened pack of yogurt, and one tube of Kalles caviar. There were spices, half a pound of coffee, and a few tea bags on the shelf above the stove. The freezer held one opened package of fish sticks. On the other hand, she found four more cans of cat food. At least Belker's needs were seen to, even though he didn't seem to have the sense to come when he was served.

The tiny bathroom also held no secrets. Neither were there clues in the hall closet. In the large living room, Irene searched through the bookshelf and then the neat pine desk by the window. She sat down on the swivel chair in front of the desk and systematically went through the contents of its one drawer.

The layout of the desk drawer showed that Linda was highly organized. The tidy piles of bills, postcards, letters, and bank forms had nothing in common with Irene's own administrative system, which was "deal with the one on top first." At the bottom of the drawer, Irene found a new passport in the name of Linda Sophia Svensson.

None of the papers gave any clues to Linda's whereabouts. Suddenly Irene realized why. There were no address books or telephone lists—not even a pocket calendar. She searched the room again and found none of these things. Nor were there any keys, nor a wallet. Nor Belker.

Irene's toes struck something. When she bent down to look under the desk, she saw an old yellow caller ID box with deep claw marks in the plastic. A gray cord had been disconnected from the telephone. Obviously the caller ID box had become a plaything for a bored Belker. Irene reconnected the ID box to the phone, but it was obvious that the device was completely dead, probably broken when it fell.

Nothing else to see here. Probably time to quit. Irene turned off the light in the room and went into the hallway. As she reached up to turn off that light, she wondered where Belker had gone to hide. A second later a tiger bolt flew from the hat rack onto her head. Belker hissed with fury, and with all the strength he possessed, the Siamese cat dug his claws right in under her chin. It hurt like hell. Irene instinctively grabbed his front leg, but then a burning pain shot through her right ear as Belker buried his teeth in it.

"OH, MY DEAR. This is really not a pretty sight."

Nurse Ellen shook her head sympathetically as she continued to clean the wound in Irene's ear. Irene's right arm was sore after a tetanus shot, but she hardly noticed that compared to the pain in her ear and under her chin.

Dr. Löwander walked into the room and put on his professional cheerfulness. "This will heal without a scar. You'll need some antibiotics, but it's too late to fill the prescription at a pharmacy. We'll start you out with a few pills from our medicine cabinet."

He sank down at the desk and pulled out a prescription pad from the desk drawer. Before he began to write, he rubbed his eyes and smiled sleepily at Irene.

"I've been up thirty-six hours, and I'm still in shock over

what happened to Marianne. And now Linda can't be found
. . . . I'm tired to death."

Irene noticed that Dr. Löwander was in fact a very attractive
man, despite the weariness etched into deep lines around his
eyes and mouth, and despite the few silver streaks in the hair by
his temples and forehead. As always, unfair, Irene thought.
Women go gray, men become distinguished. She made a mental
note to call her hairdresser for a color and cut.

Dr. Löwander wrote some scrawls on the prescription pad
and ripped off the page. With that same sleepy smile, he
handed the prescription to Irene. His eyes were bloodshot from
fatigue, but their green still shimmered.

Impulsively, Irene said, "Let me give you a lift home. I've
got to get home, too, and if I stayed here, I wouldn't be a very
good advertisement for Löwander Hospital." She gestured at
her head, covered with bandages. Her protruding right ear was
especially comical, packed into a compress carefully taped in
place.

"Don't worry. It will heal just fine. And yes, I'd be glad to
have a ride home," he replied.

Superintendent Andersson rolled into the door just as
Sverker Löwander was rising to leave.

"Time to go home?" he asked.

Löwander nodded in response. Before he walked out the
door, he turned back to Irene and said, "Could you wait just a
minute? I need to change."

The chief inspector raised an eyebrow meaningfully once
Löwander had left. "So? You're going out with the doctor?"

Why did she find herself blushing? Irene sat up straight and
hoped some of the redness in her face was covered by the bandages. "I thought I could chat with him on the drive home.
He's the head doctor here, after all, and he must know a lot
about his staff."

Andersson agreed. "I interviewed him this afternoon. He says he didn't know Marianne Svärd very well. Partly because she worked the night shift, partly because she wasn't the chatty type. Pleasant and extremely professional about her work. And that's all he'd say about her. On the other hand, he seemed very worried about Linda Svensson. Understandable, after the murder. He told me that Linda was a happy person and good at her job. Of course, he knows her better since she works the day shift. But to be honest with you, something tells me that Marianne's murder and Linda's disappearance are not related. The murder happened at the hospital. Linda was off duty then and now has disappeared from her home. We need to find the boyfriend. I called Birgitta Moberg and told her to flush him out."

Andersson sank onto the desk chair, which groaned under his weight. He stared at Nurse Ellen's back as she sorted pills into small red plastic holders.

"Excuse me," Irene said politely.

Nurse Ellen turned and nodded.

"I've seen different nurses at this hospital all day, and I was struck by one thing. The nurses here are either very young or over fifty. Where are all the thirty- and forty-year-old ones?"

Nurse Ellen sighed deeply. "They were all laid off in the late eighties. The hospital closed an entire ward. Only we were left, but we were younger then."

"How did Marianne Svärd, Linda Svensson, and Anna-Karin in ICU get their jobs?" Irene wondered.

"Three old nurses retired within six months of one another, so Marianne, Linda, and Anna-Karin were hired around the same time."

"Are there more nurses retiring soon?"

"This year there will be three: Siv Persson, Greta at reception, and Margot Bergman in ICU."

"I've already talked to both Margot Bergman and Greta— let me see . . . what was her last name?"

"Norén," Ellen informed her.

"Right! Thanks. Neither of them seemed to know Marianne and Linda all that well. Nurse Margot thought that Marianne was a hardworking, pleasant person. And that was it."

Ellen Karlsson gave Irene a long look before she said, "That seems reasonable. They're pretty different in age. They wouldn't be meeting each other on their off hours. Just at work."

So Anna-Karin was the only other person who'd socialized with Marianne and Linda. Irene still felt that the murder and the disappearance were connected, even though her boss had a different opinion. She decided that she needed to keep a good eye on Anna-Karin. Although the young woman appeared flighty, maybe she knew more than she realized about the events of the last twenty-four hours. Or maybe there wasn't a logical connection? So far there was no evidence that Linda Svensson had even been the victim of a crime, and Irene hoped with all her heart that she would turn up okay.

IRENE HAD TO give up her hopes of getting more information from Sverker Löwander during the drive home. First of all, he'd fallen asleep the instant he reclined the seat back. Second, he only lived two kilometers from the hospital, on Drakenbergsgatan.

As Irene swung into the driveway in front of Löwander's home, she almost collided with a dark BMW backing out of the garage. It was one of the larger, newer models. Both drivers slammed on the brakes. The BMW's door flew open, and a woman jumped out before the car had come to a complete stop. In three strides she'd reached Irene's car.

"What the hell are you doing, pulling in to my driveway like that!" she yelled.

Sverker Löwander had been jarred awake. As the woman bent over to get a good look at Irene, who was already rolling down her window, his tired voice stopped them both.

"This is Inspector Huss. She was kind enough to drive me

home after this hell of a day. I didn't notice you offering to pick me up."

Irene was startled at how quickly the woman's face softened from twisted with rage to great beauty. It happened so fast that Irene wondered if she'd imagined the whole thing.

This woman seemed slightly shorter than Irene. She had thick blond hair, cut slightly above her shoulders. In the light from the garage, Irene could see that she was deeply tanned. Since it was just the middle of February, Irene wondered if she had a private tanning bed.

"You know I can never pick you up on a Tuesday. My job ends at five, and my aerobics class starts at six-thirty. Why didn't you just drive the Mazda home?"

Her voice was now pleasant but still had a slightly hard, metallic undertone. Irene wondered if she was hearing things. Perhaps she was just projecting her feelings onto a younger and more beautiful woman.

Löwander sighed. "I walked to work yesterday morning." He heaved his weary body out of the car and walked through the open garage door. Irene heard a door open and close. She got out of her Volvo and reached out to shake hands.

"My name is Inspector Irene Huss."

The woman's hand was cool and her handshake surprisingly strong. "Carina Löwander."

"Did you hear about what happened at the hospital?"

"Yes, Sverker called me from work this morning. But there was no time to talk."

Carina Löwander looked at her wristwatch, cupped glass with a metallic blue face. She was making an obvious point. "Excuse me, but my class begins in fifteen minutes. And I'm the trainer," she said with a smile.

She turned in her high heels and adjusted her fur coat before sliding gracefully into the BMW. The only thing Irene could do was get into her own car. She knew she didn't have the same air, not with her scuffed boots, worn leather coat, and rusty Volvo. And a head covered in bandages. No competition with fur coats and tanned skin.

IRENE'S FAMILY HAD plenty of comments to make when she got home.

"What did you do to yourself?" her daughter Katarina exclaimed.

"Just because you were at a hospital, that doesn't mean you had to go under the knife," said Krister.

One of Krister's jokes! Irene was in no mood, and she answered shortly, "Never get a cat."

Their dog, Sammie, rushed up and reassured Irene of his undying devotion. As she reached down to pet his soft, wheat-colored fur, he sniffed at the bandages on her face. Dinner was late this evening, since both Irene and Krister had been working, Katarina had jujitsu after school, and Jenny had been at guitar lessons until six-thirty. It felt cozy having everyone together for once, a rarity. Irene twirled a strand of spaghetti on her fork. She'd had to choose her words carefully, explaining the day's events to her family. She noticed that Jenny hadn't taken any of the meat sauce for the spaghetti. Since the serving dish was next to Irene's elbow, she passed the sauce to Jenny. Her daughter stared at the brownish red sauce with its delicious tomato aroma and shook her head.

"I've given up meat," she said.

"You're giving up meat? Why?" Irene asked.

"I am not going to eat dead animals. They have the same right to life as we do. Farming animals is pure and simple torture."

"And so that's why you haven't been drinking milk lately?"

"That's right."

"But milk is not meat."

"A cow's milk is for her calf, not for humans."

Krister's voice shook as he exclaimed, "What kind of idiocy is this? Have you turned into one of those crazy vegetarians?"

Jenny looked him straight in the eye. "Yes."

Silence fell over the dinner table. Katarina broke it by complaining, "She says I shouldn't wear my new boots."

"They're leather! There are boots made with fabric that are warmer and better."

"And this morning she said I shouldn't put honey in my tea."

"No, you shouldn't. The honey belongs to the bees."

The two girls stared at each other furiously. Krister's face had darkened. He had trained as a chef and was a master of a number of foreign cuisines. In a deceptively soft voice, he asked, "So what do you intend to eat?"

"There's lots of good food that doesn't come from murdered and oppressed animals. Potatoes, carrots, fruit and berries, nuts and peas—and there's even fat made from vegetables."

Jenny spoke by rote, as if she'd memorized a list of acceptable foods. She probably had. Where did all this come from?

The family dinner had taken an alarming turn. Krister was a peaceful and pleasant person, but his great passion in life, both professionally and personally, was food. His love showed in his growing girth. Could this be considered an occupational hazard? Irene thought tenderly, He'll be fifty in a few years. He should probably start watching his weight. She herself hated cooking and was glad to leave it all to him.

Krister's voice was tough and short as he said, "In that case you can start cooking your own rabbit food. The rest of us will continue to eat as we always have."

Silence settled over the dinner table once again.

Chapter 6

"TIME TO CHANGE your razor blade."

"Did you really need a face lift?"

"Wow, that cat sure did a number on you."

Witticisms rained down on Irene and her bandaged ear, but she was used to her colleagues' bantering. She knew that this was a sign of everyone's jitters right before the start of an investigation, especially one as complicated as this seemed to be. The jokes eased the tension everyone felt.

Six detectives, the superintendent, and the forensics technician, Svante Malm, were crowded around the conference table, Irene saw. The chief inspector appeared worn out and tired next to Fredrik Stridh, whose entire body pulsed with energy. Of course, Stridh was the youngest of them all, but that wasn't the only explanation. Inwardly, Irene heaved a deep sigh. Energetic and alert officers were certainly good, but murder was not solved by youthful enthusiasm alone. Boring routines, inspections and repeated inspections, interrogations and even more interrogations were required. Mind-numbing work. And after all that, just maybe you'd manage to put the puzzle together.

Birgitta Moberg was the only other female detective in the group. Last year she and Fredrik Stridh had had a romantic fling, until Birgitta went to Australia for two months and Fredrik had to stay behind. He'd been grumpy and depressed for weeks before he got back to his normal self. *His new girl's name is Sandra, isn't it?* Irene thought.

Birgitta was a beautiful woman. She had blond hair and glittering brown eyes. She seemed younger than her true age of thirty.

Detective Jonny Blom had joined the department a few years before Irene. He was married and had four children. His coarse jokes and sharp-tongued comments got on her nerves sometimes, but she had to give him credit for being an exceptionally good officer. He was, above all, a talented and keen interrogator.

Tommy Persson sat next to Irene. He was not just her closest colleague but also her best friend. The others on the team had been suspicious of their closeness at first, but now they were used to it. Irene and Tommy had gone to the police academy together and had been good friends since the day they met.

Finally Irene looked at the detective who'd been in their department the longest, Hans Borg, fifty-four years old. Hans was actually a few years younger than the superintendent, but in experience the superintendent was still wet behind the ears compared to Borg. Borg had even managed to put together his own personal safety net. He'd taken early retirement and then finagled a way back onto the job with both pension and wages.

Andersson began. "We're all here, so let's get started. First I'll review yesterday's events."

He went through the details surrounding the night-shift nurse's murder. Both the power outage at the hospital and the sabotaged reserve generator seemed to be part of the murderer's plan. On the other hand, Nurse Siv Persson's report of the ghost nurse, Tekla, was incredibly odd.

"She must have seen something, right? Or was she hallucinating?" Fredrik Stridh asked.

Andersson nodded. "She must have seen something, yes. But the real question is, what did she see? Or who?"

Jonny Blom snorted. "Just a scaredy-cat nurse afraid of the dark. A waste of time."

"Would you say the same thing if an old man had reported it?" Birgitta Moberg snapped.

Jonny Blom pretended he hadn't heard her.

Tommy Persson cleared his throat before he gave his opinion. "I believe she did see something. I believe she saw the person who sabotaged the reserve generator and murdered Marianne Svärd."

Irene nodded her agreement. "The entire hospital was in the dark. Nurse Siv was certainly shaken by the death of Nils Peterzén, the patient, and by the fact that Marianne was gone. She certainly saw someone, and I wonder if that person was the murderer."

Andersson looked at Irene thoughtfully before he replied. "It's true that she was scared, but she insists she saw the figure quite distinctly. The sky was clear, and the moon was almost full, enough to illuminate the person. According to Nurse Siv, it was a woman wearing an old-fashioned nurse's uniform: a long, black dress and a white cap."

There was a silence, and then Jonny exclaimed, "Don't tell me we have to go on a ghost hunt, too."

Andersson gave him an irritated glance. "No, but we have to ask what it is we're really hunting for." He turned to Malm and asked hopefully, "Any ideas?"

"Not much, except you should look for a murderer with an inside knowledge of the property and a key, too," Malm answered.

"A key?" Andersson repeated.

"Neither the outer nor the inner doors had any broken locks or even any damage. The entrance door is locked at five P.M. The back door is kept locked at all times."

"Someone could have come in prior to five P.M. and hidden. In the basement, perhaps?" Irene asked.

"Theoretically, yes. However, there are people manning the phones and the reception desk all day, and they are there until the doors are locked at five P.M."

Andersson sighed. "Keys and locking times are always tricky. At least this limits the number of suspects."

A few of the detectives nodded.

Malm continued his summary. "One of Marianne Svärd's shoes was found in the elevator, which makes it likely she'd been brought to the basement that way. The murderer wore rubber gloves powdered with talcum. Svärd's stockings were black at the heels, and she had white talc on her lower arms. This indicates she was dragged. She was probably already dead when she was taken into the elevator."

"To open the electrical room's door, the murderer must have had to set her down, right?" Birgitta asked.

"That's correct. And that door is always locked."

"Once the murderer opened the door, he must have pulled Marianne upright and heaved her into the room. The murderer didn't care that she landed on the reserve generator. The main thing for him was that her body was hidden," Birgitta stated.

"Just a minute," Irene objected. "That won't work. If he'd wanted to hide the body, he wouldn't have cut the power first. The electrical room would be the first place to go to see what was wrong."

Svante Malm nodded his agreement. "There was no attempt to hide the body. Sabotaging the reserve generator was part of the plan. All of its cables were sliced, which was done before the power went out."

"How do you know that?" Fredrik asked.

"When the power went out, the reserve generator would have kicked in from the drop in voltage. But its cables were already cut, so it couldn't function."

Tommy Persson thought out loud. "So it's one hundred percent sure that Marianne Svärd was murdered before the power was lost. After all, she was dragged into the elevator. It couldn't work without power. And the murderer wouldn't have been able to see very well in the basement or in the electrical room."

"That's clear," Malm replied. "We haven't found the wire cutters the murderer used to cut the cords to the reserve generator, but it must have been a big johnny."

"What about the noose that strangled her?" asked Andersson.

"It's still missing."

"I called Stridner yesterday evening, but she hadn't finished the autopsy. We're supposed to receive her report right before lunch today. I'll try to swing by the pathology lab. It's easier to just go there than wait by the phone in case she graces us with a call."

"That woman must be going through menopause," Jonny said with feeling.

Andersson did not reprove Jonny, but he did mumble something about how Stridner was a good pathologist nevertheless.

Malm cleared his throat loudly to get their attention back. "We vacuumed Marianne's clothes yesterday. With our naked eyes we could see dark strands of fiber on the back of her smock, and we've begun to examine them more closely. So far they appear to be finely spun wool."

"Lord help us! We're back to the ghost," Irene said. "The ghost was wearing a black nurse's dress."

"How do we know that the dress was made of wool?" Birgitta pointed out. "Not to mention the fact that the color might have been dark blue or dark gray or dark green. It's hard to tell colors apart in the moonlight."

"Ghosts wear transparent clothes," Jonny said sarcastically.

Andersson's face was starting to flush. "Exactly! Listen to yourselves. Police officers don't run off and hunt for ghosts, because ghosts do not exist. We hunt for live murderers. This one definitely had a physical body that could murder a nurse and snip power cables. Put the whole hospital in the dark. Ghosts don't do that kind of stuff. How do I know? They don't exist. And if they did exist, they probably wouldn't bother with the sorts of things that the murderer did at Löwander Hospital."

The superintendent had to stop for breath. No one dared point out that his last sentence made no sense. He was right, but Nurse Siv Persson's testimony, whatever she'd seen, was still one small fact to fit into the puzzle.

Malm returned to his subject. "We found one more odd thing on Marianne's smock." He held up an item in a plastic bag for all to see. In it was a thick day planner, one of the popular brands. "This isn't Marianne's day planner. Written on the inside cover is the name Linda Svensson."

Surprised silence greeted his announcement.

"Why in the world would Linda Svensson's day planner be in Marianne's pocket?" exclaimed Irene.

No one had a reasonable answer. Irene felt an icy shiver down the back of her neck. This was not a good sign, definitely not a good sign.

Since no one had any more ideas about the murder, Andersson changed the subject to Linda Svensson's disappearance. Irene described her search of Linda's apartment and how she'd been struck by the fact that she could not find anything like a day planner, an address book, or a list of telephone numbers. Also, Linda's caller ID had been broken. She did not go into Belker's attack.

Andersson took up the topic. "We put out a missing-persons call on Linda Svensson last night for the whole district. We contacted her parents in Kungsbacka, but they haven't seen or heard from her. They didn't know the new address of her ex-boyfriend."

"But I do!" Birgitta exclaimed triumphantly. "Since I had his name and old address, I was able to get the new one from the post office's change-of-address list."

"Good. Then I'll send you to interview him today. But take Tommy or one of the other guys with you. Irene?"

"I'm wondering about something Anna-Karin said yesterday. She's a nurse in the same department as Marianne, but on the day shift. Anna-Karin is just a few years younger, and the two of them hung out a bit. She mentioned that Marianne had left Östra Hospital because she could not stand running into a certain man every day. Perhaps it would be a good idea to find out which man this was?"

"That was two years ago. Still, it might give us something to go by. Head out to Östra, and while you're at it, you can check into her ex-husband as well. I have his address. . . ." The superintendent began to search feverishly among the heaps of paper on the table. He finally found what he was looking for and waved a wrinkled sheet. "Here!"

Irene took the sheet of paper and glanced at it. Andreas Svärd. Residence on Majorsgatan and attorney's office on Avenyn. Obviously a rich dude.

Andersson continued. "Fredrik and Hans, I'd like you to keep knocking on doors and questioning folks living near Löwander Hospital. We are most interested in the time around midnight between Monday and Tuesday. We should also ask around in case Linda Svensson had been seen in the vicinity. Right now it appears as if the earth just opened up and swallowed her. Maybe Linda and Marianne met that evening, especially since Linda's day planner turned up in Marianne's pocket."

Irene shivered at his last sentence. Warning bells were going off inside her head.

"Jonny, I'm putting you in charge of Linda Svensson's disappearance. Here's her passport. It was issued just last year."

"She's hot," said Jonny as he looked over the photo.

Irene held out her hand for the passport; she hadn't gotten a good look the evening before.

Linda was five feet five inches tall, according to the passport. Even Irene could see that she was quite good-looking.

Her golden blond hair cascaded to her shoulders. She had a pleasant smile and dimples in her cheeks. Her blue eyes sparkled at the camera.

Marianne Svärd's passport was also on the table. Hers was issued four years earlier. She was five feet six inches tall and also attractive, though not as pretty as Linda. She had fairly dark hair, which was thick and long. Her large brown eyes and her mouth were set in a serious expression. She lacked Linda's spark, but the two women still had a great deal in common. They were nurses at the same hospital, they were approximately the same age, and something dramatic had happened to both of them on the same day. Irene hoped with all her heart that Linda was not dead as well, but what had happened to her and where was she?

Andersson concluded the meeting. "I am going to have a chat with Marianne Svärd's parents. Then I'll head over to the pathology lab. At three this afternoon, there'll be a press conference. Contact me if you find out anything new. Otherwise we meet here at five P.M."

IRENE DECIDED TO start by calling Andreas Svärd, the attorney, at his home number. No one answered. She tried the office number. The answering machine informed her that the office did not open until 9:00 A.M. She had a half hour to wait, so she decided to ferret out more about Andreas Leonard Svärd. It appeared that both his parents were still alive and lived in the town of Stenungsund, where Andreas had been born thirty-three years earlier. On a hunch Irene went to get Marianne's parents' address from Andersson. Yes, both sets of parents were neighbors. Perhaps it wasn't important, but Irene decided it might be a good idea to eventually contact the attorney's parents.

Before she phoned the attorney's office again, Irene called her hair salon and made that appointment for a cut and color.

They had space available late in the day, when she could squeeze it in, the following week. Pleased that she'd remembered to schedule the appointment, Irene turned back to the matter at hand.

A pleasant female voice picked up. "Svärd, attorney-at-law, secretary Lena Bergman here. How may I help you?"

"Good morning. My name is Inspector Irene Huss. I'm looking for Andreas Svärd."

The secretary gasped audibly before she answered, "I'm sorry, he's not in today. He's gone to Copenhagen for a seminar, and he won't be back until this evening. I imagine this must be about that horrible thing that happened to Marianne."

Irene was surprised. So far there'd been nothing in the news about the murder, though it would certainly be in the evening papers. They'd only sent out an initial communiqué that morning.

"How did you know?" Irene asked sharply.

"Marianne's mother called just a minute ago for Andreas . . . I mean, Mr. Svärd. She was completely beside herself and weeping. When I asked what was wrong, she told me about the murder. How awful."

"Yes. Murder is always awful. Did you know Marianne personally?"

"No, I've only been working here for two years. They were already divorced when I started."

Irene thought about the date. Two years. The same length of time that Marianne had been working at Löwander Hospital. Coincidence?

"Were you acquainted with Mr. Svärd before you took this job?"

"No. I answered an ad in the paper, just like everybody else." Lena Bergman sounded surprised and slightly insulted at the same time. Irene thought that she was probably telling the truth, but she decided she'd question the secretary again another time. They said their good-byes, and Irene hung up.

She felt that her body and brain needed at least three cups of coffee as soon as possible. Once she'd had them, she'd head over to Östra Hospital and try to find out the story behind the man that Marianne could not stand to see.

THE SILHOUETTES OF the three yellow-brick buildings stood out against the blue February sky. Irene parked close to the largest building, the central complex. She guessed that Marianne had worked in this building. The other two contained the gynecological units and the maternity ward. Irene had given birth to her twins here, because they'd been living close by on Smörslottsgatan at the time.

Irene heard the sound of air pressure as the entrance doors swished open for her. She stopped for a moment to admire the tapestry on the wall before looking for a map to direct her to the ICU. She saw she had to cross the entrance to the elevators on the other side, and as she walked, she passed a large café, a hair salon, and a convenience store. An employee was just setting out the evening papers, whose headlines screamed, NURSE MURDERED. There was more, but Irene didn't bother to read it. She already knew what it would contain.

She rode the elevator to the ICU. The doors were locked, and a sign asked visitors to press the button for the doorbell. Irene rang the bell, and a nurse wearing a mask came to open it.

"Yes?" the nurse said. It was apparent she was stressed.

"Hi. I'm Inspector Irene Huss, and I'm looking for the head of the ICU."

"Dr. Alm is in surgery right now."

"Perhaps there is someone else I could talk to? This concerns a nurse who used to work here, Marianne Svärd."

The nurse pulled her face mask under her chin and looked at Irene with surprise. "Marianne? Why would the police need information on Marianne?"

"Do you know her?"

"Yes, we worked together."

"Was Marianne on the day shift or the night shift while she worked here?"

"The day shift. Why do you need to know?"

"Unfortunately, she's been the victim of a crime. How long did you two work together?"

"Two years before she took the job at Löwander."

"Why did she leave?"

The nurse bit her lower lip. Finally she smiled and said, "Even though you've got quite a collection of bandages, I don't think you need intensive care."

Unbelievable how much people made fun of a few bandages. Irene wasn't sidetracked, however. It was clear that the nurse hoped to avoid the question. Irene replied evenly, "You're right, I don't need intensive care, thank you. I do need information regarding Marianne Svärd, so I'll ask the question one more time. Why did Marianne leave this department?"

The nurse pulled her face mask back over her mouth. "Let me . . . go get the department head," she mumbled, and quickly shut the door.

As seconds turned into minutes, Irene felt her irritation grow. At last she heard steps approaching, and the door was forcefully flung open by a man who looked like Adonis. At least Irene thought so. This was the second deeply tanned person she had had run across in the past twenty-four hours. The man, lithe and muscular, was as tall as Irene was, and he wore his thick, honey-blond, and highlighted hair in a ponytail. His amber eyes were pricked with darker splashes. His face had beautiful classic features, and when he smiled, showing shining white teeth, the effect was irresistible.

"Hi. I take it you're from the police."

"Yes, I'm Inspector Irene Huss."

"Niklas Alexandersson. Head of ICU."

He held out his hand and gave her a dry, firm shake. Irene noticed that he had many tiny gold rings in both ears. He was older than she'd thought at first glance, closer to thirty than twenty.

She decided to waste no time and got right to the point. "I need someone to talk to me about Marianne Svärd. Did you work with her?"

The effect on the man was astonishing, as if Irene had switched off a light. The beautiful face lost its glow. He stood silent for a while. At length he said, "Let's go into the conference room."

Alexandersson closed the ICU door behind them and walked over to a door in the hallway, which he then unlocked. He gestured Irene in.

The room was furnished with an oval conference table, matching wooden chairs, and the obligatory overhead projector. Niklas Alexandersson walked over to a telephone next to the window, pressed a number, and spoke into the microphone: "This is Niklas. I'll be in the conference room if someone needs me, but I don't want to be disturbed except for an emergency."

"All right," a woman's voice answered.

He turned back to Irene. "Why do you need information about Marianne? And what kind of information do you want?"

"I need to know as much as possible. To start, what do you think of her as a person?"

The department head glanced sharply at Irene before putting a quick smile on his face. This one was not dazzling, but downright nasty. "Harmless and kind." It was obvious from his tone that he did not like her.

"Were you displeased with her work as a nurse?"

"No, she was competent and careful."

"She never made any serious mistakes? No mistreatments?"

Niklas Alexandersson looked surprised. "No. What do you mean?"

"Well, her colleagues at Löwander Hospital said she'd quit her job here suddenly two years ago. Do you know why?"

"I can't see why that would involve the police."

Irene captured his godlike amber gaze. Without breaking eye contact, she said slowly, "Marianne Svärd was murdered last night."

Color drained from his face, and his tan faded to a sickly gray. He looked about to faint until he reached for a chair and sank into it.

Irene continued mercilessly. "This is why the police are involved. I will now repeat my question: Why did Marianne Svärd quit her job here?"

Niklas put his elbows on the table and let his face fall into his hands. A few moments later, he rubbed his eyes and miserably replied, "She said she wanted to try something new."

"That's not what her colleagues at Löwander told us."

He stiffened but did not say a word.

Irene continued. "They said there was a man here she wanted to avoid."

He still did not flinch or answer.

Irene decided to take a chance. "If you are not prepared to respond, I believe I will have to speak with Dr. Alm."

He gestured tiredly. "No need. Everybody here already knows that I was the person she couldn't stand."

Irene was surprised. He didn't seem to be her type. "Why did she dislike you?"

A weak reflection of his mean smile returned. "I took her guy, Andreas, away from her."

"You mean . . . you and Andreas were. . . ?"

"That's right. He left her for me. Are you shocked?" As he said this, he lifted a disdainful eyebrow and looked right into her eyes. His color was starting to return.

"No, I'm not. Are you two still together?"

"Yes. We live together."

"How did Marianne react to your relationship?"

Niklas Alexandersson snorted. "She wouldn't let go of him. She was more dependent than I realized. It was hard on Andreas. And on me."

"How was it hard for Andreas?"

"She didn't give up. He didn't want to make her unhappy. And his family wouldn't accept our relationship either. She made them believe that this was just a temporary phase and Andreas would soon come back to her. She'd say, 'I'll forgive him for everything.'" As he imitated Marianne, his voice rose to a falsetto that sounded very much like a deep female voice, his hand fluttering. When he switched off the imitation, all the fake femininity vanished from his body language.

The intercom beeped. "Niklas?"

"Yes?"

"X-ray called regarding the CVC. It's the pneumothorax. He's taken a bad turn, and his blood gases are much worse."

"Not good. Have you contacted Alm?"

"No, he's still in surgery."

"All right. Call him and get him over here as soon as he's finished."

"Right."

Niklas stood up and tried to look regretful. "As you've heard, I have to go."

Irene felt as if she were caught in an episode of *General Hospital* without understanding a word. She found it tiresome. Was it truly necessary for Niklas to leave, or was it just an excuse?

"Really serious?"

Niklas stopped. "A punctured lung is life-threatening for such a sick patient. Please excuse me. . . ."

Irene was not about to let him go that easily. "When do you get home?"

It looked for a second as if he was debating whether to tell the truth. Finally he shrugged and said, "Right before six."

"Is Andreas also home then?"

"Yes, he's returning from a seminar this afternoon."

Irene thought quickly. "Here's what we'll do. Have your dinner in peace and quiet, and I will come by at seven-thirty."

"Is this really necessary?"

"Yes, it is. We are looking for a murderer."

He flinched at that last word but said nothing. He sized Irene up as he held the door open for her, *a gentlemanly gesture you don't often see anymore*, she thought.

BACK DOWN IN the grand entrance, people were having coffee at the tiny café tables. Irene found an empty table and sat down. A cup of coffee and a sandwich would be perfect right now. She hung her jacket on the back of one of the chairs and walked to the counter to place her order. She glanced at the convenience store and the newspaper headlines on display.

At first she thought it was a joke, but as she reread the banner, she realized that the *Göteborg Times* headline really did read, WITNESS SAYS: GHOST KILLED NIGHT-SHIFT NURSE.

Chapter 7

CHIEF INSPECTOR ANDERSSON hated going to Pathology. Even more, he hated talking to pathology professor Yvonne Stridner. Most of all, he abhorred entering the autopsy room, but this was the only way to get a quick response.

When Andersson asked for the professor, the security guard pointed up the stairs with a burly, body-built arm. The chief inspector was relieved that Stridner was in her office and not in the middle of an autopsy. He tapped on her closed door.

Beeeep! A red light next to the text occupied lit up. A yellow light, indicating please wait, was beside it, as well as a green one stating come in. Even though he'd spent time driving here, Andersson was glad to accept the red light and the yellow. He sat down on the uncomfortable wooden chair against the wall. He could clearly hear the professor's voice: ". . . the worst oral examination I've ever heard! You must study and be thoroughly prepared, even for an oral examination. It's incredible stupidity to believe you'd pass just because you gabbled on and on. You have to know what you're talking about. Obviously you haven't studied. Or else you haven't understood what you were studying. The latter would be even worse. The former is fixable: Go home and study properly and I will give you another examination in three weeks with every question you failed. And that exam will be written."

The door was thrown open, and a girl with short black hair rushed out, crying. The chief inspector stayed frozen to his chair. His emotions contained an element of terror as he heard Stridner's voice.

"So there you are, Andersson, taking up space."

Andersson looked like a student who'd just been caught sneaking around to steal the answers to an upcoming test.

"Uhhh. . . ." he said lamely.

"What do you want?"

"Marianne Svärd . . . have you finished the autopsy?"

"Of course. Come inside," she ordered.

Stridner turned around, and he followed her into the office. She sat down in the comfortable chair before her computer. A visitor's chair with a worn-out red Naugahyde seat stood on the other side of her desk. It was hard and lumpy, surely on purpose. You were not supposed to feel comfortable in the presence of the professor.

He sank into the chair, breathing hard. Stridner gave him a sharp look.

"Isn't there any kind of workplace health care at the police department that could organize a diet group for you? Exercise for the overweight and so forth? Or at least provide some basic nutritional information? It'd help your blood pressure enormously."

Andersson would not let himself be goaded. Mustering all his self-restraint, he replied neutrally, "I'm taking medicine for my blood pressure, and it's under control. But I really came to hear what you've found out about Marianne Svärd." He forced a pleasant smile.

Stridner's lips curled as if she doubted his statement about his blood pressure, but to Andersson's relief she kept to the official subject. "Marianne Svärd. Livor mortis, rigor mortis, body temperature, and the temperature of the room all indicate that death occurred right around midnight. Analysis of stomach contents is still in progress, as well as blood and fluid analyses. It will take a few days before those results come in.

Nevertheless, I believe they will corroborate a time of death at approximately midnight."

Stridner paused and looked for a long time at Andersson over the frames of her glasses before she continued.

"Cause of death is strangulation. The noose had sunk deep into her neck and caused strong subcutaneous bleeding and damage to the musculature and circoid cartilage. Around the ligature marks are scratches, probably a result of the victim's attempt to defend herself from the noose. Based on the appearance of the cut, I determined that the murderer stood behind the victim. It is clear to see where the noose was tied at the back of the neck. In addition, I have determined that the murderer was taller than the victim, unless the victim was seated at the time of the attack."

"What kind of noose was it?"

"Thin, smooth, and strong. I found a number of fiber strands in the wound, which I have sent for analysis. An educated guess would be that it was a thin cotton rope strengthened by smooth synthetic material. Or perhaps the entire noose was purely synthetic."

Stridner furrowed her brows as if she were thinking about something, and then her face brightened and she said, "Speaking of fiber. I did find some strands underneath the victim's fingernails on both the right and left hands. Dark, thin textile fiber."

"Wool strands." The chief inspector sighed.

Stridner looked at him with surprise. "Wool? That's quite possible. Probably the victim grabbed at the murderer's arms in an attempt to make him loosen the noose, but she only caught the fabric of his jacket sleeves."

"Dress sleeves," Andersson said, depressed.

"What do you mean by that?"

He sighed again. "We have a witness. An older nurse who insists she saw the hospital ghost at the time of the murder.

The ghost is said to be a nurse who'd committed suicide fifty years ago. They say she wears an old-fashioned nurse uniform."

"Ridiculous! Ignore that witness completely. I can tell you that this strangulation was done by a living, breathing killer with strong arms."

The professor drew her eyebrows together sharply; her expression brooked no defiance. Not that the superintendent wanted to contradict her. No, for once the two of them were in complete agreement.

"I know. But the witness was definite about what she'd seen."

Stridner harrumphed. "Ghosts! A ghost doesn't drag a victim across the floor. Don't even give a thought to such a ridiculous notion."

The superintendent muttered defensively that he didn't believe that a ghost had done it either, but Stridner was not listening to him. She said brusquely, "I have to give a lecture in an hour, and I need to have lunch before then. Let's wind this up. She was not pregnant and had never given birth. In her stomach was a rather small meal. She'd eaten approximately four hours before she died. Her food was mixed with a froth that I believe was some kind of antacid. Her stomach lining was reddened toward the pylorus, but I saw no signs of an active ulcer. I found a healed ulcer near the duodenum, but it was old. Otherwise it appears that Marianne Svärd was in perfect health. She has no other wounds besides the strangulation mark and the drag marks on her heels. I found traces of talc underneath her arms."

Andersson could imagine the scene. The ghost nurse, floating in her old-fashioned black dress, coming up behind the night nurse. The latter, clueless about her fate. Quickly, the ghost throws the noose over the nurse's head and pulls tight. The panicked young woman clutches in vain at her throat and behind her head in order to stop her killer. All she can do is grab strands of cloth underneath her fingernails.

Andersson was completely engrossed in his vision and did not hear what Stridner had just said. She frowned at him with concern.

"Are you feeling ill? Is your head spinning? Have you ever had an epileptic attack or similar?"

"No, I was just thinking. . . ."

Stridner tapped at her watch. "Well, in that case I have no more time for you. I'll send the written report in a few days." She stood up and opened the door to the depressing hallway. The chief inspector could do nothing more than slink out. He mumbled a good-bye that went unheard, as the door behind him had already been shut.

IRENE HAD PICKED up a copy of the *Göteborg Times* from the news rack at the same time she bought her food. She settled into her chair and began to read.

NIGHT NURSE KILLED BY GHOST? a headline screamed. The byline attributed the article to Kurt Höök, the permanent reporter on the crime beat for GT.

A photo of Löwander Hospital's façade covered half the front page, which indicated they didn't have much of a story yet. The caption beneath the photo read, "What horror hid behind the hospital's grand façade last night? The chief of medicine refuses to comment." A photo insert of Sverker Löwander, disheveled hair and all, had been plugged into the right lower corner of the larger image. Some of the article was completely new information to Irene, however.

A nearby resident tells this newspaper that she saw the Löwander Hospital ghost roaming the grounds at the time of the murder. Everyone in the area, as well as in the hospital, knows the story of the nurse who committed suicide there a century ago and now returns to wreak vengeance on those who drove her to it. The witness, who asks for anonymity, describes the ghost as wearing

an old-fashioned uniform and walking on the grounds around
midnight. Our witness remained awake until past 3:00 A.M. and
swears that no one else came or went that night.

After this came a great deal of filler on the history of
Löwander Hospital. Typical archival material. The anonymous
witness wasn't quoted again in the article.

Irene felt shaken. Where had Kurt Höök gotten the story of
the ghost nurse? He didn't get it entirely correct; Tekla had in
fact had died in the 1940s. So his information probably didn't
come from anyone inside the hospital.

Irene sat there for a long time thinking without coming up
with any new ideas. Finally she gave up and finished her coffee
and cheese sandwich.

She glanced at her watch. Quarter past twelve. It was time
to pay Kurt Höök a little visit.

TRAFFIC WAS HEAVY on the E6, but apart from a bit of
stop-and-go near the Tingstad Tunnel, there were no major
obstructions. The newspaper complex's great grayish white
buildings towered above the side of the highway. Their lighted
display showed that the outdoor temperature was -8 C, the time
was 12:38 P.M., and people were encouraged to buy today's GT.

Irene parked in a visitor's space and got out, locking the
door of her old Volvo. She entered through the triangular glass
doors and was welcomed by the very proper middle-aged
woman at the reception desk.

"Good afternoon. May I help you?" She had a friendly
voice and was well made up.

"I'm looking for Kurt Höök. I'm Criminal Inspector Irene
Huss."

Irene held out her ID, and the receptionist took her time
inspecting it. With a hint of a smile, she said, "Just a minute.
Let me check if Kurt Höök is available."

The receptionist phoned an internal line. It appeared that Irene was in luck. The woman nodded and pointed to the glass doors of an elevator across the entrance. "Go on up. Take the elevator to the third floor. Someone will meet you at the central desk and take you to Kurt."

Irene headed for the elevators. She passed a splendid boat hull in many-colored glass mounted on a pedestal of black granite. Even the art on the walls indicated that this newspaper was a booming concern.

A harried-looking woman with blue-tinted hair and reading glasses far down her nose met Irene and brought her to Kurt Höök's desk. None of the other journalists even looked up as Irene passed their desks.

Although Höök's chair was empty, the woman with blue hair left Irene there. Höök's computer was turned on, and the screen showed the article that Irene had just read during lunch. He didn't seem to know that at three in the afternoon Superintendent Andersson was going to have a press conference and reveal the identity of the victim. Irene scanned the notes spread out over Höök's desk in case there was a clue to the anonymous witness. She also kept one eye on the lookout and so was not surprised when Kurt Höök approached his desk. He gave Irene one of his charming smiles.

"Hi. I remember you. You're that female officer that the Hells Angels beat up in Billdal a few years back. You look like someone got you again."

This wasn't the opening line Irene was expecting, but she kept her potentially poisonous rejoinders to herself and tried to appear friendly. The wounds beneath her bandages hurt when she tried to smile. "That's right. I'm Criminal Inspector Irene Huss."

"Of course. I can guess why you're here. Sorry, the answer is no, unfortunately." His apologetic words were combined with a twinkle in his eye.

"How can you say no before I've even asked the question?"

"I never reveal my sources." He seemed to be trying to hide a smug expression.

Irene found it extremely irritating that he was fairly good-looking. She felt that the bandages on her face were the size of beach towels. "I understand, but you must realize that an eyewitness at the time of the murder is very important to us."

"I do realize that, but my answer must remain no."

Irene cocked her head and smiled slightly. "Maybe we can come to an agreement?" Höök looked uncertain, so she continued. "If I can find out as much as possible about your anonymous witness, I'll make sure you have an inside scoop on the next stage of our investigation."

Höök could hardly hide his excitement. "Concerning Löwander Hospital?"

"Yep."

The journalist bit his lower lip as he considered this. Finally he said, "I assume you know that you are breaking the law when you ask me to identify a source, and I have no idea if what you're offering would be worth it."

Irene couldn't blame him for keeping his cards close to his chest, when he didn't know if she had any aces. She decided to tempt him further. "I realize that you can't give me the name of your source, but perhaps you can give me some hints so that I can figure it out myself. On my end . . . the information has to do with another nurse at Löwander Hospital and what happened to her that same night. Of course I'll reveal the murdered nurse's name, too."

The temptation was too much. Höök's journalistic instincts took over. "All right. The ghost is yesterday's news anyway. The headline sold well, but there's nothing more I can get out of that witness."

Irene remained silent. She knew that Höök was talking mainly to himself. He ran his fingers through his hair a few times, until it looked like it had been styled with an electric mixer. He gave Irene a distrustful look.

"This particular source is rather . . . special."

Irene saw his hand move toward the tape recorder on his desk. He hesitated and looked at Irene. "Perhaps it'd be better if I gave you some background information first. Then you can listen to the tape. It's actually not all that clear. Come with me."

He picked up the tape recorder, and they walked over to a nearby closed office. Höök opened the door and looked inside. The room was empty, and he ushered Irene in, carefully shutting the door behind him.

Hesitatingly, he said, "This . . . source is . . . how can I put it? Unusual. I don't know her name, and I don't know where she lives." He fell silent for a moment, then went on. "It started like this. A guy who's given me some small tips before called me on my cell phone yesterday afternoon. He'd obviously overheard a conversation between two police officers. Since I was already in the neighborhood, I decided to hop on over and have a slice of pizza while I was at it. By the way, do you want a cup of coffee?"

"Yes, please," Irene said without thinking. Afterward she wished she'd bitten her tongue. Why would she need coffee just when Höök was about to identify the witness? Her long-standing caffeine addiction had won out.

Höök left the room and returned with two cups of steaming-hot coffee in plastic mugs. "Where was I? The guy was just about to tell me this tip when the front door opened. . . ."

Höök stopped in the middle of his story. He swallowed some coffee before continuing. "The smell . . . the smell made me turn around and look at her. The pizza place had a plastic bag full of old bread ready for her, and she sat down on one of the chairs. We ignored her, and the guy began to tell me about overhearing two officers talking about a ghost nurse who'd supposedly murdered someone at Löwander Hospital. Can you believe it? But my source was certain that's what they'd said. Then the old hag—I mean, the old lady—butted in and said, 'I've seen her. Nurse Tekla. She haunts the place to get revenge on the people who killed her!' At first we didn't pay attention. She kept nattering on that she'd seen the ghost with her own eyes. And then she said, 'I watched her come and I watched her go. Blood was dripping from her hands.' It sent shivers down my spine. And—"

Irene interrupted him. "Did she really say 'Nurse Tekla'?"

"That's right. You'll hear it yourself. I recorded what she said. I'm going to leave the room while you listen to the tape. Here's paper and a pen if you need to take notes. But don't tell anyone where you found out about this."

"I promise I'll keep it confidential."

He turned on the tape recorder. What followed was truly strange.

"My name is Kurt Höök. What may I call you?"

"Call me Mama Bird. All my friends call me that. All my lovely ones. All my children. All of Mama Bird's children."

"Do you have many friends and children?"

"Millions and millions . . . my lovely ones, my children mychildrenmychildrenmychildren . . . all of my childrenmy-childrenmychildren. . . ."

"I see. You said you'd seen a nurse in the gardens by Löwander Hospital?"

"Nurse Tekla! I am so scared of her. So scared, so scared. I have to keep special watch over my lovely ones. She will kill them, all of them, killkillkill . . . killkillkill. . . ."

"Who is she?"

Mama Bird said nothing but hummed a nursery rhyme.

"Focus a little and I'll give you some pizza."

"Beer and pizza is what I want. And bread for my lovely ones. My children. . . ."

"I see. Anything else that you know about Nurse Tekla?"

"She died . . . a hundred years ago. Deaddeaddead. . . ."

"You saw her in the park?"

"Yes, yes, yes, yes."

"What was she doing?"

A moment of silence and then Mama Bird's hoarse voice: "She went into the hospital."

"How?"

"Howhowhowhowhow. . . ."

"How did she get inside the hospital?"

"Through the door."

"Did something happen while she was in the hospital?"

"God took away all the light. She was going to do a deed of darkness. The time had come, and all light was taken away. But I kept watch, I kept watchwatchwatch. . . ."

"Did you see her come back outside?"

"Yes, yes, yes, yes."

"What did she do then?"

Another stretch of silence. "She raised her hands to God and thanked Him for revenge! Revenge! Revengerevengerevenge!"

"And then what did she do?"

"She took the bike. God punishes theft!"

"She took the bike? What bike?"

"The other one's bike. But now she's dead. Everyone goes to their death! Tremble! Keep watch! Pray! Deathdeathdeathdeath. . . ."

"So Nurse Tekla took the bike and got out of there!"

As a reply, Mama Bird began to sing in a way that reminded Irene of a Sami joik: "Hoyahoyahoyahoya. . . ."

That's when Höök had turned off the tape recorder. Irene rewound the tape and listened to it again without pausing. Then she rewound it yet again and began to take down the unusual conversation.

She had listened to the entire conversation a fourth time before Höök came back.

"You wrote an entire article based on this?" Irene asked, not trying to hide her surprise.

"Along with my other source, who had overheard two police officers discussing the same thing. Normally I would have blown it all off. But it made sense, in a weird way. If you think about what the two officers were saying, there must have been someone else inside the hospital who'd also seen the ghost nurse. Right?"

"Yes, someone did mention the old legend, but I don't remember who it was or why it came up," Irene replied before she quickly switched the subject. "What did Mama Bird look like?"

"I'm not going to tell you any more about her. You already know too much as it is." He was right, but that would not make it any easier to find this woman. "So you got yours. Time for mine."

Irene told him everything about Linda Svensson's unusual disappearance on the night of Marianne Svärd's murder. Höök took down notes as if his hand were on fire. Afterward he appeared satisfied.

"Thanks so much. Now I have to hurry over to your press conference at three. By the way, are they going to make Linda Svensson's disappearance public?" he asked suspiciously.

Irene did her best to look innocent. She was happy that her bandages hid most of her face—a little silver lining there. "No idea. Superintendent Andersson will hold the press conference. This morning we were all told not to breathe a word about anything, especially to the media. So bye for now, and thanks."

Irene tore out her pages from the notebook and got up quickly. Before too long the glass doors of the newspaper building closed behind her.

• • •

AT THE STATION everyone was running full speed before the press conference. She rode the elevator up to her office, deciding she'd hide out there to avoid Kurt Höök. He probably wouldn't be too pleased with her after the press conference.

There were two desks in her office, hers and Tommy Persson's, both of them bare. She took a tape recorder from one of her desk drawers and recorded the dialogue between Kurt Höök and Mama Bird. Her own voice sounded stilted when she read her notes, trying to re-create the conversation word for word. She made several attempts before she was relatively satisfied.

She sat at her desk for a long time afterward, lost in thought. Mama Bird was crazy, all right, but she'd seen something that night. Who had she really seen? How did she know the story of Nurse Tekla? Where had Mama Bird been standing when she saw this person moving about the hospital grounds? And, most important, who was Mama Bird?

THE PRESS CONFERENCE proceeded in the usual manner—mild tumult. Andersson confirmed that the night-shift nurse Marianne Svärd had been strangled around midnight on the eleventh of February. The murderer was still unknown. When a reporter asked about the ghost, Andersson snorted so loudly the speakers popped.

Then Andersson changed the subject to Linda Svensson's disappearance. It was an unexpected bone tossed to them, and they threw themselves onto it. They scribbled down her particulars, noting that she was last seen wearing a red down coat and brown leather boots with platform soles. Her bicycle was also missing, and it was assumed that she'd ridden it away.

"It's a city bike, light green metallic color," Andersson concluded. Unfortunately, he was still standing too close to the microphone as he said, "What the hell is a 'city' bike?"

Questions from the reporters flew through the air, but Andersson could not add much. Instead he promised another press conference within twenty-four hours.

Irene watched the clock hit 4:00 P.M. In an hour the detectives would meet again. Before then Irene decided to call home to check in with her twin daughters, who were on winter break. Jenny was happy that one of the girl cousins from Säffle had called. The girls had been invited to join their cousins in Säffle, and from there all four girls would head to the family summer cabin in Sunne, where they planned to go snowboarding in Finnfallet and do some cross-country skiing in Sundsberget. Irene gave them permission to go, even as she thought that this trip seemed rather hastily put together.

Then she collected her thoughts and wrote her report covering the day's events. Actually, quite a bit had happened. She'd just finished when it was time to go to the conference room. She took the tape recorder and a new notebook. On the cover she wrote "Löwander" in black ink. She opened to the first page and wrote "pizza" in neat letters.

ALL OF THEM had written their food orders on the list, and the orders had been called in.

"Everybody here?" Andersson said to open the meeting. "I see Jonny is missing. I imagine he'll be here soon. Let's get going."

He took a breath and began to tell them about the morning's phone call to Marianne Svärd's parents, who had been extremely upset and shocked. The superintendent felt they'd need a few days before they were questioned again. Both parents agreed they'd never known of any threat to their daughter, nor had she behaved any differently when they'd last seen her over the weekend. That was two days before she'd been killed.

After that, Andersson summed up his conversation with Yvonne Stridner in Pathology. As he was wrapping up, Jonny appeared in the doorway, one eye covered with a bandage. His right hand was also wrapped up.

Irene tittered. "Hello. It looks like you've met Belker." she said in her mildest voice.

Jonny's flushed face contrasted nicely with his white bandages. He sank down into the nearest chair. "That damned cat jumped on me from the hat rack. I had to go to Mölndal Hospital for treatment. Including a tetanus shot. While I was defending myself from that cat, guess what? A little old lady came into the apartment and what does she say?" Jonny cleared his throat and proclaimed in perfect falsetto, "'Are they being mean to you, little Belker?'"

Everyone around the table burst into laughter.

"Then she just picked up that tiger, and wouldn't you know that little devil curled up in her arms and began to purr. She asked me to bring the cat's feeding dish and water bowl into her apartment, because now she was going to take care of the poor little pussycat."

Irene was happy to hear the last bit—both because Belker and Ruth Berg were going to keep each other company and because Linda's apartment would now be terror-free for the police.

"Anything new about Linda Svensson?" asked Andersson.

"I went to Kungsbacka and talked to her parents. She's an only child. They're beside themselves with worry. I asked them if her ex had ever hit her, but they didn't believe he had. According to them he's not the violent kind. Otherwise nothing new turned up in Linda's apartment. I searched the area around the apartment building for the bicycle, but I didn't find it. The building manager lent me a master key, and I looked in the basement, the laundry room, and the garbage room. The building has two stairways, and there are nine apartments on each floor. None of the other inhabitants saw or heard anything around the time Linda disappeared. Well, except the old lady who took in that man-eating beast. She says she heard Linda leave her apartment on the tenth of February at eleven-thirty P.M. Not a trace since. She and the bicycle are just gone."

Andersson frowned. He thought for a long time before he finally said, "Jonny, you keep working on finding Linda. Fredrik, too. It feels like time is running out on us. Birgitta, did you reach Linda's ex?"

"Yes, but only by phone. He's taking a seminar in Borås and won't be back until late tonight. He works for some kind of computer company."

"All right. You talk to that young man tomorrow. Take Jonny with you. Try to lean on him to see what he knows."

"Okay," said Birgitta.

Irene observed that Birgitta did not look at Jonny while she nodded. On the surface she didn't show any discomfort, just seemed to accept the assignment. But Irene sensed the tension between Jonny and Birgitta, and she wondered why. Of course, all Jonny's off-color jokes offended some people, but Irene hadn't been a policewoman seventeen years for nothing. Her instincts told her there was more to it than that.

"Should we request a reverse search on Linda's phone?" Birgitta asked.

"Reverse search?" Andersson echoed.

"Linda had an ID box on her phone, which, unfortunately, the cat destroyed. But we can ask the telephone company to check who called her phone number on the tenth of February."

"Is that possible?" Andersson asked, surprised.

"Yes, but it's not cheap. We have to go through the prosecutor's office."

"Inez Collin," Andersson said gloomily.

"That's right."

Andersson sighed. "Okay. I'll talk to Her Highness and arrange it. It sounds like something that won't happen overnight, though."

"I've got to leave at seven," Irene put in. "But I want you to know that there were more than one person attending seminars on the night in question."

She quickly explained the gist of her interview with Niklas Alexandersson, that he and Andreas Svärd were living together, and that she planned to interview them together in their home at seven-thirty.

"I just don't get that kind of thing at all." Andersson shook his head. "Two guys living together? And one of them once married to a really cute girl to boot."

"A cute girl who's now dead," Jonny pointed out.

"Exactly." The superintendent thought a moment. "Tommy, go with Irene. It's better if there are two of you."

"Will do."

"Fine. The pair of you will take care of our little pansies, ha! Hmmm." Andersson cut his laughter short when he saw that only Jonny was laughing with him. He quickly turned to Irene. "Was that everything?"

"No. I went to the GT home office and had a chat with Kurt Höök." Irene repeated her conversation with the journalist. Everyone else in the room had already read the article, and it had led to speculation about possible leaks. Here was the answer. As the icing on the cake, Irene played the tape she'd made of the conversation with Mama Bird. When she turned off the tape recorder, Jonny snorted.

"You're terrible at re-creating conversations. But regardless, that is one crazy old lady. No reason to pay any attention to her."

Irene nodded, ignoring his criticism of her dramatic-reenactment skills. "Of course, she's mentally ill. But listen between the lines. She knows about Nurse Tekla and the story going around the hospital. She may have gotten the wrong date for Tekla's death, but she knew it was a suicide. And she mentions that the building went dark. She must have been near the hospital when the power went out and the murder took place."

Andersson's face flushed with excitement from cheeks to ears, and he slid forward on his chair. "You're absolutely right. We have to track down this . . . Mama Bird. You and Tommy get on it right away tomorrow morning."

"Aye-aye." Irene made a joking salute to her boss, but he'd already turned his attention to Tommy.

"So what did you do today?"

"I was supposed to help Birgitta interview Pontus Olofsson, but since he was gone for the day, I decided to help Hans and Fredrik canvass the neighborhood. We went to all the apartment buildings and single-family houses around Löwander Hospital. No one had seen or heard anything on the night in question. One person walking his dog around eleven-thirty P.M. said that the dog went crazy while they were walking through the park behind the hospital. The park there stretches all the way to a stream at its south side. On the west it meets the edge of a forest. That's where the dog owner was walking his dog. The dog suddenly began to growl in the direction of the grove. The man couldn't see anyone but felt uncomfortable, so they left right away."

If the murderer hid in the grove of trees at the edge of the forest. . . . If Mama Bird also was in the vicinity. . . . They would have to find her. But where should they start to look for her? Maybe in the park. . . .

Irene's thoughts were interrupted by her pager.

"Come get your pizza," said one of the men from the front desk.

Irene and Tommy got up to get the food. In the elevator Irene said, "This evening we're going to talk to Andreas Svärd and Niklas Alexandersson. Then tomorrow morning we'll have to search for Mama Bird. We'll have to go to Löwander Hospital and see if there's anything in the grove, if someone was perhaps waiting there. Perhaps she's homeless? Höök said she smelled awful."

Tommy nodded in agreement. "Seems reasonable."

"There's a lot of pressure on us right now, especially about Linda Svensson's disappearance."

"The two must be connected somehow. Marianne had Linda's day planner in her pocket." Tommy was thinking out loud. "And, for a night nurse, no flashlight? Very strange."

And worrisome, Irene thought. Very worrisome. Yes indeed, why did Marianne, the night-shift nurse, have Linda's day planner but no flashlight in her pocket?

THE POLICE OFFICERS had eaten their pizza and worked out their assignments for the following day when Irene and Tommy headed out to interview Marianne Svärd's ex-husband.

Finding the address was not easy. Many of the stone buildings near Linnégatan had been torn down in the 1980s when a changing water table had rotted their support pilings. Architects attempting to re-create a turn-of-the-century atmosphere had not always been successful, but now pleasant pubs, small boutiques, and proximity to the large forest of Slottsskogen had made this area extremely popular. House prices and rents were sky-high.

They finally located the address; A. SVÄRD and N. ALEXANDERSSON were on the nameplate by the entrance. Irene called on the intercom and heard Niklas's sour voice. "I'm opening," he said crossly.

The front door buzzed and let the police officers into an airy hallway. The light gray marble floor and warm, champagne-colored walls with their iris-blue borders were very attractive. The elevator was the same champagne tone as the walls, so as to not disturb the aesthetics.

The elevator swished silently to the top floor. Just as Irene was about to press the doorbell, the door was yanked open. The angry twist to Niklas's mouth took away from his handsomeness. "Is this really necessary?"

Irene replied mildly, "And a good evening to you, too, sir. Yes, our errand is really necessary, since Marianne has been murdered."

Niklas jerked at her last word but said nothing else. He still wore the sour expression as he led them through the entry hall over a rug that was soft underfoot. He motioned them toward a large, cozy living room. The furniture and the artwork gave the room an upscale feeling. A man was sitting on the silver-gray sofa. He stood and offered his hand.

"Hi. I'm Andreas Svärd."

"Hello. I'm Criminal Inspector Irene Huss."

"Tommy Persson here. I'm also a criminal inspector."

"Welcome. Please sit down." Andreas Svärd was a pleasant contrast to Niklas. He treated them as welcome guests. As Irene sank into one of the plush leather armchairs, she observed the lawyer before them. Andreas Svärd was six feet tall and slender. He had thick blond hair and a fairly ordinary face. Irene knew he was thirty-three years old, but he appeared younger. He wore a light gray silk shirt, chinos in a darker gray, and a wine-colored lamb's-wool sweater—casual but obviously expensive. To her surprise, Irene could tell that he'd been crying.

"I understand why you're here. This has been a real shock for me . . . what happened to Marianne, that is. In spite of how our relationship ended, we were actually still close."

Andreas Svärd turned his face away. Irene looked at Niklas, who glowered even more. Andreas appeared to be mourning, but Niklas just seemed angry.

Irene cleared her throat. "When was the last time you saw Marianne?"

Andreas cast a sidelong glance at Niklas before he answered. "We had lunch two weeks ago."

Niklas seemed even angrier, so Irene turned to him. "What about you?"

"I haven't seen her since last Christmas," he growled.

"How was that?"

"She came to dinner here."

It was obvious that he wasn't the one who'd invited her. Irene turned back to Andreas. "Did you get together often?"

"Not that much."

"How often?"

Andreas looked nervously at Niklas but seemed determined to tell the truth. "About once a month."

"Why did you meet?"

The lawyer seemed truly surprised by her question. "We've known each other all our lives. We grew up together on the same street. Over the last year, we'd sometimes have lunch together."

"At which restaurant did you last have lunch?"

"The fish restaurant Fiskekrogen."

Niklas could not contain himself any longer. Half suppressing a swear word, he swiveled on his heels and stalked from the room. Andreas looked after him thoughtfully but said nothing. It seemed he was willing to tell the truth even if it enraged Niklas. At any rate, now it would be easier to interview Andreas, one-on-one. "Would it be possible for you to come down to the police station tomorrow afternoon?"

"Sure, but not till after four."

"That'll work for me, too."

The police officers stood up and shook hands. Irene noticed Andreas's hands were unusually small and well formed.

In the apartment's hallway they saw no sign of Niklas. Irene did not raise her voice as she said, "Niklas, I need to talk to you."

A door opened, and Niklas stuck his head out. "What do you want?"

"We need to talk to you some more. I would like you to come down to the police station tomorrow. What time can I expect you?"

"I work until four-thirty. I can't get there until five, but five-thirty is more likely."

Tommy let his eyes wander to the artwork in the hallway. He pointed to a framed poster. "Is that you?"

Irene turned to look at the poster. *Drag Show Fever* was written in Gothic letters. A slim, long-legged woman wearing fishnet stockings and impossibly high stilettos climbed a staircase, a black G-string cutting between her two firm buttocks. The back of her sequined top was low, and her long hair flowed over her shoulders. Her head was slightly turned away, but even through the woman's false eyelashes and makeup, Irene was able to recognize the cool, amber-eyed gaze. Surprised, she turned to Niklas and exclaimed, "It is you!"

His smile was both amused and vicious. "Shocked again?"

"No, not this time either. But what's the poster for?"

"I was a drag-queen dancer. A poor nursing student who needed some extra cash to fill in the gaps left by his student loans."

"Are you still dancing?"

"No."

Niklas opened the front door to let them out.

Chapter 8

AT SEVEN-THIRTY IN the morning, Irene and Tommy began their workday at the edge of the forest grove on the far side of Löwander Hospital's park. Since it was a long time before full daylight, they decided to wait half an hour. The park was large and overgrown, so it would take some time to comb through it, even though the trees were bare of leaves. During the night the temperature had risen to around freezing. The sky was dark gray, which could mean either snow or sleet.

They began their search near the small grove of fir trees. There were many footprints in the thin layer of frost, but also paw prints both large and small. This was clearly a favorite spot to take dogs for walks. Where the grove ended, deciduous trees took over. Most of them had been planted more than a century ago, when the park was first founded. Right behind the hospital itself were big clumps of lilac and golden chain. As the two of them examined the densest bushes more closely, they could see that once upon a time this had been a lilac arbor. Decades of neglect had made it as thick as rain-forest vegetation. Deep among the branches, they could make out a hut.

Irene and Tommy searched for a way in and found an opening almost completely hidden by overgrowth, which appeared to be the former entrance to the arbor and from which they could clearly see the hospital's employee back door.

They stood in the middle of the thicket. The lilac bushes grew several meters high and concealed almost totally the tiny, green-painted hut. It seemed to be surprisingly new, with a ramp leading up to the wide door. Tommy approached it and tried the handle. With a protesting creak, the door opened. Tommy went inside but came out just as quickly.

"Goddamn it. We've found her hidey-hole."

Irene looked inside. A stench assaulted her nose. Its source was clear. Right by the door was a plastic bucket filled with urine and excrement. The hut was apparently a gardening shed: shovels, rakes, and other gardening tools were lined up neatly against the wall. In the middle of the floor stood a riding lawn mower. There was not much space around it, but here was where Mama Bird had made her home.

At the back of the room, she'd heaped newspapers and flattened cardboard boxes. On top of that was an old sleeping bag covered with a bloom of mildew. She had a plastic bag stuffed with newspapers and rags as her pillow. Irene felt a lump grow in her throat when she realized that Mama Bird had actually made up her bed with a bedcover. On the lower end of the sleeping bag, she'd spread a grimy baby blanket. Once upon a time, the tiny hopping lambs on it must have been pink.

Irene peered into the large plastic bag at the head of the bed. "Here's the rest of the bread she got yesterday from the pizza joint."

Examining Mama Bird's home was a quick job. They stepped outside into the much more pleasant fresh air.

"It looks like she didn't sleep here last night. She got the bread the day before yesterday," Irene said. "I imagine she'll be coming back."

"Do you think she has a number of hiding places?"

"Possibly. I wonder if anyone at the hospital knows that someone is living here?"

"No idea. We'll have to ask them later. Now let's go back to the grove."

Even though it was lighter now, they still had to use their

flashlights to see in the darkness beneath the fir trees. Farther in, the trees grew close together, and it was difficult to make their way between them. They found condoms, empty containers, and dog shit. Beer cans, empty cigarette packs, candy wrappers, potato-chip bags—city people have great faith in nature's ability to break down waste.

Half an hour later, they'd gone over the whole area. Irene was sweating and disappointed. Tommy plucked pine needles out of her hair and pointed to his own forehead. "Check this out. I was so focused on looking at the ground that I banged my head on a branch."

Irene stared at him, thinking about what he'd just said. "If we could hardly see in broad daylight, how about someone in the middle of the night?"

"Anyone hiding here wouldn't have to go in very far."

"Maybe we should be smarter, then. Concentrate near the hospital and not go too deeply into the woods. And we need to look at the branches, too. Something might have caught in them."

They did another round through the grove. A few minutes later, Tommy called out.

"Irene! Come here!"

She made her way through the tangle toward Tommy. Without a word he pointed up at a stout fir, about a half meter over the ground. There were some dark fibers hanging on its outer branches.

He pulled a plastic bag from his pocket, slipped it up his arm, and took hold of the branch. He broke it above the fibers and enclosed it in the bag, textile fragments and all, then carefully pocketed it. They continued searching but found nothing more beyond further evidence that many people had come here with their dogs. Maybe the forensic technicians could have found something more, but they weren't here. An ice-cold rain was starting to fall.

"Nothing more here," Tommy said. "Let's go inside and ask if anyone knows about Mama Bird's nest."

Irene agreed that it was hopeless to continue the search. The rain poured down, making the prospect of shelter tempting. Their boots squelched as they rounded the hospital toward the front just in time to catch a glimpse of Superintendent Andersson disappearing through the grand entrance.

THE WOMAN AT the reception desk looked up from her keyboard, and Irene nudged Tommy. He was good at handling middle-aged women.

"Hi. Do you mind if I bother you for a moment?" Tommy asked in a friendly manner. He looked into her eyes with his kind, puppy-dog gaze.

The receptionist patted her age-inappropriate blond hair, straightened her glasses, and let a pleasant smile appear on her well-reddened lips. "Sure. But I do have a great deal of work to do."

"I wonder if you've seen an elderly lady around the hospital grounds. She looks like she's probably homeless."

"A homeless person? Here at Löwander Hospital? Don't be silly. What would a person like that be doing around here? They usually keep to Brunn Park."

"You haven't heard any talk?"

"No."

"Is there anyone else here who might know about her?"

"Our security guard, Folke Bengtsson, usually knows everything that goes on around here."

"Where can we find him?"

"One floor down. His room is on the left at the bottom of the stairs." The phone rang, and the receptionist picked it up, answering with professional warmth: "Löwander Hospital. How may I help you?"

They headed down to Folke Bengtsson's door.

security guard was not in, but his door was unlocked, so they went inside. The room was fairly large, with a basement window set high up. When Irene stood on her toes, she could catch a glimpse of the lilac arbor. In silent accord they began to explore the room.

There were a number of Track & Field World Cup posters on the walls. Tommy pointed at a large tool bag hanging near the door. They gave it a quick search but couldn't find any large wire cutters. On the shelves various things were jumbled together: cardboard boxes with lightbulbs, plumber's snakes, rolls of steel wire, and a carton labeled *Flags*. There was an old brown lamp on the desk, as well as a coffeemaker. Irene pulled the desk drawers open. She found only a tin of snuff, some invoices and order forms, pens, and two well-thumbed sports magazines. The upper drawer was locked, and she couldn't budge it. She was just about to try to force the lock when Tommy signaled to her to stop. They heard heavy footsteps coming down the basement stairs. Irene stepped away from the desk, turning her back to it, and pretended to be looking out the basement window. She said loudly, "You can just about see the tops of the trees in the park."

"It's not like they were generous with the view," they heard a bass voice from the door.

Irene whirled around and tried to appear surprised. "Hi! We were looking for you." She smiled and held out her hand. "Criminal Inspector Irene Huss. I saw you early Tuesday morning, but we didn't have a chance to talk."

"Hi, I'm Folke Bengtsson. Lots of other officers were talking to me."

They all shook hands. Without even asking, Bengtsson took the glass carafe from the coffeemaker and disappeared into the hallway. They heard him fill it with water from a tap. The security guard was back in an instant and began to measure pleasant-smelling ground coffee into the paper filter. Without his knowing it, Folke Bengtsson was rising in Irene's esteem. A guy who started the coffee machine right away must be a good guy, at least in her opinion. Her coffee gene was already crying out for a cup.

Folke Bengtsson was about sixty years old, bald and stocky. He reminded Irene of a hefty tree stump. Irene, who kept herself in shape, could tell that this man was still active in some kind of sport, so she began her interrogation with a question. "These posters from the world championship are really great. I was dumb enough to get rid of mine."

"I took vacation and was able to watch almost the whole thing," Bengtsson said contentedly.

"Are you active?"

"Not any longer. I coach several young guys, but these days I just lift some weights."

Judging from the biceps under his blue plaid flannel shirt, Bengtsson lifted a great many weights. He handed plastic mugs filled with coffee to Tommy and Irene, keeping a porcelain mug with the text *I'm the Boss* in English for himself. He took the large key ring from his belt and opened the desk's top drawer. Irene craned her neck to see what was inside: a packet of cookies and a number of other keys. Bengtsson took out the cookies and shut the drawer.

Irene thanked him for the cookie, drawing the aroma of fresh-brewed coffee into her nostrils. "Excuse me, Folke, for changing the subject. I do have to ask you about keys," she said. "The murderer must have had keys to the hospital. There is no trace of forced entry anywhere in the building, and I'm wondering about master keys. How many are there?"

"Two. I have one and Dr. Löwander has one."

"What kinds of keys do the other employees have?"

"One to the outer doors. It's the same key for the front and back doors, and it also works for the employee changing room here in the basement. Then they have a separate key for their department."

"So the employees of the care ward would have keys to the care ward and surgery employees for the surgery department?"

"That's right."

"But you keep extra keys for everything in that drawer?"

"Yes, but I'm the only one who has a key to this room, and I lock it when I go home for the day. This desk drawer is always locked, and I'm the only one with a key." Bengtsson appeared satisfied with his mastery of the key situation.

"But this room wasn't locked when we got here."

"No, it's open during the day."

"But the top drawer is always locked."

"Always."

"Where do you keep the master key?"

"Here." The security guard pulled the key ring out of his pocket and showed how it was attached to his belt. "And here's the key to the top drawer."

Irene saw that she wasn't going to get any more information about keys, so she decided to change the subject and ask about Mama Bird.

"Are you aware that there's a lady living in the toolshed?"

Bengtsson stiffened. He looked down into his steaming coffee mug and mumbled, "Hmm, there is?"

He was truly a terrible liar.

"Didn't you see yesterday's GT? Didn't you read about the woman who had seen old Tekla haunt the place on the night of the murder?"

"Well . . . yes . . . I saw it. Where did they find out about that?"

"The journalist who wrote the article had interviewed Mama Bird."

Bengtsson looked up from his mug, surprised. "An interview? In her state?"

"So you know her?"

The security guard sighed, defeated. "Yes, I know her. Or at least I'm aware of her. I found her right before Christmas."

"Found?"

"Yes, she was wrapped up in a garbage bag and had huddled against the basement heating exhaust, on the other side of the electrical room's wall. At first I thought that someone had dumped garbage on the property, and I was furious. I walked over to get it and drag it to the garbage room when I realized that there was a human being inside."

"Did you bring her into the building?"

"No. She stank to high heaven. It made you want to throw up. And she was totally off her rocker. I couldn't get a word of sense out of her."

"So you decided to let her sleep in the toolshed."

Bengtsson nodded, resigned. "What else was I supposed to do? The hospital was closing for Christmas. She obviously had no home of her own. I unlocked the garden shed for her. She seemed to be very happy. Sometimes I hang a plastic bag with sandwiches on the door handle, and they're gone the next morning. Though I have to say that I once saw her crumbling them into bits so she could feed the birds."

"Where did you see her do that?"

"Here in the park."

"Does anyone else know about Mama Bird?"

Folke Bengtsson shrugged his massive shoulders. "Don't know. Maybe."

"Do you know her real name?"

"No idea. She only babbled about being Mama Bird. But really, I haven't talked to her much since that first morning."

"Does she stay in the shed during the day?"

"No, she's always gone in the morning. I arrive at six-thirty A.M. I never catch a glimpse of her then."

"Have you looked inside the toolshed?"

The guard swallowed and nodded. "Yes, it's pretty damned awful. . . . But she can stay through the winter. After that I'll throw her out and lock the door again. I'll deep-clean the shed and then repaint it thoroughly. No one will ever have to know that she lived there."

It was obvious he was pleading with them not to tell. He seemed to feel sympathy for the homeless woman.

"Do you know where we can find Mama Bird during the day?"

"No idea. But. . . ." He hesitated, thought awhile, then said doubtfully, "One Saturday morning a few weeks ago, I saw her in Drottning Square. She came out of the shopping center with a big plastic bag in each hand, singing to herself as she walked by."

"Did you hear what she was singing?"

Bengtsson looked surprised. "No. I kept my distance."

"Did she see you?"

"No. She went to Hotel Eggers and sat down right by the entrance. Then she opened the bags and began to crumble up loaves of bread and scatter oats until she was covered with pigeons. Disgusting."

The woman's curious stink had an explanation, Irene thought. "When did you last see her?"

"Well . . . she's not easy to spot. I only saw her that one time in Drottning Square. She comes to the shed late at night and leaves in the early morning. Last Monday night I hung a bag of sandwiches for her, and they were gone Tuesday morning."

So Mama Bird was definitely nearby on the night of the murder. It was urgent that they find her.

"What does Mama Bird look like? How is she dressed?"

Bengtsson took some time to think before he answered.

"Well, it's hard to tell how old she is. Perhaps a bit younger than me. Short and thin. Though it's hard to see what she really looks like. She wears a large man's coat. She wears a knitted cap—I believe it's pink. She keeps it pulled over her ears and nearly over her eyes. You don't see much of her face."

"What color is her coat?"

"Don't know. Brown. Gray. She wears it with a rope tied around her waist. She has big gym shoes on her feet, and she stuffs them with newspaper."

"Anything else?"

"No. Yes. She has hardly any teeth."

Tommy and Irene thanked him for the coffee and got up to leave. As they walked through the hallway, Irene stopped by the door marked central electricity.

"Have the techs searched the entire basement?" she asked.

"Yes, but they didn't find anything outside of this room," Tommy answered. "They also made a sweep of the elevator. Malm believes that she was killed in the ICU. She must have opened the door for the killer, since the lock can only be turned from the inside. Looks like she knew the murderer."

"Unless the murderer had a key."

"It's possible. But the techs couldn't figure out where in the room she was killed. During the outage Dr. Löwander and the old nurse were fumbling around and knocking stuff over. By the next morning the young ICU nurse had already cleaned it all up. Anna-Karin. She knew Marianne and was Linda's friend."

Again Irene had the feeling that Anna-Karin knew more than she was letting on. Still, it was only a feeling, and she couldn't press the nurse further just on a hunch. She turned to Tommy and said, "I'm going up to the care ward. Nurse Ellen promised to take a look at my cat scratches."

"All right. I'll ask around and see if I can get anything more on Mama Bird."

• • •

IRENE CLIMBED THE stairs up to the ward. At the nurses' station, she found her boss in happy conversation with Nurse Ellen Karlsson. They were laughing heartily together at a good joke. Irene tried to remember when she had last heard him laugh like that. When he saw her, he stopped abruptly, and his face turned red. *He had the look of a kid with his hand in the cookie jar*, Irene thought. But there should have been nothing for him to blush about.

Nurse Ellen followed Andersson's glance and spun around in her chair. "Well, hello. How are you feeling? Your scratches giving you any trouble?"

"Thanks, I'm fine. As long as I don't laugh."

"Let me take a look. Let's go to the exam room."

Nurse Ellen got up from her chair, and Irene followed her. As they left, Irene shot a glance back at her boss, who looked very ill-tempered. Maybe he was up to something after all.

The nurse began to pick out the supplies she'd need. Sterile saline, new bandages, skin-friendly adhesive, and tweezers. She chatted as she assembled everything on a trolley.

"Things are quiet today. Dr. Bünzler has gone to his cabin in Sälen with his children and grandchildren. Konrad Henriksson, our anesthesiologist, has also gone on winter break. So it's just Sverker Löwander in surgery, and he's only doing minor operations using local anesthesia in the polyclinic. So there's not a lot going on." Nurse Ellen stopped in the middle of the flow of words. Her voice filled with worry. "Is there any news about Linda?"

"No. Sorry. No trace yet."

"The whole thing is unbelievable. First Marianne is murdered, and then Linda disappears."

"It's strange, all right. Did you read yesterday's newspaper? The woman who claimed to see Nurse Tekla?"

Nurse Ellen began to carefully remove the bandages from Irene's face. It still hurt. "Yes. Who would say a thing like that?"

"There seems to be a homeless woman hanging around. Do you know anything about a homeless woman on the property?"

She paused to think about what Irene had said. "A homeless woman? There can't be too many of those. No, I haven't heard anything. What does she look like?"

"Short and thin. Wearing a pink knit cap and a man's coat."

"She could be the one I saw at Burnsite."

"Burnsite?"

"That's what we call it around here. Kind of a joke. There used to be a huge doctor's mansion close to the hospital. It burned down eleven years ago, and the grounds were made into a parking lot for the employees."

"I see. No one wanted to rebuild instead?"

Nurse Ellen stopped cleaning Irene's face for a moment and bit her lower lip. For the first time in their conversation, Irene had the feeling that Nurse Ellen was deciding whether or not to tell the truth. Finally she said, "Mrs. Löwander went nuts and said that Carina had set the place on fire."

"Isn't Carina Mrs. Löwander?"

"She's Mrs. Löwander Number Two. Barbro was Sverker's first wife. He and Barbro moved into the mansion one year after old Dr. Löwander died. They were barely settled in the place when Dr. Löwander filed for a divorce. Barbro was totally devastated."

"Do they have any children?"

"Yes, John and Julia. John lives in the States, and Julia's there this year as an exchange student."

"So Barbro stayed in the mansion by herself?"

"No, she left, and Sverker lived there alone."

"Why would Carina set fire to the place if she planned to live there with Sverker?"

"That's just it. She didn't want to live in an old mansion. According to Barbro."

"So she decided to burn the place down? That sounds far-fetched."

"Yes, everyone else thought so, too. Barbro was unbalanced at the time, so nobody paid much attention to what she said."

"So the house burned to the ground?"

"Yes. Oh, people managed to save a few things, but Carina refused to have them in the new place, so Sverker put them in the attic here."

"Are they still here?"

"Most likely. I saw the suitcases they were in when I went to get the Advent lights last year. That part of the old attic was never renovated. It's just used for storage."

"Was that where Nurse Tekla hanged herself?"

"Yes."

Irene decided to change the subject and go back to Mama Bird.

"You said that you might have seen the homeless woman near Burnsite?"

Ellen Karlsson relaxed again. "Yes, about two weeks ago. It was around six in the morning. I'd gotten here extra early. I still had things to finish from the night before. I just caught a glimpse of her underneath a streetlight. Then she disappeared into the park."

"You never saw her again?"

"No." The nurse cocked her head and inspected Irene's cleaned wounds. "It's healing nicely. You will still need one bandage, but the rest can be covered with surgical tape. You're keeping up with your penicillin, I trust?"

Irene nodded obediently. "Did you know Dr. Löwander's first wife, Barbro?"

"Oh, yes. She was a medical secretary here at the hospital. After the divorce, though, she took a new job at Sahlgren Hospital to avoid Carina. You see, Carina also had a job here."

"What did she do?"

"Physical therapist. Sverker and Carina met here."

"But Carina doesn't work here anymore either, right?"

"No, she started to work in wellness care instead. She's leading the fitness program for Corporate Health Services. I'm sure it suits her perfectly. She can hang out with people she likes."

There was a sharp tone in that last comment, but just as Irene was about to follow up on it, someone knocked on the door. Ellen Karlsson didn't have time to speak before the door flew open and Anna-Karin stuck in her head.

"Hi, I just got a call. The other night nurse has the flu, and Siv Persson is still out. So what do we do now?"

Nurse Ellen's soft, friendly face suddenly sagged. Her exhaustion was audible in her voice. "Oh, dear Lord. I have no idea. I'm almost at my limit. I've already covered Linda's shift twice."

Anna-Karin thought quickly. "I'll call Källberg Hospital and see if they have anyone in the pool that can be sent over."

The image of a swimming pool filled with nurses flashed through Irene's mind. Along the edge a desperate group of personnel administrators and exhausted hospital employees were trying to fish for people. Nurse Ellen's stern voice snapped Irene back to reality.

"Please excuse me, Irene, I have to run. You can take the tape off on Sunday. Bye, now."

The next moment Irene was left alone in the tiny examination room. She got up from the table she'd been sitting on and walked over to the window, which looked out on the park. Right beneath her was the lilac arbor and the garden shed. Although the leaves were gone, it was still hard to see its tarpapered roof. Mama Bird's nest was well hidden. Irene looked past the park to the heavily visited cluster of evergreen trees. Beyond them she could see a three-story apartment building. She could see a car or two passing by on the road below. The traffic crossed the stream via a narrow bridge, on the other side of which she could make out a streetcar stop. This was probably the route Mama Bird used to get here in the evenings. She came by streetcar from town, got off at the stop, made her way over the bridge and through the park to her nest.

Maybe they ought to keep watch by the shed and try to wait for her? If they couldn't find her today, this would be a last resort. Still, it would cost time and resources, and it looked as if the woman had other hideouts as well. What if she didn't show up several nights in a row? They'd have to check in with the superintendent if they couldn't find her.

IRENE FOUND TOMMY PERSSON in a secretary's room by the reception desk. He was talking on the telephone, the notebook page in front of him scribbled full.

"By lot? And then how do they find out about it?" He listened to the voice on the other end of the line, rolling his eyes when he spotted Irene. "I see. And what if they have no address? . . . You can't? You can't do anything about it? . . . I see. Thanks so much."

Tommy slammed down the receiver and sighed dejectedly. "This is crazy. There are human beings in our society who officially do not exist. They've been administrated out of existence."

"What do you mean?"

"I've been calling around to our welfare offices and asking them if they know Mama Bird. They're helpful at first, but then they want her real name, her personal number and address. Since I can't answer a single one of those questions, they can't help me. When I mention that she's homeless, they turn frosty. Homeless? Can't help you there. Then they say a polite phrase or two and hang up. I decided to press this last person for more details, like their routines for homeless people. Do you know what they do with them?"

"No, what?"

"They pick a part of the city to place them in. By lot."

"By lot?"

"Yep. Mama Bird could have been assigned the social-welfare office in Torslanda, and they would be in charge of her welfare. But how is she supposed to know that? There's no address to send her the information. Her true address is the garden shed in Löwander Hospital Park. It's a great system. They raffle responsibility to someone who has never met the homeless person in question. This person is now the homeless person's caseworker on paper. Society has done its duty and made sure that the homeless person has his or her own caseworker. And the two never meet."

Tommy looked at the telephone bitterly, as if it represented the social-welfare offices.

"I assume there's no need to bother with the welfare office."

Tommy nodded and shrugged. "So it seems. We'll have to search all the city districts. But I don't think that'll lead anywhere."

"What should we do, then?"

"Let's go try the Salvation Army or the City Mission."

"How about lunch?"

"Okay, lunch first."

IT WAS THREE in the afternoon by the time Tommy and Irene got out of the car at the police station. Tommy was to continue calling to find out about Mama Bird. He borrowed Birgitta and Fredrik's office, since Irene would be hosting her interviews in the office he shared with her. Irene decided to put her report together before Andreas Svärd showed up.

At exactly 4:00 P.M., Andreas Svärd knocked on Irene's door. He was dressed as elegantly as he'd been the previous evening. His pale color was underscored by the dark blue overcoat, black pants, and black shoes he wore. As he took off his coat, Irene saw he was wearing a black jacket, a dark blue tie, and a white shirt. Obviously Andreas was dressed in mourning, and his face reflected his sorrow. His eyes were still bloodshot. Irene wondered if he'd had a fight with Niklas about his lunch outings with his ex-wife.

"Have you learned anything new?" Andreas asked directly.

"No, but we have a possible witness."

"The one mentioned in the paper?"

"Yes, among others."

Irene was purposely vague. It was obvious that Andreas Svärd was affected by the murder, but he could also be afraid of what the police would find. She decided to feel him out.

"How did you and Niklas start your relationship?"

"Is this of any importance?"

"Absolutely. It seems to be what motivated Marianne to leave Östra Hospital for Löwander."

Andreas sighed, resigned. "We had an open-house party, Marianne and I. We'd bought a house in Hovås, and she was so . . . happy." His voice turned raspy. "We'd never had many people over, and we certainly didn't have large parties. But now we had the space, and Marianne thought that for once we should have a really huge party. We invited all our friends and co-workers. Of course, Marianne invited Niklas. So that's how we . . . got to meet."

"Had you had any homosexual relationships prior to meeting Niklas?"

Andreas started. "No."

"When did Marianne find out about this one?"

"A half year later. Things happened the way they always do. Everyone knew about it but her. I tried to break off things with Niklas, but I just couldn't. . . ." He fell silent and swallowed with a gulp.

"How'd she take it?"

"She took it hard."

They sat silent until Andreas was ready to continue.

"She couldn't stand seeing Niklas every day at work, so she decided to find another job."

"When did you and she start meeting again?"

"Except for the first six months after the divorce, we saw each other all the time. When my father had his sixtieth birthday, we invited Marianne and her parents. Our parents had been friends all their lives, and they're also next-door neighbors. Marianne and I started to talk, and she was so . . . good. She didn't blame me a bit."

"Was Niklas also invited to the birthday party?"

"No."

"How did he react?"

Andreas sighed heavily. "He has a real temper. It's always difficult."

"Your relatives have never met him?"

"No."

"And how did Marianne and Niklas get along?"

"Obviously not at all." Andreas gave Irene a tired smile. "Marianne tried to have a neutral relationship, but Niklas . . . he just kept getting angry."

"Why did you and Marianne decide to start meeting for lunch?"

Andreas closed his eyes and didn't answer for a while. "We've known each other a long time. Our relationship is very special. There was a great deal between us that just couldn't be erased."

"Did you only meet at restaurants? You never went to Marianne's place?"

Andreas understood right away what she was indicating. "We only met to talk and eat," he answered sharply.

Irene tried to form her next question as tactfully as possible. "Did it ever seem that Marianne would have wanted to reenter a sexual relationship?"

"No." His answer was short and swift, but he did not look at Irene when he answered. His fingers moved over his pant legs, and he started to pick at invisible lint.

Irene decided to widen the question. "She never talked about meeting another man?"

He looked up at her in surprise. Obviously the thought had never crossed his mind. "No. Never."

"Do you remember the last time you saw her?"

He bent down and snapped open his slender briefcase, which was made of soft brown leather. "I checked my calendar this morning. Tuesday, January twenty-eighth."

"And that was when you ate at the Fiskekrogen restaurant?"

"Yes."

"It seems Niklas did not know that the two of you got together so often."

"No. I told him that we got together now and then, just in case we were ever seen together. I was forced to let him know it did happen."

"But not how often."

"No."

Here was something Irene could set her finger on, but she did not know how to pursue it. This was a classic triangle: ex-wife, new lover, and the man they both wanted. Was Andreas Svärd ambivalent about his feelings? This was an angle of approach that Irene had to try. Neutrally, she asked, "How would you have reacted if Marianne had told you she'd met a new man? Maybe that she'd even stop meeting you for lunch?"

"I actually hoped she would. But at the same time . . . I needed her."

"Why?"

"Together we had a sense of belonging and . . . peace."

"You didn't have that with Niklas?"

"We have something else. Passion."

"Which you also can't be without."

It was not a question but a statement. Andreas just shook his head slightly in response.

"Do you have any idea what might have happened the night Marianne was killed?"

Andreas shook his head again.

"You were in Copenhagen, and we have checked your alibi. Do you know where Niklas was that night?"

"Niklas? I assume he was home sleeping. He's the head of his department, and he has to get up early every morning."

Irene decided to finish up. Andreas looked as if he couldn't slump any further into his chair.

They made their good-byes, and Irene reassured him that she would contact him the minute anything turned up. Andreas Svärd slipped his elegant coat back on and stepped into the hallway. Quietly, Irene shut the door behind him.

SHE SAT FOR a long time staring at the worn veneer of her office door. Her tired thoughts revolved around all the information she'd received, but nothing useful turned up. She suddenly had the urge to go home, although she knew there'd be no decent meal on the table and no one would be home to greet her. Krister worked until midnight every Thursday, and the twins were up in Värmland province enjoying their winter vacation. It would be just Sammie tonight.

Sammie! She'd forgotten no one was around to pick him up from doggie day care. She leaped from her chair and snatched the phone.

The voice of her doggie day care's mama was tired, but once Irene promised to pay double overtime, she agreed to keep Sammie until seven that evening. Not one minute longer, though, since she and a neighbor were going to bingo. Irene promised to be there on time.

Just as she placed the receiver back in the cradle, a hard

knock sounded on her door and Niklas Alexandersson's tanned face appeared in the doorframe.

"Hi, I'm here early."

His smile was blinding white. He surveyed her with his amber eyes.

"Come on in and sit down." Irene gestured at the visitor's chair.

Niklas slid smoothly into it. He was wearing a honey-colored heavy cotton shirt and nougat-brown chinos. His body seemed bathed in golden light, as if the entire man were gilded. No one could expect mourning for Marianne from Niklas. He watched Irene quietly and waited for her first question.

"Yesterday when I talked to you at the hospital, I gathered you found Marianne somewhat irritating."

Niklas replied by rolling his eyes heavenward.

Irene said sharply, "Did I misunderstand you?"

Niklas stopped his theatrics and said shortly, "Yes."

"Well?"

"You're wrong. I did not find her somewhat irritating. I found her totally irritating."

"How so?"

"Everything about her was an irritation. She hovered over Andreas and even his relatives in Kungälv. 'Patient, understanding little Marianne.'"

"What do you mean when you say 'hovered over'?"

"She didn't accept that their marriage was finished. She got both her parents and Andreas's parents on her side. They've never accepted our relationship. She wanted him back."

"What about Andreas himself?"

Niklas drew out his answer. "He wanted to live with me. I knew that our relationship was something special," he said triumphantly.

Just how Andreas had described his relationship with

Marianne not more than one hour before. Irene decided this was nothing to share with Niklas.

"You did not know that Andreas and Marianne were meeting as often as they did."

His face clouded over immediately. "No."

"What did you think about it once you knew?"

"I found out about it only yesterday. And now it doesn't matter." He smiled an evil smile.

For a second he reminded Irene of Belker. This was how the cat must have looked just before he'd dug his claws into the soft skin of her face. Niklas's smile disappeared quickly. He leaned over her desk and stared her in the eye.

"I know what you think. You believe that I killed Marianne so Andreas would never go back to her. But I can assure you that I did not kill her. Of course, I'm not a hypocrite. I'm not grieving her death. But how she died . . . no. There was no reason for me to kill her."

"Why do you say that?"

"Andreas will never leave me."

"Where were you at midnight between the tenth and eleventh?"

Niklas grinned again as he answered. "Believe it or not, I do have an alibi. I was at a pub with three friends all night long. And I'm going to hand you their names and addresses right now." He pulled out a folded piece of paper, obviously ripped from a notebook, and set it in front of Irene.

She did not glance down but kept her gaze steady on Niklas. "Let's hear your entire alibi."

Niklas leaned back and looked at her through half-shut eyes. Finally he said, "I do hope that Andreas will not learn of this. He doesn't know anything about it."

"What doesn't he know?"

"That I met these old pals. We've been friends for a long time, and they're not people he knows."

"What time did you meet them and at which pub? Remember, we will be checking up."

"Of course. I have a set time at the gym every night. I went straight to the gym after work on Monday. That's the address furthest down on the list. Then I went in the sauna and spent some time in the tanning bed. Probably left around seven-thirty. Then I went straight to Johan's place. His address is there, too. We waited for the other two, had a good dinner together, and then we went out."

"When did you leave Johan's apartment?"

"Around eleven P.M. We went to the Gomorrah Club and were there for the rest of the evening."

"When did you return home?"

"Three A.M. Alone. I had to get up early to go to work the next morning. That morning was hard, but I made it. I hardly go clubbing anymore. People get older and more stable." He smiled derisively.

"So you were with your pals the whole time."

"The whole time."

His self-assurance gleamed over his head like a halo. Of course all this had to be checked out carefully, but Irene felt he was telling the truth.

"And you would prefer that Andreas did not find out."

"Preferably not."

There was only a touch of worry in his voice.

Chapter 9

"MORNING. BEFORE WE get started, let's welcome an old friend," Superintendent Andersson said as he started the "morning prayer." "Hannu Rauhala from General Investigations has worked with us before."

Inspector Hannu Rauhala nodded and raised his hand in greeting. Most of the people working in the Criminal Investigation Division knew him, since he'd worked with them on a dicey case a few years earlier.

The superintendent continued. "As many of you have noticed, Jonny isn't here this morning. His entire family has the stomach flu. I went over to General earlier this morning and talked their superintendent into letting us borrow Hannu for a while as a substitute. Since Jonny isn't here, could you fill us in, Birgitta, on Linda's former partner, Pontus?"

Hans Borg took a deep breath, which made Irene look at him. She was surprised at his expression. His eyes were wide and frightened. The strangest thing of all was that Borg was staring at Birgitta Moberg. Birgitta noticed it as well and stared right back. He quickly looked down at his empty notebook, but Irene could see how his cheeks and ears were burning.

Birgitta nodded at her boss but shot Borg another direct stare before starting her report.

"Jonny and I headed over to Axel Dahlström Square, where we met Pontus Olofsson. He's subletting an apartment on the tenth floor of the skyscraper there. It appears he moved in last week and had his final few things moved from Linda's apartment on Saturday."

"That is to say, Saturday the eighth," the superintendent noted.

"That's right. Pontus didn't hide the fact that he took the breakup pretty hard. They'd moved in together just one year ago. According to Pontus, everything was fine until the beginning of January. Then Linda suddenly said she wanted a separation. To Pontus this came straight out of the blue. He had no clue why, but she wouldn't change her mind. Around the same time, Pontus had a friend who was leaving to spend a year in the United States, so he was able to rent his friend's apartment."

"So Pontus was not happy about separating," Andersson said.

"No, not at all. He said he didn't have the slightest idea why Linda wanted him to move out. He asked her over and over if there was someone else, but she said that there wasn't. She only said that she did not love him anymore. So he picked up his stuff and moved into the apartment in Högsbo."

"What kind of alibi does he have?"

"Airtight. I checked it. He was in Borås taking part in his employer's personnel-training program between Monday morning and Wednesday afternoon. He shared a hotel room with one of his co-workers. The night between Monday and Tuesday, he was in the hotel bar with this co-worker, and they were busy raising their glasses at around two in the morning, after which they went to bed."

"So it seems he's in the clear. Does he have any idea what might have happened to Linda?"

"No, but he's extremely worried."

"He didn't have a clue as to where she might be?"

"No. But I did ask him about Linda's day planner. He says she always had it with her. And when she takes her bike, she always wears a mini-backpack of light brown leather. So the missing items are these: one bicycle, one brown backpack, and Linda herself."

"But we have her day planner, and later today the techs will give it to me to go through. Hannu will be put on Linda's disappearance," declared Andersson. "Hans, did you find out anything more during your house-to-house by Löwander Hospital?"

Hans Borg had returned to his usual lethargic self, but by the way he fiddled with his pen Irene could tell he was still nervous.

"Nothing new. None of the renters or homeowners near the hospital has seen a thing. I also asked about Linda yesterday. Again nothing. No one has seen anyone fitting her description around there since late Monday evening."

"Damn it all, it looks like Linda went up in smoke," Andersson exclaimed glumly.

The other officers in the room could only agree.

The superintendent sighed deeply and turned to Irene. "What have you got on Andreas Svärd and his boyfriend?"

Irene summarized the interrogation of Marianne's ex-husband and his present partner. Hannu Rauhala nodded at her suggestion that he follow up Niklas Alexandersson's alibi.

Then Irene took up Mama Bird. She repeated her conversation with Folke Bengtsson and related the search of Mama Bird's shed shelter.

Andersson seemed surprised. "Doesn't the welfare office take care of people like her?"

Tommy flipped through the pages of his notebook before he answered. "I spent a great deal of time calling around yesterday. All I can say is that bureaucracy has managed to make some people invisible to us—and even, maybe, to themselves. They're bounced from department to department in the system until they finally cease to exist."

"But we've all seen homeless people," the superintendent protested.

"Homeless folks are not all alike. Many are drug-dependent. But the folks I'm talking about are mentally ill. Strange people who cannot make it in our society on their own. Or outside of society, for that matter." Tommy stopped to sip the last of his coffee before he continued. "Homeless people are almost impossible to trace via the welfare system without a name, number, or address. All we know about Mama Bird is her nickname, as well as the fact that she tends to feed the birds when she's at Drottning Square and that she's been staying at Löwander Hospital's shed since this past Christmas. We also have Irene's imitation of Mama Bird's speech pattern from the notes she took off of Kurt Höök's recording. They certainly show that Mama Bird is mentally ill. I've also contacted people at the Salvation Army and the City Mission, and they've told me that help for the mentally ill is different from that for addicts. There's a few treatment residences for the addicts, but nothing for the severely mentally ill."

"There has to be someplace they can go!" Birgitta protested.

"The reform that included closing mental hospitals and letting the mentally ill become integrated with society has worked for many people who have families and are in contact with the social-welfare offices. But they forgot about one group of people. Those who can't take care of themselves, even within a mental institution, are suddenly expected to handle their personal hygiene, their living quarters, their food, and their money. Many of these people also have no contact with relatives and often no friends. Many of them have committed suicide."

"How many commit suicide?" wondered Birgitta, upset.

"No one has kept any such statistics. No one wants to know."

"So where do these people hang out?" asked Andersson.

"They show up at cafés that the Salvation Army and other organizations run. People from City Mission drive around at night in a bus, and they'll creep out of their hiding spots for some sandwiches and coffee."

"So they take care of themselves as best they can." Birgitta was more upset than ever.

"Right. The City Mission and the Salvation Army do their best to take them in if they show up. Otherwise no one bothers about them. Last night I brought this up to my better half, who's a nurse, and she said that our society has returned them to the medieval state of the village idiot. I think she's probably right."

"But," Irene countered, "you said many other mentally ill folk have better living arrangements after the reform."

"That's certainly true, and many people were freed from confinement, but they probably were not the long-term mentally ill. The rest have no one to take their hand, and they've fallen through all the cracks in the system. Nobody seems to care about them."

"Why not?" asked Irene.

"People who need so much help cost society a great deal of money. This way they cost the state nothing. The best answer for politicians cutting the costs of government. It's their own final solution, so to speak."

Tommy paused, and no one else spoke up. "Anyway, today I believe I'll contact our colleagues in Nordstan shopping mall and see if they know where Mama Bird can be found. If we don't find her during the day, we'll have to stake out the garden shed at night. Let's hope she decides to show up to sleep."

"Fine," said Andersson. "Tommy and Irene are in charge of finding the bird lady."

Irene watched Hans fidget in his chair. He obviously wanted to get away, which was not like him at all.

The superintendent turned to him. "Hans, put on an intensive search for Linda's bicycle. Maybe it's been stolen. Maybe someone has turned it in to one of the other police stations. We have its brand and serial number. If we find the bike, maybe Linda will be found close by."

Irene thought the way Andersson put it was certain to bring bad luck, although of course he didn't mean it like that. She watched Hans Borg nod even as he got up. He was really in a hurry to leave. Irene was surprised to see Birgitta simultaneously rise and follow him. Instinctively, she got up to follow them both.

Irene watched Birgitta sneak around the corner a few meters ahead of her. Silently, Irene followed her, and just as she was rounding the corner, she heard Birgitta's angry voice: "Let go. That was in my in-box."

Irene saw Birgitta snatch at a brown internal-mail envelope that Hans had just taken from the box next to Birgitta's office. Borg didn't reply, but he also didn't let go of the envelope. Birgitta then kicked him in the shin. Borg yelled, and Birgitta took her chance, grabbing the envelope and dancing away with it. Irene saw Hans lower his head to charge Birgitta, and instantly she stepped between them. She blocked Borg's hand with her forearm, pushed away his hip with her left arm, and dropped him backward with an osoto otoshi. This was not hard to do, since he had the training and quickness of a sloth. She used a firm grip to keep him down. He whimpered that she was hurting him, but she didn't care. As long as she had a jujitsu black belt, third dan, no one would hurt a colleague. Borg now was painfully aware of that.

Andersson and Fredrik Stridh had also rounded the corner. Irene still kept her grip on Borg while he moaned. Birgitta stood holding the brown envelope tight to her chest. When she saw Andersson, she said, "Sven, we need to talk to Hans."

Andersson took one look at the brown envelope and

blanched. "What the hell! Of all the bastards!" Andersson's neck and face went from pale to beet red. All his officers knew that this was bad indeed.

"Irene, take Hans into my office," Andersson commanded.

Fredrik Stridh looked like he was dying to ask, but he knew enough to duck into his own room. Irene was still in the dark, but Birgitta and Andersson seemed well aware of the significance of the brown envelope. And Hans, too, of course. Without loosening the grip on his arm, Irene pulled Hans to his feet. As he straightened, she whispered into his ear, "Don't forget I'm right behind you."

Hans didn't answer.

Andersson gestured to Hans to take a seat in front of the desk. Hans slumped into the chair with no resistance.

Andersson sorrowfully shook his head. "Why, Hans, why?"

Borg said nothing.

"Answer me or this goes right to Internal Investigation. I've seen the other pictures. Disgusting."

Irene took the envelope from Birgitta, opened it, and pulled out some pictures. One glance was all it took. Not soft porn, either.

"That. . . . She . . . kept thinking she was so damn good and . . . clever. . . . Knew computers and was always up on the latest . . . All she had to do was wave her tits and get the best assignments and benefits. Talk about affirmative action. She was showing it off to everybody. But I saw through her."

Hans looked up at Birgitta as he spit out his venom. Even though his ranting was ridiculous, Irene could see that Birgitta was holding back tears. She was smart and talented with computers, but she wasn't the kind to flirt and flaunt. She and Fredrik had been in love at one time, but that wasn't what Borg was spouting about.

It was hard to imagine a deeper shade of red than the red on Andersson's face. He said nothing, however, just drew his hand over the sparse hair at the back of his neck. Finally he leaned across his desk and stared right into Hans's eyes with barely controlled anger.

"Bullshit. Birgitta's a good cop. You seem to have some problems, though. Go home and take a few days sick leave. This can't be swept under the rug, you understand. I'll have to report this to a higher level."

Hans sat motionless. Birgitta seemed as if she wanted to speak but bit her lower lip instead.

"You can go," Andersson dismissed Hans. "I'll call you this afternoon."

With one last spiteful look at Birgitta, Hans got up and lumbered out of the room. The superintendent sighed heavily and gave Irene a weary glance.

"This has been going on a while. A year and a half ago, Birgitta came to me and said someone had been sending por-nographic pictures to her by internal mail. Something hap-pened . . . that made her think Jonny was behind it, but Jonny denied that he was involved."

Birgitta could not keep silent any longer. "I didn't think it could be anyone but Jonny, the way he was always trying to cop a feel ever since I started here. Not to mention all his sex jokes. And the insinuations—" She stopped abruptly and tried to calm herself down before she continued.

"The whole thing started four years ago. Every few weeks an internal envelope would appear in my in-box with these porn pictures. When Fredrik and I were going out together last spring, it dropped off. But it all started again when I returned from Australia in October. I decided to hand over the enve-lopes to Sven."

The superintendent nodded. "I have five sets locked in my drawer. We checked for prints, but there weren't any. The last two had been addressed to Birgitta with a green felt pen. This morning Birgitta saw a similar envelope addressed with a green felt pen. I'd just walked into the hallway when she spotted it. I'd been out seeing about getting Rauhala on our team. Jonny couldn't have left it, since he was out sick since last night, but I was the only person who knew that Jonny wasn't coming in today. Birgitta and I decided to leave the envelope there and see if something happened, and it did."

He absentmindedly stroked the nonexistent hair on his bald head. He seemed old and worn out. "I'll deal with Borg now. Go on back to work."

Irene and Birgitta left his office in silence. They stopped outside Birgitta's room.

"I don't know what to say. This is . . . unbelievable," Irene exclaimed.

Birgitta nodded glumly. "No less true, though. In the beginning I just ignored those pictures. Thought that the whole thing would blow over. But . . . it never did."

Impulsively, Irene laid a hand on Birgitta's arm. "Let's go get some coffee. I could use a bucket of it after this."

Birgitta smiled. "Your universal cure for all problems—coffee."

TOMMY HAD ALREADY started phoning to set up interviews.

"First we're going to Nordstan shopping mall to see whether Mama Bird is hanging around there. The patrol cars are alerted, and they'll keep an eye out for her. A foot patrol will check the garden shed all night at regular intervals just in case she shows up. At least we won't need anyone posted there. The weather sucks, and it's supposed to be bad all through the weekend."

Irene looked out the window. The weather was truly bad, but at least she could stay inside where it was warm and dry. The foot patrol that she and Tommy would check in with had no such luck.

"Then I've made an appointment with one of the field-workers at the City Mission. We're supposed to meet him at three-thirty if we haven't found Mama Bird by then. He'll also ask around in case one of his co-workers knows anything. I gave him my cell number."

"But first it's over to our colleagues in Nordstan."

"Yep."

POLICE INSPECTOR STEFANSSON had recently been appointed squad leader for Nordstan's relatively new police station. Both Irene and Tommy knew him well from previous work.

He was sitting at a shiny new desk and seemed blinded by its glare. He wasn't much for desk work, but it came with the promotion. He looked at them thoughtfully before he said, "Yes, I know who you're talking about. A short, bony lady who feeds birds. It has to be her."

Irene was surprised when Stefansson tittered. He stopped as soon as he saw their raised eyebrows. "We've had to deal with her quite a bit, actually," he said. "At least once a week, someone from a grocery store calls and screams at us: 'She's here again.'"

"What does she do there?" Tommy asked.

"Steals, but only bread and other stuff you can feed to birds. She takes a shopping cart and fills it up with what she wants and then heads through the checkout line without paying. That's when the fur flies."

"Do they yell at her for taking stuff?"

"No, she yells at them for insisting she pay. She's even thrown bread loaves at people's heads and spit on them."

"Do you know her real name?"

"No, I don't." Stefansson shook his head in apology.

"Where's the most likely place we could find her?"

"Since it's raining cats and dogs out there, I suspect she's

trying to keep dry inside the mall, in one of the shops or maybe
the parking garage. Let me check with foot patrol to see if
anyone's seen her today."

Stefansson called both foot patrols on duty inside the Nordstan shopping mall complex, but neither of them had seen
the bird lady for a while. Shrugging in apology, Stefansson said,
"Sorry, you'll have to search for her yourselves. At least she
hasn't been taken to jail lately."

AFTER THREE HOURS going through stairwells and
parking garages, Tommy and Irene gave up, went to McDon-
ald's, and had one Big Mac apiece. It appeared that Mama Bird
was nowhere to be found in the entire Nordstan shopping
complex. Stefansson had called different shops to check
whether anyone had seen her, but all his results were negative.
No one seemed to have seen her the last few days.

"Where can she be? She's not here. She's not at the shed."
Irene sighed.

"I'll give Kent Olsson at City Mission a call." Tommy fished
his cell phone from his pocket and produced a wrinkled piece
of paper bearing the squad leader's telephone number.

"Hi, this is Tommy Persson again. We haven't found a trace
of the lady here in Nordstan. Have you had better luck?"
Tommy's face lit up as he listened. "Really? That sounds promising. We'll be there as soon as we can." He hung up.

"Kent's found a woman who knows Mama Bird. He told her
we'd buy her a half special if she stays until we get there."

"Finally a lead on the bird lady."

THEY HAD THE good fortune to find a parking spot on
Allmänna Vägen. In spite of the fact that they didn't have to
walk far to the City Mission Café, they were soaked through
when they crossed the threshold. Kent Olsson was standing
right inside the door waiting for them. He was a short, strong

man in his early middle age. His reddish hair and impressive beard framed a face with friendly gray-blue eyes. After saying hello, he said, "Mimmi, the woman you are going to meet, now has a tiny apartment of her own nearby. She usually comes here to our café every day just to have someone to talk to. Her sister died five years ago, and Mimmi was able to take over the apartment. It's her way back into society."

"How old is she?" Irene asked.

"About sixty. But she's able to take care of her own cooking and cleaning with only a little help from home services. She's proud of that. But, unfortunately, she's very lonely. She and her sister were the only two left in her family, and once her sister died, she was all alone. She has us, though."

"Do many mentally ill people come here?" Tommy asked.

"Yes, we have many. A few here at the café, but most when we're out in our deacon bus."

As they were talking, they reached a door with the word café on it. Kent Olsson held it open for them. The odor of unwashed human bodies was noticeable. There weren't all that many people around the table, which was surprising, since the weather was so bad.

"Not many people today," Irene stated.

"No, most of them had to leave already to find a place to sleep for the night," Kent Olsson answered.

Over by the window sat a small, plump woman. She wore a red headband and a torn jacket that had once been orange. Her smile was toothless and filled with anticipation. She got up from her chair with difficulty and held out a knobby hand. Irene took it warmly and did her best to ignore the strong urine smell the woman gave off.

"Hi. I'm Inspector Irene Huss."

"Hi. I'm Mimmi."

Mimmi's voice was grating and raspy. She cleared her throat

a few times and wet her lips with her tongue. It didn't seem to help, since her tongue seemed just as dry.

"Hi, Mimmi. I'm Inspector Tommy Persson."

From the corner of her eye, Irene noticed how some of the people closest to them listened as they introduced themselves. Then, one by one, they slunk out the door.

Irene decided to be direct. "Kent said you might know the name of a woman we're looking for. She calls herself Mama Bi—"

"Peep! Peep! Gunnela has peeps!" Mimmi giggled.

"Her name is Gunnela?"

Mimmi nodded enthusiastically.

"Do you know her last name?"

"Hägg."

Tommy was taking down everything in his notebook, so Irene continued. "How do you know Gunnela?"

"We lived on the same floor."

"At the mental hospital called Lillhagen?"

Mimmi nodded again and tried to moisten her dry, cracked lips.

"How many years did you know each other?"

"All of them."

"You mean all the years you lived there?"

"No, all the years she lived there."

"How many years was that?"

"Don't know."

Mimmi appeared uninterested and tried to keep her shaking left hand still by covering it with her right hand. The result was that both hands began to shake.

"How many years did you live at Lillhagen?"

Without looking away from her vibrating hands, Mimmi answered, "Thirty-two years, five months, and sixteen days."

"How old are you?"

"Fifty-six."

Irene quickly did the math in her head. Mimmi must have been around twenty-four when she'd been admitted to the mental hospital. Mimmi looked at Irene again.

"I tried to live outside of Lillhagen, but it didn't work. Now it's better with my shot once a month." She smiled.

"Is that all the medicine you need?"

A single nod was her answer. If the medicine lasted an entire month, it must be one powerful dose. No wonder the woman was constantly shaking.

"How old is Gunnela?"

Mimmi shrugged.

"Is she older than you are?"

"Younger. She's much younger."

Irene was surprised. She hadn't expected that. "Do you know how much younger she is than you?"

Mimmi just shrugged again.

"Did she feed the birds when you were living on the same floor?"

"Every time we went outside, she fed them. She could speak with the birds. So she said."

"Did you hang around with Gunnela very much?"

"No. She was younger."

"Do you know where Gunnela went to live?"

The tiny woman appeared surprised. "She lived at Lillhagen, of course."

"Do you know where she went to live after she left Lillhagen?"

"She lived at Lillhagen." Mimmi was certain.

It appeared that Gunnela Hägg was still living in the mental institution when Mimmi had moved out. At least now they knew the name of the bird lady; they'd be able to start with Lillhagen's records.

"Mimmi, did Gunnela have any family?"

Mimmi concentrated but finally shook her head. "No. She never had visits. I had visits."

Irene reminded herself that they'd promised Mimmi a half special—a grilled hot dog with mashed potatoes on top. They decided to take Mimmi with them and bought her one at the nearest hot-dog stand before she went on her way.

TOMMY CALLED THE station and asked Hannu Rauhala to find out as much as he could at Lillhagen about Gunnela Hägg. Since they'd worked with him before, both Irene and Tommy were well aware that Hannu had phenomenal ways of finding vital information out of thin air. Before Tommy hung up, Hannu let them know that Niklas Alexandersson's alibi held. He'd checked the three friends as well as employees of the Gomorrah Club. He also let them know that there'd been no progress on Linda Svensson's disappearance. They'd sent out a missing-persons bulletin covering the entire country now.

Tommy ended the call and stared out the windshield, depressed. The world around them was dissolved into fragments of light broken by cascading rain. Irene started the car resolutely.

"It's almost five o'clock, and I have to pick up Sammie. My dog-sitter will have a fit if I'm late two days in a row."

Tommy nodded. "By the way, do you know if there's a florist nearby?"

"Why do you need a florist?"

He laughed. "I have to take care of my sweetheart. Don't you know it's Valentine's Day?"

Irene had forgotten, but she said quickly, "Good idea. I need a bouquet for Krister, because he'll be home earlier than usual. We're going to have a wonderful Valentine's Day dinner."

She really longed to get home.

• • •

IRENE TOOK SAMMIE for a walk in the pouring rain. Afterward she arranged the bouquet of tulips in a vase in the center of the dinner table and put out the good china. She had no idea what Krister was going to prepare, but he would have to buy ingredients on the way home, since the refrigerator was empty. She'd need to write a shopping list and get more groceries tomorrow, because Krister would be working all weekend. At least he didn't need to go in until late afternoon. Tonight they'd have a pleasant evening. A tingling of expectation warmed the spot between her legs. It would be wonderful to spend Valentine's Day evening without the children at home. As the clock ticked toward nine, she decided to call Glady's Corner.

The maître d' told her that Krister was still in the kitchen. Irene asked to speak to him. After she'd waited what seemed like an eternity, Krister came on the line.

"Hi, sweetheart. Sorry, I haven't even had a free minute to call you. We're totally swamped here, and Svante called in sick."

"When do you think you'll be home?"

"Probably ten-thirty at the earliest."

"Oh." Irene couldn't hide her disappointment. At the same time, she felt so hungry she couldn't stand it. Carefully, she asked, "Well, what should we do about our Valentine's Day dinner?"

"Valentine's? That's today? No wonder there's such a rush here. Well, we'll have to have a Valentine's Day lunch tomorrow instead. I'll be dead on my feet when I get home. I've been working since nine this morning."

They kissed through the phone and hung up. Irene irrationally felt abandoned. And there was nothing here for a real dinner.

She fried an egg and put it on a slice of bread that had been sitting in the bread box for a few days. Searching through the cupboards, she found a can of tomato soup, which she warmed up. There wasn't even any near beer in the house. Her meal did not put her in a festive mood.

She turned on the TV and settled on an American cop show. Her movie counterparts killed six people in a matter of minutes with no consequences. She found that it all made her feel somewhat ill. Maybe she should just go to bed.

As she lay awake, she thought about many things. Life at home wasn't running as smoothly as it had when Krister worked only thirty hours a week. Back then the fridge was always full and dinner was always made. He'd also done most of the grocery shopping and cleaning. Now that he was working full-time, and overtime to boot, he wasn't able to plan things the same way. Jenny and Katarina were probably a bit spoiled. They never had to cook, go shopping, or clean. Of course, they were busy at school with their studies and their activities. How much did it cost to have someone come in and clean? Certainly that would be politically incorrect. But they probably could afford someone. It would be wonderful to come home to a clean house. Then maybe she and Krister would have enough energy for shopping, cooking, and being with the family. Not to mention the dog, Irene reminded herself, as she felt Sammie turn over in his sleep and land on her feet.

Their sex life was suffering. Suffering? Nonexistent! It must have been at least two weeks since they'd last had the chance to make love. Krister was often too tired. And, to be honest, she was often much too busy at work. But she was always too busy at work. The unbidden memory of the reporter Höök's mischievous, glittering blue eyes under a shock of blond hair came into her mind's eye. He was certainly very charming, that reporter, and he even resembled Krister, just ten years younger. With the kind of energy Höök gave off, he'd never be too tired to. . . .

The last time she glanced at the clock before she finally fell asleep, it was ten after eleven, and Krister still had not come home.

Chapter 10

Snores were rattling the windows at 6:34 a.m. when Irene realized that she was awake for good. Krister was on his back, sleeping with his right arm thrown over his head. Sammie was also lying on his back at the foot of the bed, and he was also snoring, though not as loudly as his master. When Irene got up to put on her jogging clothes, Sammie squirmed up to the warm spot she'd left behind. You can't wake up a sleeping dog, he seemed to say, but Irene saw that he did look at her through half-open eyes.

It was still raining, although not as hard as yesterday. She pulled her nylon rainwear over her jogging suit. Jogging was not her favorite sport in this kind of weather, but it was the easiest and fastest first thing in the morning. A rainy Saturday before 7:00 a.m. should guarantee peace on the bike trail down to Fiskebäck's boat marina.

As she started, her right knee ached from an old injury, but as she went on, it loosened up and the pain disappeared. The rain lashed her face and began to soak through her cap. Her mind was beginning to clear from its morning drowsiness, and she felt her heart pump oxygen-rich blood into her system. Once she reached the harbor, she turned and jogged up past the summer cabins. She made her way through the elegant mansion area and from there onto Stora Fiskebäcksvägen. She imagined that most people in those apartments were still sleeping, although she could see the shimmer of TV screens behind a few curtains. Small children were probably sitting and watching videos so that their parents could sleep in. After she passed Björnekulla, she continued to Berga, and then turned toward home. A six-mile run was certainly long enough.

SHE FORCED SAMMIE outside to pee before she went to take a shower. As the warm water streamed over her, she felt rewarded for her hard work in the cold rain. She wrapped a towel around her hair and walked naked and steaming into the bedroom. Krister was awake, his eyes partly shut against the light coming through the hallway's skylight. Irene lifted her arms to slowly rub her wet hair with the towel. This trick was amazing for shaping breast contours. One could say it was low-budget plastic surgery. The trick had the desired effect on her husband. When she crept back into bed with him, she could tell plainly that he thought she was the sexiest woman on the planet.

THEY DID MAJOR grocery shopping later. When they came home again, Krister whipped up a fantastic lunch: a shrimp stew with the delightful aroma of garlic, wild rice, and a salad on the side. It more than made up for the lost dinner the night before. A piece of chocolate and coffee finished it off. Full and content, Irene looked at Krister from her sofa perch. He'd been her husband for fifteen years now. Krister had sunk deep into his armchair, his head resting on the back and his eyes shut. His reddish blond hair was thinning, and more of his forehead was visible. Around his eyes were new crow's feet. He'd always laughed easily, so she could consider them laugh lines. In just three years, he'd turn fifty, one of life's greatest milestones.

In the beginning she'd fallen for his wonderful smile, and it was still the heartwarming and mischievous smile it had always been. He was one inch taller than she was. In his opinion he was still fit from years juggling heavy restaurant pots, but he probably should have added some training at the gym. He'd put on close to fifty pounds the last few years, and his waistline showed it. A wave of love washed over her. She got up, went to him, and kissed him gently on the forehead while settling onto his lap. Luckily, she hadn't gained weight at all after she'd had the twins. Her lips touched his cheek as she said softly, "What are you thinking about?"

He sighed and opened his eyes. "The meaning of life. Is this what it's all about? Coming home absolutely exhausted? Today there are so many unemployed folks aching for a chance to work, while those who have jobs are working themselves to death."

"I have to agree with you. Those poor nurses at Löwander Hospital are wearing themselves out, but the hospital keeps cutting staff. The ones still on the job are just getting older and more worn out, while the young folks today want to study media or music. The dream jobs seem to be hosting for a music channel or actress on a soap opera."

Krister laughed. "Someone in charge has made a real mess of things."

"What do you think the twins will want to be?" asked Irene.

Krister thought a moment. "Katarina will probably be a gym teacher or a jujitsu instructor, if you could make a living at that. She'll probably do languages. Jenny probably will focus on music. Maybe she'll be a veterinarian, though she doesn't have the grades for it—you need a fairly high grade-point average to get into vet programs. Or she'll start farming vegetables."

His mood grew darker at the thought.

"So you're not thrilled with her becoming a vegan."

"Hell, no. I'm a culinary professional. We've always had good, well-balanced meals in this household."

Irene understood that Krister was taking Jenny's veganism very hard. She tried to comfort him. "It's probably just a phase."

"I certainly hope so," he grumbled.

• • •

LATER THAT AFTERNOON Krister headed off to the restaurant. Sammie showed that he had to go, and there was nothing else for Irene to do but go back outside in the rain. When they returned, Sammie was wet through and through, so Irene thought she'd just as well give him a bath. It had been a while, and he was starting to smell. After the usual fight, the bathroom was soaked, so Irene decided it was a good time to clean it. The kitchen floor also needed a thorough scrubbing, but perhaps it would be better to vacuum the whole house first. She was not often hit by the urge, but today, as she felt crumbs crunching underfoot, she was seized by cleaning mania. Not to mention the piles of laundry stacking up; it was hard to imagine how high they'd get once the twins returned the next day and unpacked after their ski vacation. And the heap of ironing had become gigantic. But there Irene drew the line. Those who needed something ironed would just have to do it themselves.

Even though Jenny and Katarina cleaned their rooms themselves as part of their allowance agreement, Irene decided she'd still vacuum in there to catch the biggest dust bunnies. Sammie was cowering beneath Katarina's bed, so she didn't send the hose under there. Although he happily fought cats and badgers up at their summer cabin in Värmland, he was scared to death of the vacuum cleaner. He wouldn't come out until it was put away again.

She did vacuum under Jenny's bed. The vacuum cleaner hit something, and a large, gray rolled-up poster came out. Curious, Irene peeked into it. She could see handwritten red letters: SLAUGHTER IS TORTURE. She shook out the contents, four handwritten posters with various slogans: DON'T USE ANIMAL-TESTED PRODUCTS! SPRAY-PAINT FUR COATS! EAT MEAT = EAT CORPSES!

Irene sank down onto Jenny's bed. There was a sticker on

one of the posters bearing the initials ALF. Like most police officers, she knew that ALF stood for Animal Liberation Front. It appeared that Jenny was not only a vegan refusing animal products for ethical reasons, but that she was also an animal-rights activist. Irene remembered that the shop selling fur coats in the center of Göteborg had had its windows smashed and all the fur coats on display spray-painted. Had Jenny been a part of that?

"Give me strength. What am I supposed to do now?" she said out loud to herself.

As she looked inside the roll again, she saw a smaller piece of paper. She pulled it out and smoothed it down.

It was obviously a hand-drawn map. On the top was written "Liberation Zoo FS." Irene sat for a moment studying the map and suddenly put it all together—the pet-store break-in at Frölunda Square. She got up resolutely and went to the phone in the hallway.

She called a few colleagues in the Västra district and finally found out what had happened.

On the morning of January 27, a report had been filed concerning a pet store at Frölunda Square. The owner had just opened the shop and had gone into the storeroom to get food for the animals. When he came back out, a youth wearing a black hoodie ran out the door. The owner tried to catch him, but he got away through the square's automatic glass doors. There was an old VW bus outside the building. Its engine was running, and its license plate was covered with mud. It shot away toward Tynnered. The police had not found the perpetrator, the bus, or Putte, the dwarf rabbit that had been the only animal stolen.

Jenny could hardly have been involved in this so-called liberation. She didn't declare herself to be a vegan until two weeks later. She'd still been happily eating hot dogs and chicken at the time of Putte's rabbit-napping. But why would

Jenny have these posters and this map under her bed? Irene decided that it was clear there'd have to be a serious talk with her daughter once she'd returned.

She finished her cleaning halfheartedly, her thoughts elsewhere.

IRENE WAS WATCHING the news on TV when the phone rang. She put down the plate of microwaved leftover shrimp strew. She had a feeling she knew who was calling and felt a twinge of guilt. She was right.

"Hi, Irene, it's Mama. It's been a while since I heard from you."

Irene made the usual excuses: too much work, too much stuff to do, she'd planned to call.

Her mother would soon be seventy but was still energetic and healthy. She hadn't married again after Irene's father passed away ten years earlier. They agreed that Irene would come over for Sunday lunch before she'd have to go get the twins from the central train station at 4:30 P.M.

She'd barely finished her cooled off leftovers before the phone rang again.

"Hi, Huss. It's me, Lund."

Her former colleague and old friend Håkan Lund, now superintendent of Central Station, had never called her at home before. Irene managed to hide her surprise as she said, "Hi. Nice to hear your friendly voice."

"Same here, but that's not why I called. We just received a call from Löwander Hospital. There's been a fire on the grounds. Apparently some kind of garden shed. I couldn't contact your duty officer . . . let me see . . . Hans Borg. Since I know that you're involved in the murdered-nurse case over there, I thought you might want to know."

Andersson had obviously forgotten that Hans Borg had weekend duty when he'd sent him home, and Borg's name was still up. Not surprising. With Jonny out, too, there was a lot to keep track of. Irene debated for a moment what to do.

"Thanks for calling, Håkan. I'll head out to the hospital right away."

"Okay Hope this helps."

WHEN IRENE ARRIVED, the fire was out. The fire truck was parked in front of the building and the hose had been dragged around the perimeter, but the firemen were already winding it up. Irene spotted the fire chief a moment before he was about to drive away. She ran up to his red Volvo and knocked on the window.

"What do you want?" The chief had a deep, warm voice with a touch of a Scanian accent.

"Hi, I'm Criminal Inspector Irene Huss, and I'm working on the case of the nurse murdered here earlier this week."

"I read about that."

"What happened? Was anyone injured?"

"No, no one is hurt. There was no one in the shed when it caught fire. We got here quickly, but it was thanks to the guys in the patrol car the whole thing didn't go up in smoke."

"They called in the alarm?"

"Yes, it seems they were looking for someone. As they got near the shed, they saw the fire. One of the guys ran back to the car and gave the alarm. Then he brought the tiny fire extinguisher from the patrol car. It's not much, but it was better than nothing."

"And you made sure no one was in the shed."

"Right. There was just a heap of trash inside that was on fire."

"Do you think it was set?"

"Hard to say, but I believe it was. The fire inspectors should be able to give you an answer, but they won't be here until early tomorrow morning. Right now it's still too hot to go inside."

Irene thanked him. The fire truck started its engine with a deafening rumble, and both vehicles disappeared through the front gate. After they left, the silence was palpable. Irene got her flashlight and walked toward the park behind the hospital building. It was spooky to have the large, dark building behind her. A hospital should be a hive of activity, not a monument of black silence. I imagine Nurse Tekla is making her night rounds now, Irene thought with a grimace in the darkness.

As she rounded the building, the smell of smoke became heavy, almost suffocating. She switched on her flashlight and walked toward the overgrown garden. At the opening made by the wild lilac arbor, she turned. If Mama Bird had been standing in this spot, she would have clearly seen a person entering the hospital building, but what about when the person left? It must have been pitch-black after the electricity went out. Wait a minute. Of course, the moon, she thought. There had been a full moon that night. Siv Persson swore she'd seen Nurse Tekla in the bright moonlight. Irene shivered. All this talk of ghosts was starting to get on her nerves.

She shone the beam of her flashlight directly through the arbor. The garden shed was still standing but appeared to be burned out. Irene tried to peer inside, but it was hopeless. Everything was black as soot. Better to let the technicians look at the residue in the morning. There was nothing she could do now. The lawn sucked at her rubber boots as she squelched back to her car.

She pulled off her muddy boots and changed to her jogging shoes from the trunk. If the weather was going to stay like this, she wouldn't want to go jogging. She'd have to exercise indoors instead. Tomorrow she taught a women's group, something she enjoyed. She'd been training eight female officers in jujitsu for the past year. The suggestion had come up at last year's annual meeting, and having Irene lead the class was a given. There was no other female black belt, third dan, in

Sweden. Without giving it a second thought, Irene took on the job. Sometimes she brought Katarina with her and used her as an assistant trainer. Her pupils had been extremely hard-working, and the way they were going, they'd soon be on a par with the men.

She sheltered from the rain in the car to dial Superinten-dent Andersson's number. Ten rings, no answer. She dialed Central Station and reached Håkan Lund again. There was nothing for it but to tell Lund that she'd be on call the rest of the night. Birgitta Moberg was scheduled on Sunday. Then everything would be back to normal.

IRENE'S PHONE RANG at 2:25 A.M. She was awake imme-diately and quickly threw on her clothes. Krister did not stir at the sound. He'd just gotten home one hour earlier and was in deep sleep.

This new case was not pleasant, but not unusual. A man had beaten his wife to death in their Guldheden apartment building.

When Irene arrived, the husband had already been taken down to the station. The woman was lying in a pool of blood in the bathroom. Her face was misshapen after a beating gone berserk. The technician was already in the middle of investi-gating the crime scene. Irene didn't recognize him and decided to wait with her questions until he was finished.

In the meantime she did a hasty reconnaissance. It was a five-room apartment, complete with kitchen. The place was tidy and well cared for. In the largest bedroom, there was a huge, unmade king-size bed. The sheets were rose-colored. There was a great deal of blood there as well. It appeared that the beating had begun in the bedroom and culminated in the bathroom. In the photo of the woman on the dresser, she seemed young and beautiful, and she was smiling at the pho-tographer.

The technician appeared to be wrapping it up. He stood and wearily pulled off his gloves as Irene walked toward him with a friendly nod.

"Hi, Irene Huss. Inspector in the Violent Crime Division."

The young man looked at her gloomily from behind glasses as thick as bottle bottoms. Maybe it was his thin black hair, parted on the side, that made Irene think of a vampire. He was unusually tall, thin, and sallow besides.

"Hi, I'm Erik Larsson, Åhlén's substitute."

"How do you think this happened?"

"Major trauma to the head and neck. The back of the skull is broken. The victim reeks of alcohol, as does the perpetrator."

"Where's the patrol car?"

"They got another call. I told them they could take off, since you were on the way. This lady and I could take care of ourselves in the meantime."

Maybe he said it as a joke, but Irene still shivered. Where had Svante Malm dug up this guy? Probably in the nearest crypt.

The men from the funeral home arrived. They packed up the body and then drove off to Pathology. Irene left the technician in the apartment. As she walked into the hallway, a neighbor stuck her head out from her front door.

"So did he finally beat her to death?"

It was five in the morning, and the woman was dressed in sweats and a sloppy cotton sweater. Her hair was greasy and gathered in a ponytail. Even though she wasn't as tall as Irene, the woman gave the impression of being fairly large. She probably weighed over two hundred pounds. Irene's experience told her she'd found a witness eager to talk. She showed the woman her police ID by waving it just like they did in Hollywood.

"Morning. Criminal Inspector Huss here. May I come in and have a little chat with you, as long as you're awake?"

"Sure." The woman couldn't hide her pleasure and eagerly backed up to let Irene come through the door.

Irene automatically let her eyes sweep through the room. She concluded that this was a woman who really needed a cleaning service. The hat rack was covered in clothes, and the floor beneath it was layered in shoes of various styles. Irene's feet crunched crumbs and other debris as she walked over the floor. In the minimal kitchen, the counter was piled with dirty dishes, which she thought might have been the source of the odd smell in the place. However, when Irene entered the living room, the smell's origin was clear. It had probably not been cleaned in a year or more, and cats filled the place. There were at least nine that she could count. Unconsciously, she touched the surgical tape beneath her chin.

"Please go ahead and sit down," the woman said. She gestured toward a worn-out armchair of an indistinct gray, its seat cushion covered with stains.

Irene gave the cat colony a mistrustful look. "No, thanks. I'm not going to stay long. Excuse me, I didn't catch your name."

"I probably didn't say it. I'm Johanna Storm."

"How old are you?"

"Twenty-five."

"Profession?"

"I'm studying psychology. I have one year left until I take my qualifying exams."

Mostly for appearance's sake, Irene wrote the details in her notebook. "What did you mean by asking if he'd finally beaten her to death?"

"Just what I said."

"So he often beat her up?"

"Yup."

"How often?"

"Since Christmas it's been every weekend. Maria—the wife, that is—is Polish and can't speak Swedish."

"When did she come to Sweden?"

Johanna thought about it. "I don't know. She moved in

with Schölenhielm last summer. But she's probably less than half his age. What a horny old goat!"

"Were you the person who called the police?"

"Yes, because it was worse than usual this time. The police have been here lots of times before. At least five or six. This time she screamed so horribly, one long scream, and then everything went totally silent. My cats got really nervous, and I just knew something terrible had happened."

"That was right before two?"

"Right."

Johanna Storm didn't know much more about the couple in the neighboring apartment than that Maria had stayed at home during the day and Schölenhielm was a used-car salesman. "Would you like a cup of tea?" she asked.

Irene declined politely. Although she'd recently had her tetanus vaccination, she doubted she would survive drinking tea from one of Johanna's mugs.

IT WAS ALMOST eight o'clock when Birgitta stuck her head through the door of Irene's office. "Hi, what are you doing here?"

Irene explained the unfortunate circumstances that had brought her to the office that Sunday morning. When she mentioned Hans Borg's name, Birgitta's face clouded over.

"Andersson is going to let him off. He called me yesterday and said he and Bergström had decided to let Hannu Rauhala and Borg switch jobs. On paper, Borg is still with us in the Violent Crime Division. But the exchange is made already."

"So no internal investigation?"

"Nope. The bosses say that there's already too much bad publicity. It wouldn't look good after the incident with the woman walking her dog in Stockholm."

"You and I both know that similar incidents happen all the time that never get reported to the media."

"That's exactly what I told Andersson. Unfortunately, I got really upset and said a few things I probably shouldn't have. But I was so damned disappointed. Andersson told me to think everything over. If I argued too much, he'd consider moving me, too."

Irene contemplated her colleague. "So what you're after is revenge on Hans Borg?"

"Of course! He made my life hellish for years."

"Then you want to move to another department?"

Birgitta stiffened. "No."

"Well, then listen to me. Forget fantasies of revenge. Of course what Borg did was disgusting. But if bosses feel backed into a corner, they'll lash out. At you. If you keep pushing, you'll be transferred, and there will be a write-up in your file about how uncooperative you are to work with. They'll bury you in the bowels of the department without a chance of any career advancement."

Birgitta didn't answer.

Irene continued calmly. "This whole time you've kept your cool. Wait it out. Don't show your feelings."

"So if they smell blood, they'll attack, is that what you're saying?"

"Something like that."

The atmosphere became tense. Finally Birgitta broke the silence. "Finish your report on the Guldheden incident, and I'll take over."

"I've already written up my questioning of the neighbor, Johanna Storm, as well as my report of the crime scene."

Irene pulled the disc from the computer and handed it to Birgitta, who took it without looking at her. With a curt "Thanks," she disappeared into the hallway.

THE HOUSE WAS empty and silent. Krister had taken Sammie for a walk. The rain poured down in sheets outside so solid it looked like laundry hanging between the trees. Irene gratefully crawled into bed at ten in the morning. Before she fell asleep, she set her alarm for two hours later.

WHEN IRENE WOKE up, Krister had already left for Glady's and Sammie was in his dog bed, his paws in the air, almost dry from his walk in the rain. On the other hand, Krister had gotten his half of the bedsheets so wet they needed to be hung up to dry so that they would no longer be damp that evening. Irene felt as if she were hungover, an effect of sleeping during the day. A long shower alternating between hot and cold water helped her wake up. Since her mother's lunches tended to be filling, all she needed was a cup of tea and a hardtack sandwich for breakfast before she headed out to teach the women's class. Sammie had to come, too, and wait in the car. He was so thrilled to realize he was going for a car ride that he hardly took the time to lift his leg on the spirea bushes along the garage wall. In Sammie's mind the car was his, though he was generous enough to let his masters drive him.

IRENE'S MOTHER, GERD, still lived in the apartment she and her husband had bought when Irene was born. The three-story brick town houses lining the hill along Doktor Bex Gata always brought back memories of Irene's childhood. In those days people thought of it as the outer suburbs, but now Guld-heden was considered centrally located.

The wind blew stronger up here, and the rain came down harder. Even Sammie didn't think a walk would be pleasurable, and he hurried up the stairs.

"Hello. My, how late you are. I called, but there was no answer, so I thought that you were already on your way here. But when you still hadn't arrived, I thought something might have happened and—"

"Hi, Mama. Do you have a towel for Sammie? I forgot to

bring one." Irene said this to stop her mother's habitual tirade. Maybe she was just lonely? No, Irene told herself, in order to placate her conscience. Her mother had always found ways to keep active.

Lunch was a wonderful flounder gratin with heaps of fresh shrimp, and they both enjoyed it. They were drinking coffee afterward when her mother suddenly said, "In three weeks I'm traveling to the Canary Islands."

This took Irene totally by surprise, but she managed to stammer, "How . . . nice." As far as she knew, her mother had never traveled to anywhere but Denmark.

Gerd took a deep breath and looked her only daughter in the eye. "We, I should say. Sture and me."

"Who's Sture?"

"A man I met at the tea dances. You know I go there every Thursday."

"How long . . . have you . . . ?"

"Known each other? Half a year. He started coming to the dances last fall. His wife died two years ago, and he had a tough first year, but then he began to go out and meet other people. And then we met at the dances . . . and, so . . . that's how we met."

"But why didn't you say anything to me? He could have joined us at Christmas—"

"Last Christmas he was with his daughter in Örebro and I was with you. And New Year's Eve he was with his son here in Göteborg. But we had a nice Twelfth Night together."

Her mother's cheeks turned pink. It was a strange feeling to be sitting across the table from her newly in love, almost-seventy-year-old mother.

"How old is he?" Irene asked.

"Seventy-two. He's healthy and active. Though he does have a little asthma."

"What's his full name?"

"Sture Hagman. He's a retired postmaster. He lives on Syster Emmas Gata. He sold his house after his wife passed."

Now it was almost time to pick up the twins. Irene hugged her mother and wished her happiness with Sture.

IT WAS HARD to find parking. Irene had to circle around for quite some time before she found a spot. Once they entered the elegant train station, Sammie's little terrier heart rejoiced at all the new people. The hissing, braking train inspired him to go for much bigger game than his usual mopeds. Irene scolded him and tried to calm him.

The train from Karlstad pulled in to the station, and Katarina and Jenny were the first ones out the door. Sammie was beside himself with joy and had no intention of listening to nonsense about behaving.

The girls looked happy and healthy. After hugs and kisses, they began to tell their stories about what had happened on vacation, speaking over each other. Irene listened with half an ear, her attention drawn to the headlines posted on the Pressbyrån newspaper kiosk.

WHY WAS NURSE MARIANNE MURDERED? WHERE IS NURSE LINDA? TIME IS RUNNING OUT!

In her own mind, Irene added a few more headlines: WHERE IS MAMA BIRD, AKA GUNNELA HÄGG? AND WHY DID THE GARDEN SHED BURN? And another one: WHY DID NURSE MARIANNE HAVE NURSE LINDA'S DAY PLANNER IN HER POCKET? Irene had the strong feeling that she did not really want to know the answer to that last question. But of course she did. That was part of the job.

Chapter 11

THE RAIN STOPPED during the night, and the streets were slick. The temperature was just below freezing, and the traffic was as bad as it usually was during the winter in Göteborg.

Irene was late for "morning prayer," but as it turned out, everyone else was late as well. Svante Malm was the last one to come through the door. An expression of relief passed over the superintendent's face when he saw Malm. Technical investigations ought to be finished by now; maybe there would be some answers.

"Good morning, everyone!" Andersson began heartily. Irene understood this to be an attempt to energize the group, but both Birgitta and Jonny seemed to need more than a cheerful greeting. Jonny's pale appearance probably was the result of having the stomach flu, but Birgitta's face was also pinched and white. Maybe she was just tired from the weekend shift, but Irene feared she was holding in real anger.

However, the superintendent maintained his cheerful demeanor. "Hans Borg has asked to transfer to a less challenging job for now, so he's moving to general and Hannu is joining us."

Irene, Birgitta, and Hannu were the only ones who showed no surprise. Andersson ignored the shocked murmurs and plowed on. "Anything turn up on Linda Svensson?"

Fredrik and Birgitta shook their heads. "No one's seen her

since she left work last week," Fredrik said. "We have only her neighbor's testimony that Linda left her apartment at eleven-thirty that night, a strange time to leave on a Monday. There's nothing to go on."

"She certainly wasn't dressed for a bar," Birgitta added. "According to Pontus, the only things missing from her apartment are a red down coat, black stretch jeans, and a light blue angora sweater, her favorite one. But she'd never wear that sweater to a bar. She never wanted it to smell of smoke."

"Angora sweater. Belker . . . she's a cat lover," Irene said, apropos of nothing.

"That could be important. She loves Belker and would never leave him without food," Birgitta said. "The passport found in her apartment indicates that she's not abroad. And if she'd left voluntarily, she certainly would have arranged a cat-sitter. Pontus Olofsson said this about her a number of times. And I think he's right."

Andersson looked at Birgitta a moment. "So you really feel she didn't leave on her own."

"No, she didn't."

Silence fell over the group. To everyone's surprise, Hannu was the person who broke it. "I've made the rounds this weekend, and no one has seen her."

Irene almost asked if he'd been trolling his underground Finnish contacts, but she managed to stop herself in time. The man had amazing sources. Irene remembered the first time that they'd worked together. Hannu was able to flush out things no one else could find. Whether all his methods were legal, she couldn't say. At times she wished she knew, but at other times she suspected it was better not to know.

"I looked into Niklas Alexandersson. His alibi checks out. Three of his pals as well as employees at the Gomorrah Club saw him until two in the morning," Hannu continued.

"Damn, he would have been perfect. Sneaking around the hospital in a nurse's dress and murdering his rival," muttered Andersson.

"Any clues in Linda's day planner?" asked Birgitta.

Andersson shook his head. "No, I didn't find anything. Maybe you should look through it again, though. A woman might see something a guy wouldn't."

He pushed the day planner across the table toward Birgitta. Without looking at her boss, Birgitta took it.

"I have a question. Where is Marianne's pocket flashlight?" Irene asked.

All the others looked at her in surprise.

"I've been turning it over in my mind. Marianne was a night nurse. All the night nurses carry a pocket flashlight. But Marianne didn't have one. All she had was Linda's day planner."

"It wasn't in the ICU?" Birgitta asked.

"No. I asked about it when I was there getting my scratches checked out. No one had seen Marianne's pocket flashlight."

"Strange. And the thing with Linda's day planner is also weird. Maybe Linda lost it before she went home and Marianne found it," Birgitta mused.

"Maybe Linda was biking back to pick it up," Fredrik suggested.

"Not in the middle of the night," Irene pointed out. "She'd have called and asked Marianne to put it somewhere where she could find it the next afternoon."

"Maybe there was something really important in it, so she needed it right away." They could hear that Birgitta didn't believe her own suggestion, but it wasn't much worse than any of the others.

The superintendent broke in. "If she hasn't left of her own free will, we must consider she might be dead. If so, where would her body be?"

"Perhaps she didn't get far," Jonny said.

"I agree," Fredrik said. "The farther she biked, the more chances that someone would have seen her."

"It was late, almost midnight, and at least ten degrees below freezing. So there probably weren't many people outside," said Irene.

"Okay. We'll keep on pounding away on Linda's disappearance. Hannu, Birgitta, Fredrik, and Jonny will continue that search." Andersson slammed his palm onto the table's surface so hard that his mug leaped and spilled coffee on the table— which didn't matter much, since it was marbled in old stains already.

"Irene and Tommy, what's up with the bird lady?"

Tommy told what they'd found out about Mama Bird. Then Hannu asked to take the floor again.

"I've contacted Lillhagen. Gunnela Hägg had been in care there since 1968, when her alcoholic mother died. The death of her mother triggered a psychosis. Schizophrenia, in her case."

"How old was Gunnela when that happened?" Irene asked.

"Eighteen."

Irene was surprised to hear that Gunnela was only forty-seven years old. Most of the witnesses that they'd questioned seemed to think that she was closer to sixty. Life had definitely not been kind to tiny Mama Bird.

"During the seventies and eighties, they'd tried to get her back into society, but were unsuccessful. She was just too sick."

"Any support from the family?"

"No. Her father and one of her brothers are deceased. Gunnela's younger brother works as a businessman and wants nothing to do with her. I called him, but he got angry. His family doesn't even know that she exists." Hannu's calm face, with its high cheekbones and icy eyes, did not reveal his personal feelings, but a slight sharpening of his tone perhaps indicated some compassion for poor, disowned Mama Bird.

"When did she leave Lillhagen for good?" asked Tommy.

"She moved to an apartment on Siriusgatan in the fall of '95. After a while a group of drug addicts took that over and she was booted out."

"Where's she been living since then?" Irene asked.

Hannu shrugged.

"I see. At least we know that she found shelter in the garden shed next to Löwander Hospital last Christmas. She was there as late as Tuesday night. That's almost a week ago now. Where is she? Was she the person who set fire to the garden shed Saturday night?"

Irene turned to Svante Malm in expectation.

Svante's freckled horse face broke into a smile. "I have no idea where she is. That's your job. The fire inspectors took a look at the shed yesterday. It was a good thing that the patrol caught it before the fire could spread. Otherwise the hospital could have burned down. The fire was definitely arson. It started in a corner heaped with rags. The technicians found a charred candlestick. The person who started the fire probably lit a candle and then held some flammable like paper right next to it, counting on the fact that the fire would spread to the rags."

"No sign of gasoline?"

"None. Underneath it all was an old sleeping bag covered with some kind of cotton blanket. Over that was a blackened layer of thin wool. And this."

From a pocket in his jacket, Malm pulled out a murky plastic bag, within which was a flower shape with four visible blooms. Malm turned the bag over to show the soot cleaned away there. The silver metal inside contrasted brightly with the dark soot.

"This is a nurse's brooch."

They could hear Andersson inhale sharply; color flared up in his face. Malm did not notice. "Yes, I've talked to the school of nursing. This brooch is from the H.M. Queen Sophia University College of Nursing in Stockholm."

Malm noticed the odd looks on the faces around him, and his proud smile faded. Andersson seemed dangerously close to having a stroke. Malm sat quietly, wondering what kind of apoplexy this was and whether it would pass.

Andersson looked down at the table and said in a controlled voice, "Excuse me, Svante, it's just that damned ghost coming to haunt us again."

Malm knew enough not to ask any questions. He just nodded. "The woolen cloth on top of the rag heap is extremely interesting. I studied it all yesterday afternoon. The fibers we found on Marianne's smock, as well as the ones that Tommy found on a pine branch, came from this wool, which seems to be part of a dress. We found buttons and what was apparently a belt made from the same fabric."

If Malm had imagined that this information would have been accepted calmly, he now could see he was wrong. The officers around the table were leaping to their feet. Irene stared at the technician. Strange. Now we're back to where we started. Löwander Hospital and Nurse Tekla's ghost."

"I'm a scientist. I would like to point out that my results indicate a living person. The talc on the victim's underarms reveals that the murderer wore gloves. Threads and fabric remnants indicate a dress. The brooch is real. And what's more, so is the fact of Marianne's murder," Malm said.

"Thank you for bringing us all back to earth," the superintendent said darkly. He gave Irene a disgusted look. "From now on, no more talk of ghosts."

Irene had not meant she really believed that it was a ghost, but she let it go. Instead she said, "I think Löwander Hospital is at the center of all this. Both Marianne's murder and the disappearances of Linda and Mama Bird. The fire . . . it all goes back to the hospital."

"Then I suggest you go back there and poke around some more. Tommy can keep searching for the bird lady. God knows whether she's even important in this investigation." The superintendent's voice was sour.

But without knowing why, Irene believed in her bones that Gunnela Hägg was extremely important.

IRENE SAT AT her desk and stared, unfocused, at her computer screen. Absentmindedly, she sipped her fourth cup of coffee of the morning. The caffeine was beginning to have the desired effect; her thoughts were clearing. She suddenly thought of something no one else had. Marianne Svärd was not the only person who had died that night. Nils Peterzén had been a fairly wealthy man. Perhaps the old banker was the intended victim and Marianne Svärd had just been in the wrong place at the wrong time.

Irene turned the idea over in her head. She found Doris Peterzén's telephone number, lifted the receiver, and dialed. The line was picked up after two rings.

"Doris Peterzén."

"Good morning, Mrs. Peterzén. It's Criminal Inspector Irene Huss. We met after the sad event concerning your husband."

"Good morning. Of course, I remember you. I'm sorry I was such a mess . . . but it was just too much. All of it."

"I understand. I wonder if you have time to talk with me for a little while today."

"Ye-ess . . . Göran and I are invited to lunch at one, but I could meet you before then."

"Is Göran coming to you?"

"Yes, an hour before we have to leave. There are still many details we have to decide on about the funeral. Maybe that's just as well. This way I don't have to think so much."

Irene looked at the clock. "I can be at your home in half an hour. Would eleven work for you?"

"That'll be fine."

They said their good-byes and hung up. Irene thought through the scenario again: The murderer sneaks into Löwander Hospital, dressed as the hospital ghost. He is just about to kill Nils Peterzén when Marianne Svärd catches sight of him. The killer has to get rid of the night nurse because she would be able to recognize him. Perhaps she already knew him! Old bankers. A great deal of money. Often the sole motive for murder.

THE PETERZÉN HOME was one of the largest and oldest houses in the area. It had been built on top of a hill and had a wonderful view of the ocean. It was somberly whitewashed, the black tile roof coated with a shimmer of frost. The pale sun did its best to thaw out the icy shell encasing Göteborg. At least it had warmed the air to above freezing.

Irene struck the door hard with the bronze lion's-head knocker. The heavy oak door was opened by Doris Peterzén. She looked wonderful. Her silver-blond hair was combed into a thick pageboy. A necklace glimmered thinly over beautifully contoured décolletage. Her dove gray Thai silk dress matched her eyes perfectly.

Irene suddenly realized where she'd seen Doris Peterzén before. "It was kind of you to make time to speak to me."

"Come on in. I wasn't kind. I am angry. I want to know more about that ghost they wrote about in the newspaper. Was it really the person who sabotaged the electricity and stopped Nils's respirator?"

Doris moved aside and let Irene in. She hung up Irene's old, ratty leather coat next to her own beige mink without any reaction. Irene pulled off her brown boots furtively. They'd never looked worse than compared to Doris Peterzén's elegant leather stiletto boots.

Her hostess walked before her through an airy hallway and into an enormous reception room, the whole west wall of which was made of glass and faced the ocean. Along one of the shorter walls was a lengthy dinner table surrounded by an incredible number of chairs. The view from the room was fantastic. Irene was taken by the bleak February sunshine glittering on the ocean's lead-colored waves.

Doris Peterzén seemed used to the view. Without a single glance out the window, she invited Irene to sit down. They sat together on an oxblood sofa group of English design, less comfortable to sit on than to look at.

"Would you like a cigarette? We don't have to be so formal."

"No, thanks," Irene said. "I don't smoke. But informal is good."

"Have you found out who shut off the electricity?"

"No. We know there was a witness, but we still haven't tracked the person down."

"Who is it?"

"I can't tell you because it's still part of the investigation."

Doris Peterzén shook a long cigarette from a gold package. She needed both hands to lift the heavy crystal table lighter. She took a deep drag and blew out the smoke with evident enjoyment.

"The first time I saw you," Irene began, "I thought I knew you from somewhere, and today I remembered. I've seen you in my mother's magazines. You used to be a model."

Doris Peterzén smiled weakly. "That was a long time ago. I was a successful model. Very much in demand during the sixties. During the seventies not as much. You age quickly in that field."

"How long were you married to Nils?"

"Nineteen years. We met at a yacht-club ball."

"Was he divorced?"

"No, a widower. His wife had died from cancer the previous year."

"There's a large age difference. . . ."

Doris Peterzén stubbed out her cigarette in an ashtray that matched the table lighter. "Yes, people talked about it. There's twenty-six years between us. They said I was marrying him for his money. But I really did love Nils. He gave me . . . peace. Love. I have Nils to thank for everything I have in life."

"How did you choose Löwander Hospital for your husband's operation?"

Doris's beautiful face showed true surprise at Irene's change of direction. It took her a moment to answer. The Peterzén family has always trusted Löwander for our medical procedures. Kurt Bünzler, the plastic surgeon, is our good friend and neighbor. He's also helped me with a few things."

She unconsciously touched the back of her ears with her fingertips. Irene had already concluded that the smooth skin and the sharp features were the work of a fine plastic surgeon, and now she knew who'd done the job. She briefly glanced at Doris's perfect bustline and surmised that Dr. Bünzler had been doing his good work there, too.

"But Kurt Bünzler didn't operate on your husband."

"No, it was an inguinal hernia. Dr. Löwander does the normal surgery at the hospital. But the operation took longer than planned. Nils . . . bled a great deal. He obviously had adhesions that no one had expected. His lungs couldn't take the long anesthesia. Emphysema. He had to be put on a respirator."

Doris sniffed. Her deep grief seemed real, but Irene had seen a number of good performances during her police career. She changed direction again.

"Your son, Göran—when did he get home?"

Doris Peterzén blew her nose discreetly into a tissue she

made appear from nowhere. She pulled her voice and her face together. "He arrived on Thursday. I faxed a message to him on Tuesday."

They were interrupted by a metallic knock on the front door. Doris got up and swept out of the room. The word that came to Irene's mind as a good description of Doris was "regal."

Irene took the break to stand up and stretch her legs. She saw that the ocean now shimmered bottle green, the peaks of the waves reflecting silver light.

Doris Peterzén's pleasant voice brought her back from her reverie. "This is Detective Inspector Irene Huss. Irene, this is Göran."

Irene swung around and looked right into a pair of friendly blue eyes.

"Nice to meet you," Göran said as he offered his hand.

He was tall and muscular. Irene's brain short-circuited for a second. The son was older than the mother. It took Irene a moment to realize that Göran must be Nils Peterzén's son from his first marriage. Her eyes were drawn to the oil portrait hanging on the wall. The resemblance was striking. Nils Peterzén had a stricter mouth, however, and his gaze was sharp and hard. The son's expression was jovial, happy, and almost carefree. His elegant dark gray suit was strained across his back and rear but still had the look of expensive English tailoring.

Irene took his hand, which was dry and warm. Once they shook, Göran clapped his hands together and looked at his stepmother with playful horror.

"But, my dear Doris. We're letting the inspector die of thirst. Let's have a small aperitif before we all have to go."

He said the last sentence with his head cocked. His tone was easy, but Doris was not deceived.

"No. You have to drive. I'm still taking sleeping pills, and they affect me until the afternoon. It's probably time to start weaning myself. . . ."

Doris hadn't seemed medicated to Irene, but perhaps only Doris could feel the effects.

Göran's face reflected his disappointment, but he quickly overcame it and gestured to a white leather seating group. It looked much more comfortable than the one in red.

"Please, sit down," he said.

Irene sat on one of the armchairs. It was as comfortable as it appeared. Doris went to find a pack of cigarettes. When she came back, she draped herself in one corner of the sofa and lit one of the long cigarettes. Göran sat down in the other arm-chair. He crossed one heavy leg over the other until his tai-lored seams seemed to creak.

He watched Irene steadily as he reached out and took Doris's lit cigarette. She lit another one immediately. Göran drew the smoke in greedily and let it flow from his nostrils. When he spoke, small puffs exited from his mouth and nose.

"Why do you need to talk to us?"

"As Doris has probably told you, or perhaps you read it in the paper, a murder was committed in the hospital the same night your father died. The killer sabotaged the electricity, and your father's respirator quit working. We have a number of dif-ferent leads we have to investigate. One possibility might be that the sabotage was directed at your father."

The smoke production came to a standstill; both Doris and Göran seemed to be holding their breath. Before either of them could compose themselves, Irene continued. This is not our first line of inquiry, but all eventualities must be ruled out. Do you know of anyone who might want to hurt your father?

Göran let out a great puff of smoke and shook his head forcefully. "I hear what you're telling me, but I can't believe my ears. That anyone could consider murdering Papa? Never! He was too old to have enemies. Anyone who might have been one is already dead or decrepit. He and Doris have had a good life these past few years. Traveled. Played golf. Right, Doris?"

Doris sat up straight. "Indeed we did. Göran took over the business many years ago, but Nils still had a hand in. He had difficulty stepping back and just being retired."

Doris gave a suggestion of a smile to Göran, who grimaced and rolled his eyes. "That's the truth. Business was his life. Actually, it'll be tough to get along without him. He was a clever fox. He knew a lot and had a lot of important contacts." He looked worried. He stubbed out his cigarette with force. "Well, Doris, I think we'd better get going so we won't be late."

The three of them stood up and went to the door. Chivalrously, Göran took Irene's leather jacket from the hanger and held it for her. As she pulled up the zippers on her old boots, she keenly felt her lack of fashion sense.

Chapter 12

MICROWAVED LEFTOVER SHRIMP stew was not the worst possible lunch. Irene was seldom able to have lunch at home when she was working, but today she'd managed, since it wasn't far between Hovås and Fiskebäck. She quickly heated a mug of water in the microwave as she sorted the mail. Ads for miracle diets and rebates for gym memberships to prepare for the coming bikini season were predominant.

Absentmindedly, Irene scooped three heaping spoons of instant coffee into the hot water. As the coffee cooled, she went to the hall mirror and took a good look at her reflection. Her hair was passable. Reddish brown and shoulder length with some wave and a touch of gray. It needed to be cut, but she had an appointment tomorrow for that, she reminded herself. Her face was oval, and her wide mouth had good teeth. A bit baggy under the eyes, though. She tried lifting the edges of her eyes with her fingertips on her forehead. Her eyebrows rose and the bags disappeared, but she acquired an expression of chronic surprise. Not a good look for a criminal inspector. You probably shouldn't go around with a face that said, "Really? You don't say!" every time you visit the scene of a crime or bring a suspect in for questioning. That rationalization was easier than admitting she didn't have twenty thousand crowns for a face lift. Sighing, she let go of her forehead and looked at the clock. Time to head to Löwander Hospital.

• • •

AS SHE NEARED the exit for the hospital, she spotted a gang of boys busy on the bridge over the stream. Curious, she slowed and saw that the stream had swollen from the torrential rains during the weekend. On an impulse she parked at the side of the road and strolled over. The boys were about middle-school age. A muscular boy in a muddy snowboarding jacket dangled dangerously from the railing while he scrabbled industriously in the culvert underneath the bridge. He had a broken Christmas-tree branch to help him.

One of the smaller boys saw Irene and said, "He's only trying to get rid of what's blocking it."

Now Irene was able to realize that the creek had risen only on the upstream side. Farther down, the stream was flowing normally on its way to Mölndal River.

The boy with the stick was groaning from his effort. "There's something . . . here. . . . I feel it. . . . Damn! It's stuck! Now it's coming loo—"

The boy almost lost his grip on the bridge fence when the branch came unstuck with a jerk. It took Irene's brain a few seconds to register what her eyes saw. A soaking-wet pink beanie was dangling on the end of the stick.

THE FIRE STATION'S divers helped recover the body. Irene had immediately called Superintendent Andersson and Tommy Persson, who were now at the scene. The three police officers stared unhappily at the mangled corpse of Gunnela Hägg. Life had certainly been hard on Mama Bird, but her death had not been more merciful. Small animals had gnawed off her nose and lips. While waiting for the forensic doctor, they decided to place a gray tarp over her. The body was so emaciated that there were hardly any contours under the stiff plastic. They turned and walked heavily over to the other discovery the divers had made.

Linda Svensson's bicycle lay on the bank. It had been

wedged sideways in the culvert and had anchored Gunnela
Hägg's body in the rapid runoff of the melting snow. Superintendent Andersson inspected the bicycle morosely, mumbling
so quietly that only his people could hear him, "I see. That's
what a city bike looks like."

He straightened himself and turned toward the fire station's
chief. "I'd like your divers to comb the area around the bridge
and a bit farther downstream. Maybe the murderer threw in
something else."

The familiar white Ford Escort zoomed toward the bridge,
Yvonne Stridner's frizzy red hair visible behind the windshield.
Irene was extremely relieved to see her, although her boss was
not. Irene wanted someone as competent at Stridner at the
murder scene.

"The bike is here, but where's Linda?" the superintendent
asked himself.

"Linda? Is that the name of the victim?" asked Stridner.
She'd parked and walked up to the group, giving the gray tarp
an appraising look.

"No, Linda is the missing nurse. Her bicycle is over there.
The victim is Gunnela Hägg, a homeless woman," Andersson
said.

"I see. Well, tonight she'll be inside for a change. I won't be
able to do the autopsy this afternoon, so it will have to wait
until first thing tomorrow morning."

Irene thought, *Too bad some people have to die in order to be
indoors.* She was startled back to attention by Yvonne's brisk,
"Turn her over!"

The command was directed at two of the firemen, who
complied immediately. One of them rushed off to vomit into
the stream immediately afterward. Stridner didn't say anything, but her expression said, *wimp*, loud and clear. She pulled
on her rubber gloves and protective smock and began to
examine the body on the ground.

The police officers watched her in silence. All three felt oppressed by the shabbiness of life and death.

Ice-cold certainty began to seep into Irene's consciousness. Her lips were reluctant to form the words coming from her brain. "She's here."

Andersson was jolted from his thoughts. "Who? Gunnela Hägg?"

"No, Linda."

Tommy and Andersson looked at her and started to nod at the same time.

"She biked away around midnight. Her bike is here. Ergo, so is she," Tommy agreed.

They began to search. There were overgrown bushes all along the banks of the stream, as well as a number of fir trees whose long branches swept the ground. Linda could be under any of these. She certainly wasn't in the grove by the parking lot.

"We'll have to bring in a dog," said Superintendent Andersson.

Irene pulled out her cell phone and arranged for a canine patrol.

The sun had already gone down behind the buildings. The shadows under the trees began to deepen. None of the police officers wanted to talk. They stood lost in their own thoughts as they waited for the pathologist's preliminary results.

Finally Yvonne Stridner got to her feet. She waved majestically at the body, which the men from Funeral Services understood they could now take to the pathology lab. She ripped off her protective covering and stuffed it into a plastic bag. Irene realized then that Stridner was wearing rubber boots. They were uncharacteristically plain for the pathologist.

"Large, deep wounds on the back of the head. One or more powerful blows to the base of the skull. Again, we're dealing with a strong killer. I estimate she's been dead for a number of days. It's been cold until Thursday evening, which hinders decay. I will have to examine her more closely tomorrow."

"She must have been left on top of the ice, because the stream was frozen until last Thursday," Tommy pointed out.

Stridner nodded. "I'll have to keep those factors in mind when I perform the autopsy. She hasn't been in the water all that long. I'll get in touch tomorrow afternoon."

Mud squishing under her boots, the pathology professor turned to go to her car.

Andersson glared after her. "Why is she always in such a hurry to get back to work? It's not like her patients pick up and go home when they're tired of waiting."

Gunnela Hägg's body was carried away inside the discreet gray station wagon. The technicians had arrived and were wrapping the bicycle in the same gray tarp that had earlier covered the body. One of the divers shouted and triumphantly waved a muddy tool. Irene came closer and saw that it was a large pair of pliers. She did not doubt for a minute that they were the wire cutters. One of the technicians wrapped them in a large plastic bag.

Andersson looked extremely tired.

"I don't know about you, but I need coffee, preferably intravenously," Irene said.

The superintendent gave her a grateful look. It was starting to get dark in the ravine. The Canine Unit arrived, and two eager German shepherds were let out of the backseat of a Volvo. The superintendent was happy to see they were on a leash. He was not particularly fond of dogs—nor any other animal for that matter. He nodded and said, "Since Irene wants coffee, let's go back to the station and get some."

THE ENTIRE TEAM had assembled in the conference room. The superintendent briefed the rest on what had happened near the hospital that afternoon.

"Even though Gunnela Hägg was totally bonkers and completely harmless, she was a danger to the murderer. He must have understood that she had seen something the night of the murder when he read Kurt Höök's article," Tommy said.

Irene nodded. "So he knew who Mama Bird was, and he knew how to get her." She thought a moment. "When I asked around at the hospital, I had the feeling that very few people knew she'd stayed in the garden shed. Gunnela came late in the evening and left early in the morning."

"The murderer must have been waiting for her there," Tommy said.

"Nurse Ellen saw her once right after six A.M.," Irene said. "A hasty glimpse at the parking lot. They call the area Burnsite, by the way."

"Why is that?" asked Birgitta.

"There used to be an old mansion there, but it burned down eleven years ago. According to Sister Ellen, Sverker Löwander's ex-wife, Barbro, accused his present wife, Carina, of arson."

"Why would she want to burn the place down?"

"Because she didn't want to live there."

"Seems improbable. . . ."

"Stop all that side chat," growled Andersson. "We have to focus on last week at Löwander Hospital." The superintendent took a deep breath. "How do we explain Linda's bike? The canine patrol has found nothing. They'll try again tomorrow when it's light."

Hannu indicated he wanted to say something. "The bicycle was ahead of the body."

Everyone sitting around the table blinked. A second later Irene realized what he meant. "It was already in the culvert and kept her body from washing away. Therefore, it was there first," she explained.

"Maybe the bike could have been shoved in on the other side?" suggested Fredrik.

"Maybe so, but most logically the bicycle was thrown in

while there was still ice. It also would have been easy to push Gunnela's body over the ice to the culvert. If the weather hadn't warmed so quickly, they'd still be hidden. Bad luck for the murderer, but good luck for us," Irene concluded.

"Bad luck for Gunnela that she ran into Kurt Höök," said Tommy glumly.

Jonny turned to Irene. "That tape you listened to . . . did Gunnela Hägg say that Linda rode her bike from the hospital?"

"That's right. Should I get the tape?"

"Go ahead." The superintendent nodded.

While Irene went for the tape, Birgitta called in the evening's pizza order for delivery.

Everyone concentrated on the tape. Irene heard her own voice imitating Kurt Höök's as he asked Mama Bird how the nurse left Löwander Hospital after her revenge, then her imitation of Mama Bird: "She took the bike. God punishes theft!"

"Good heavens. That's the only place on the tape where she answers a question directly. But does she really mean that the person dressed as the ghost nurse biked off wearing the old-fashioned nurse uniform?" Irene wondered.

"Not all that improbable. The bike was shoved under the bridge. Then our murderer could have gotten out of costume."

"But then why burn it up in the garden shed as late as Saturday?" Irene asked stubbornly.

"Maybe just to get rid of the evidence," Tommy said. "No garden shed, no proof that Gunnela was staying there. No nurse's uniform, no proof that someone was wearing it to spook the nurses at Löwander Hospital."

Jonny looked at the tape player thoughtfully. "Gunnela said that the ghost nurse stole the bicycle. It was Linda's, of course. Maybe it was Linda who had dressed up as a ghost to haunt the hospital? She left her apartment early enough to play the spook. So perhaps she was the one who murdered Marianne?"

Irene nodded slowly. "Not so crazy. But some things still don't work. First, the night nurse who saw her was sure it was Nurse Tekla. I've seen a photo of Tekla. She was a large, strong woman, almost as tall as me, but bustier, with such thick hair it couldn't be hidden by a nurse's cap. Linda would never have been able to play Nurse Tekla. But I've met a woman who could."

"Who?" everyone asked in chorus.

"Doris Peterzén."

"Doris . . . ? Why the hell would she want to kill Marianne Svärd?" the superintendent sputtered.

"Money. The most common motive in history. She's inheriting millions. You should have seen her mansion in Hovås."

"She doesn't get anything from killing Marianne Svärd."

"Sure she does, if the idea was to create an accidental outage so that the respirator goes out and Nils Peterzén dies a natural death due to unfortunate circumstances. Marianne would be able to do CPR until the power came back on. Marianne had to be taken out of the game."

"But was killing her really necessary?" asked Tommy.

"Maybe it went wrong. Maybe Marianne was stronger than she appeared," Irene suggested.

Birgitta shook her head. "No. She was strangled with a noose. Was it brought along? I think the purpose was to kill her right from the start."

"You're right. Honestly, though, it doesn't seem to be Doris Peterzén's style," Irene admitted. "Cutting off the power to the respirator, committing a bloodless murder—that would not be out of the question. But killing an innocent nurse by strangling her . . . no. It's hard to reconcile that with Doris Peterzén's personality." She thought glumly for a moment, then brightened up. "Then again, we have Göran."

This statement was met with a polite, questioning silence from her colleagues. They knew that Irene's brain worked so quickly she ran through ten sentences before speaking the eleventh.

Andersson sighed. "Göran who?"

"Peterzén. Göran Peterzén. Nils Peterzén's son from his first marriage. He's almost sixty years old. Seems to have been under his father's boot his entire life. He said it would be hard to take care of business after his father's death, and I find that suspicious. A man who is almost old enough to retire himself can't run the bank without Daddy's help? And of course he stands to inherit a great deal of money, too."

Irene's cheeks had gotten slightly pink from the ideas that came pouring in. Jonny brought her right back to earth. "And this Göran would look like the perfect Valkyrie in an antique nurse uniform?"

Irene thought back to Göran's appearance and sighed. "No, he's almost six feet tall and weighs well over two hundred fifty pounds," she admitted. Her mood fell.

Jonny scoffed. "So Doris Peterzén, wearing a nurse's uniform, drives over to Löwander Hospital to cut the power so the respirator stops working. At the same time, she strangles Marianne Svärd. After that she pedals away on Linda Svensson's bicycle, wearing the uniform, and then shoves the bike down the culvert. She's shocked the next day when she reads that there's a witness and in some supernatural manner knows that this must be Gunnela Hägg. Maybe she's psychic? Then she kills Gunnela. On Saturday she returns to set fire to the garden shed and the nurse's uniform. And where does Linda fit into all this? Irene, I believe this is one of your worst theories ever."

Irene sourly thought that some people seem to recover more quickly than others from stomach flu. The worst thing was that Jonny was right. Linda's disappearance did not fit into her theory, and, of course, Linda was involved. Her day planner was in Marianne's pocket, her bicycle was in the culvert, and she'd been gone ever since Marianne's murder.

The pager buzzed to let them know the pizza had arrived. Irene and Tommy volunteered to go pick it up.

In the elevator Tommy said seriously, "We have to find Linda. Dead or alive. We won't understand how the murders of Marianne Svärd and Gunnela Hägg are connected until we do."

"So you believe it's the same killer?"

"Oh, yes."

THE SUPERINTENDENT STILL looked tired, Irene thought. This case was wearing him down. No one knew better than Andersson that they hadn't gotten much further than they'd been a week ago, when the only thing they worried about was Marianne Svärd's murder. So far the media hadn't found out that Gunnela Hägg was dead. As soon as they did, they'd bite. Andersson didn't realize that he'd sighed heavily, but everyone else heard it. Tactfully, they pretended that they didn't notice. At his age he was allowed a few small eccentricities. Not to mention he was the boss.

"I want to hear that tape again," Tommy said.

For lack of other alternatives, Irene started the tape from the beginning. Tommy leaned forward and listened closely until the end. "She took the bike. God punishes theft!"

"Yep! That's exactly what she says." Tommy looked at his colleagues in triumph. They all tried their best to appear as if they understood what he was getting at. "Don't you hear what she says? 'She took the bike. God punishes theft!' So the bike did not belong to 'Nurse Tekla,' but she was the one who pedaled away on it." Tommy used air quotes around the ghost nurse's name.

"So you mean that Gunnela Hägg saw Linda arrive and park her bike at the hospital but it was not Linda who biked away again," said Irene.

"Yep."

"And the person didn't resemble Linda," Jonny pointed out.

"Why would Linda park her bicycle and then disappear completely?" Irene countered.

Jonny glared, but he was forced to agree.

They listened to the tape one more time, but there was nothing to add.

"If Tommy is right, Gunnela Hägg saw Linda leave her bike in the hospital park. You could wonder why she went in the back way during the middle of the night. It's a little creepy, and she had a key for the much better-lit front door." Irene fell silent for a moment. "Did Gunnela see her actually enter the building? We don't know. But let's say she did."

"Okay. Let's say she did," Jonny snapped. "And then what?"

Irene pretended he'd said nothing. "Gunnela says that Nurse Tekla came out, took Linda's bike, and rode off." She paused to see if her colleagues were following her. Everyone kept silent, so she continued. "Gunnela said nothing about seeing Linda come out again."

Andersson glowered at her mistrustfully. "Still in the hospital? Ridiculous!" He thought it through. "But then again there's nothing to indicate that she ever did come out."

Chapter 13

THEY STARTED AT exactly 7:00 A.M. Everyone from Criminal Investigation as well as a Canine Unit convened to search the building from top to bottom. Another Canine Unit was assigned to the ravine.

The superintendent had collected the entire group in the basement, right outside the elevator door. "I talked to the technicians yesterday evening. They've already gone over the entire basement, the elevator, the stairway up to the ICU, and the entire ICU ward. We're going through the entire place one more time, every nook and cranny in this entire building, anywhere someone could hide a body."

Andersson surveyed his people. No matter how used to death they were, confronting it always lead to sorrow and depression. He sucked in another lungful of air. "We've gotten a master key from Bengtsson, the security guard. For our benefit he's also made available separate keys for each floor. Fredrik and Jonny will take the basement. The dog unit is also going to start in the basement and move on up. Birgitta and Hannu will go through the polyclinic and the entrance level. I'll take the care ward and the ICU, which is probably the least likely place she'll be found. If she's even here. Irene and Tommy will check surgery and the other rooms on the top floor."

Each team took its specific keys and scattered throughout the hospital building.

Irene and Tommy left Andersson at the care ward and

continued up to the top floor. Outside the surgical ward, they saw a young nurse trying to edge a gurney in through the doors. Tommy rushed forward and politely held the door open for her.

"Thanks," she said. "The automatic door isn't working. These old wires and fuses break down regularly." She smiled with sparkling energy at Tommy. Once she'd pushed the gurney inside, she turned in the doorway and asked, "Why are you here so early in the morning?"

Tommy inclined his head. "We're going through the entire hospital with a fine-toothed comb. Didn't you read the paper this morning?"

The nurse shook her head, surprised.

"Well, a murdered woman was found yesterday underneath the bridge at the back of the hospital's park."

"Good Lord! Terrible! Is it . . . was it . . . Linda?"

"No, a homeless woman. We've found out she sometimes slept out there in the garden shed. Had you heard any rumors about that?"

"No. I didn't even know that there was a shed. Not until the fire there, at least."

"Who told you about the fire?"

"Folke Bengtsson. He knows everything that goes on here."

"And you never heard a thing about the homeless woman?"

"No." The nurse's voice showed her distraction. She expertly slid the gurney against the wall to leave just enough room so another could pass. The hallway was certainly narrow. On the left were two operating rooms and on the right storage rooms and an office. The hallway gave the impression of being crowded and overstuffed.

"If you want to look around the operating rooms, you'll have to change clothes. If you're just going to stay in the hallway, please put on foot coverings," the nurse said. "Actually, right now would be the best time for you to look around. Surgery is scheduled in an hour."

The police officers peered in through the doorways of the operating rooms and saw immediately that there was no room to stash a body there. Just bare walls, operating tables, operating lamps overhead, anesthetic machines, and a few rolling tables and footstools. The only way to get rid of a body in this room would be to dismember it and mingle the pieces with the rest of the surgical waste.

The surgical ward was equally cramped; it would be just as impossible to hide a body (or pieces thereof) anywhere in it.

They walked the full length of the surgical ward's hall. As soon as they exited, they stripped off the blue plastic foot coverings to throw them in a waste basket.

Directly ahead was Administration. Irene peered into the elevator stopped on that level. It was small, with a maximum capacity of four people. It would be impossible to roll a gurney or a bed into it. To transfer a patient, then, the larger elevator at the back of the building would have to be used.

Tommy opened the first door, marked SECRETARY. Two desks were pushed together to face each other in the tiny room. A computer, surrounded by heaps of paperwork, stood on each desk. One entire wall was taken up by racks of folders with different-colored spines.

The next room had an imposing bronze plaque that proclaimed doctors' offices, but the room itself was not much larger than Tommy and Irene's office at the police station, perhaps even smaller. Here there were also two desks, two computers, and a shelf with folders and books. In one corner was a low armchair and next to it a floor lamp.

The bathroom beside it was minimal. One would either have to back up into it to sit or decide ahead of time to stand up to pee.

The cleaning closet was unlocked; this made Irene's pulse quicken for a moment. Perhaps a body would fit inside. But it held just cleaning supplies piled together in the small space.

"So the only room left is the on-call apartment," Tommy said, without much hope in his voice.

They unlocked that room and stepped inside. Just as Irene was about to switch on the light, she stopped. Heavy snoring vibrated throughout the room from the bedroom adjacent to the office. She motioned to Tommy to follow her as she sneaked toward the bedroom. She stretched her hand around the doorway and flipped the switch for the ceiling light.

The snoring stopped immediately. With an inarticulate sound, the person in the bed sat up. Sleepily, Sverker Löwander blinked at the police officers.

"Who . . . who are you? Oh, yes, the police. . . . Good Lord, what time is it?"

He looked just as disheveled as he sounded. His unwashed hair was sticking out in all directions.

"Quarter to eight," Irene answered.

"I have to get to the operating room in fifteen minutes!"

Löwander leaped out of bed. Irene was surprised to note that he was sleeping with his jeans and socks on. His upper body was bare, and his muscled chest, with just the right amount of hair, showed that he worked out to keep in such good shape for his age. There was not a spare ounce of fat on him. Irene found him fairly attractive. In spite of the fact that he was sleeping when they'd entered the room, he did not look rested at all. Just the opposite—he looked as if he hadn't slept in days. Irene hoped that the scheduled operations weren't complicated, for the sake of the patients.

Tommy cleared his throat. "Why are you sleeping here? Were you on call last night?"

Sverker Löwander stopped halfway in the middle of putting on his T-shirt. He lowered his arms and looked directly at Tommy.

"No, I wasn't on call. It might look odd, but . . . I was working on some calculations last night, and suddenly I was so exhausted I thought I would faint. It was four A.M. I don't even remember going to lie down, but obviously I must have."

Now both police officers noticed that the desk in here was covered with paper and notebooks as well as an old-fashioned adding machine. Long loops of paper tape printed with numbers hung from the table all the way to the floor.

"Did you figure it out?" Tommy asked dryly.

"No. No matter which way I run the numbers, it's still too expensive. I'm in a hurry right now. Can we continue this after lunch? I have no operations in the afternoon."

"That works for us. Let's say one P.M.?"

"Fine." Löwander was already running toward the operating room.

Together Irene and Tommy walked over to the desk and began to lift each sheet of paper carefully. Most of them seemed to be bids from various contractors. One was for roofing and another for drainage and pipe systems.

Tommy waved his hand over the mess. "Looks like old Löwander Hospital needs a big transfusion of cash. I wonder whether Sverker Löwander is suited to all this. Maybe there's a system here we can't see."

Irene glanced at the paperwork on the table critically. "Hardly."

They left the disorder of the desk. In the doorway of the on-call department, Irene turned to look back. "Do you wonder whether Löwander ever sleeps at home?"

"Couldn't prove it to me. We're always finding him sleeping here."

"LET'S FIND ANDERSSON and see if anyone else has stumbled across anything," Tommy said.

They were waiting by the small elevator when the door to the operating room was flung open and the young nurse peered out.

"The guy with the dog wants to talk to you," she said.

They followed the nurse back through the surgical ward, where more nurses were making their way between the gurneys. Irene realized guiltily that neither she nor Tommy had remembered to put on blue plastic footies. The nurses cast disapproving glances at their street clothes and shoes. Irene picked up her pace.

In the hallway was the canine patrolman with his German shepherd. The dog did not turn its head when Tommy and Irene entered but kept staring at a nondescript door right next to the larger elevator. A deep growl rumbled in the dog's throat.

Irene turned to the nurse. "Where does this door lead?"

"To an old attic storage area," the nurse answered with a tremor in her voice. She swallowed before continuing. "It's still used for storing stuff that isn't used much. Christmas decorations and that kind of thing."

The nurse looked from the door to the dog. "Oh, my God . . . that's Nurse Tekla's attic. I mean . . . the attic where Nurse Tekla died."

FLOODLIGHTS ILLUMINATED LINDA Svensson's body. She looked as if she were kneeling, her body hanging forward on the noose suspended from the ceiling beam, her calves touching the floor. Her long hair had fallen in front of her face. Beneath the window a rib-backed wooden chair rested on its side. Next to it was a red down jacket. The stench made it clear there need be no hurry to cut her down.

The technicians walked around taking photos from different angles. The police officers stood outside the attic room and watched the scene through the open door. The atmosphere was heavy, and no one wanted to break the silence.

The patient elevator hummed as it came to a stop and the door swished open.

"It looks like it's time for me to set up a forensics branch right here at Löwander Hospital," declared Yvonne Stridner.

It was entirely possible that she was trying to make a joke, but none of the officers laughed. Unperturbed, she scrutinized the hanging body as the technicians went about their work. Then she turned back to the officers, her expression grim.

"That's our strong-armed murderer again. It's hard work to pull up a dead body, even if, as in this case, the body was not raised to its full height. What frightens me the most about the three crimes here is the real cold-bloodedness of the killer. He seems to murder spontaneously."

"You think he did in the homeless woman, too?" Andersson said with surprise.

"Yes. The first blow was perfect—immediate death. The victim had no chance to cry out. Then the body was hidden in a culvert. I call that cold-blooded. What if someone had happened by?"

"And Marianne?"

"Same thing there. Powerful strangulation and quick death. The body hidden where the killer already planned to take out the power. One tough guy."

For once Andersson seemed to agree with Stridner. Mournfully, he nodded toward the hanging body. "How long has she been dead?"

"The attic is not heated, but it hasn't been below freezing in here. My informed guess would be about a week."

"So she died at the same time as Marianne," Andersson concluded.

"Possibly. I'll do the autopsy this afternoon."

With a nod to no one in particular, the pathologist disappeared down the stairs, leaving the faint scent of Joy de Jean Patou in the air.

Andersson sneezed when the perfume tickled his nose. After he collected himself, he said, "We're closing the hospital.

The entire place will be combed through—every square inch. All operations must be halted, and every single person in this place will be interrogated. Everyone! The techs will keep working in the attic while we check the rest of this building."

"Tommy and I made an appointment with Sverker Löwander right before Linda was discovered. Should we go ahead?" Irene asked.

"Do that. Birgitta, Fredrik, and Hannu will talk to everyone else in the operating ward. Jonny and I will take the care ward. Then we'll all go through the basement. Although the only person down there is the security guard."

"Let Tommy and me see him. We've talked to him before," Irene said.

"Fine," Andersson said. "Let's go, then."

TOMMY AND IRENE found Sverker Löwander back in the on-call apartment. He had sunk into the armchair, hands over his face. The noises coming from him sounded suspiciously like sobs. Irene and Tommy could think of nothing to say, so they let the doctor break the silence.

"What's happening to my hospital? Who's the crazy person running around here killing people?"

His last sentence sounded like a call for help, which it probably was. Irene saw his hands shake as he ran them through his hair. He was so beside himself that the police officers couldn't help but feel sorry for him.

Irene took the desk chair and turned it toward him. She sat down silently, while Tommy sat on the rumpled bed. Tommy cleared his throat and said, "Honestly, we don't know. But it's so serious we've decided to close the hospital today. We'll do all we can to solve these . . . occurrences. We would be extremely grateful if you were up to answering a few questions. Or would you like to wait until later?"

Sverker Löwander shook his head. "No! Now! I want these

murders solved! We can't afford to close for long. It will break us financially."

Tommy assessed him for a moment. "Perhaps that's where we should start. If I've understood correctly, Löwander Hospital is in economic difficulties. How serious is it?"

Sverker Löwander sighed heavily. "Very serious. The hospital will soon be one hundred years old. It needs a new influx of cash. For example, we need to drill a well. It's going to cost several hundred thousand crowns. The Civil Defense Corps has decided that all hospital facilities in the country must guarantee an in-house water supply in case of possible disruption to the water system. In addition, we have to install a drainage system around the entire building and replace all the old water pipes. The insurance company has condemned the old ones. The roof leaks and will have to be replaced. The copper tiles will cost me the shirt off my back. The safety engineer has given us six months to replace the ventilation in the operation ward. It no longer meets minimum standards for a hospital. During the renovation, activity must be shut down. So we have loss of income while employee salaries must still be paid. All of this together will cost at least five million crowns. That kind of money doesn't exist."

Tommy looked at the doctor in surprise. "Why is all this coming at once?"

Sverker Löwander stood up, mumbled an excuse, and went into the bathroom. The two police officers could hear him blow his nose and turn on the faucet. When he came out, Irene noticed that he'd washed his face and tried to fix his hair by wet-combing it. The result was not successful. But his eyes. . . . For a second, Irene met his gaze and found herself swirling into their sea-green depths. The man was dangerous!

An instant later that impression was gone; the man who drew up a chair appeared anything but a heartbreaker. Irene was ashamed of her thoughts and sat up straight. *Just like a romance novel*, she thought. She had to pull herself together and be professional. But before she was able to collect herself enough to ask a halfway intelligent question, Löwander began to speak.

"My father took care of all the investments and the renovations. He put a great deal of money into building that new stairwell so we could have a true hospital elevator. We moved the operation ward to the upper level and built the ICU," he said.

"When was this?" Irene asked.

"Late fifties. He managed the financial side until his death, about fourteen years ago."

Irene felt she had to ask another question to quell her curiosity. "Why is Källberg Hospital in the black while you're in the red?"

"They have much greater resources. They have specialists in all areas. They had money and investments and made their renovations before the crisis in health care. Now they are one of the most modern hospitals in Göteborg."

"And Löwander Hospital?"

"Basically, we're bankrupt."

A long silence followed this revelation. Irene broke it by saying, "So what are you going to do?"

"No idea. No one wants to buy the building to run it as a hospital." He laughed dryly. "Carina has the idea of opening a fitness center here."

"What do you think about her idea?" asked Irene.

"The way I feel now, I don't give a damn." He covered his face and bent forward.

Tommy and Irene shared a look over Löwander's back. Using the most comforting voice she could muster, Irene said, "We understand that you've been under a great deal of stress. First all your worries about the hospital and now these murders. If you would like to take a break, we can continue later this afternoon."

Löwander nodded. His head down, he disappeared into the bathroom again. Irene and Tommy stood but waited for him to return.

When he reappeared, he looked totally beaten.

"Would you like a lift home?" asked Irene.

"No . . . thanks. I'll stay here and try to pull myself together."

"Would it be all right if we came back at three this afternoon?"

"Yes. Thank you."

WHEN THEY REACHED the landing outside the care ward, Irene said thoughtfully, "He looks like he's heading for a nervous breakdown."

"No kidding."

"What do you think about these kinds of private hospitals?"

"Not a good thing. But if the public system can't provide good health care, it shouldn't stand in the way of our getting help elsewhere. Even going to private doctors. Dying while waiting in a line for care is completely crazy."

They continued in silence down the stairs to Folke Bengtsson's domain.

THE DOOR WAS wide open. They found an empty office. Everything looked the same, except that the cardboard box marked *Flags* was on the desk. Irene was looking inside when they heard Bengtsson's heavy tread on the stairs. He sounded rushed. Irene took a step back and turned toward the doorway as Bengtsson appeared. He was out of breath and seemed agitated.

"Finally! Somebody who will listen," he exclaimed.

He headed straight for the desk and opened the cardboard box. Triumphantly, he pulled out a roll of white rope.

"Look! What did I say?"

"Excuse us, Folke, but what did you say?"

Bengtsson looked from Irene to Tommy uncertainly. "But . . . I thought they sent you here to check it out."

"Check what out?"

"The rope! The flag rope!" Bengtsson exploded.

"What about it?"

"Someone has cut off a huge length of the rope. I went up to the attic, but the police wouldn't let me look. I said I had to see, but they still wouldn't let me in."

"Why did you need to see Linda?"

"Not Linda! The rope. The rope she hung from. I believe it's a piece of this."

He held out the coil to Irene, who took it with surprise. The rope was strong but soft and supple. Perfect for strangling someone. She didn't remember what the rope around Linda's neck looked like, but she needed to check it out immediately.

"You're probably correct. We'll go right away and see."

"I'll go. You two talk," Tommy said. He took the rope and headed out the door.

Bengtsson dried his face with a reasonably clean handkerchief that he pulled from one of the many pockets in his blue overalls. He blew his nose while he was at it. Then he smiled weakly at Irene. "Want a cup of coffee?"

"Thanks, I would." What a saint! *It was certainly past time to have a cup*, Irene thought.

"Make yourself at home." Bengtsson pointed at the rickety rib-backed chair and went to fill the coffeepot.

As the water began to percolate and the room filled with the blessed aroma of brewing coffee, Bengtsson searched for mugs and cookies. He exhibited a restlessness he hadn't last time they were here. He put his white mug with the English *I'm the Boss* on the table, sank down into his desk chair, and pulled out his handkerchief again, repeating the face-wiping procedure.

"You have to understand. . . . This morning a policeman

came with the wire cutters, which they'd found in the stream. Near the dead . . . Mama Bird. Who for the love of Christ would ever kill that poor woman?" He kept dabbing at his forehead. "The wire cutters belong to the hospital. I'm absolutely sure of it. Earlier I was searching down here for something that Marianne's killer could have used to sabotage the reserve generator. Then I wasn't able to find the wire cutters. They were missing from the toolbox." Bengtsson pointed indignantly at the toolbox on a nearby shelf.

"So they've been missing since Marianne was murdered," Irene concluded.

"Right."

Bengtsson got up to pour the coffee. "Last night I couldn't sleep. All sorts of thoughts were tumbling through my head— you know, Marianne's murder . . . the bird lady—and I thought it was nasty that the killer had been in here, in my room, and found himself a weapon."

Bengtsson stopped when he heard noise at the door. It was Tommy returning.

"You were right," Tommy said, his face grave. "It's the same rope."

Bengtsson nodded grimly, as if he'd been sure the whole time. He poured coffee into another mug for Tommy and took up his tale again.

"This morning I overslept, which is unusual. When I arrived at the building, I ran right into a German shepherd in the hallway. I asked the officer with the dog what they were up to, and the guy said they were looking for Linda. It was such a shock. That she'd still be in the building. Then I heard all the commotion in the surgical ward. . . ."

"Did you know Linda well?"

"I know everybody here. We would chat now and then. She was always energetic and happy. I can't understand why anyone would do that to her. Or the other two, for that matter. Unbelievable." Bengtsson shook his head sorrowfully.

"So how did you think of the flag rope?" Irene asked.

"Oh, yeah, that. I'd rushed upstairs and heard that she was . . . hanging in the attic. One of the operation nurses told me. Then I thought of something." Bengtsson paused, then spoke each word with emphasis. "I thought that if that devil had stolen one murder weapon from my room, he could steal another. I remembered the rope for the flag that I bought last fall." He said nothing for a moment. "I came down here and pulled down the box. When I bought the coil of rope, it was twenty meters long. Now it's hardly fourteen. I'd measured with my thumb, you see."

"So six meters are missing," Tommy said.

"Right."

They finished their coffee and found nothing more to say.

"IT'S ALMOST TIME for lunch," Irene said. "There's something we can do between lunch and when we meet Löwander at three."

Tommy sighed. "It's been my experience that your little ideas tend to take more time than we expect."

"Not this one. You and I should go see the old nurse who was working the night Marianne was murdered."

"The old lady who saw the ghost? Siv What's-Her-Name?"

"Siv Persson. Remember the brooch found in the shed? At the time I didn't recall this, but now I remember that Siv Persson wore a similar brooch that morning after Marianne's murder."

SIV PERSSON LIVED in a four-story apartment building of yellow brick only a few blocks from Löwander Hospital. Irene had called ahead from the Chinese restaurant where they'd had lunch—beef with bamboo shoots—to make sure she'd be home.

Siv Persson welcomed a visit from the police. Apparently she'd heard about the murder of Gunnela Hägg and was worried about Linda. Irene did not mention that Linda had been found dead. She decided it would be best to tell her in person.

SIV PERSSON LIVED on the fourth floor. The building had no elevator. After trudging up three flights, Irene rang the doorbell next to the teak door. It was a while before they heard noises inside. Irene put on a friendly expression, knowing they were being scrutinized through the peephole. When the door finally opened a few inches, Irene was reminded of a little mouse peeping from its hole. Nurse Siv was wearing the same gray woolen poncho she'd worn the first time Irene met her. Her hair seemed to be made from the same skein of the yarn. Underneath was a beige-brown dress. Even the most charitable person would not be able to say the dress was attractive. The only touch of color came in the light blue frames of her glasses, and even they looked faded.

"Good day, Nurse Siv. I'm Inspector Irene Huss. I just phoned you. And this is Inspector Tommy Persson."

"Good day." Nurse Siv opened the door and invited them in.

The hallway was so tiny that Nurse Siv had to back into the kitchen to give Tommy and Irene enough room to take off their coats. From her spot in the miniature kitchen, she said, "I remember you, Detective Huss, from that horrible morning after . . . the murder. But I'm sorry to say I do not remember Inspector Persson. There was so much going on. Please, though, let's not stand on formalities. Would you like some coffee?"

"Thanks, I'd love some. That is, if you were going to make some for yourself," Irene added quickly.

Siv Persson smiled weakly and turned on her coffee machine. She'd obviously prepared everything needed for a proper coffee hour. The living room's well-polished coffee table was set neatly with coffee cups and chocolate-filled cookies.

"I'm sorry, I have no coffee cake and didn't have time to run out and buy some."

"This is fine." Tommy smiled. "We're used to simple spreads with our coffee."

Siv Persson seemed pleased and tripped along to the kitchen. She returned with a sugar bowl and a creamer.

The moss green sofa with its beige armchairs—all straight lines and shining polished armrests—brought Irene back to her childhood living room. The low oval table matched the wood on the arms of the furniture. The pile on the shag carpet was red and green. The entire living room breathed the fifties. It wouldn't have surprised Irene for a second if Bill Haley's "Rock Around the Clock" suddenly blared from the speakers.

The art on the walls shattered that impression. The pieces could be measured in square yards and all seemed to be painted by the same artist. The color scale was strong and saturated, gorgeous landscapes with bluish mountains and lush green valleys.

The late-model TV had the largest screen Irene had ever seen. On both sides of the screen were huge speakers.

"My brother painted them." Siv nodded proudly at the artwork.

"They're wonderful. Was he abroad when he painted them?"

"Yes, he lived in Provence during the last twenty years of his life. He died ten years ago."

Was there a colorful person behind Siv Persson's gray exterior? When she sank her thin body into the beige armchair, it seemed as if she melted into it and disappeared. Only the light blue frames of her glasses remained floating in midair. Irene shook the image from her brain and decided it was time to get down to reality.

"As you probably figured out, we're here for something more concrete about what you saw the night of the murder," she began.

"I've told my story several times," Siv Persson said. There was a hint of worry in her voice.

"Of course. But now a week has gone by. Perhaps some things have gotten clearer to you or some new detail came to mind?"

The nurse pressed her lips together and shook her head slightly. Irene did not let herself be dismissed.

"Have you heard about the garden-shed arson?"

"Yes, it was in the paper . . . but that can't have anything to do with Marianne's murder, can it? Or Linda's disappearance? I didn't even know there was a garden shed back there."

"I assume that you know about the murder of the homeless woman."

"Yes, that was also in the paper. What is going on at Löwander Hospital?"

"That's exactly what we're trying to find out. And we need your help." Irene let her last sentence sink in. Then she said emphatically, "The murdered homeless woman lived in that shed."

Siv Persson's expressions ranged from suspicion to surprise. She wrinkled her forehead. "That can't be possible, can it? Living in a garden shed during the middle of winter?"

"She was probably grateful to have a roof over her head. Have you ever seen her around the hospital grounds?"

"What did she look like?"

"She was short and very thin. She wore a large man's coat held together by a piece of rope. Pink knitted cap."

"No. I've never seen anyone who looked like that. I certainly would remember it if I had," Siv Persson said firmly.

"Back to the fire on Saturday night. It was arson. The homeless woman had a bed of blankets and a sleeping bag.

The arsonist set fire to everything after he'd put a black wool nurse's uniform on top. We also found a nurse's brooch among the remains. It belonged to a nurse who graduated from the Sophia nursing school. I remembered you had a brooch that matched."

Without saying a word, Siv Persson stood up and disappeared behind a closed door that Irene guessed concealed her bedroom. Tommy and Irene exchanged looks. They could hear the nurse rummaging around. A few minutes later, Siv Persson came back. Somehow she reentered the room as a different person, straighter, with an air of authority. She'd transformed into a nurse right to the ends of her fingertips.

She wore a white hat with a wide black band; on the edge of the band was a narrow, crisp ruffle. The blindingly white dress collar had at its center the shining silver nurse's brooch. The black dress itself had puffed, capped sleeves lined with buttons. The bodice was short, a tight row of more black buttons running down to the waist. The pleated skirt came to the middle of the calf, revealing black stockings and shoes. Over one arm she had a neatly folded apron.

"This is how she was dressed," declared the nurse. She turned slowly so that the police officers could see the uniform from all angles. "But one thing was missing."

"Missing?" echoed the officers.

"Yes, missing. The apron was gone. This is how it's supposed to look."

Siv Persson shook open the crackling, starched apron so they could get a closer look. It had a gentle golden tinge, an indication of its age. "At home you always wear the apron."

"At home?"

"If you are working on a ward, you are at home in that ward. Then you wear the apron but not the belt."

"So when you're away from your department, you take off the apron and put on the belt? Do I understand you correctly?"

"That's right."

Irene and Tommy both got to their feet to inspect the dress more closely.

"It's not black. More like dark blue," Tommy said.

"But it wouldn't be practical to work in that uniform, would it? Hard to wash."

Nurse Siv snorted. "We certainly didn't work in this uniform! This is a dress uniform for important events. The daily uniform was a light blue cotton one. No puffed sleeves or all these buttons."

"And the person you saw the night of the murder was dressed just as you are now?"

"That's right. Tekla was also a Sophia graduate. Since the beginning of the twentieth century, it has been the tradition at Löwander to have nurses trained at the Sophia nursing school."

"But isn't Sophia in Stockholm?"

"Yes, but it was always the most prestigious school. Plenty of Göteborg girls applied to Sophia for their training. I did. Many of them wanted to return to Göteborg after graduation, and Löwander Hospital was happy to hire them. In those days working at Löwander brought status. Dr. Löwander's mother was also a Sophia nurse."

"You mean the younger doctor?"

"Yes."

"Are all the nurses at Löwander Hospital still graduates of the Sophia nursing school?"

"No, just Ellen and myself. All the others were educated here in Göteborg, except Margot. She got her education in Karlstad."

Irene tried to remain casual. "You are absolutely sure that it was Nurse Tekla you saw that night?"

The nurse sighed, and then she wilted. "I know it sounds unbelievable. But the moon was shining brightly—it was almost like broad daylight when the clouds broke up. I was about to enter the nurses' office and happened to look at the glass doors. And I saw her as clear as day."

"What did she look like? Did you see her face?"

"No, I saw her sideways, from the back. But she was tall and . . . stately. She'd set her hair up according to regulations. You were supposed to be able to see all the way around the collar."

"Did you see the color of her hair?"

"Blond. The light of the moon was reflecting off it. She looked just as she did in the picture I showed Superintendent Andersson."

"But she was 'away.' No apron."

"That's right."

Tommy hadn't said much, but now he squeezed in a question. "What was Nurse Tekla wearing when she was found hanging in the attic?"

Siv Persson looked at him with distaste. "She was wearing the daily uniform."

"With cap and apron?"

"Yes."

"How do you know?"

"Gertrud told me. She was there and helped cut Tekla down. Gertrud had taken over Tekla's position after she'd quit. So the two of them never met—in life, that is."

Tommy nodded as he reflected on her statement. Then he said innocently, "Why does she haunt the hospital in her ceremonial uniform when she hanged herself in her daily uniform?"

Siv Persson pressed her lips together. "I'm going to change," she said.

Irene stifled a smile and wagged her finger at her colleague in admonition. Perhaps he was correct in his suspicions, but there was no point in antagonizing Siv Persson. She was their most important witness, since she'd seen the murderer. The only other such witness had been silenced forever. At least they had Irene's transcript of Kurt Höök's tape recording. It was time to find the connection to Gunnela Hägg's murder. One thing on the tape troubled Irene, and perhaps Siv Persson would be able to enlighten her.

Irene did her best to appear pleasant when the nurse returned wearing her dust-colored clothes. She smiled as she said, "Perhaps you can help us with the other murder. The homeless woman, Gunnela Hägg. Does her name ring a bell?"

Siv Persson wrinkled her tiny face in concentration, then shook her head. "At first I thought . . . but . . . no. I don't recognize the name."

"Gunnela's statement was recorded the day after Marianne's murder. She told a reporter the story of Tekla's suicide. She even calls her by name."

Siv Persson appeared surprised. "Strange. Maybe she worked for us?"

"Hardly. She was an inpatient at Lillhagen for over twenty-five years and—"

"That's it!" Siv Persson leaped out of her armchair. Her pale face was brightened by a slight flush. "Was she at Lillhagen . . . let's see . . . thirteen years ago?"

"That's right."

"Then she could have been one of the ten patients we took in from Lillhagen when they closed for the summer. Löwander Hospital did it to generate extra income. We signed a contract with the hospital's board and took a number of patients from different medical institutions." She fell silent to think for a minute. "All the following summers we had no mental patients, thank God. Löwander Hospital is not set up for long-time care and certainly not for mentally ill people. It was the worst summer of my life. At least as far as my work was concerned."

"That could be something to check out. Let's ask Hannu to follow up on that."

Irene's last sentence was directed to Tommy, who pulled his cell phone from his jacket.

Irene also stood and took Siv Persson's hand. She thanked her for the coffee and the inestimable help she'd given them. As she put on her jacket, mostly to have something to say, Irene asked, "When are you going to return to work?"

Siv Persson crossed her arms on her chest as if the room had suddenly gotten very cold. "Not before my own surgery in two weeks."

"An operation? I hope it's not serious."

"No. Cataracts in one eye."

Irene froze. She remembered her mother complaining before her cataract surgery about how fuzzy everything appeared and how difficult it was for her eyes to adjust between light and dark. Trying not to show her agitation, Irene asked, "Do your cataracts bother you much?"

Tommy lifted an eyebrow questioningly. But this could be important.

"Oh, yes. It's worst when I read. All the lines meld—" The nurse stopped suddenly and glared at Irene. "I know what you're implying. But I saw her clearly. The clouds parted, and the moonlight flooded in through the windows. I saw her!"

Irene chose her words carefully. "I have no doubt that you saw a woman. But it was no ghost. You saw a murderer dressed up. Put aside all thoughts of a ghost. Think about a real person. Who might it have been?"

Siv Persson didn't answer, just hugged herself more closely. Tommy walked over to her and set a hand gently on her shoulder. She trembled but didn't shrug his hand away.

"We don't want to scare you, but we believe that Gunnela Hägg was killed because she'd seen the murderer. Her statement indicates that she had." Tommy paused and let his words sink in before he continued. "You are now the only surviving witness. This is a dangerous killer. You must take precautions.

Do not open the door if someone rings and you don't know who it is. Even if you do know someone, think back and make sure that it isn't someone who could have dressed up as Nurse Tekla."

"Well, you are certainly scaring me now."

"With good reason. We found Linda this afternoon. She's dead."

"No!" Siv Persson reeled as if she'd been hit. Irene took her arm and led her to the chair. Nurse Siv sank into it heavily and stared straight ahead. She whispered, so softly they could hardly hear her, "How did it happen?"

"You mean how did she die?"

She nodded wordlessly.

"She was found hanged in the same place that Nurse Tekla hanged herself. From a beam in the attic ceiling. The pathologist believes that she's been dead for a week."

"So she died the same night as Marianne," Siv Persson said emotionlessly.

"That's more than possible, but we don't know for sure."

"Was it . . . suicide?"

"We don't know. We have to wait for the autopsy results. But I agree with my colleague. Think about what happened to Marianne and Gunnela Hägg. Be careful. Please, stop thinking that you saw a ghost. Ghosts don't commit murder. That's left to the living."

The nurse's face looked like a death mask, but she nodded to show she'd heard what Irene said.

"Will you be all right? Shall we call someone for you?" Irene asked.

The nurse shook her head heavily. "I'm used to taking care of myself. But . . . how can anyone be so cruel? Kill young girls like that. And that poor homeless lady. . . . It's horrible!"

Both police officers nodded. Senseless atrocities were playing out in the old hospital.

• • •

IRENE SIGHED. "NURSE Siv is right. It makes no sense only because we don't have a motive. If we had a motive, we would be able to close in on the murderer."

Tommy nodded. They were in the car on the way back to Löwander Hospital. It was going on three and time to continue their talk with Sverker Löwander.

His cell phone rang, and Tommy answered. He didn't say much. After he clicked off, he said somberly, "That was Andersson. Stridner has just called from Pathology. Linda was definitely murdered."

They completed the drive in silence.

SVERKER LÖWANDER WAS as pale as a corpse. Irene was starting to wonder if he had already gone over the edge. His hair had still not been washed, and he smelled strongly of sweat. He looked like a man who had lost his whole world. *Which he probably has*, Irene thought. In spite of his worn appearance, she still found him extremely attractive. Obviously some people have it and some people don't. Unfair.

"Sit down," Löwander said, skipping any small talk. Tommy sat down on the bed, and Irene pulled out the desk chair. They were all sitting exactly where they'd been that morning. Only one thing had changed: Now the police knew that Linda Svensson had been murdered.

"I want to ask you about Linda," Irene began.

Löwander looked nauseated. After drawing a few deep breaths, he said, "Excuse me, but all of this has been . . . just too much."

"I understand. First the economic difficulties and now the murders. Not exactly the kind of advertising a private hospital would want," Irene said.

"No hospital in the world would want any of this." Löwander sighed.

"Returning to Linda. When did you see her last?"

"Monday the tenth. I saw her briefly during the morning rounds. I swung by the nurses' station to look for some misplaced paperwork. It was supposed to have been sent up to the operating room."

"Which paperwork?"

"What's that got to do— Nils Peterzén's medical consultation. His heart and lungs weren't in the best shape. There wasn't much time to read through it before surgery."

"How did Linda appear the last time you saw her?"

"Appear? The usual for a Monday morning with a full operation schedule. Stressed. Not more than average, though. She was her usual self."

"Did she say anything to you?"

Löwander's forehead wrinkled in thought. For a brief moment, he showed his fifty years. "We said hi and complained about the cold. . . . I asked where the paperwork was, and she helped me look for it. She was the one who realized that it was probably still down at the secretary's desk."

"Did you see her later that day?"

Löwander shook his head. "I spent the rest of the afternoon and the evening in the ICU. Peterzén was in bad shape. I might have caught a glimpse of her around five when she was leaving for the day. But I couldn't say for sure if it was that specific Monday or the Monday before. . . . I'm so tired. I'm totally exhausted." Löwander covered his face with his hands.

"What is your opinion of Linda as a person?" Tommy asked.

"Happy and pleasant. A good nurse."

"Have you ever seen any indications that she might have a problem?"

"What kind of problem?"

"Maybe a drug addiction or something similar?"

The doctor shook his head emphatically. No, absolutely not. Marianne Svärd didn't take drugs either. I didn't know

Marianne as well as I did Linda, because Marianne worked the night shift. But I'm absolutely sure neither of them had a drug problem."

"We've received some information from the pathologist. Linda Svensson did not commit suicide. She, too, was murdered."

At that, Löwander vomited so quickly that he barely had time to lean forward. Not much came up, just fluid from an empty stomach. "Excuse me," he said.

He stood on shaky legs and headed for the bathroom. They heard the sound of the faucet, and he returned with a bit of toilet paper to wipe up the vomit on the rug. He headed back to the bathroom.

When he returned again, the first thing he did was open the window, for which they were all grateful, as the sour stench of gall had permeated the room. He sat back down in the armchair but no longer appeared so hopeless. There was an air of caution about him that had not been there before.

In a formal tone, he said, "Please excuse my behavior."

Tommy smiled in his friendly way. "We understand you're not feeling well."

Our plastic surgeon, Kurt Bünzler, told me last week, right before he went on vacation, he was going to retire this June. Today our anesthesiologist, Konrad Henriksson, turned in his resignation. He's found a new position at Källberg Hospital."

"So they're looking ahead."

"That they are."

"Will it be difficult to find replacements?"

"Not just difficult. Impossible. Who wants to sign on to a sinking ship?"

"And you have the same problem finding nurses?"

"Of course. It's been hard the past few years. We had the luck to find a few good nurses, although they were young when they started here."

"Linda, Marianne, and Anna-Karin, you mean."

"Right."

Of those three, only one is still alive, Irene thought. She mentally made a note to talk to Anna-Karin as soon as she could.

"If you can't find replacements, what are you going to do?"

Löwander sighed. "I made up my mind this afternoon. I'm going to close the hospital this summer."

"You're giving up?"

Löwander nodded tiredly.

Irene cleared her throat. "I have a practical question. How many master keys are there for this hospital? The door to the attic, where we found Linda, was locked, and there were no signs of forced entry on the door or on the lock. Just as with Marianne's murder."

"There are two. Bengtsson, the security guard, has one. I have the other."

"No one else has one?"

"No one."

"Do you have yours with you now?"

"Yes." The doctor stuck his hand into his pocket and took out a key ring. He snapped it open and looked through the keys before pulling one out. "It's this one. This is the master key."

He extended the key ring to Irene, who took it and examined it. It was a normal ASSA key with a large L engraved on one side.

"Do you always keep these keys with you?"

"Always."

So all the master keys were accounted for. If it wasn't one of these two men, who was it? Inadvertently, Irene thought, *Only ghosts can move through locked doors.*

She handed the key ring back. On impulse she asked, "What will you do after you close the hospital?"

"No need to worry about me. My patients will follow me to

another clinic. Perhaps Källberg, I hope. I'm not sure where I'll go, but it'll work out somehow."

"The other employees will lose their jobs," Irene stated.

"Yes, they will. Unfortunately."

"What will happen to the hospital building?"

"No idea. I'm going to put it up for sale as is."

They could tell from his voice that he couldn't care less what happened to the building. Irene and Tommy exchanged glances. They silently agreed there was nothing much more they could find out right now.

Just as they were getting up to go, Irene's cell phone rang. Irene took it from her pocket. "Irene Huss."

"Hi, Mama." It was Jenny's voice on the other end. "Your hairstylist just called. She was really mad you missed your appointment. She said you'd have to pay for it anyway."

"Damn."

SUPERINTENDENT ANDERSSON LOOKED glum. Questioning the hospital employees had not yielded any leads. No one had noticed any change in either Marianne or Linda in the days leading up to the murders. Both had been acting normally. Only Nurse Ellen hadn't been reinterviewed; she'd been sick and hadn't been in. Andersson sighed and rubbed his bald head.

His investigators were starting to trickle in. Birgitta and Hannu were the first ones back. Birgitta said, "I've gone through three interrogations with that swine Schölenhielm. He's out of his mind!"

Andersson tried to think. Who was Schölenhielm and how did he fit in at Löwander Hospital? Maybe he was the security guard? No, that guy was called Bengtsson. . . . He gave up. "Who is Schölenhielm?"

"The guy who beat his Polish girlfriend to death last Saturday. Maria Jacobinski."

"What? What are you doing with that case? You re supposed to be dealing with this Löwander problem."

"Who else was available? Irene had to take over the shift for Hans Borg Saturday night because you forgot to have it covered."

That last sentence came out a bit more spitefully than she intended, and, observing the shifting color of her boss's face, she hurried to continue.

"I took over the case on Sunday. It's clear-cut. The forensics team faxed the preliminary report yesterday. She was beaten all over, and her body had massive signs of earlier beatings as well. Two fingers had been broken, and from appearances they healed without treatment. The back of her skull was beaten in—that was the killing blow. During my first interrogation, the used-car salesman insisted that he'd lost his memory. I would rule it a massive hangover. But today he had a completely new story."

In spite of himself, Andersson was curious. "Let's hear it." By now most of the group had arrived and was listening.

"He says that the Polish mafia forced their way into his apartment that evening and forced him to drink an entire quart of Grant's. Then they beat his girlfriend to death. There was nothing he could do, since the alcohol had incapacitated him. He was helpless as he watched them kill his girlfriend."

Jonny snorted. "Well, that's a new spin on an old story. What was his name again?"

"Sten Schölenhielm. He took the name twenty years ago. He was born Sten Svensson. Probably thought that a name that sounds vaguely noble would be good for business."

"All right, let's ignore the salesman and his Polish whore for now. Birgitta, see if you can find someone to take over that investigation. Maybe Tomas Molander— What's wrong now?"

Birgitta's back was as straight as a board as she leaned over the table and stared into Andersson's eyes. She said in an ice-cold voice, "How would you know?"

"How? What?"

"How do you know she was a whore?"

Andersson stared at Birgitta in surprise. "Everybody knows that's what they're all like."

"All like what?"

"They hang around in bars picking up tourists. Find a rich foreigner and get off the street and away from their miserable lives."

"And they're all like that?"

"Well, maybe not all, but most of them."

"And you know for a fact that Maria Jacobinski was a whore?"

"Yes . . . no . . . but she had to be."

Birgitta and Andersson glared at each other like two roosters ready to fight. The air seemed to vibrate between them. Irene understood what was behind it. It had nothing to do with Andersson's thoughtless comment regarding Maria Jacobinski. Birgitta still felt bad about Hans Borg, and Andersson had not backed her up. Birgitta wanted Hans Borg's head on a platter. And Andersson couldn't understand Birgitta's reaction. He felt he'd made a smooth move as an administrator and solved the problem by exchanging Borg for Hannu Rauhala. No gossip and no leaks to the media about sexual harassment inside the police force.

Irene also knew that Birgitta would never win this fight. Perhaps she realized this herself, as she rounded off her harangue. "Most of those women are lured here by promises of marriage only to find they're sex slaves in a foreign country. The cost of returning is just too high. And even if they manage to return, they end up having to take up the life anyway. Even if Maria Jacobinski had been a streetwalker back in Poland, that's no reason for denying her justice here."

"I never said she wouldn't get justice." Andersson bristled, outraged. His glare let Birgitta know she'd gone too far. "Forget about Tomas Molander. You're still on this investigation." He nodded toward the door.

Birgitta looked at him, not comprehending.

"Go and deal with your used-car salesman and Polish lady."

Teeth clenched, Birgitta stood up and collected her papers. Without looking at anyone and with her back still straight, she walked right out the door.

An unpleasant silence filled the room until Jonny broke it by saying, "What a bitch!"

Jonny and Andersson exchanged a look of male camaraderie. Irene bit the inside of her cheek to keep herself from speaking up. Like Birgitta, she knew that this was a fight she could not win.

"Back to Löwander Hospital," said Andersson. "We haven't gotten the final pathology reports on either the bird lady or Linda. Stridner promised we'd have both reports early tomorrow morning. We'll go over them during morning prayer at seven-thirty." A few members of the group nodded. "Stridner could tell me, however, that Linda was strangled and then hung up on the ceiling beam by the doubled flag line."

"Why was she strung up?" asked Hannu.

"Maybe so it would seem like suicide?" Jonny suggested.

"No, he left the rope used for the strangulation embedded in her neck," Hannu said.

The group pondered this for a minute until Irene said, "I believe Hannu has raised a good point. The intention was not to make it appear like a suicide. The murderer had something else to say. Otherwise it would have been enough just to strangle her and throw her behind the door of the locked attic."

"As he had with Marianne," Fredrik Stridh interjected. "Just throw her into the room."

"Another strange detail. If it's a detail. Why go down the elevator with Marianne's body and drag her into the generator room when it would be easier to throw her into the attic, too? It took a lot of extra time." Irene was thinking out loud.

"Time," Hannu said.

Everyone in the group remembered Hannu's succinct way of speaking from previous cases and knew it was best not to press him for more. When he was ready, he was ready. He wouldn't say a word before then, which really got on the nerves of everyone else. However, every word he said was golden.

Andersson usually had great respect for the Finn's acumen, but because he was still mentally off balance after his confrontation with Birgitta, he snapped. "What the hell do you mean?"

Unperturbed, Hannu continued. "The murderer needed time. That's why he sabotaged the electricity. The respirator stops. The doctor and the nurse have to hurry to take care of the patient. The murderer can return to the attic and get on with stringing Linda up."

The entire room fell silent. Most of them were surprised at such a long statement from Hannu, but what he said gave them much to think about.

"Continue," Andersson said.

"The murderer has to go the electrical room anyway to sabotage the electricity. He takes Marianne's body there because he knows that it will be found as soon as someone comes looking to see what's wrong. That's exactly what he wants. It might delay the discovery of Linda's body."

"That's exactly the hell what happened—a whole week!" The superintendent stared gloomily at his underlings. No one said a word, because if Hannu's theory was correct, it was a coldly planned trap and they'd all fallen into it.

"It's pretty clear now that the murders of the two nurses are connected. But the murder of the crazy bird lady? Someone else?" Jonny asked.

Tommy shook his head. "No, Stridner believes it's the same killer. 'Brutal and strong,' she said. And the probable murder weapon, the wire cutter, is the same one used to sabotage the electricity that night. Remember, it was found on the stream bank near Gunnela Hägg's body."

"Keep in mind, too, that everyone says that Linda and Marianne were acting totally normal right before they were murdered," Andersson pointed out.

"There's one niggling detail about Linda," Irene said. "She asked her partner to move out, since she no longer loved him. Was she in love with someone else, even though she denied it? Perhaps we should look into this separation some more. Of course, this doesn't explain where Marianne comes into the picture, not to mention the murder of Gunnela Hägg."

"It's all about the hospital." Hannu's calm voice.

Irene was startled. She'd also had that feeling many times. "I agree. We keep circling around Löwander Hospital and what happened a long time ago—"

The superintendent groaned. "Please don't bring up that damned ghost."

"No, not the ghost. We're searching not for a phantom but a killer. But there's something connected to the story of Nurse Tekla. Remember, the killer hung Linda's body in the same place where the nurse hanged herself fifty years ago. That must mean something."

"Such as?"

"No idea. We have to keep looking into the stories sur-rounding the hospital. Maybe the dead can lead us to the killer."

"Have you lost your mind? We can't keep digging into old shit when we're up to our knees in what's going on right now," Jonny exclaimed.

Andersson quietly looked from one of his inspectors to the next. The superintendent was inclined to agree with Jonny, but he also felt there might be something to Irene's point of view. Resolutely, he proclaimed, "Hannu, Irene, and Tommy, you dig around the hospital history. Fredrik, Jonny, and Birg— I mean, and myself will keep talking to the living."

"SO HOW SHOULD we go about this?" asked Hannu.

The members of Irene's group, which Jonny had already nicknamed the "Ghostbusters," were sitting in Irene and Tommy's office.

"I'll track down Sverker Löwander's first wife, Barbro. She knew Sverker's parents and certainly knows some of the hospital stories. And I'd like to hear more about her accusations against Carina regarding the fire at the doctor's mansion," Irene said.

Tommy nodded agreement. "I'll try to speak to Siv Persson again. I want to track down any of Tekla's relatives, if any are still alive. And I want to know exactly where in the attic she was supposed to have killed herself. Did Linda's murderer hang her in the exact same spot? And then the obvious follow-up question: Why?"

"How could the murderer know the exact place?" Hannu said.

Irene felt absolutely sure they must follow this trail. Everything was tied up in the history of the hospital. The ghost disguise was a smart move, but it might be the murderer's downfall. Knowing the exact spot where Tekla had died made for a limited field of suspects.

"I'll follow up the patients at Löwander Hospital during the summers of '83 and '84," Hannu said.

Irene nodded and tried to hide a yawn. It had been a long day, and tomorrow hardly promised to be a shorter one.

She'd have to remember to call her hairdresser for another appointment.

Chapter 14

BARBRO LÖWANDER WAS now a medical secretary at Sahlgren Hospital. Irene had called her first thing in the morning. Barbro did not want to speak to a police officer and wanted nothing to do with Löwander Hospital. Irene pressed her case, using a thinly veiled threat of interrogation in the police station, and Barbro gave in. They agreed to meet at 11:00 A.M. at the main entrance of Sahlgren Hospital.

This worked for Irene. She'd be able to attend Andersson's morning prayer and catch up on some of her paperwork, not to mention calling her hairdresser for a new appointment.

"LET'S START WITH Gunnela Hägg. Was anyone at the autopsy?"

No one in the room had gone.

Andersson rustled two faxes and put on his reading glasses. He cleared his throat. "Gunnela Hägg. Born January nineteenth, 1950. According to the police report, found dead in a culvert underneath a bridge. Near the body a pair of large wire cutters was found, with traces of blood and hair. Massive fractures of the skull. Skull shattered near its base with a great deal of bleeding in the brain. Autopsy shows she died from that blow. The combined picture indicates a homicide. A complete toxicological examination will take place. Samples have been taken for forensic examination.'"

The superintendent finished reading and looked up over the

top of his glasses, the cheap square kind that can be bought at any drugstore or gas station. He slowly folded them and took up the thread again. "I managed to reach Professor Stridner this morning before you arrived. She tells me that the murderer is right-handed and strong. Her theory is that the killer hit Gunnela Hägg with the side of the wire cutters many times, using much more force than necessary to kill the little old lady."

The "little old lady" was thirteen years younger than the superintendent. Irene would refrain from commenting on that.

"The murderer felt threatened," Jonny said.

"He knew that she'd seen him," added Hannu.

"The newspaper article led to her death," Tommy said.

Irene put in, "He knew that Gunnela saw him do something incriminating. Perhaps that he rode away on Linda's bicycle and dumped it in the culvert?"

"Yep. That's what I think. I also believe that the murderer took off the uniform under the cover of the bridge. Then he walked up onto the road and headed away. Maybe even in a car," Tommy said.

"That sounds entirely possible." Irene nodded.

"Can you park a car somewhere near the drive?" asked the superintendent.

"No, not at the actual drive," Irene conceded. "But it hit me that there was a fantastic parking spot very close to the murder scene. In fact, barely thirty meters away."

"Where?"

"Behind the grove of fir trees. Visitors' parking."

The others pondered and began to nod. Encouraged, Irene continued. "It's the perfect place for the murderer to park. As he sneaked toward the hospital, Gunnela watched him from the lilac arbor. She knew the ghost story and of course believed that she'd seen a phantom."

Irene looked around. It seemed to her that they were following her reasoning. "The most important thing is that Gunnela kept standing there. She saw Linda arrive at the hospital. She saw that the killer, dressed as a nurse, later came out, took the bicycle, and rode away. On the tape she says, 'She took the bike. God punishes theft!'"

"How can we know that it wasn't Linda coming back to get her own bike?"

Andersson started to say something and in his excitement hit his palm on the table. His paper cup of coffee overturned, and the coffee spread over the faxes. To save them he quickly wiped them with his sleeve. Irene sighed and went to get some paper towels from the bathroom. As she returned, she noticed Birgitta in the other end of the hallway. It appeared she didn't see Irene—she definitely didn't wave back.

As Irene reentered the room, she heard Andersson's excited voice.

"Jonny and Fredrik, head back to the apartment building near the hospital. See if anyone noticed a strange car in the visitors' parking lot around midnight on the night of the murder. If only we can get a make or model, perhaps this devil's luck will finally run out."

Andersson's breathing was audible. Irene felt her usual worry over her boss's blood pressure. But since he was touchy about that, she kept silent.

The superintendent lifted the second page of the fax and waved it in the air to dry it. He said, "Did anyone attend this autopsy for Linda Svensson?"

Fredrik Stridh lifted his hand and then leaned across to take the damp fax. He went over the paper quickly before beginning to read aloud:

"'Linda Svensson. Born January twenty-third, 1973. According to the police report, found dead in an attic, hanging from a ceiling beam. Found almost on her knees with her upper body hung by a doubled flag line. The rope went under the chin and up over the back of her head. The body appeared discolored on both the left and right sides of the face, and there were external abrasions on the right side of the neck. Lesions visible on the skin of the neck. A thin rope remained embedded in the wound. Underneath it bleeding in the soft tissues and musculature. Broken thyroid cartilage and hyoid bone. Also spotty bleeding in the eyes and the oral mucosa. These findings indicate that death resulted from strangulation. Probable time of death: midnight between the tenth and eleventh of February, as concurrent with the changes apparent within the body. Complete toxicological examination still ongoing. Samples have been taken for forensic examination.'"

Fredrik looked up as he threw the report on the table.

"Sick! The murder is sick in and of itself, but to hang her body up like that. Hanging her was some kind of ritual. And a sloppy one."

"Yes, it is sick, and the murderer, in his sick mind, meant something by it," Irene said.

"Keep digging, Ghostbusters," Jonny cackled.

Irene refused to rise to his taunt. He did not realize how right he was. They had to search back in time, into the tangle of legends, ghosts, and lies. Right now everything felt at a standstill, she admitted to herself. But she'd never admit that to Jonny.

"We'll meet again here at five in the afternoon. Svante Malm will bring some of his lab results," Andersson concluded.

THE SAHLGREN HOSPITAL'S buildings were a hodgepodge of styles thrown together by a crazy architect, Irene thought. Every single style of architecture from the previous century was represented. It was neither beautiful nor functional.

Irene walked toward the complex's main entrance. She could see a woman waiting by the glass doors, sheltering from the wind. She just had to be Sverker Löwander's ex-wife. Carina and she were remarkably similar, blond and tall, although Barbro was eleven years older according to the files. She wore her hair just like Carina, but there were some streaks of gray in her blond. *Another woman who needs an appointment for a color job,* Irene thought to herself. Barbro Löwander's skin was sallow. Although Irene was not a big believer in makeup per se, she thought that Barbro Löwander really ought to get some help from the cosmetics industry. A touch of bronzer, a little mascara, and some nice lipstick would make a world of difference on this colorless face. Adding to the miserable appearance was the beige down coat. Was she consciously trying to downplay her looks? All these thoughts swirled through Irene's brain as she held out her hand to the woman and said with a smile, "Excuse me, are you Barbro Löwander?"

"Yes, that's me."

"Hi, I'm Criminal Inspector Irene Huss. Can we go somewhere we can talk?"

Barbro Löwander nodded in reply and turned toward the automatic glass doors. For a second, Irene imagined that the sensor wouldn't react to such a colorless woman and the doors wouldn't open.

Sahlgren Hospital would never win a prize for the most welcoming entry. Even though someone had stuck a bubbling fountain next to the window, the good impression was lost among the floating cigarette butts.

They marched down the wide hall that ran the length of the building. They did not exchange a word as they passed the cafeteria and exited the building again through the glass doors on the other side. Barbro Löwander bent over into the strong wind and hurried toward an older, dark brown brick building. Through the windows they could see a number of white-clad people moving about, protected from the wind and the rain. Irene had a feeling that her interview would not be easy.

Once inside, Barbro headed up some worn stairs, looking

neither right nor left and saying not a word to Irene, who followed her glumly. Barbro stopped on the third floor, and Irene could hear the rustling of a key chain. Barbro Löwander unlocked the door and said, without much enthusiasm, "Come in. This room is empty, as its occupant is on vacation."

The room was spacious and airy, with two large windows overlooking the botanical gardens. Not much to see in February, but it was not hard to imagine how spectacular it would be in spring when all the green plants came to life.

"Does this building have only offices?" Irene asked.

"For the most part," Barbro replied.

She hung her jacket on a wall hook, and Irene did the same with her leather jacket.

"Were there care wards here before?" Irene continued.

"No, this was a nursing school."

Irene suddenly understood that no brand of cosmetics in the world could make Barbro into a beautiful woman. The thickest layer of makeup couldn't hide the fretful bitterness on her face. Irene moved a pile of papers from a chair and sat down, trying to figure out what made Sverker's ex-wife tick.

Barbro plopped down on a desk chair next to the large computer. She withdrew a pack of cigarettes and impatiently shook one out. Apparently smoking was forbidden in the building, as she did not light it but nervously rolled it between her fingers.

"I really don't understand why I have to be dragged into all that mess over at Löwander Hospital," she exclaimed.

To her surprise, Irene saw tears spring up in the other woman's eyes. Irene asked her next question carefully. "Did you know either of the murdered nurses?"

"No. I haven't set foot in that place in eleven years. I had nothing to do with any of the employees either. I broke away completely from all of that . . . then."

"When you divorced?" Irene clarified.

Barbro nodded in response. Irene looked into her blue-gray

eyes and could see the pain. She was surprised. A lot of time had passed since the couple had split up. Perhaps the divorce was still an open wound that was best left undisturbed. She decided to try another approach.

"It's not the murders or the divorce that I came to ask you about. We need your help." Irene let her words sink in.

Barbro's tense shoulders relaxed slightly, but her voice was still suspicious as she asked, "Why would you need my help?"

"Well, you worked at Löwander Hospital for many years. You were married to Sverker for . . . how many years?"

"We were married for thirteen years. I worked at Löwander for six years. I started half-time after Julia was born."

Barbro snapped her mouth shut as if she felt she had given away too much. Irene could hardly agree. She tried a new question.

"What kind of people were your in-laws?"

Barbro could not hide the look of surprise that flickered across her face. Finally she shrugged and said, "I can hardly see how they'd have anything to do with the murders. Just as little as I would." She thought for a moment. "Sverker's mother died when he was nine years old. My ex-father-in-law, Hilding, died the year before our divorce. He was eighty-nine. A strong man until his last year of life. Then he had a stroke, and . . . everything went downhill fast. He was furious."

The hint of an affectionate smile played at the corners of her mouth. Irene was surprised. Apparently Barbro had liked her father-in-law.

"Why was he furious?" Irene asked.

"He was forced to loosen his grip on Löwander Hospital. The hospital was his life. He'd stopped performing surgery years earlier, but he did all the administration work and the day-to-day running of the place."

"How did Sverker feel about that?"

Barbro gave Irene a cold look of disdain. "He thought it was just fine. He had all the time in the world to run after Carina."

"So Sverker did not want to run the hospital."

"No."

"Did your ex-father-in-law ever remarry?"

"No."

"Do you know of any stories circulating around him . . . about other women . . . ?"

Irene left her sentence unfinished on purpose to see if Barbro would swallow the bait. She did, with a bitter grimace.

"I read the article in the paper about Nurse Tekla. Of course I'd heard her story. Everyone who worked at Löwander knew it. I don't believe it. Ancient gossip and rumors."

"It looks like Sverker didn't know anything about any relationship between Hilding and Nurse Tekla."

"Well, it's possible. He did know that she'd hanged herself in the attic, and people said she haunted the place. But he never talked about any of it. Perhaps no one dared mention the gossip to his face."

"So there never was another woman in Hilding's life as long as you knew him?"

"Never, but he was seventy-two when I met Sverker."

"I understand that his parents were fairly well along in years when Sverker was born."

"Yes. Hilding was fifty, and Lovisa must have been . . . almost forty-five. Oh, I'd never thought of her as that old. She'd been dead many years by the time we got married, and Sverker never talked much about her. But then there were many things he didn't talk about."

Barbro was back to the divorce like a tongue probing a loose tooth. Even though it hurts, you can't stop.

"So he never told you he'd started a relationship with Carina?"

"Of course not! I was the last to know, as usual. I was presented with a fact. Carina was expecting, and so now he wanted a divorce. For the baby's sake. Not thinking he already had two children. He never gave them a thought while he was busy chasing that cat's tail, just like she'd planned. He fell into the oldest trap in the book."

Obviously Barbro saw Sverker as an unknowing victim of Carina's wiles. *It takes two to tango*, Irene couldn't help thinking. She kept her thoughts to herself and carefully posed the next question.

"How long had their relationship gone on before you knew about it?"

"About six months. The worst thing was his lying and sneaking around. That they were doing it almost right in front of my eyes. I've never been so humiliated in my whole life."

Finally some color had come into Barbro's face and a spark into her eyes, but it was not attractive. Her hate and bitterness shone through.

Irene felt it was time to ask the most important question. "Someone at the hospital told me that you accused Carina of setting fire to the old mansion. . . ."

Barbro sat silent for a moment. Then she said stiffly, "No one would listen to me. No one believed me. But I saw her."

"Where did you see her?"

"Outside the house. She was circling it. I saw her try the basement door, but it was locked. Then she moved backward to look up at the upper floors. She stood there for a long time. I heard her laugh to herself and saw her raise her fist and shake it at the house. Like this."

Barbro bent her head back and laughed a hissing laugh. She shook her fist toward the ceiling.

"Were you still living in the house at the time?"

"No, the children and I had moved out."

"What were you doing there?"

Barbro looked depressed, but now she was more willing to talk. "There was a police investigation after the house burned down. The police asked why I'd been there. I'll tell you what I told them: I wanted to see what Sverker and Carina were up to."

"So you were spying on them?"

"Yes."

"Was Carina living in the house with Sverker?"

"No, she hated that house and never intended to move in. That's why she burned it down. She and Sverker denied it during the investigation. They said I suffered from a jealousy bordering on mental illness."

Again the deep pain appeared in her eyes, and she pressed her lips together. Irene realized that would be about all she would give. She thanked Barbro Löwander for her time, lifted her leather jacket from the hook, and left.

FOR THE REST of the afternoon, Irene busied herself with all the paperwork that had collected on her desk. She read through her report of her conversation with Barbro Löwander several times without feeling any wiser. It was not pleasant to meet with such hatred and pain. Irene had the impression that Barbro was the kind who cherished her grudges, whether they were real or imagined. It looked like she was the one who had suffered the most from the divorce, since her mental health appeared so unstable. Was there any truth in her accusations against Carina Löwander? It certainly was high time to meet Carina herself.

Irene's colleagues were all taking their chairs in the conference room. To Irene's surprise, Birgitta was back in her seat. She nodded in reply to Irene's greeting. The superintendent did not comment on Birgitta's reappearance but handed the floor to Svante Malm immediately.

"I can begin by saying that we found the same kind of dark

fibers on Linda Svensson's clothes as we had on Marianne Svärd's clothes. The fibers seem to have come from the same garment—namely, the nurse's uniform found in the burning garden shed last Saturday evening. There was enough left of the uniform dress so we could establish that fact with absolute certainty."

"No such fibers on Gunnela Hägg?" Tommy asked.

"No. On the other hand, Gunnela had a great deal of talcum powder on the upper part of her skirt. We even found a fuzzy handprint. The murderer appears to wear size seven and a half in gloves."

"Large female hands or small male hands," Irene pointed out. She wore size eight in gloves, size ten in shoes. If you're five-ten in stocking feet, that's how it is.

"We'd also found glove talc on the two nurses. The murderer wore medical gloves while he committed all three murders. In addition, we were able to secure blood and hair samples from the wire cutters. Both came from Gunnela. We believe that we have also found the murder weapon used to kill Marianne."

Svante Malm flipped through his notebook. Everyone else was silent.

"As you know, the killing length of rope was still around Linda's neck when she was found, even though she was hung up after death. This rope was deep in her musculature, and the murderer did not bother to remove it. Marianne was also strangled, but the ligature was not still on her body. We wondered why, and now we know. The murderer still needed it."

Svante said nothing as he bent down to pick up a paper bag by his chair, and he drew out a clear plastic bag containing thin, white rope. Before opening it, he pulled on a pair of thin latex gloves.

"This is the rope for the flag that was stolen from the security guard's roll. There's almost six meters of it. One meter was cut off and used to strangle Linda. That's this piece."

Malm took out a meter-long piece of rope. It was darkly stained in the middle.

"The strange thing was that there was also a stain in the middle of the rope used to raise Linda's body. We thought it must be blood, but of course we had to analyze it. And it was blood, but not Linda's. It was Marianne Svärd's blood."

The superintendent's breathing had become labored, and he started to gesture wildly. "Wait a minute. This sounds nuts. First strangle Marianne and then bring away the rope because it's still needed to hang up Linda? And Linda left with the shorter part still stuck around her throat? There's no rhyme or reason to any of this."

To everyone's surprise, Hannu corrected the boss. "First Linda. Then Marianne."

Andersson glowered at this suggestion. "Explain," he said shortly.

"First he strangled Linda with the short piece of rope. Then he strangled Marianne with the long piece. He took it back because he needed it to hang up Linda's body."

The timeline might be correct, but why? Why was Linda hung up in such a way?

Andersson turned to Irene to hear if Barbro Löwander had brought any leads. After Irene summarized her interview, it was Tommy's turn.

"I met with Siv Persson, the old nurse, today. She was practically one hundred percent certain that the nurse who cut down Tekla had said that Tekla had hanged herself from the ceiling beam closest to the window. We didn't find Linda there. She was on the beam two in from the window."

"Is this important?" asked Jonny.

"Don't know. Maybe it was enough to hang her up in the same room where Tekla had been but not necessarily from the same ceiling beam."

"What would that indicate?" asked Irene.

"The murderer knew only part of the story," said Hannu.

A vague idea flashed in Irene's brain. This was important, but she still didn't know why. She nodded at Hannu. "The murderer didn't know all the details of Nurse Tekla's death. Gunnela Hägg didn't know them either. She knew the story, but she didn't know the details. Has anyone confirmed whether she'd ever been at Löwander Hospital, by the way?"

"Yes," said Hannu. "A group of Lillhagen's mental patients were at Löwander Hospital one month in 1983. Gunnela was one of those."

Yet again things were beginning to fall into place in the puzzle. Irene was staring at Hannu in concentration when she became aware that Tommy was laughing quietly beside her.

"Hannu found all that out by lunchtime, so I called Siv Persson back. I asked her if she might know how any of the mental patients could have known the story of Nurse Tekla. She was angry at me at first and said she had no idea, but in the end she confessed. She'd told them the story herself."

"Why in the world would she tell this story to a group of mental patients?" Irene asked.

"So that they'd stay in their rooms and not sneak out at night. She made them afraid of the ghost."

"Lord help us!"

Here was the reason that Gunnela knew the Löwander Hospital ghost story, which led to a newspaper story, which in turn led to the poor woman's death.

Svante Malm had more to say. "There were two large suit-cases and a smaller, older leather briefcase up in the attic as well. We're going to take a look at them. Their locks were broken rather recently, and they were wiped down with a cloth afterward, so there was no dust on them at all. We've taken all of them to the lab, and they'll be ready tomorrow afternoon. Would any of you like to look at them then?"

Without a moment's hesitation, Irene said, "Yes!"

Svante Malm nodded and wrote something down in his notebook. "Tomorrow afternoon at the earliest," he said.

No one had any information on possible cars at the visitors' parking lot behind the spruce grove. No new witnesses had been flushed out of hiding that day. The only ones who'd made any progress were the members of the "Ghost Group," as Andersson called them, and he decided to let them continue.

The superintendent wished his people good luck in their investigations the following day. He then requested they throw their empty pizza cartons into the large plastic bag by the door.

Chapter 15

THE FLAYED BODIES hung close together, making it difficult for Irene to move. She crept forward carefully and tried
to avoid touching them. Thick slime on the floor engulfed her
feet. From far off she heard Jenny's cries for help. She knew
that forcing her way through would not work, because the
heavy bodies would fall off their hooks and cover her. The
slime rose further, and she realized she'd soon be trapped
among the cadavers. Jenny's desperate voice was getting
fainter. Soon she'd be beyond all help.

IRENE SAT UP straight in bed, covered in sweat. Darn it, she
still hadn't had a chance to ask Jenny about the posters rolled
up under the bed. Sunday evening, after the girls had returned
from their skiing trip, had been too busy. The girls had so much
to tell, and all their suitcases needed to be unpacked. Last
night she hadn't had any time either.

Irene lay back down and tried to calm her thoughts. She
turned her head cautiously to look at Krister. He was sleeping
on his back, right arm stretched over his head, and he was
snoring loudly. Irene nudged him. Without waking up he rolled
onto his side and grunted. His snoring quieted.

Irene hadn't told him about the posters. It was pure cow-
ardice on her part, she knew. On the other hand, she didn't
know how he would react if she told him Jenny had a stash of
protest placards for the Animal Liberation Front hidden under

her bed. He'd been so unhappy about her veganism; this was one step further and obviously much more serious.

It was useless to stay in bed and stare into the darkness. There was only one thing to do—this evening she'd have to talk to Jenny.

Although she'd made up her mind, she still couldn't fall back asleep. Of course, her alarm clock rang just as she dozed off.

TO IRENE'S SURPRISE, Svante Malm was at morning prayer.

"Morning, everyone," Andersson began. "Svante has other places to go, but he has something important to say. Go ahead, Svante."

"Yes, well, I forgot to inform you that we secured evidence in the dust on the floor of the attic. Just inside the doorway, we saw signs that a body had lain on the floor. We identified strands of Linda's hair there and also signs of a body being dragged to where she was hung. There was a great quantity of dust from the floor on her clothes. We have concluded that her body lay on the floor right behind the door and only later was dragged to the place where it was found."

"So yesterday's summary of what might have happened appears correct. Linda was murdered first and then Marianne," Irene said. She nodded at Hannu. He barely nodded in return and kept his calm gaze on the technician.

"There was a shoe print in the dust as well. There were a number of scuff marks, but only one clear print. A well-built female shoe with a heel. Probably size eight and a half or nine."

Svante Malm raised his hand in good-bye and hurried out of the room.

There were a few moments of silence after he left. The superintendent stared gloomily at the door, then barked, "Ghosts don't leave shoe prints."

No one had anything to add after that, and they all quickly decided to get on with the investigation.

• • •

IRENE, TOMMY, AND Hannu discussed ways to proceed with their assignment.

"I want to talk to Carina Löwander," Irene said. "Anyone want to come with me?"

"You go," Hannu said, nodding toward Tommy. Hannu didn't say what he planned to do, and something made his colleagues decide not to ask. Instead they agreed to meet again at three in the afternoon.

SOMETIMES YOU GET lucky, Irene told herself when Carina Löwander answered the home phone.

"Good morning. This is Criminal Inspector Irene Huss. I'm wondering if we could meet today and have a quick talk."

"Yes, that's fine," Carina said, sounding very interested.

"Can we come now?" Irene asked.

"Sure."

Carina sounded wide awake and energetic. She'd probably already concluded her first round of exercises and had eaten a biodynamic breakfast of granola and sun-ripened grapefruit. Then she'd taken an ice-cold shower before she applied her makeup and dressed in her best Armani jacket.

Irene scolded herself for having those thoughts. Simply a case of jealousy. Carina Löwander was beautiful, in great shape, and drove a BMW. And was married to Sverker to boot.

THE POLICE CAR was light blue, the color of the Swedish flag. A practically new Ford Fiesta. Irene parked it on the blacktop driveway in front of the garage. The Löwander residence was a large modern house, plastered in a warm apricot color with doors and window frames picked out in a reddish brown brick color.

Carina Löwander opened the door at the same time they

rang the bell. She looked every bit as fresh as Irene had imagined.

"Hi. Come on in. I've just made coffee. Would you like some?"

"Yes, please," Tommy and Irene said in unison.

Carina ushered them toward the living room, which Irene immediately baptized "White Sea" in her head. The room was large and airy. Light streamed through colossal bay windows framed by thin white silk curtains. The walls were painted a bright white. The sofa group was also white, and the stripes on the black-and-white abstract rug were just as blinding. The rug must be at least thirty feet square. Irene pictured someone trying to carry it outside to beat it clean. Impossible. Supposedly an eleven-year-old girl lived in this house. Irene thought about how her house had looked when the twins were that age. Crumbs and chips all over her rugs. This rug might not require a beating, as it appeared neither children nor adults spent time in this room. Everything was clean and clinically white. Cold and perfect.

Three enormous paintings were hung on the wall. All three had different color schemes, but the motif was the same—large waves at sea. In one of the paintings, sunlight struck deep into the waves, giving them a turquoise glow.

Carina came through the doorway with a percolator in one hand and three ceramic mugs clustered together by their handles in the other. "Milk or sugar?"

Irene and Tommy declined, both preferring black. After she filled the mugs, Carina sat in one of the armchairs. She was wearing black stretch pants, a black silk top, and a clear blue jacket that matched her eyes. Her skin was faultlessly tanned, and her face could have belonged to a fashion model. Close up she appeared thirty; no one would have imagined she was really thirty-six. It pained Irene to admit to herself how beautiful Carina was.

"You're in luck that today's Thursday. I go in to work at noon on Wednesdays and Thursdays, but I work until ten at night. Tuesdays are the worst. I start working at Corporate Health Services in the morning and finish with aerobics at night."

"Sounds like a tough schedule to me," Tommy said. "We've gotten some information that we need to run past you—just routine. Hope that's okay."

"Sure, no problem."

"Can you tell us more about your work?"

"I have two jobs. I have a half-time position leading a rehabilitation group at Corporate Health. My other part-time job is more fun. I lead aerobics and exercise groups at a gym. I like aerobics the best. But still, I do use my real training more with the rehabilitation group."

"I've heard you're a physical therapist," Tommy said.

"That's right, but after a while I realized I wanted to work with healthy people, too. That's the real way to go. If people exercised regularly, they wouldn't need rehabilitation."

"Have you worked at Löwander Hospital as a physical therapist?" Irene asked, although she already knew the answer.

"Yes. My first job was at Löwander."

"And that's where you met your husband?" Irene asked innocently.

A gleam of mistrust appeared in Carina's eyes. "I took it for granted that you'd already heard the old gossip. It goes around at the speed of light at Löwander."

"Was that why you quit your job there?"

"In part. Many people there liked Barbro and thought that Sverker and I . . . betrayed her. The whole thing was awful. Barbro had had periods of depression long before Sverker and I became a couple. She was psychologically unstable, you could say. Sverker and I had a passionate relationship. When we realized it was serious, we hesitated to tell her because of her nervous temperament. We didn't want to hurt her. But once I knew I was pregnant, the whole thing came to a head. But we still didn't know what to do. And then one of the gossips at the hospital called Barbro and told her everything. It was . . . horrible. She totally fell apart."

"Do you know who told on you?" Irene asked.

"No. I kept working at the hospital a few more years before I decided to change jobs. But I was never able to find out who told her."

"Is there anyone you suspect?"

"Well, there are a few old nurses and secretaries who were openly hostile toward me. They could never accept that Sverker and Barbro divorced and blamed me. But I never knew which one was the snitch."

"What happened to Barbro right after the divorce?"

"She was in and out of a mental hospital. Several times. Like I said, she fell apart as soon as she knew that Sverker and I had a relationship. I believe she still takes a bunch of pills. I really don't know for sure. But at times she's really . . . strange."

"Do you run into each other often?"

Carina looked at Irene in surprise. "No. Never. She's refused to meet me since they divorced. We just talk on the phone when it's necessary. Nowadays John and Julia are all grown up, so there's hardly any reason for us to contact each other."

"Do you find it difficult to deal with her?"

"Not really. But she can't stand me. I believe that we should get over our differences for the sake of the children and at least be polite. She refuses. The worst of it is that she's turned the children against me and Sverker. Only God knows what nonsense she's stuffed into their heads, but Sverker and his children have never gotten along."

Irene thought it was time to get down to the real business at hand. "We're here today mostly to listen to your version of what happened when the doctor's mansion burned down. We know that Barbro accused you of setting the fire and that there was an investigation."

A shadow of rage passed swiftly over Carina's face but disappeared just as fast. Her voice did not even hint at irritation, but rather at deep sorrow.

"Unfortunately, this was at the same time that Barbro was at her worst. Of course we all felt sorry for her. Jealousy made her paranoid, and it spilled over. She wanted me in jail for arson. She even suggested Sverker had a hand in it so that he could get the insurance money."

"What were her reasons for suspecting you of arson?"

"Supposedly I set fire to the house because I didn't want to live there. Sverker was supposed to have wanted the insurance money so that we could buy this house for ourselves."

"Did she make it up out of thin air?"

"Completely! Sverker had just inherited a great deal of money from his father. Almost three million crowns. He didn't need insurance money. He would have been better off if he'd just sold the mansion outright. The profit from its sale would have been more than insurance, let me tell you."

"And the idea that you didn't want to live there?"

Carina's face had turned an indignant red. It intensified the blue of her eyes. "I was only twenty-four. I thought the mansion was too old and too big. Barbro and Sverker had begun renovations, but they hadn't gotten very far. The expense weighed on them. The entire place was run-down, and nothing had been done to it since the end of the nineteenth century. For me it was mostly because Barbro had lived there and set her stamp on the house. She has no taste. But I would have accepted living there as long as I was with Sverker."

"So you're saying that Barbro's accusations are without merit," Irene summarized in her most neutral voice.

"That's right. And if I didn't want to move into the mansion, I just would have refused to do so."

"But you were pregnant," Tommy said.

"That wouldn't have changed anything. I wanted to live with Sverker, even in the mansion if that's what he wanted. But he didn't want to either. Before we'd decided what to do, the place burned down."

"Was anyone at home when it caught fire?" Tommy asked.

"No. The fire started around ten in the morning. Both Sverker and I were at work. Of course, it's just a stone's throw away, but neither one of us was at home."

Irene pondered this for a minute. Then she asked, "Could Barbro have set the fire?"

Carina sighed again. "They investigated everything at the time. There was never any proof of arson. The final decision was that there had been a short in the electrical system. The house was really extremely old."

The police officers drank the last of their coffee, stood up, and thanked Carina for her time.

Carina walked them to the doorway and waved good-bye.

Reflexively, Irene waved back.

"SHE WAS NICE. And boy, she's a beauty," Tommy said.

Irene was not able to stop herself, but to her dismay she heard herself say, "Not to mention thin."

Tommy laughed out loud, and she was relieved that he thought she was joking.

He glanced sideways at her and said, "And her husband's not that bad either. Kind of like Pierce Brosnan—you know, the guy who played James Bond."

Irene did her best to appear indifferent. Tommy continued, "Speaking of Dr. Löwander, don't you think it's time to pay him another visit?"

OF COURSE ALL surgery was canceled at Löwander Hospital. They found Sverker Löwander in the office, flipping through sheets of paper. He'd had the chance to take a shower since they'd last seen him. He was no longer wearing a white coat, and his outfit, a royal blue polo shirt and jeans, should have given him a more relaxed look. The tired lines in his face told Irene he wasn't relaxed at all.

"Excuse us, may we come in and talk to you for a moment?" Tommy asked.

"Sure. Come on in. One of you can take that chair and the other the armchair."

Irene walked over to the armchair and let herself sink in. It was surprisingly comfortable. Tommy started his line of questioning at once.

"We've been following up a number of rumors regarding the house fire eleven years ago."

Sverker Löwander said sharply, "Why?"

"Honestly speaking, there's no clear answer to that. We've got to follow every rumor or idea that comes up in order to find this murderer. Sometimes there are red herrings, of course, but that's the way it goes in an investigation."

The doctor didn't seem convinced. Finally he shrugged. "So what do you want to know?"

"Your first wife, Barbro, accused Carina of arson. Why would she do that?"

Löwander took his time answering the question. "She's mentally unstable, and she took our divorce fairly hard."

"Did she have psychological problems before?"

"No . . . well . . . when Julia was born, she suffered from preeclampsia. That's a poisoning of the system due to pregnancy. Then after she had the baby, she suffered from postpartum depression for a few weeks. But it passed without further treatment."

"No other signs of depression before the divorce?"

Löwander appeared both surprised and irritated as he answered, "No, and what does this have to do with the murders of Linda and Marianne?"

"Investigation technicalities."

Tommy then went through the events at the time of the fire and the testimony that Barbro had given. Sverker agreed with everything Carina had said. Finally Tommy asked, "Could Barbro have set the fire to take revenge on you and Carina?"

The doctor rubbed his eyes tiredly before he answered, with great conviction, "That was brought up in the previous investigation. I am absolutely sure that the answer is no. Barbro loved that old mansion. More than I did, in fact. Even though it was my childhood home."

"A few old suitcases were saved. They were stored in the hospital attic. Were you aware of that?"

Löwander's surprise was absolutely genuine. "Suitcases? I had no idea that they'd been saved. It would be—" He stopped himself and looked straight into nothingness before slowly beginning to speak again. "That's right. I remember. I was cleaning the basement the weekend before the fire broke out. I'd put some old suitcases I was going to throw away right next to the door. Were those the ones that were saved?"

"I don't know. Probably. What did they contain?"

"Old stuff that belonged to Mama and Papa. Papers, old clothes . . . nothing important."

"Who decided they should be stored in the hospital attic?"

"That could have been me. . . . Things were so crazy back then. I don't remember. And I've never set foot in the attic. When I was young, the door was always locked, and once I was grown, I had no reason to go there."

Irene decided it was time for her to chime in, even though it was not a pleasant question she had to ask. "Another rumor has cropped up. It also doesn't seem relevant to our investigation. But since the murderer was dressed as Nurse Tekla, I have to ask. . . . What do you know about Nurse Tekla?"

Sverker lifted an eyebrow, and a hint of a smile played across his lips. "That came out of the blue. Of course, I've heard about the hospital ghost. She was fired or she chose to leave and went to Stockholm to work there. For some reason she returned and decided to commit suicide in the attic. I asked Papa once why she chose our attic and not Stockholm. He said she was mentally ill."

"Was that the only time you asked about Nurse Tekla?"

"Yes. He didn't like to talk about her. My father was a down-to-earth, practical man. He had no respect for ghost stories and that kind of thing."

"An old rumor says that your father and Nurse Tekla had a relationship. Have you heard anything about that?"

"Not at all. That's ridiculous. Papa and some old nurse!"

"She was only thirty-five, and your father was fifty," Irene countered calmly.

"No, it doesn't fit. She hanged herself in the spring of '47. I was just a few months old then. Mama and Papa had given up hope of ever having children, so I was the miracle child. Mama was already fairly old, and she had to be under the supervision of specialists during her entire pregnancy. Would Papa do something while . . . ? No! It's just not possible."

Irene decided to change the subject.

"Your mother passed away when you were fairly young?"

"That's right. She had an aneurysm. What does this have to do with the murder investigation?"

"We don't know yet. We're trying to find out. As we said, many of our leads point backward in time."

"Damned strange."

"That's what we think, too. So we're not letting go of this line of investigation until we're sure it won't have relevance in the present. The only people who have seen the murderer are Siv Persson and Gunnela Hägg, the homeless woman in the garden shed, who was killed. You didn't know of her existence, you said."

"No. I've already told you that."

Nodding toward the heap of paper, Tommy said, "Have you found a way to save the hospital?"

"No, it can't be done. I've decided to close it at the end of the summer. I'll be informing my employees next week."

Irene felt some sympathy for him, but still, how much of this failure could be laid at his door? A good doctor, yes, but the administrator of a hospital? He couldn't blame circumstances entirely. Perhaps he was too weak and indecisive. *Handsome but hopeless*, she thought sarcastically as she contemplated the defeated figure in front of her.

AFTER TAKING IN a bowl of soup in the police cafeteria, Irene and Tommy headed up to their department. They'd begun to sort through their impressions of the Löwander couple when Hannu Rauhala appeared, holding a large, old-fashioned suitcase of brown leather.

"Hi. Here's the arson investigation's results."

He set the suitcase down and pulled out a thick envelope from the waistband of his jeans. Irene decided that Hannu must be clairvoyant. Although neither she nor Tommy had mentioned it, Hannu had tracked down all the papers pertinent to the investigation of the mansion fire. Since they already knew the result of the investigation, they decided to take a look inside the leather suitcase.

"So this is from the attic?" Irene asked.

"Yes, the lab's finished with it. We'll get the other two tomorrow. Apparently they contained traces of something," Hannu replied.

"What kind of traces?"

"No idea."

Irene walked resolutely over to the suitcase, grabbed it by the handle, and heaved it onto the desk.

"Whose is it?"

"Lovisa Löwander's. Says so on the inside."

The suitcase was unlocked, but the metalwork of the hinges was rusted shut. Finally it creaked open, and Irene lifted the lid.

On top lay a dark blue dress uniform belonging to a Sophia nursing graduate. Between the yellowing halves of the collar, the flower-shaped, four-edged silver brooch was proudly pinned.

Irene could hardly believe her eyes. Once over her initial surprise, she cautiously lifted the dress. It was exactly like the uniform Siv Persson had modeled for them, but in a much smaller, even a child's, size.

"Yet another nurse's uniform. But didn't Siv Persson mention that Lovisa had been a graduate of the Sophia nursing school?"

"It's rather small," said Hannu.

"She must have been under five feet. Unbelievably short and thin."

Underneath the uniform they found a nurse's cap and apron so small that they had to belong to the same person who wore the dress. They began to take the other contents carefully from the suitcase and array them on the desk. In addition to the pieces of the uniform, there was a pair of black dress pumps. Irene estimated that they couldn't be larger than size four.

Beneath the clothes were some framed photographs wrapped in yellowed silk paper. The first one must have been Hilding and Lovisa Löwander's wedding photo. The stamp of the studio could be seen at the bottom-right-hand corner. The year 1936 was written in black ink. The handwriting was elegant.

In many ways the bridal couple was a remarkable sight. Hilding stood ramrod straight, his right hand tucked into his tuxedo lapel, his left hand resting on the bride's right shoulder. This man knew how to wear a tuxedo. He was tall and stylish and had a self-confident smile on his face. He looked straight into the camera. His bearing, his features, and his thick hair shared a family resemblance with those of his son. Irene peered closer to see if Sverker's sea-green eyes had also been inherited from his father. It didn't appear so. It was hard to say, since photograph had been tinted, but Hilding's eyes seemed to be a kind of grayish blue.

Irene turned her attention to Lovisa. The tiny bride barely reached her husband's chest. She also stared directly into the camera, but her hands were grasping her bridal bouquet tightly. The bouquet was oversize and bursting with roses and cornflowers. Or more likely the bride was so undersize that the bouquet was in fact normal. She was wearing a lace veil, and her dress had a high collar and long sleeves. It was heavy white silk.

For a long time, the three police officers studied the photograph without saying a word. Finally Tommy said, "She's hardly more than four and a half feet tall."

"She looks like a little girl," Hannu said.

Irene did the math quickly in her head. "Lovisa was actually thirty-three years old when she married Hilding. They were married for eleven years before Sverker was born."

"It must have been difficult for her to bear children," Tommy commented. He knew what he was talking about, since he'd attended the births of his three children.

Irene was surprised that Sverker had not inherited the brown eyes of his mother. Her face was cute, but fairly average. Her dark hair was curly under her veil. Sverker seemed to completely take after his father.

The other two photographs showed Sverker as a child. Both were framed in silver. In the first one, Sverker was a newborn, and in the other he was about three years old. The latter was a studio photograph. Sverker held a teddy bear and was laughing at the photographer. Happiness glittered in those large, sea-green eyes.

The last silk paper bundle revealed itself to be Lovisa's record from the Sophia nursing school. Her highest grades were in bedside manner and pharmacology. All the other grades were nearly as high. Lovisa had been a good student. Irene couldn't help giggling at one of the teacher's comments: "Although she is small, Lovisa wears her uniform beautifully." Irene hoped Lovisa had taken it as a compliment.

There were some books at the bottom of the suitcase. They were all textbooks from Lovisa's training. After that the suitcase was empty.

"Why did they let you take this suitcase?" Irene asked Hannu.

"The locks had been broken, but the contents weren't disturbed," Hannu replied.

"So the technicians think that someone was digging around in the others?"

Hannu shrugged. "Apparently."

They carefully put all the articles back into the suitcase. Irene looked at her male co-workers and said, "We should wait for the technician's reports on the other suitcases before we return this one to Sverker Löwander."

Hannu nodded his agreement.

IRENE SPENT THE rest of the afternoon writing her reports and studying the results of the investigation into the fire at the doctor's mansion.

The fire had burned rapidly, taking the old wooden building down to its foundation. If the fire had been set, the arsonist had luck on his side to have it destroyed so completely.

Chapter 16

FOR ONCE IRENE arrived home before the twins. On Thursdays they didn't come home until six in the evening, because they both had basketball practice right after school. Irene found a wonderfully aromatic chicken stew in the refrigerator, which Krister had made the night before. She only had to use her culinary skills to put the rice up to boil.

Still, she had to check one thing before the girls came home. She took the stairs two at a time to Jenny's room. The poster roll was still under the bed. Not that it made things easier, but it could be a starting point for a discussion.

And maybe it would have been, if Jenny and Katarina hadn't come in through the front door at that moment.

"Things are going down. They call it 'direct action.' These are great guys who know what they stand for. Not meek weaklings who are all talk and no fight. And they're feminists, too. They think women and men are equal. That kind of stuff."

Jenny's voice was crystal clear to Irene as she stood there in her daughter's bedroom. Without knowing exactly why, she swiftly crossed the hall to her own room. Sammie made a tumult downstairs greeting the twins, and it overrode the girls' voices. Irene quietly pulled her door almost shut, leaving a small crack in order to listen and look out.

"How nice of them," Katarina said sarcastically. "And if we weren't, would we even be protected under their animal-rights legislation? Or would we be of less value than a hamster?"

"God, you're so mean. It's great that they're on our side."

"On our side. As long as we agree with them, sure. Just try stating your own opinion and they'd kick you out quicker than you could say jackrabbit."

"No they wouldn't. I can say what I believe. There's a lot of girls in our group. We can say what we want. And it's not a problem, because we all agree anyway."

Angry stomping on the stairs followed Jenny up to her room. Irene heard her messing around for a while, before she stomped back down. From the kitchen came the familiar sound of the refrigerator door opening.

"Did you drink all the apple juice?" howled Jenny.

"There was just a little bit left."

"How damned considerate. You know I don't drink milk."

"Fucking ex-cuse me."

The tone as well as the language were so horrendous that Irene fantasized going downstairs to tell them to wash their mouths out with soap so their tongues wouldn't turn black and fall off. Then she heard Jenny say, "You're just mad that I'm actually doing something to change the world. This evening we're going to—"

Jenny stopped talking, and Irene froze.

"So what's your big plan?" Katarina scoffed.

"Direct action."

A moment of silence. Finally Katarina said, "What do you have there?"

"None of your business."

"You're an idiot."

Irene peeked down the stairs and saw Katarina head toward the bathroom door in a rage. Katarina slammed the door and locked it dramatically. At the counter, Jenny was drinking a glass of water, the poster roll jammed up under her left arm. She held a tomato sandwich in the other hand. She had her jacket on. Then she headed for the door, opened it, and left.

The second the door closed behind Jenny, Irene shot down the stairs. Without making a sound, she pulled on her jacked and slipped out after her daughter.

It was dark and below freezing outside. Irene saw Jenny in the light of a street lamp and realized she was heading for the bus stop. Irene whirled back toward the garage and got into her car. She drove slowly toward the bus stop and parked the car in the darkness between two streetlights a short distance away. As she turned off the motor, she saw Jenny appear by the bus shelter. A few minutes later, the bus arrived, and Jenny climbed aboard. Irene followed at a distance.

Jenny got off the bus at the Frölunda Square stop. She started to walk toward one of the apartment buildings. Irene was distracted as she parked the car and paid the fee. She lost sight of Jenny. She knew only the building Jenny had entered, but not which entrance she'd used.

Irene cursed her own idiocy. What would it matter if she'd gotten a parking ticket? Now she had to sit and wait, since there was nothing else she could do. As she waited, she took out her cell phone and called Katarina.

"Hi, sweetheart. I'm going to be a little late this evening. There's chicken stew in the fridge. Could you boil some rice and throw together a salad? . . . Oh, so you already had a sandwich, I see . . . But maybe you'll want some dinner once I get home. . . . All right. I understand. Could you at least take Sammie out for his walk before you head over to Anna's? . . . Okay, thanks. Be home by ten. School tomorrow. Bye, now."

Irene hung up and prepared to wait for Jenny to reappear. She waited a long time.

Her car was freezing cold, and it was almost nine in the evening when she saw her daughter again. Jenny was not alone. She was in the middle of a gang of six people; it was hard to say whether they were girls or boys. All of them wore hoodies that shadowed their faces. The young people headed over to an old Volvo 240. It was hard to tell its true color under the predominant color of rust. It was a real clunker. Irene had almost wanted to go see if its inspection was current when she'd first caught sight of it. One of the taller people, who Irene assumed was a boy, opened the trunk. He searched for something, then pulled it out and handed it to Jenny. Jenny took off her jacket in spite of the cold weather to put on this new article of clothing. Irene had a chill down her spine when she saw that it was a hoodie, too. Jenny pulled the string on the hood so that little could be seen of her face. Now she looked like all the others.

The whole gang hopped into the car. It protested loudly at being started, but finally it began to move. The thick exhaust made it impossible for the kids to see Irene following them. She could have been only five yards behind them and they wouldn't have seen her through the smoke. Nevertheless, she kept her distance.

The car turned onto Radiovägen and headed toward the suburb of Mölndal. Irene had no difficulty following them, since the Volvo could hardly go more than forty-five miles an hour. Its engine sounded like an old sewing machine set at zigzag.

They passed the Radiomot and kept going until, to Irene's surprise, the car signaled a left turn. The car drove up Viktor Hasselblads Gata. Irene dropped back a little more, since there was not much traffic here at this hour. The rusty clunker slowed even further and began to creep along the road. What were they up to? Irene's worst suspicions were confirmed when the car turned off onto a small side street. She hit the gas and went on past. She was able to see the neon sign reading NISSE'S MEAT AND DELI.

Irene switched off her headlights as she turned down a neighboring side street. She got out of the car as quietly as possible and closed the door carefully. She decided to head back via the roads behind the industry buildings along Viktor Hasselblads Gata. It would have been much easier to walk down the main street, but she was sure the gang would have assigned someone to keep watch.

It wasn't easy to find her way among the confusion of side streets. Finally she was able to recognize the back side of the neon sign for Nisse's Deli. A high fence surrounded the large parking lot behind the building, but at the corner there was a clump of bushes that would provide a good hiding place.

Irene peeked out between the branches. All she could make out were three parked refrigerator trucks. The back of the building and the loading dock near it were brightly lit. She figured that the distance between the dock and the trucks was about five yards. Everything appeared calm and silent, except for a repeated metallic snipping sound. Someone was cutting through the chain-link fence. Then she saw five dark silhouettes moving into the lot next to the trucks. She'd been right. One of them was standing watch.

Slowly, she moved closer to the fence. She had a good guess where the hole had been made and gingerly felt along the fence until she found the cut-open space. She passed through carefully and took cover in the darkness at the side of the building.

The group of shadowy figures was gathered just out of range of the light near the front of the closest truck. The tallest one lifted his arm over his head and measured a blow with the heavy pliers. The memory of a different set of wire cutters sprang into Irene's head.

She fished out her cell phone, and at the same time as she heard the shattering of glass, she called emergency services, 112. As the wick of the gasoline bomb caught fire, she reached someone on the other end.

"Firebombing of a refrigerator truck. Militant vegans. Högsbo industrial area, Viktor Hasselblads Gata. Nisse's Meat and Deli. The activists are driving an old, rusty Volvo 240. License number N—"

She was so concentrated on the fire breaking out that she didn't notice someone creeping up behind her. Just before everything went dark, she thought she heard Jenny's horrified scream: "Mama!"

IRENE CAME TO a few moments later. She heard running footsteps across the asphalt and the slamming of a car door. In spite of her ambivalent prayer to the contrary, the car's motor started right up. Her skull throbbed, and she felt extremely nauseous. With great difficulty she lifted her head to look around. She saw a flamenco dance of flames before her eyes and felt the heat on her face. When the world finally stopped spinning, she saw that the truck was burning. It took her a few more seconds before she heard the sobbing. Irene slowly turned to look behind her and saw a huddled figure she intuitively knew was Jenny. She began to crawl toward her daughter. She didn't dare stand. She feared she'd pass out if she did.

Jenny didn't appear to be hurt, although she was down on the ground. Her entire body was shaking from sobs. Or perhaps from the cold. To her surprise, Irene realized that Jenny wasn't wearing any coat, not even the awful hoodie. Which Irene was glad to see. But now she had on only a T-shirt. Her skin was ice-cold when Irene reached her and stroked her arm with a shaking hand. "There, there, sweetheart," she said. "Come on, let's get out of here before my cronies get here."

Jenny swallowed her sobs and nodded. Shakily, she stood up and tried to help her mother, but Irene was unable to stand.

"I'll just crawl for a bit," Irene said.

As quickly as she could, she made her way to the opening in the fence. It was easy to find now in the light of the blaze. She used the fence to help her get to her feet. Extremely slowly, she headed toward the bushes in the corner. They could hear police sirens coming closer. The moment the first flash of blue light appeared, Irene ducked behind the bushes and pulled Jenny after her. She wrapped her arms around her daughter to both keep her warm and comfort her. They sat stock-still.

They heard the slam of a car door and footsteps on the asphalt.

"Damn, it's locked. We have to pull the alarm— Wait, is that a car from the security company? Hey there, guys! I'm glad you're here. The fire truck will be here any second. Hurry and open the fence."

Now or never. The activity around the fence and the approach of the fire truck distracted the policemen and firemen just enough so that Irene and Jenny could sneak away. Irene supported herself with a hard grip on Jenny's shoulder, and they headed together toward the tiny side street.

Step by step they wobbled toward the car. Irene felt that they had walked for miles, even though it was hardly a hundred yards. She was no longer dizzy, but she felt weak and shaky. Her clothes clung to her body with sweat.

Before she opened the car door, she thoroughly wiped the cell phone on her sweater and then, with all her remaining strength, threw it into a clump of rhododendrons nearby. It would lie there undiscovered for a long time, if she were lucky.

She fumbled with the lock on her car door and sank down into the driver's seat. She unlocked the passenger door for Jenny, whose teeth were chattering from cold. Irene took off her leather jacket and gave it to Jenny. Her daughter began to cry softly again but pulled herself together enough to put the jacket on. Her voice trembled as she said, "Mama . . . I thought . . . we were just going to put up . . . some posters. . . . Not set . . . a car on fire. And he . . . hit you! I saw it. . . . I screamed. . . ."

Now Jenny dissolved into violent sobs. Irene started the car and carefully backed onto the main road. She began to drive away, well under the speed limit but putting as much distance as possible between themselves and the burning truck.

Jenny blew her nose and dried her face with the cloth Irene kept in the glove compartment. Irene used the cloth to wipe the insides of the windows when they fogged up, so it was not the cleanest. Jenny's face now looked as if she'd put on camouflage makeup. Irene decided not to mention it and asked instead, "What happened to you?"

Jenny blew her nose again into the cloth and tried to control her voice. "When Tobi—one of the guys—realized that you were . . . you were my mom . . . he called me a traitor and slapped me on the cheek and demanded the hoodie back."

Irene glanced at Jenny and realized that the red in her face was not just from crying. There was a sharp mark just at the line of Jenny's cheekbone that would certainly blossom into a black bruise.

Irene drove back toward Frölunda Square. As she entered the square, she was happy to see that a police car and a police bus, blue lights flashing, were parked next to the ancient Volvo 240.

IT WAS EXACTLY 10:00 P.M. when Irene and Jenny opened the door to their house. Irene was relieved that Katarina was not yet home. Irene's rattled brain was beginning to clear and she'd started to make a plan. She turned to her daughter, who looked forlorn and frozen, and said, "Hurry up and take a shower. Use steaming-hot water. Then go right to bed and pretend you're asleep. Do not talk to Katarina. I'll bring you a sandwich in a minute."

Jenny nodded and hurried upstairs. Irene hopped into the downstairs shower. She threw her dirty clothes directly into the laundry. Then she called her colleagues in Frölunda to report her telephone stolen. She said she believed it had been stolen while she was shopping, around six that evening. Her

voice didn't tremble and the other officer promised to cut service to her number.

Fifteen minutes later she went up to Jenny's room with a let-
tuce-and-tomato sandwich on a plate and a mug of hot tea. At
the last moment, she'd remembered not to add honey. Jenny was
just coming out of the bathroom in her thickest flannel pajamas,
the ones she'd gotten for the ski trip to Värmland. She snuggled
down into her sheets as Irene sat on the edge of the bed.

Irene said, "We won't mention this to anyone, not even
Papa or Katarina. No one at all."

Jenny's eyes were red from crying, and the mark on her
cheek was beginning to take on a purplish hue. She nodded
without saying anything.

"We're going to say that you hit your face on the railing of
a stairway and that gave you the bruise." Irene considered.
"You left your jacket in the trunk of that Volvo. Is there anything in the pockets that could lead to you?"

Jenny thought for a moment and shook her head. "I had my
wallet in my jeans, and my keys, too. It was an old jacket, and
I'd just washed it, so I'd taken everything out of the pockets.
They . . . they said to wear dark clothing. So we wouldn't be
seen. I thought we were going to hang . . . those posters."

"I know, sweetheart. But it's worked out okay. Everything's
fine now. Just promise me you'll never get in touch with them
again. Do you think they might turn you in?"

Jenny shook her head violently. "We never talk to the pigs.
Never!"

The mother pig smiled and stroked her militant daughter's
face above the bruise now turning blue.

IRENE WAS IN bed when she heard Katarina sneak in
through the front door. She heard Katarina try to muffle Sammie's joyful barks, hissing, "Shh, Sammie. You'll wake them all
up. Stop."

The sounds of careful tiptoeing up the stairs. Irene closed her eyes and pretended to sleep as her daughter peeked through Irene's half-open bedroom door. She must have put on a good act, because Katarina slowly closed the door and slipped into the bathroom. Irene glanced at the clock on her nightstand: 23:08.

Katarina ran water from the faucet, flushed the toilet, and then crossed through the television room to go to her bedroom.

Irene lay for a long time and stared into the darkness. It did not feel right to have secrets from the family. But right now Krister was under tremendous pressure at work. He didn't need to know about this latest adventure. Perhaps this would be the end of Jenny's foray into the animal-rights movement. She could be a vegan as much as she wanted, which would be enough of an irritant for her father. This just wasn't necessary for him to know.

A new worry began to rattle around in her brain. Why was Katarina out so late? Of course, the girls were in the last year of their basic schooling and would be fifteen next month, but coming home after 11:00 P.M. on a normal weeknight was much too late. Perhaps she hadn't even been at Anna's house at all. What was she up to? Did she have a boyfriend? Irene was wide awake now and imagining one scenario after the other. Had she warned the girls enough about HIV and using condoms under any circumstance? Had she talked to them about other sexually transmitted diseases? What kind of birth control would be best for fifteen-year-old girls? Finally she calmed herself down. She would have to trust her daughters a bit. They probably knew more about all this than she did. But she would make sure to have another chat with them anyway.

Perhaps it was a good thing that Katarina had come home late. Nothing need be brought up about what had gone on this evening. They all seemed to have their own little secrets.

• • •

THE EVENING MOVIE on Channel 5 was over. Siv Persson felt content and even somewhat tired. The movie had been a romantic comedy, not one of those unpleasantly graphic mysteries with all those deaths and murders. Nothing to remind her of the previous week. She'd come out of that fairly well, she thought. Her anxiety was no longer so bad, and there were even stretches of time when she hardly thought about the hospital at all. Now she'd do her best to relax in the days before her cataract surgery.

The memories of that terrible night were still vivid, especially when she tried to fall asleep. Then the images became as sharp as those on her big-screen TV. Cold moonlight. The tall blond woman in the nurse's uniform, her face turned away. Then the woman began to turn her face back. . . . Siv shut down the memory as quickly as she could.

She got up to go into the kitchen. It was almost eleven in the evening and time to get her medicine ready. She usually put the tablet into an egg cup and brought the cup and a glass of water to her nightstand. Now that she could no longer read before sleeping, she had taken up the habit of listening to the music on the radio's Channel 2. At midnight she'd take her medicine. Then she'd be able to sleep until eight.

Siv Persson had just put her little white pill in the porcelain cup when she heard a soft knocking at the door. At first she doubted her ears and stood still in the kitchen with the open bottle in her hand. A moment later the knock repeated, just as quietly as before. Her heart began to thud, and she felt her fear grow. She heard the male policeman's voice inside her head: You are now the only surviving witness. This is a dangerous killer.

Whoever would knock on the door at this time of night? She certainly wasn't expecting visitors.

Her mouth was dry, and her tongue stuck to her teeth. She could hardly breathe. Screaming would not help, and she wouldn't have been able to make a sound anyway. Who could she call for help? She hardly knew the neighbors. They'd exchange greetings when they ran into each other on the stairs, but that was it. The police? They already thought she was crazy. She walked to her door quietly and looked through the peephole.

Empty. No one was on the other side. She almost laughed out loud from relief, but her laugh lodged in her throat. Even if she didn't see well, there was nothing wrong with her hearing. The sound out there was barely audible, detectable only by someone whose senses were on high alert. Clothes rustling. Someone was pressed next to the wall beside her door. Someone was hoping that she'd open it.

Her heart leaped, and her ears hummed. *Don't faint! Don't faint!* she told herself as she took deep breaths. She tried to calm down. Her door was sturdy and equipped with dead-bolt locks. She'd locked them all, even with the risk of being caught inside in case of fire. She'd been doing this ever since Marianne Svärd had been killed.

Her pulse had calmed somewhat when she noticed that the lid of the mail slot was slowly opening. There was a slight creak. To her horror, Siv realized that the killer could probably see her ankles and her feet. She quickly moved back. Slowly, the lid closed again. Hasty footsteps away from the door clicked toward the stairs. At first Siv Persson stood paralyzed, but once she heard the footsteps in the stairwell, she rushed to the peephole.

She caught a glimpse of a black hat with its brim turned down. Underneath the hat she could see blond hair.

Chapter 17

Cold rain teemed from the dark gray skies; it was a day when the curtains of downpour would never part.

Irene stared gloomily into her first cup of coffee of the day. The injury on the back of her head was throbbing and aching, but she still slept until six-thirty.

She felt sick as soon as she woke up. Her skull hurt, and her eyes felt filled with a shovel of sand. A badger also seemed to have crawled into her mouth and died. Judging by the smell of her breath, he'd been rotting for some time now. That's what I get for not brushing my teeth before I went to bed, Irene condemned herself in no uncertain terms.

Krister was asleep beside her and didn't notice as she slowly got up. After a brief shower and a quick application of makeup, Irene went downstairs to make breakfast. The twins managed to show up by seven. Katarina appeared to swallow the story that Jenny had fallen down the stairs. She started to chatter about anything else but the events of last night, just as Irene had expected.

Göteborgs-Posten had a huge headline on the first page: MILITANT VEGANS BURN TRUCK. Underneath that, a subhead: POLICE BELIEVE ARSONIST CAUGHT. Jenny quickly folded the paper with the first page inside.

AT THE STATION everyone's spirits were down. The investigative group held a brief morning prayer. Andersson announced that the technicians had found a few new leads. One of the suitcases had long blond strands of hair. The strands were fresh. They hadn't been permed or bleached, and they were about four inches long. It was possible that they might have come from a wig. Hair samples from all blond female suspects would be collected and tested. Fingerprints, fresh and clear, had been found on the inside edge of the second suitcase. Fredrik had been given the task of collecting the samples.

The Ghostbusters Group could pick up the suitcases if they wished. They did.

HANNU, TOMMY, AND Irene were given four paper bags filled with the contents of the suitcases. Irene took the time to look through both of the empty suitcases before they left the building. These two were larger than Lovisa Löwander's had been. One was made of thick leather with reinforced corners. The monogram H.L. was on the edge. Obviously Hilding Löwander's.

The other one was made of heavy yellow-gray cardboard. There were two wide leather ropes wrapped around it. A name tag with a yellowed celluloid window was attached to the handle. The name Tekla Olsson was faded but still legible, written in old-fashioned black-inked letters.

Svante Malm entered the laboratory. He pointed at the paper bags and said, "I wrote their initials on the outside." The technician was as overworked as always and disappeared out the door as fast as he'd entered.

Two bags were marked H.L. and the other two T.O.

"So who shall we start with?" Tommy asked as he placed the bags on his desk.

"Tekla," answered Irene and Hannu at the same time. They moved the two bags marked H.L. to the floor.

Methodically, Tommy started to unpack the things Tekla Olsson had left behind.

Uppermost was a knitted shawl in thin black wool. No moths had nibbled their way through it, which was understandable, since the unmistakable smell of mothballs spread through the room. Next Tommy unpacked a sturdy pair of walking shoes. They were made of brown leather and had low, thick heels. Also two pairs of underwear, rather large, in white cotton. Then a long white slip with embroidery around the neckline, and then a thin, armless nightdress in cotton satin and a pair of heavy black socks.

Irene held the clothes up next to her body. "She was almost as big and tall as I am."

The next bag contained more interesting items: a number of envelopes and sheets of paper. At the bottom there were some thin books.

"Let's divide the papers between us," Tommy suggested.

The bag's contents were quickly separated into three piles.

"I'm taking my share to my office," Hannu said. He nodded and left carrying his share of papers under his arm.

AN HOUR LATER Hannu reappeared. Irene had finished going through her stack, and Tommy had only one more envelope to open and read.

"These can wait," he said. "They're mostly rent invoices anyway." He set the envelope down again. "Who'll start?"

"I can," Irene said. She began to go through the papers in the order she'd looked at them. "I have an identification card made in the name of Tekla Viola Olsson. Born October eighteenth, 1911. On the line where the reason for wishing an identification card is given, someone has checked 'New Employment.' Maybe that's when she started working at Löwander Hospital?"

"That's correct. I have her proof of employment," Hannu said.

Tommy said, "I have a number of letters from one of her friends. According to the return address, this is Anna Siwén.

Her address is Rörstrandsgatan in Stockholm. Mostly she writes about her husband and her small child. In her last letter, judging by the date of October 1946, she seems to have had another child, a girl. Her first child had been a boy.

"I also have three letters from Anna Siwén. In the earliest letter, dated April 1943, she writes: 'Mother's difficult bout of pneumonia is almost past. She will make it this time, too.'" Tommy placed the letter he'd just read from back in the pile and took up another one. "The next one is a short letter, which says, 'Mother much worse. She is asking for you. You must come home.'"

Tommy then picked up a third letter. He didn't read it out loud but looked directly at his colleagues. "This is a long letter dated June first, 1943. The mother has died, and Anna writes about her deep sorrow and says things like, 'We'll make it through our grief together' and 'it's hard to believe that our parents are gone.' I believe that Anna is probably Tekla's sister."

"She had no relatives," Hannu reminded them in his quiet way.

This was true, unless Anna Siwén and her entire family were gone before Tekla died. This didn't seem probable.

"Siv Persson said that Tekla had a cousin. This cousin was supposed to come down to Göteborg and pick up this very suitcase but never came. Perhaps Anna was Tekla's cousin?"

"If that's so, they seem very close. Judging by these letters, you would assume Anna and Tekla had the same mother," Tommy said.

"I have the death certificates of her parents," Hannu said. He placed the yellowed sheets of paper next to each other on the table. Tekla's mother had died three days after giving birth to her. Tekla had been the only child. Her father had passed away two years later. He was almost twenty years older than her mother.

"Two years old and already an orphan," said Tommy. "Poor girl."

"Do you think she was placed in an orphanage?" Irene wondered.

"I'll track down Anna Siwén and her relatives," Hannu said.

Irene and Tommy were grateful to hear that. They were confident that whoever was left in Anna Siwén's family was as good as found.

"Tekla had good grades from the Sophia nursing school. Not as fantastic as Lovisa's, but still fairly high. She received her nursing diploma in 1934."

"Did they both attend Sophia at the same time?" Tommy asked.

"No. Tekla was seven or eight years younger than Lovisa. Since Lovisa moved back to Göteborg after she graduated to work in her father's hospital, they couldn't have met before Tekla started working at Löwander."

"And by then Hilding and Lovisa were already married," Tommy said thoughtfully.

"Yes, they'd been married for six years."

Irene waved her hand over her stack of papers. "Most of the rest of these are Christmas cards and other greetings from friends. Probably fellow students from Sophia."

Tommy nodded. "Same thing here. But I have two letters from a man as well. They're love letters. Both are dated July 1942. No return address, but he signs his name as 'Erik.'"

"I have Erik's last letter," Hannu said. He pulled a thin envelope from his pile. "He's calling it off. He met someone else."

"What is the date of the proof of employment at Löwander?" Irene asked eagerly.

"November first, 1942."

"That explains how she ended up in Göteborg. The same old story. Unhappy love," Irene stated.

Tommy thought a minute before he said, "Wonder where she lived."

"At the hospital," Hannu answered. He flipped through his papers and found the sheet he was looking for. "Appendix to the employment contract. The hospital provided her housing. One room. She had to share a kitchen and a bathroom with two other nurses. But there's another employment contract, too." He pulled out a thick white envelope from the bottom of his pile. "This is from 1944. Nurse Tekla achieved a new rank as head nurse. The hospital would provide a one-room apartment with kitchen and bathroom just for her."

"Sounds like the apartment for the doctor on duty," Irene said, surprised.

"Let's have another chat with your doctor," Tommy said.

"He's not my doctor." To her embarrassment, Irene felt a blush come to her cheeks. Perhaps she was already getting high blood pressure like Superintendent Andersson?

Tommy gave her a teasing look but changed the subject. "All her books are collections of poetry. We can put them aside and assume she liked poetry. Should we get something to eat before we go through Hilding's bags or wait until afterward?"

"Tekla's things took us two hours to go through, so I vote we eat first," Irene said.

THEY ATE AN uninspiring potato-and-egg hash in the employee cafeteria. The red beets on the side seemed designed to remind them of a violent crime. They finished quickly and decided to take their cups of coffee back upstairs.

They sat down around the desk and found spots for their mugs. "Let's pack up Tekla's things before we open Hilding's," Irene said. They finished their coffee and then cleared everything away.

"Nice to see the surface again," Tommy said. "It's been weeks."

He lifted one of Hilding's bags and was just about to unpack it when Hannu said, "Could the two of you go through these bags on your own?"

Tommy looked at him, surprised. "Sure. What are you going to do?"

"Find Anna Siwén or her relatives. And Tekla's death certificate."

Hannu was already out the door. Tommy raised an eyebrow meaningfully toward Irene. Neither of them said anything; they weren't about to contradict Hannu.

These bags contained no clothes, only books, envelopes, and files. The books were textbooks with titles such as Organic Chemistry, General Anatomy, and Dictionnaire Étymologique de la Langue Grecque. All the books were bound in dry brown leather.

"I refuse to read these books, and I'm sure it's unnecessary. Let's concentrate on the envelopes and files," Irene said.

Just as they'd done with Tekla's things, they separated the remaining contents of the bags into two piles. They sat down at their respective desks and began to read.

As they read, one or the other would exclaim out loud, but they'd promised not to interrupt each other until they were both finished.

IRENE LEANED BACK in her chair. She stretched her shoulders and spine; there was the sound of cracking. Then she contemplated the papers as ideas jelled in her mind and a theory formed.

Tommy slapped his papers with his palm. "Unbelievable! I think I've found something completely—"

"Wait. Me, too. But let's take it systematically from the beginning."

"Okay. I have his university transcript. Top grades. In those days his name was Hilding Svensson. Later he changed to Löwander, probably because it sounded more upper-class."

"Maybe. On their marriage certificate, it's noted that the couple would take the bride's last name. Much less common in those days."

"I have a letter from an old classmate or colleague. This letter congratulates Hilding on the event of his marriage, but at the same time it adds condolences on the death of his father-in-law."

"So Lovisa inherited the hospital but it was Hilding who took it over."

Irene thought about the wedding photo from 1936—tall, stylish Hilding Löwander, born Svensson, and doll-like Lovisa. Sweden in the 1930s was going through a major depression and hard times. Hilding, on the other hand, had acquired money, a powerful position, and social status via his marriage. He didn't get a castle by marrying his princess, but he did get a hospital. A good catch for a hardworking, career-oriented doctor without a fortune of his own.

"Three of my files concern the restoration and renovation of Löwander Hospital. There are drawings of the plumbing system, the elevators, and the operating rooms. Hilding was a stickler for order and kept everything."

"Which year did they start the renovation?" Irene asked.

"In the mid-fifties. The drawings date from '56 and '57."

"So the actual renovation was probably '58 or '59."

"Yep."

Tommy picked up a thin blue cardboard file and waved it in the air. "This one has completely different stuff. Personal bills. It's very interesting. Look at the index."

He opened the first page and held it toward Irene. In confident handwriting were alphabetized entries: under A, "Automobile"; F, "Freemasons"; G, "General." Under T, Hilding had written "Tekla."

Tommy opened the T file and pointed to a bunch of receipts. "During the entire fall of '46, Hilding Löwander paid Tekla's medical expenses. There's seven of them here. And there's one for a fourteen-day hospital stay from January first until January fifteenth, 1947."

"This confirms my suspicions!" Irene found the file that had interested her. It was marked "Private" on its linen spine. It crackled as she opened it. "Rumors tell us that Lovisa Löwander wanted Tekla to leave the hospital. It was during the same time she became pregnant. My theory is that Tekla went into a deep depression. Hilding paid for her visits to the doctor and her hospital stay. We know that her depression culminated in her suicide two months later."

Irene flipped the pages in her file folder to find what she was looking for. She nodded to herself. "I believe that Lovisa and Hilding thought they couldn't have children. Nothing happened for years. Perhaps Lovisa was feeling worthless and wasn't able to demand an end to Hilding and Tekla's relationship. Maybe her pregnancy was what gave her the power to stand up for her principles. And here's a piece of paper dated March fifth, 1956."

"Read it out loud."

"It's a doctor's evaluation. Dr. Ruben Goldblum. He writes, 'Since Lovisa Löwander suffers from Turner syndrome, there are valid reasons to consider adoption. I have known the Löwanders for many years and can bear witness to their good character and reputation. Although Lovisa Löwander is over forty, this is no reason for avoiding adoption. She is unusually intelligent, hardworking, and healthy. Dr. Löwander is a well-respected doctor and a fine person besides. These two people would make excellent parents."

"Soooo . . . they were considering adoption."

"Yes."

"What kind of doctor was this Goldblum?"

Irene held the sheet up to the light to help her read the blurred stamp. "It says 'Doctor of Gynecology.'"

"All right. So what is Turner syndrome?"

"No idea."

"Anything else?"

"Yes, there's a rental contract for a studio apartment with kitchen on Drottninggatan. It's made out to Lovisa Löwander for a four-month period from November '46 to February '47."

"Did she have Sverker in Stockholm?"

"It appears so. I remember him saying that she had to have expert care during her entire pregnancy. It was quite complicated, he said."

Irene flipped until she found some small, thin pieces of paper. "Here we have bank receipts. At the end of each month, Hilding put two hundred crowns into an account. The first deposit is the last day of August '46 and they end on the last day of February '47. He didn't need to make a payment in March because Tekla had already hanged herself."

"You think the money was for Tekla?"

"Yes, it's the right period of time. Probably he was trying to deal with a bad conscience."

"Did she ever have another job?"

"No idea. Maybe she was too depressed to work."

They fell silent as they contemplated this new information. Finally Tommy said resolutely, "I have to know what kind of illness this Turner syndrome is. I'm going to call Agneta."

He picked up the receiver and quickly dialed his wife's work number at Alingsås Hospital. She was soon on the line. Tommy said, "Hi, darling, can you help me out? I need to know what Turner syndrome is."

Tommy said nothing else but began to write in his notebook. Two times he lifted his eyebrows toward Irene, but he remained silent and continued writing, turning pages as he ran out of room. Irene wondered if he was in the midst of composing a medical dissertation.

Finally, after a long time, Tommy stopped writing. He put

down his pen, thanked his wife for her help, and kissed into
the receiver. Once he'd hung up, he looked Irene right in the
eye and said, "Hold on to your hat. Lovisa Löwander never
could have had children. She didn't have working ovaries."

Tommy sat down and began to read out loud from what he'd
written in his notebook.

"'Turner syndrome is a chromosomal disorder that only
affects girls. Normally, boys have the chromosomes XY and
girls have XX, but girls who have Turner syndrome have only
one chromosome, and therefore it's noted as XO. These girls
are short and do not undergo puberty. They can be treated with
female hormones in order to develop breasts and the like'—but
I imagine that wasn't a possibility during the twenties, when
Lovisa was young. 'Regardless, girls with Turner syndrome are
always sterile.'"

"Sterile! But how—"

She was interrupted when Hannu knocked on the door and
came in. He had a number of faxes in one hand.

"Hello. So what did you find out?" Tommy asked.

"Lots. Anna Siwén is deceased. I reached her son Jacob
Siwén. He still lives in Stockholm."

"Were Anna and Tekla related?" Irene asked.

"Yes, they were cousins. Tekla's mother died when Tekla
was born, so Anna's parents took her in. Tekla's father started
to drink heavily after the death of his wife and was unable to
care for a child. He died two years later and left Tekla some
money."

"Does Jacob Siwén remember Tekla at all?"

"Not well. He was six years old when she died. He says that
he remembers one Christmas when a lady who cried all the
time stayed with them. He believes this must have been Tekla.
He had some letters Tekla had written to his mother that she'd
saved. He faxed them to me. And I also found a photograph of
Tekla in one of the envelopes."

Hannu handed all the papers to Irene. The photograph was on top. Nicely printed on the back were the words "Tekla Olsson. Graduation from nursing school, June 1943." Irene turned it over.

In spite of the fact that the photo was faded with age, Irene saw at once something that made her head spin. She took a deep breath and let it out slowly. "Tekla is Sverker's mother."

Her two colleagues looked at her in surprise.

"How can you say that?" Tommy asked.

"Look at her eyes."

Tommy grabbed the photo and looked it up and down. "How can you tell in this black-and-white picture? Cute face, though."

The white cap with its black band was placed firmly on tightly pinned blond hair. Tekla's face had regular features, and her laughing mouth revealed perfect teeth. Tekla Olsson had been quite a beauty. Although the photo was black and white, and somewhat yellowed at that, Irene imagined that her eyes were greenish blue, the color of clear seawater.

"Lord in heaven! I really believe Sverker knows nothing about any of this. And yet we are now certain that Lovisa was sterile and never could have had a child."

Hannu regarded her, contemplating. "He should have known. Both his parents are deceased. It would have been on the death certificates if he were either their natural-born or adopted child."

Tommy and Irene both looked at Hannu. Tommy was the one who said it first. "Do you think you could track down those death certificates?"

Hannu nodded and headed out the door.

Irene began to search through the file marked "Personal." She was sure she'd glanced at something behind one of the tabs. There! She pulled out the sheet of paper.

The top of the yellow sheet stated "Delivery Record."

"Look at this! A delivery record for Mrs. Lovisa Löwander. January second, 1947, at Sabbatsberg Hospital in Stockholm. There's a lot of strange jargon—'nulliparous' . . . 'pelvimetry carried out' . . . 'shows tendency to . . .' Here! A male child was born without complications at 4:35 P.M. Weight at birth, seven pounds, six ounces." Irene looked up from the sheet. "What's this all about? We know that Lovisa couldn't have children. Probably Tekla Olsson and Hilding Löwander are Sverker's parents. How can there be a delivery record under Lovisa's name?"

"Who wrote the record?"

"Let's see. . . . Well, what do you know. Our friend the gynecologist who wrote the adoption certification. Here he is again: Dr. Ruben Goldblum."

"The very good friend of Mr. and Mrs. Löwander."

"He must have helped them create a fake delivery record."

"Why?"

"No idea. Perhaps something to do with biological versus adoptive children."

"Maybe. And remember, that recommendation for adoption was never sent. It's still here."

They both thought a minute.

"If Hilding was Sverker's biological father, he wouldn't have to adopt his own son," Tommy said. "But Sverker could not have been Lovisa's son. We know that. Therefore she must have adopted him. Right?"

Irene thought again and nodded. "Yes, I think you're right. That's what happened."

"Know what I think? The whole arrangement with the fake delivery record and all that talk that Lovisa was under a specialist's care was just an attempt to hide a scandal—that Hilding had gotten another woman pregnant."

"Perhaps Lovisa had a deep need for a child—even an adopted one. There weren't any alternatives in those days. Not like today, when a fertilized egg can be inserted into a sterile woman's womb."

"Yes, that's done these days."

"But not fifty years ago."

"No."

Hannu stuck his head into the doorway. "On the death certificate, Sverker is registered as Lovisa Löwander's biological son."

"Hannu, come take a look at this."

Tommy held out the faked delivery record. Hannu read it without expression.

"That could have worked," he said at last. "There were no central data registries then. An unwed mother could give her child up for adoption at birth, and the new parents could take the child at once. This must have happened in Stockholm. If the adoptive mother came back to Göteborg with papers that proved she'd given birth, there's a good chance that the church registry would accept it."

"Especially if the parents were upper-class and were considered respectable. And they must really have played the game well. I expect Lovisa wore a pillow under her clothes before she left Göteborg for Stockholm," Irene said.

"Wait a moment! Tekla. The envelope with the rent receipts." Tommy began to shuffle papers as he looked for the right envelope. He quickly pulled out the receipts. "Here! Seven rent receipts at one hundred crowns apiece. Under the name Tekla Olsson. No address, unfortunately."

"Let's take another look through these file folders and see if we can find a rental agreement," Irene said.

She was only able to open to the index when the phone rang.

"Inspector Irene Huss."

"It's Siv Persson. Something's happened!"

"What?!"

"The killer! The blonde! Yesterday evening. Right outside my . . . my door!" Siv Persson stammered.

"We'll be right there. Don't open the door for anyone but us, even if it's someone you know."

"I promise. Thank you for coming."

Irene hung up and repeated the short conversation to the others. They decided to split up. Hannu and Tommy would go to Siv Persson, while Irene would stay to keep sifting through the papers and letters.

She hardly wanted to admit it even to herself, but she was intrigued, almost excited, to poke around among these relics of the dead. But would she turn up anything relevant? She'd have to trust her intuition, and she had a hunch these clues from the past were important. The need of the murderer to kill, on top of all these secrets, told her that.

Irene was unable to find a rental contract, so she went over the letters, which were much more interesting. There were nine of them. She arranged them according to their dates.

The first one was from July 19, 1945. A poem was quoted as a superscription above the greeting. Following the poem, the letter read:

Dearest Anna!

My vacation weeks are the last week of July and the first week of August. I will arrive at Stockholm Central Station on July 26. We can head straight to Ingarö as far as I'm concerned. It sounds absolutely wonderful that you've managed to rent a house on the island! I feel that I need to rest up. This year has been filled with work, and it's much harder to be the house mother and head nurse than I thought it would be! But now I have a nice, comfortable apartment. What a difference from the tiny room I had before, where I had to share kitchen and bathroom. . . .

Irene quickly read the rest of the letter. Not one word about Hilding or Lovisa Löwander. She sped through the other letters as well. Same negative result. Not one word about love—or any other emotions, for that matter—just small stuff about happenings at work and in daily life.

The last letter was entirely different. It also began with a poem, but there were only a few lines below the quote. Irene felt strong emotion at the date: March 21, 1947. It must have been written a day or two before Tekla hanged herself.

Irene leaned back in her chair and tried to think. Why had Anna kept these letters of all letters? Did they contain some important information somehow? Tekla and Anna had grown up as sisters. Did they have a secret code?

She felt her brain slow to a stop. No use continuing. Time to go to the coffee machine and get another cup.

She'd just dropped the required two crowns into the machine when she heard a familiar voice.

"There you are. Any scoops for me today?"

Kurt Höök didn't sound angry, just sarcastic. Extremely sarcastic, actually. Perhaps he was entitled, Irene told herself.

She turned around with an innocent smile on her lips. "Well, hello. Can I offer you a cup of coffee? Not as good as yours over at GT, but this will have to do."

Höök shrugged and mumbled something that Irene took as a yes. She stuffed two more crowns into the machine and handed him a steaming-hot cup. She hadn't thought of any strategy, just walked ahead as Höök followed her to her office. He stopped with raised eyebrows as he reached her door.

"Are you moving in or moving out?"

Irene laughed, but she could understand his quizzical expression. Files, folders, and paper were strewn everywhere. The paper bags containing Tekla's and Hilding's books and clothes stood on the floor.

"You won't believe me. These things belonged to the ghost nurse. They fill two whole bags."

"Somebody is putting you on. People here didn't have paper bags back then. Especially not ones with a grocery-store logo on them."

Amazing how this guy spotted things. He was right, of course. Irene hoped he wouldn't ask about the suitcases.

"Where did you find all this stuff?" Kurt Höök asked. "And is this everything?"

Irene could almost sense his professional antennae go up. She was just about to give him a noncommittal answer when something occurred to her. Someone had broken into the suitcases recently. What had been taken from them?

She was jolted from her musings as Höök added, "And why are you wasting time sorting through it?"

Irene waved his questions away and pointed him to a chair. Her brain went into overdrive as it tried to churn out a story not too far from the truth. She made a tentative effort.

"As you know, we found Linda Svensson hanged in the hospital attic at almost the same place where the ghost nurse Tekla had hanged herself way back when."

Irene took a large sip of coffee as she decided where to go next.

"In one corner of the attic, we found three old suitcases. They'd been recently broken into. One of them belonged to Tekla Olsson, and the other two belonged to Mr. and Mrs. Löwander—that is, Sverker's parents. Now I'm sorting through them to see if anything here is important, especially since someone had broken the locks to get into them. Whoever it was must have been looking for something, but what?"

"If they found it, it would be long gone," Höök pointed out.

"True. Still, we have to sort through everything just in case there's something we missed. Probably not, but you never know. . . ."

She let her sentence trail off for a reason. She took another long sip of coffee. Höök bent his long body over the desk and picked up the pile of faxes before she had a chance to stop him.

"What are these?"

"Old letters Tekla wrote to her foster sister in Stockholm."

"Why in the world would you read these?"

Irene didn't like his inquisitive stare and sharp questions. Why did she ever invite the most inquisitive journalist in all of Göteborg into her office? But here he was!

"We were tracking down Tekla's sister, but, unfortunately, she's deceased. We did find her son, and he was the one who faxed these to us."

"Why would these letters be of interest?"

"Don't know."

Irene could tell how dumb she sounded but decided to maintain her tack. She watched Kurt Höök flip through the letters. Then he started to arrange them by date. Thoughtfully, he read through them and hummed to himself. Finally Irene couldn't restrain herself and burst out, "Do you think they might be in a secret code?"

Höök gave her a sharp look. "What do you expect to find?"

She decided to tell the truth without revealing everything. "Details about an affair. We know that an unhappy love affair was behind Tekla's suicide."

Höök looked at the pile of papers with renewed interest. Still reading the letters, he said, as if it were just a passing thought, "And why would the reason behind an old suicide be of interest?"

"Honestly, we don't know. However, we believe you found the truth in your article. The murderer was wearing an old-fashioned nurse's uniform so that he would be taken for Nurse Tekla. We believe that Mama Bird saw him that night. We believe that's why she was killed. Once your article was published, the murderer knew that Gunnela Hägg had seen him.

We believe that the killer knew of her existence prior to the nurses' murders, since he knew immediately she was the 'anonymous neighborhood woman.'"

Höök's face darkened, but his voice had a bit of belligerent guilt. "You can't say that my article was the reason she was killed."

"No, we'll never know that for sure. These are our hypotheses."

Silently, Höök read through the letters a second time. At length he shook his head and said, "No, there's nothing in the text. It must be in the poems."

"The poems?"

"Every one of her letters starts with a poetry quotation. Maybe this was a trick they used to convey something to each other they didn't want to write down."

"Maybe. But Anna didn't use poetry in her letters."

"But Tekla did in the letters that Anna saved," Kurt Höök replied.

That thought hadn't crossed Irene's mind as she'd read. She'd only glanced at the poems.

Now she read them again, and with the recent revelations the poems seemed to fit into what Irene knew of Tekla's life history.

The poem in the first letter, dated July 19, 1945, was a happy summer poem and contained no hidden message as far as Irene could tell. On the other hand, the second letter, dated August 25, appeared more somber:

As friendly evening stars burn
And send their rays down to the valley,
He looked at his servant,
See! He saw as the loved one sees.

WAS TEKLA TRYING to say that Hilding had declared his love for her? "His servant" seemed fairly belittling, but maybe that's how Tekla saw her relationship to the much older head doctor.

The two poems following also did not appear to have any connection to a love story, but the poem of the fourth letter, dated December 10, 1945, made Irene's jaw drop.

Take me.—Hold me.—Touch me softly.
Embrace me gently for a moment.
Weep awhile—such a sad truth.
Watch me sleep a moment with tenderness.
Do not leave me.—You want to stay,
Stay then until I myself must go.
Place your loving hand on my forehead.
Yet a little while longer we are two.

"This is not a love poem. It's so . . . filled with pain and sorrow," Irene said.

Höök nodded. "Certainly it was a painful love story, especially when you consider she killed herself."

Of course Tekla's illicit love affair gave her great pain. Having to give up her lover and then even her child would still be in the future here. This poem was simply about her pain in the relationship with Hilding. Irene didn't mention this to Höök, but she had to give him credit for his intuition. Surely an invaluable quality in a journalist.

There seemed to be no connection to the love affair in the letters written between January and April 1946, as far as Irene could tell. On the other hand, the letter dated June 7, 1946, was as clear as a bell:

He came like a rushing wind.
What does the wind care for what is forbidden?
He kissed my cheek,
He kissed all the blood from my skin.
The kisses should have ended there:
He belonged to another, he was on loan

One evening only in the time of the lilacs
And in the month of golden chain.

"Well, that takes the cake! I know this poem. Hjalmar Gullberg. You can't get any clearer than this. She regrets having an
affair but finds she can't resist him. 'He comes like the wind . .
.' and she just toppled right over!" Kurt laughed.

"Hjalmar Gullberg. She had one of his poetry books, I
remember."

Irene went to the small pile of books. On the top was a
poetry collection by Hjalmar Gullberg. She flipped through its
pages until she found the poem. It took a second for her to
realize that the quote had been changed.

"Look here. Tekla writes 'He belonged to another, but in
the book it says 'You belonged to another.' And she also writes
'He kissed my cheek . . .' while the book says 'He kissed your
cheek. . . .'"

"Well, there's your code," Kurt said calmly.

Irene could hardly restrain herself as she flipped to the next
poem. The letter was dated November 30, 1946:

We women we are so close to the brown earth
We ask the cuckoo what he expects from spring
We throw our arms around the cold fir tree
We search the sundown for signs and comfort
Once I loved a man, he believed in nothing. . . .
He came one day with empty eyes
He left one day with forget written on his forehead
If my child does not live, it is his. . . .

It was a horrible poem, heavy with anger and a reproach to
the callous, coldhearted father of her child. Probably well
deserved.

The last poem, which headed the letter Tekla wrote just

before her suicide, at first appeared to be totally innocuous, but Irene shivered as she realized how the few lines connected to Tekla's death:

> I intend to undertake a long journey
> It will be some time before we meet again
> This is not a hasty escape, this plan has been in my mind for
> a long time
> Though I could not speak of it till now

She must have been declaring her intention to commit suicide. And she had taken a trip, if only to Göteborg.

Kurt Höök stood up and stretched his long body. "How about we have a Friday-night drink?" he asked.

Irene almost said yes, but then Hannu and Tommy appeared at the door. They threw questioning looks at Irene and Kurt.

"Sorry, we're not done working yet," Irene told Kurt in a light tone. "Thanks to you, we've solved the mystery of the letters."

Kurt nodded, wished them all a good weekend, and disappeared down the hallway.

Tommy lifted an ironic eyebrow and did an imitation of Höök. "'How about we have a Friday-night drink?' Since when has he ever offered someone a drink? Watch out for the fourth estate, Irene. The mass media can do a number on a tiny little police officer."

To her annoyance, Irene could feel that she was blushing. It was crazy how Tommy suddenly had so much to say about the men around her. *He must think I'm going through a midlife crisis*, Irene thought, and she started to laugh. That was the least of her problems!

"He was just helping me figure out if there was a secret code in these letters. How are things with Siv Persson?"

"We drove her to the airport and made sure she was on the evening flight to London. Her son lives there. I called him, too, and we all agreed that was the best plan. She was extremely relieved. These past twenty-four hours have been rough on her."

Tommy told Irene about Siv Persson's late-night encounter with the blonde. She couldn't say if the person was a woman or a man dressed as one. Both Tommy and Hannu were convinced her story was true.

"We have to believe that this murderer is likely to kill again. Siv Persson is the last living witness," Tommy concluded.

Irene turned to the letters and showed them how the poems that began them contained hidden messages.

Hannu nodded and said, "It's as if she's left word for us from the other side of the grave."

IRENE'S HOUSE WAS filled with the tempting scent of good food. Only Sammie noticed as Irene came through the door, but he exhibited his usual joy. She could hear cheerful chatter and the clatter of utensils in the kitchen. Both girls were home and helping their father make dinner. It sounded very pleasant. Irene's mouth was already watering as she followed the wonderful aromas into the kitchen. Filled with expectation, she heard her husband say happily, "Hello, sweetheart. Dinner's almost ready. Go ahead, sit down, pour yourself some beer."

Krister bent to take a bubbling casserole from the oven.

"We worked together on dinner tonight. And guess what. Papa's going to go on a diet." Jenny said, beaming.

"So what's the menu you've created?"

"Endive gratin covered in cheddar cheese, served with boiled sugar peas and a tomato salad," her daughter said with pride.

"And?"

"And what?"

"And what's for dinner?"

Her whole family looked at her in surprise and answered in chorus:

"This is the dinner!"

Sadly, Irene anticipated lean times at the Huss household.

Chapter 18

SATURDAY FLEW BY in a blur of long-overdue tasks. Clipping Sammie's coat was chore number one, certainly high time by now, since he was beyond shaggy. He hated every minute of it, but once it was over, he pranced about and showed off. *Must feel great to be rid of half a paper bag's worth of excess coat,* Irene thought. She hadn't clipped him too severely, since winter wasn't over yet.

Afterward the entire family pitched in with the cleaning, laundry, ironing, and weekly shopping.

To Irene's great relief, Saturday's dinner included meat: a wonderfully aromatic pork-chop stew with the last frozen chanterelles and lingonberries from their fall harvest. Krister had purchased a red Chianti slightly flavored with black currant. Jenny happily microwaved the leftovers from yesterday's vegetarian dinner, while Katarina opted for the pork. Both girls had soda.

Krister lifted his glass, cleared his throat, and said, "Skoal, my girls. To my new life!"

Irene's expression probably revealed her questions about his resolve, but she lifted her glass anyway.

"Jenny and I talked through things yesterday afternoon," Krister continued. "Vegetarian food is trendy, and I've had a number of customers asking for more vegetarian dishes. And I need to lose at least forty pounds." He grabbed his big belly and hoisted it up. He had really gained weight the past few years.

He turned to Irene and asked, "Sweetie, did you notice any difference in flavor in this dish?"

"No, it's really good."

Krister appeared content. "Great. Instead of heavy cream, I used half-and-half. It's the first time I've tried it. My old kitchen chef used to say, 'Real ingredients should never be compromised. Real butter and real cream, boys.' But the real deal has its disadvantages." Again he grabbed his belly and jiggled it.

"Perhaps you should also take up jogging," Irene said thoughtfully.

"Are you crazy? Do you want me to have a heart attack? Jogging is not my style. But I've promised myself that I would take Sammie on a one-mile walk every day, in all weather. And every Sunday I'm going to do laps at the Frölunda community pool."

Irene could hardly believe her ears. They never had much in common when it came to exercise. Irene enjoyed jujitsu and jogging on her own. Not to mention handball and weight lifting, though she'd quit handball after the twins were born. Something had to give. At least weight training was part of her job and she was paid for those hours.

"Jenny and I decided that we'd be eating vegetarian three times a week and the other days would be fish or meat. What do you say?"

"Can you really lose weight that way?"

"Yes indeed. If you don't add too much cream and are easy on the oils. Jenny doesn't eat dishes with cream, so her food will have even fewer calories."

"But I do have to keep eating sunflower seeds and nuts to get the energy I need," Jenny added.

Katarina shrugged. "Fine by me."

Irene was still inwardly convinced that hard times had certainly come for the normal eater at the table.

• • •

IRENE WOKE UP on Sunday morning feeling that she'd had a restless night. She should have been well rested; it was already after 8:00 A.M. But one question had been gnawing away at her subconscious: What had been taken from Hilding's and Tekla's suitcases?

Irene took Sammie on a quick walk so he could pee before she jogged away by herself. She took a shorter route today, only five kilometers. That was enough. Maybe she'd keep Krister and Sammie company on their walk later. Before then she hoped to solve this riddle that wouldn't leave her in peace.

Back home she took a shower and prepared breakfast. Krister came down, and they drank their coffee and decided who'd read which part of the newspaper. Once they'd finished breakfast, Irene said, "I'm going to head down to the station. We didn't finish everything last Friday, and there's something important I want to get done before tomorrow morning."

Krister nodded. "Fine. I'm going to go swim in half an hour. Drop me off at the pool on your way in, and then I'll take the bus home."

PILES OF PAPER were strewn over Irene's desk, just as she'd left them. Carefully and thoughtfully, she began to repack Tekla's things into the paper bags, trying to pin down what might be missing.

First she replaced the poetry books, then the papers and letters. After that she started repacking the clothes. The brown shoes, the shawl, the underwear, the nightgown. . . . What had been taken? What ought to be here?

Irene sat down in her chair and pondered, until suddenly it came to her.

When Tekla was found in the attic, she was wearing her daily uniform, according to Siv Persson. Her daily uniform was a light blue dress, a hat, and an apron. Where was her dress uniform? It should be among her things. It wasn't there because the murderer had taken it to wear on the night of the murders. The uniform cap and black shoes had probably been in the suitcase as well.

So what would be missing from Hilding's suitcase? Irene started to unpack all the folders, files, and books and flip through them, but it was hard to tell if any particular piece of paper was missing. She replaced them neatly.

Then she drove home and took her dog and her husband on a walk.

THE MORNING MEETING had a typical Monday atmosphere; most of the officers were blinking and trying to jump-start their brain cells with coffee. As usual, only Fredrik Stridh appeared energetic. *The man is a living advertisement for vitamin-packed fruit juice,* Irene thought sourly. She should feel rested, but she'd had a late night. Krister had extra energy from all his exercise, and to cap off his first day of his new life they'd spent the night burning it off with passionate lovemaking. It wouldn't surprise Irene if Krister needed a few days to recover, but it had been a wonderful. . . .

She was jerked back into the present by Fredrik's engaging voice: " . . . if no one else has anything against it. I have fingerprints and hair from Doris Peterzén and Birgitta Löwander. I wasn't able to get Carina Löwander's prints until last Friday evening. She asked me why we needed anything from her. I told her that we'd found a number of clues at the scene of the crime. 'Which crime scene?' she asked. 'You mean by the suitcases?' I asked her if she knew anything about the old suitcases. 'Sure I do,' she said. 'I didn't have the keys, so I broke them open.' Apparently she was looking for the architectural drawings of the building, because she was planning a renovation."

"For a fitness center," Irene added. "So when did she break into them?"

"Last Christmas."

"Did she find the drawings?"

Fredrik looked a little sheepish. "I didn't think to ask her."

Irene thought for a minute. Now they knew who'd broken into the suitcases and they also knew what had been taken from Hilding's suitcase. No drawings in it now. Did Carina take Tekla's clothes, too? Not necessarily, but there was certainly reason enough to go for another chat with Carina Löwander.

As if he were reading her thoughts, Superintendent Andersson said, "We should keep a close eye on this Carina. Though I must admit I find it hard to believe that a woman would kill three others. Women don't usually strangle people."

"What does a typical female murderer do?" Birgitta had to ask.

"Well . . . poison or a small-caliber pistol. . . ." Andersson attempted.

Irene could think of at least ten murders during the past few years where the killer had been female and both knives and heavy objects had been the murder weapons of choice. No point in saying anything, though, as this discussion would lead nowhere. On the other hand, she wanted to be the one to check up on Carina Löwander as soon as possible.

"But why would Carina Löwander kill them?" Tommy said. "It doesn't fit. One night nurse, one day nurse, and a homeless woman. Why? What did her plans for a fitness center have to do with the killing of these particular three women? None of them would have been able to stop her plans for the hospital."

Obviously, beautiful Carina had impressed Tommy, since he was so quick to defend her. *Perhaps he's also approaching his midlife crisis?* Irene thought snidely. But he did have a point.

A secretary knocked on the door and stuck her head in. "Telephone for Irene Huss. Superintendent Danielsson from Västra Frölunda."

Irene nodded and stood up to go to the phone. She had a suspicion she knew what the call was about, but she picked up the receiver calmly. "Irene Huss."

"Hi, Danielsson in Frölunda here. You reported your cell phone missing last Thursday night. Correct?"

"That's correct."

"We were investigating an arson near Högsbo Industrial Area that night. You probably heard about the refrigerator truck that was fire bombed."

"I read about it in the paper."

"We'd gotten a tip right before the arson broke out. We traced the call. It was made from your phone."

Irene did her best to sound surprised. "Why . . . what are you saying? That's strange. . . . Can you tell if the phone's been used for other calls?"

"No. Nothing else."

"Have you found my phone?"

"No. Do you have any idea who might have taken it?"

"No. It disappeared from my bag when I was grocery shopping near Frölunda Square. I didn't notice it was gone until later that evening. Then I called right away to report it missing."

"I see. Well, in any event it was put to good use." In a pleasant tone, Danielsson added, "By the way, do you have any children who might be vegetarian?"

"No. My husband is a chef, and he'd go crazy if anyone in the family turned vegetarian on him." Irene also spoke pleasantly and added a light laugh to the end of her statement even as she felt her heart salsa up into her throat.

"Never mind. It was just a thought. Thanks for your time."

"Bye and thanks."

Her hand was shaking as she replaced the receiver in the cradle.

• • •

THE FIRST THING she did when she returned to the conference room was ask, "Has anyone checked Linda Svensson's phone calls yet?"

"Yes. There was a call from her mother and one from a young nurse working in ICU. The one with spiky blond hair. Anna-Karin something . . . Anna-Karin Arvidsson." Jonny's face lit up as he remembered the nurse's name.

Anna-Karin again. Irene had not had time to follow up with her questioning of Anna-Karin, in spite of her intentions to do so earlier. The young nurse hadn't mentioned that she'd called Linda that evening. Anna-Karin was priority number two after Carina.

Jonny continued. "We also found a cell-phone number. That call came at six-thirty. We've traced it to Sverker Löwander. When we talked to him before, he said he didn't remember calling her. But then he did remember he'd called Linda about some missing paperwork. She didn't know where it was. Löwander said he found the papers later that evening."

That was interesting. Neither Anna-Karin nor Sverker had mentioned that they'd been in contact with Linda only hours before the murder. They'd remembered after being told that the calls had been traced. Linda's day planner also contained Sverker's cell-phone number. Priority number three.

"We have to get to the bottom of this," said the superintendent. "We have to assume that Linda was lured back to Löwander Hospital. But why would it be so important that she'd have to bike over there in the middle of the night?"

"We never found Marianne's flashlight either," Irene commented. "The killer must have taken it."

"And why kill the bird lady, Gunnela Hägg? Nobody should have cared that she was telling ghost stories," Fredrik said.

"Too many questions. Now get me some answers," barked the superintendent.

"Tommy and I can go to meet with Carina and Sverker Löwander," Irene said. "We've talked to them quite a bit already."

• • •

THE LÖWANDERS PROVED hard to reach. Sverker was in the middle of surgery at Källberg Hospital. "It was an absolutely necessary operation, which Dr. Löwander decided to perform at Källberg now that Löwander is closed on Wednesdays," the nurse told Irene.

Carina Löwander was busy giving a lecture on ergonomics for secretaries, Irene was told. The seminar would be going on all day.

Irene and Tommy decided to catch the Löwanders at home that evening.

Tommy leaned back in his chair. He stretched his arms behind his head and looked curiously at Irene. "So," he said. "You've decided the killer took Tekla's dress uniform from the suitcase. And we found a letter that seems to confirm the truth in the rumor of a love affair between Tekla Olsson and Hilding Löwander. But you didn't mention in the meeting that Tekla was Sverker's real mother."

Irene sighed. "I really don't know how we should handle this. It's not directly connected to the murder. Sverker doesn't know anything about Hilding's betrayal of Lovisa. He believes that they are his parents. If a fifty-year-old man finds out that the real woman behind the ghost myth is his mother . . . how do you think he'd handle it?"

"That's a tough one. Poor, sensitive little Sverker has to be protected from all possible emotional crises, especially now when he has a bankrupt hospital to deal with, not to mention these horrible murders."

Sarcasm coming from Tommy was so unusual that Irene looked at him in surprise. Then she became angry.

"It's not like that."

"Isn't it? Then what is it like?"

Irene opened her mouth, but no answer came. She closed

her mouth again and thought. What was it like? Really? She swallowed her irritation and said, "It's just . . . like pulling a chair out from under someone. Losing an identity. He feels secure as Hilding and Lovisa's son."

"But it's a lie. A lie behind his whole life."

Irene didn't have an answer to that. Tommy was right. She was still not going to be the person to tell Sverker the truth about his background.

To change the subject, she said, "I need to have another chat with Anna-Karin Arvidsson. Since surgery is temporarily suspended, she can't hide behind being too busy. She'll have to speak to us. She never mentioned her phone call to Linda. I'd like to ask her about that. And much more besides."

ANNA-KARIN WAS SCRUBBING out the medicine cabinet when the police officers arrived at the tiny ICU, and at first she didn't notice them watching her from the doorway. She just continued to scrub away with a rag soaked in smelly disinfectant. Irene was ready to put her money on Anna-Karin. The bacteria didn't stand a chance. As her rag swished around each bottle, Anna-Karin checked the expiration dates and tossed the expired ones into a cardboard box marked pharmaceutical returns. This job shouldn't be all that stressful, but Anna-Karin's face was flushed with effort.

Tommy cleared his throat to get the nurse's attention. Anna-Karin jumped at the noise.

"God, you scared me," she exclaimed. She stopped the frenetic scrubbing. The rag dangled from her hand.

"Excuse us, we didn't mean to startle you," Tommy said. "We just need to talk to you for a moment."

He smiled and gave Anna-Karin with his best cockerspaniel-puppy face. Irene had tried this technique herself, but it never worked. People would get nervous or ask her if something was troubling her, so she'd quit attempting it.

"Can't now. I have a great deal of cleaning to catch up on," Anna-Karin said.

"The dust bunnies won't run away," Irene said.

Tommy looked at Irene with irritation, but she couldn't help it. This little nutcase wasn't going to hide behind her jobs anymore. Time for her to spill the beans—right now!

Anna-Karin ground her teeth together. They could see the muscles working in her jaw, but she remained silent. Finally she threw the rag onto the desk. "All right, but I've already told you everything."

"No, you have not," Irene replied.

The effect of these words on the nurse was electric. All the color fled from her face; her blue eyes widened. Her right hand fumbled for the desk chair, which she drew toward her and sat down in heavily. Her blanched face then turned red, but she still said nothing.

Irene was surprised at such a strong reaction. Her police instincts went to high alert, and she turned her internal lie detector all the way up. Did Anna-Karin have a bad conscience about something? Or was she frightened?

"Please tell us a bit more about Linda's sudden breakup with her boyfriend," Tommy began gently.

Anna-Karin relaxed, and her answer was calm. "We never had the chance to talk about it. It happened so fast. One day she just told me that Pontus was moving out."

"That must have been around February first. Am I right?"

"Yes, that sounds right to me."

"Before that moment you had no idea that things were not going well between them, if I understand you correctly," Tommy continued.

"Not a clue. But I've told you all that already."

"We know. We want to hear it again," Irene said.

"So the two of you had no chance to talk about the reasons

behind her sudden breakup, if I understand you right," Tommy said.

"No. Things were too stressful here at work," Anna-Karin whispered.

"And therefore you never got together alone after the separation?"

"No. She helped Pontus pack and . . . we never had time."

"But you talked on the phone."

"No."

The trapdoor closed, and Anna-Karin was caught. She still didn't realize it, but she was about to.

"We know that you're lying now. It would be much easier for you to tell the truth at this point. We know that you called Linda the last evening she was alive. You called her from the hospital. The call was traced."

Yet again Anna-Karin's face blanched and then reddened. It did not look good on her either.

"Yes . . . I forgot . . . that call. Was it Monday night? I thought . . . it was on the weekend."

"What did you talk about?"

"Linda was planning a party the following weekend. She wanted to borrow my waffle iron. We were going to have waffles and cloudberry ja . . . ja . . . jam," Anna-Karin's voice broke, and she started to cry.

Tommy and Irene exchanged looks but said nothing. They waited patiently until Anna-Karin finished her crying fit.

She rubbed at her runny nose with her cleaning rag. Her nose flamed red at once. Irene realized that the chemicals must be truly powerful.

"This has all been so awful. Everything about Linda and Marianne. And I've had to work overtime. And Siv Persson is gone, too. It's all too much, and my brain is mixing everything up. I really thought it was Sunday afternoon when

Linda and I last talked. It was just a few words. About the waffle iron."

Again Anna-Karin clammed up. It was clear she would stick to the waffle-iron story.

Irene said calmly, "I'm afraid we'll have to ask you to come down to the station."

"Why would I have to do that?" Anna-Karin said with terror in her voice.

"For an official interrogation. Our theory is that Linda was lured to the hospital in the middle of the night. Probably by a phone call. Why else would she come there at that time? In the winter, no less? Linda did not call you about borrowing a waffle iron. You were the one who called her."

The fear was palpable. Anna-Karin was almost screaming. "Linda and I had already talked about the waffle iron before. I didn't know if mine worked, and I was just calling her back to tell her it was okay. That's the truth!"

Maybe it was, but all of Irene's instincts were crying, Lies! "A waffle iron. Is that so?"

"Yes."

"We'll be checking to see if Linda already owns a waffle iron, and whether you have one or not."

Anna-Karin didn't reply, but she looked up straight into Irene's eyes. Irene stared back. Anna-Karin was the first to look away.

"MAYBE WE SHOULD have brought her to the station," Tommy said as they sat in the police car on the way to lunch at a Chinese restaurant.

"No, her nerves are already on edge. We should give her some time to sweat. She probably won't be able to sleep. She knows something that she doesn't want to tell us. That's obvious. Tomorrow she might be more ready to spill it."

"You think? She seems like she's holding fast to her story."

"We'll see. We're not done with our little lady."

Irene managed to parallel-park the police car into a tight spot in front of the Chinese restaurant. They ordered pork in sweet and sour sauce. A cup of coffee and a fortune cookie were included in the fifty-crown price.

Irene's fortune cookie read, "Don't stare blindly into the fog. Gather your strength until the fog clears and you can see." Irene laughed but still thought it sounded pretty wise.

BIRGITTA MOBERG WAS in her office about to undertake the mission of locating Linda's waffle iron. Before she vanished through the door, she said, "The lab called. Both the hair and the fingerprints on the suitcases belong to Carina Löwander. By the way, Jonny and Fredrik are going through Marianne's apartment one more time. The last time we didn't find any indication that there was a new man in her life."

"The man in her life was Andreas," Irene said.

"Obviously. Some people are monogamous by nature," Birgitta said as she disappeared down the hallway.

Her words struck something in Irene, but she didn't have time to puzzle about it further. Hannu took Birgitta's place at the door. He must also have heard Birgitta's last sentence; Irene noticed how he glanced back at her. For a fraction of a second, she thought she caught a glimmer of affection, but when his ice-blue eyes turned back to Irene and Tommy, they did not reveal any sign of sentiment. He was merely his usual unflappable self.

"Death certificate for Tekla Viola Olsson. One son. Father unknown." Hannu held out the sheet of paper.

Tekla Olsson, born October 8, 1911, Katarina Parish. Death by suicide March 28, 1947. One son, born January 2, 1947, Bromma Parish.

Tommy flipped through his desk calendar. "January second. That's the name day for Sverker."

"Tekla is buried in Stockholm," Hannu informed them.

Tommy sighed. "Let's hope she can finally rest in peace."

HURTLING AROUND THE corner, brakes screeching, Irene turned in to the asphalt driveway.

"Answering an alarm, are we?" Tommy said.

Irene didn't reply. Maybe her driving was a bit careless.

They rang the doorbell, then had to wait a long time before the door was opened by a small, chubby girl. Irene was confused at first and wondered if they'd come to the wrong house. The girl stared sulkily at them from behind her thick blond bangs and didn't say a word.

"Hi," Tommy said in a friendly voice. "Is your mommy or daddy at home?"

"Mama's home," the girl said shortly.

The girl's gaze went from Tommy to Irene. The girl, who had to be Sverker and Carina's daughter, had inherited the same sea-green eyes as her father and grandmother had. Other than that she didn't resemble either. Irene remembered that the girl's name was Emma and that she was eleven. Emma turned her head and yelled toward the interior of the house. "Mama!"

They had to wait for a minute or so longer before Carina Löwander came to the door. Irene heard Tommy's quick intake of breath. She had to admit that Carina was striking. Her blond hair was swept up in a ponytail high on her head. She was wearing a short, baby blue aerobics outfit with a deep décolletage. The knitted leg warmers matched her outfit, and to accentuate her small waistline she wore a black knitted belt. The decorative thong was also black. Carina's tanned skin glistened. Maybe she'd oiled it; a slight scent of coconut wafted in the air. To her chagrin Irene noticed that Carina did not smell of sweat.

"Hi. Excuse my outfit. On days when I'm not working at the gym, I work out at home. Please come in."

Carina gave them a friendly smile as Irene and Tommy hung their coats on a heavily lacquered black hat rack.

Tommy cleared his throat. "We'd like to talk to you about what you found in those suitcases."

"I understand. How stupid of me not to tell you earlier. On the other hand, it was a while back, and I had no idea that they'd have anything to do with . . . what happened to Linda."

She turned and led them into the house.

Irene noticed how Tommy was staring at the black thong sliding between Carina's butt cheeks. She walked vigorously as well as beautifully. *That woman doesn't have a single ounce of fat on her body, only muscles!* Irene thought with envy. Irene kept in shape, but she never went that far, working every single muscle to make sure it appeared as beautiful as possible. She also didn't understand the sick desire. Fitness center indeed! There was something indecent about the whole thing.

Carina led them down the stairs to the basement. Once upon a time, it'd probably been a den, but Carina had fashioned it into a home gym. As far as Irene could tell, the room had everything piece of equipment needed. There were even mirrors on the walls.

Carina walked through the gym and opened a door on the other side. "This is my personal office. Here you'll be able to see exactly what I took from Hilding's suitcase."

Irene and Tommy stepped inside the surprisingly spacious room. Underneath the large basement windows, there was a desk pushed against the wall. On it stood a computer, a fax machine, and a telephone. Three storage shelves from IKEA stood along the side wall. The rest of the wall space was covered by posters of male and female bodybuilders. On the kitchen table in the middle of the room were a number of carefully rolled papers. Carina turned on the ceiling lamp and bent over the table, going through the rolls until she found what she was looking for.

"Here they are. The original architectural drawings of Löwander Hospital."

The paper was faded from age. The year 1884 was written in the bottom-right-hand corner. There was no doubt these were the original drawings.

Irene noted that the area where both Tekla and Linda had been found dead was designated "Attic Storage Space." The modern-day operating rooms were over four rooms marked "Nurse Apartments." At the end of the hallway, there was a shared kitchen and bathroom area. On the other side of the hallway, there was a room for a doctor on call, a house mother's office, and the apartment now meant for the on-call doctor. This apartment had been named "House Mother's Apartment."

Inside her head Irene imagined Hilding Löwander carefully opening the door from the on-call room and glancing around to see if the coast was clear before he hastily crossed the hall to Tekla's apartment.

The plans for the care wards were identical to the present layout, except for a room identified as the "Operation Room," which had been transformed into the ICU room.

The stairway and the patient elevator were not on the drawings, of course, since they weren't added until seventy-five years later.

The basement had a kitchen as well as the usual basement storage areas. Irene was reminded of something she'd barely considered. Where did the food for the patients come from now? Did they have a contract with a restaurant to send in food? Or did the patients diet so they'd look slim as well as younger after getting their faces expensively lifted?

"Why did you need these old drawings anyway?" Irene asked.

Without speaking, Carina lifted another roll of paper and spread it over the older drawing. She had chalked the hospital's outer contours and drawn in the additional stairway and elevator. She'd marked all the load-bearing walls correctly. There the resemblances to the old Löwander Hospital came to an end. Where the present operating rooms existed, "Massage and Relaxation Room" was marked. The on-call apartment and two offices were marked "Employees." The third office and the attic were "Storage."

The care wards had been changed to one large gymnasium, or "Acrobics Room" as Carina had written on her drawing. The ICU and one of the care wards had become "Weight Training." The first floor had "Reception," "Cafeteria," "Mani-Pedi," and "Hair Salon."

The basement was similar to the present configuration. There was an employee changing room, a furnace room, a power room, and the usual basement storage, but where the security guard's room had been was now marked "Changing Room—men" with showers, hot tub, and a sauna. A similar space was set up on the other side of the basement for women.

Tommy lifted his gaze from the drawing and looked at Irene. Then he asked, "When did you take these drawings from Hilding's suitcase?"

Her brow wrinkled as she thought back. "It must have been sometime between Christmas and New Year's Eve. I had my vacation until St. Knut's Day on January thirteenth."

"How did you know where the drawings were?"

Carina shrugged impatiently. "I didn't. It was a wild guess that turned out to be right." She walked over to her desk chair and sat down. Before she started to talk, she fixed her gaze on one of the bodybuilder posters showing a woman glistening with oil. "Here's what happened. All this fall Sverker complained that he couldn't see a way to keep the hospital profitable. It needed too much money to maintain as a hospital. He would have had to fix the roof, the pipes, and who knows what else. He wanted to sell the building. Then I got the idea of converting it into a fitness center. A calm, rural atmosphere in the middle of the city. Perfect for stress-filled city folks who don't have time to get away to a spa for a few days to relax. I believe in my concept. It's modern. More and more people are realizing the importance of taking care of their bodies. If people took care of themselves, there wouldn't be a need for so many hospitals."

"What did Sverker think about it?"

Carina didn't answer for a second. Then she replied, "He hasn't made up his mind yet, but I believe he was coming around."

"Tell us why you had to break into the suitcases," Irene said.

"I'd been thinking about my concept all through December, and on Christmas Eve I told Sverker about my thoughts regarding the future of the Löwander Hospital building. I asked him if he had any of the original drawings, but he said he didn't. He said that they'd probably burned up in the house fire. Then he thought that they might be somewhere in the hospital. He loaned me his key, and I was able to search the hospital in peace, since it was closed for Christmas and New Year's."

"So when were you at the hospital searching for the drawings and when did you find the suitcases?" Irene asked.

"I went over there for the first time the day after Christmas, and I found the suitcases on the following day. There weren't any keys for them, so I had to break them open."

"How did you break open the locks?"

"With a screwdriver."

"Where did you get it?"

"I had it with me."

"From home?"

"No, I have a tool chest in the car."

"Did you see a nurse's uniform in any of the suitcases?"

Carina thought for a long time before answering. "There

were a great deal of old clothes in the largest suitcase. Maybe a nurse's uniform was among them. I don't know. That's not what I was after."

"You were after the drawings. And you found them."

"That's right."

"What did you do with the suitcases once you'd found the drawings?"

Carina looked surprised. "Nothing. I left them right where I found them. The locks were broken, though, of course."

"You didn't wipe down the suitcases or the locks after you were finished?"

"No, why would I do that? I wasn't doing anything wrong. The suitcases belonged to my husband's family."

She had a point. If she hadn't wiped down the suitcases, someone else must have done so. Probably the murderer when he removed the nurse's uniform for his masquerade.

He? Why were they always calling the murderer a he? Irene thought about Superintendent Andersson's earlier comment, that strangulation was not a "female" method. The killer could be female. Irene took a close look at Carina and her glistening muscles. Yes, indeed, Carina was certainly strong enough to strangle someone. All the victims had been small women. Yet Carina had no motive. She had plans for her future, and it looked as if everything was going her way. She'd have no reason to kill Marianne Svärd, Gunnela Hägg, or Linda Svensson. She had all the reason in the world not to have Löwander Hospital connected to murder and scandal if she planned to open an exclusive fitness center there.

"I believe that we have enough for today. Where can we find your husband?"

"He gave me a phone call a moment ago. He's playing squash with Konrad Hendriksson at Landala Sporthall. They've had a standing appointment there for years."

"When will he be home?"

Carina appeared apologetic. "Probably not before nine this evening. They usually go to the sauna and then have a beer together afterward. Sverker needs to get back into his daily routine. This has been an extremely difficult time for him."

"Would you tell him that we're going to show up at the hospital at eight A.M. tomorrow? If he prefers that we come here instead, he can call Tommy or me before seven-thirty."

She handed her card to Carina, who set it down without looking at it. She graciously stood up and led them back through the home gym and up the stairs to the hallway.

As Carina was shutting the door behind them, Irene heard her yell toward the interior of the house. "Emma! Won't you come downstairs and exercise with me? You really need it!"

As an answer, Irene heard the volume on the Backstreet Boys CD crank up.

"IF YOU THINK Sverker Löwander looks like Pierce Brosnan, I have to tell you that Carina looks like Sharon Stone," Irene said.

Tommy nodded. "Not a bad comparison, actually. Poor little Emma. She doesn't look like either of her parents."

"With those eyes she'll be just fine," Irene said.

Tommy just smiled.

AT HOME IRENE smelled freshly baked bread, and she drew the wonderful aroma into her nostrils. Sammie came thundering toward her and tried to convince her that he'd been all on his lonesome for hours, but his wet paws betrayed him.

"You'll have to wait until after dinner," Irene said as she burrowed the cold tip of her nose into Sammie's warm fur.

With high expectations, she went into the kitchen.

Jenny was bustling around with the flush of the hot kitchen on her cheeks. She had baking sheets filled with dinner rolls.

"Hi. I'm making graham rolls," she said happily.

Krister was at the stove, stirring a pot. There were no cutlets or freshly rolled meatballs anywhere Irene could see. With trepidation she went over to her husband and kissed him on the neck before she asked, "What's for dinner?"

Smiling broadly, Krister turned to look at her. "Russian beet soup. I've made real smetana."

Irene tried to comfort herself by thinking that the graham dinner rolls were bound to be at least as tasty as they were filling.

Chapter 19

Sᴠᴇʀᴋᴇʀ Lᴏ̈ᴡᴀɴᴅᴇʀ ᴍɪɢʜᴛ have felt mentally recharged after his squash match, but he didn't look all that physically refreshed. Tommy and Irene had arrived at exactly 8:00 ᴀ.ᴍ., and they were now sitting in his office at Löwander Hospital.

"Carina said you'd visited her yesterday. Sorry I wasn't home. I've started to get back to exercising again. I feel I really need it. Time to return to my routines." Sverker's voice faded, and he looked down at his hands, which were folded and resting on his desk.

"We just have a few follow-up questions for you," Tommy said.

"That's fine."

Tommy wore his most innocent look; Irene knew that he was going to cut to the chase. "Why did Linda have your cell-phone number in her day planner?"

It was obvious that Löwander didn't expect the question but was doing his best to maintain an impassive expression. "I've already explained that."

"It would be better if you explained it again," Tommy said in a friendly but unyielding manner.

"It happened last fall. I was at a seminar at Hotel Gothia, and I gave Linda my cell phone because one of my patients wasn't doing well. She was working that day."

"Wouldn't it have been more logical for her to jot it down in the department's phone book?" Tommy objected.

Löwander shrugged. "Maybe so. But she didn't."

"You never saw where she wrote it down?"

"No."

"We have traced a phone call from your cell phone to Linda Svensson the evening of February tenth. It was recorded at six thirty-five P.M."

Sverker Löwander rubbed both eyes hard before he replied. "I'd forgotten that completely. Things were crazy after we found Marianne. And then when Linda. . . . I'd forgotten that." He took a deep breath before he continued. "It concerned the snafu with Nils Peterzén's medical paperwork. It wasn't there the morning of his surgery. I was searching for it and asked Linda about it in case she'd seen it somewhere on the ward. It was in the secretary's office. I was able to glance through it as I headed up to operate. Of course I should have read it more thoroughly. His vitals weren't good. He should have been seen by a lung specialist before we operated. His blood results and oxygen rate hadn't been included in the charts. . . ." He sighed heavily. Then he turned his hypnotic green eyes toward Irene and said, his voice pleading, "Nils Peterzén seemed to be in good shape. He was optimistic and in an upbeat mood. He even joked on the way to surgery. He didn't want to put off the operation."

Sverker fell silent and looked morosely at the two officers. "After he took a turn for the worse that evening, we got the acute readings regarding his blood gases. Of course they were abysmal. I was worried and wanted to know what the original levels had been. I couldn't find the record anywhere. Nurse Ellen had the evening shift, but she hadn't seen his chart that day. Then I called Nurse Linda, but she hadn't seen those values on Peterzén either."

"So she was home when you called."

"Yes."

"How did she seem to you?"

"What do you mean?"

"Was she happy? Tense? Worried?"

Sverker looked doubtful as he answered. "I didn't notice anything unusual. She seemed her normal self. But I had other things on my mind."

"So you're worried that the reason Nils Peterzén died was really your own carelessness."

Löwander sank lower into his chair and nodded reluctantly.

"Do you remember when Carina began to talk about her idea for the fitness center?" Tommy asked.

Sverker looked surprised. "Yes, last Christmas. Why?"

"Did you lend her your master key so that she could search for the architectural plans of the hospital?"

"Yes."

"When did she return them?"

Löwander wrinkled his brow as he thought. "Don't know for sure. Sometime before New Year's Eve. I came here, too, to look through the building before we headed off to Thailand on vacation. We celebrated my fiftieth birthday in Phuket."

"When did you leave?"

"On New Year's Eve. We returned on January thirteenth."

"Did you want to avoid a big party with family and friends?" Irene asked.

Sverker smiled. "No, they all came over the following weekend. You can't escape a fiftieth birthday."

"Did you go into the attic when you searched the building before your trip?" Tommy asked.

"No, there wasn't any reason to go there. Nothing to see."

"So there was no indication anyone got into the hospital building while it was closed?"

"No, only Carina, but I knew that already, of course."

For the moment it looked as if nothing more could come out of this interview. The police officers stood up and thanked the doctor for his time. Then Irene was struck by a thought.

"Does your ex-wife, Barbro, know that you're going to shut the hospital?"

Sverker looked at her quizzically. "No, why would she know that? We're not in touch at all, especially after John and Julia moved to the United States."

"Do you have contact with your children?"

"Of course," he replied tersely.

"Do you think that she might have heard from them about Carina's plans to start a fitness center?"

For the first time during their conversation, Sverker looked irritated. "No, they hardly talk to her. Why are you asking these kinds of questions anyway?"

"Just a thought. Barbro has tried to throw suspicion on you and Carina before. Like the time when the mansion burned down."

"We didn't take that seriously. Nobody believed her. It was clear that she wasn't in her right mind. Barbro would never hurt a fly."

That might depend on how strong her desire for revenge is, Irene thought.

IRENE AND TOMMY swung by the ICU to have a chat with Nurse Anna-Karin.

"I believe she's hiding something," Tommy said.

"Why do you think that?" Irene asked.

"Just experience and a cop's nose."

They decided they'd bring her to the police station if she didn't cooperate about what she knew.

When they pressed the door opener to the ICU, nothing happened. The door stayed shut. Tommy knocked hard, and they could hear approaching footsteps.

"Who is it?" a voice called.

It wasn't Anna-Karin's voice but that of a somewhat older woman.

"Inspectors Huss and Persson," Tommy said.

The door was opened carefully. The elderly nurse introduced herself as Margot.

"We're looking for Anna-Karin," Tommy said in his friendliest voice.

"Anna-Karin isn't working today. There aren't any operations planned, so she took the day off."

Not what they expected to hear.

"Do you know where we can find her?"

Margot smiled conspiratorially and lowered her voice. "I believe she's found herself a boyfriend. It's a new relationship. I'm not supposed to tell anyone, but since you're police officers. . . . He lives in Varberg."

"Varberg? Do you know where?"

"No, but I think her friend is a teacher. Or somebody who works in a school. Maybe he's a principal. No, I really don't remember. Why are you in such a hurry to find Anna-Karin? Nothing else . . . horrible has happened, has it?"

"No, we're not in a rush. We can talk to her tomorrow," Tommy said.

Something occurred to Irene. "If she didn't go to Varberg, maybe she's at home. Could we have her address?"

"Sure. I have it written down in here." Nurse Margot walked over to her desk and opened the bottom drawer. She took out a black address book similar to the one at the reception desk. "Here's her apartment on Munkebäcksgatan. She is subletting it from someone. And here's her phone number."

The nurse handed the slip of paper to Irene, who immediately asked if she could borrow the phone. She dialed the number on the slip. The phone rang, but no one answered. A shadow of worry passed over the elderly nurse's face.

"If she hasn't gone shopping in town, then she must be in Varberg," Irene said, giving the nurse a soothing smile.

As soon as the heavy ICU door closed behind them, Irene

turned to Tommy and said softly, "Let's get to Munkebäcks-gatan right away."

THE REDBRICK, FOUR-STORY building appeared peaceful. The keypad at the entrance was broken, so all they had to do was push open the door and go right in. They found Anna-Karin's apartment on the second floor. She'd written her name on a bit of surgical tape and stuck it over the nameplate. They rang the worn-out doorbell a number of times, but no one answered. Irene opened the mail flap and glanced inside. She could see a number of advertising flyers on the floor inside.

"She's not home," Irene said.

"I WAS SURPRISED how freely Löwander admitted his medical mistake in the case of Nils Peterzén but how close-mouthed he was about Linda and his ex-wife," Tommy said. They were driving back to the station in the squad car.

"You think? I bet that his mistake about Peterzén has been eating him up inside and he needed someone to talk to about it."

"He doesn't need to worry about the police as much as he has to worry about the National Board of Health and Welfare, that's for sure. But listen to yourself. You're trying to defend Löwander's behavior. I'd guess that women often are willing to make excuses for that guy."

"You do?" Irene said weakly. She'd been thinking about Birgitta's comment that some people were born to be monoga-mous. Now she also thought about Tommy's words, and some-thing began to stir deep in her mind.

THAT AFTERNOON BOTH Tommy and Irene spent planted squarely in front of their computers catching up on paperwork, lost in concentration.

"There must be a common motive for all three murders," Irene said. "We just haven't figured it out yet."

She paused in her typing and watched Tommy peck away with his one-finger method. His only reply was, "Hmm."

"We've got to get Anna-Karin to talk. I just know she's sitting on something big."

"Hmm."

Irene gave up and went back to her typing.

THAT EVENING THE town house was filled with the wonderful smell of crispy fried fillets of flounder and mashed potatoes. Jenny was enjoying a bowl of lentil soup and eating a side dish of raw carrots. Krister dipped his spoon into Jenny's bowl for a taste.

"Well, it's edible," he declared. "But I don't think it tastes all that great."

"Nothing should lose its life for my meals," Jenny pronounced.

"Did you hear that vegetables scream when you harvest them?" Katarina asked, a mischievous look on her face.

"They do not," Jenny replied.

"They sure do. Russian scientists have proved it. They've measured—"

"Katarina, cut it out," Krister ordered.

Both daughters shut up and stared at their father. He seldom became angry, but once he did, they knew to watch out.

Irene was grateful that her husband had stopped that particular argument in its tracks. She had no illusions about Jenny. If she began to feel sorry for vegetables, she might just stop eating them, too. And once she'd stopped eating vegetables because the poor things screamed when harvested, she would starve to death. There were limits to what parents could put up with.

Chapter 20

"A NEIGHBOR DISCOVERED the fire shortly after midnight. Arson. The technician—that Svensson guy—called me from the scene of the fire and told me that he's absolutely sure it started in the hallway. The whole apartment burned up, even though other units in the building were not damaged as much. It looks like someone poured flammable liquid through the mail slot and then set it on fire with a burning rag or the like." Superintendent Andersson, in deep gloom, surveyed his investigators. No one commented on his report, but they all were unusually alert, especially for that hour of the morning. "The technician also said there was no one in the apartment at that time."

Irene had a fledgling idea. "Did Anna-Karin contact us?" she asked.

"No, but it's only been eight hours since the fire broke out. I doubt it'll even be in the paper this morning. In any case, as soon as she hears about it, she'll contact us, I'm sure."

Tommy said thoughtfully, "One of the nurses in the ICU told us that she was planning to be at her boyfriend's place in Varberg."

"Do you know his name?"

"No, and when we asked, she said she only knew he worked in a school."

The furrows in the superintendent's brow were so deep he was beginning to look like an English bulldog. After a moment his face relaxed and he recovered his voice. "This is what we'll do. Call the radio stations and have them send a bulletin out instructing her to contact the police immediately."

"You can only do that in a case of life-and-death danger," Jonny pointed out.

The superintendent bellowed, "This is a case of life-and-death danger! Anna-Karin is the killer's next victim."

TWO HOURS LATER a frightened Anna-Karin called Superintendent Andersson's direct line. He told her that something serious had happened, but not what it was. He said that she had to come to the station immediately. He was sending a squad car to pick her up and bring her to the Göteborg Central Police Station.

Irene and Tommy found the wait tedious. Irene kept mulling over her thoughts.

Some people are monogamous. And now another fire had broken out.

ANNA-KARIN WAS WHITE as death and obviously terrified. As she walked between two uniformed patrol officers, she looked as if she were heading to her own execution. Irene felt sorry for her, but she also felt that this was a self-inflicted wound. She should have spoken up right from the start.

Irene ushered Anna-Karin into their office and thanked her Varberg colleagues for their help in bringing her in. Tommy started to exchange pleasantries with the young woman.

"I'll go get three cups of coffee," Irene chirped as she headed down the hallway. She wanted Anna-Karin to relax with Tommy before she would hit her full force.

Anna-Karin was sobbing when Irene came back. Tommy was sitting next to her and petting her hand comfortingly as he murmured consoling words. He was great at this. He glanced up at Irene with a look that said, Let's give her a few more minutes.

"I've just told her about the fire in her apartment and that it was arson," Tommy said.

Irene nodded and set the coffee mugs on the table. She calmly sipped from hers while she waited for Anna-Karin to stop crying. Just about the time Irene wondered if she'd ever stop, Anna-Karin began to pull herself together. She blew her nose into a paper tissue that Tommy pulled out of nowhere for her. Her voice shook as she asked, "Who would have done this? Why would anyone. . . ."

Quietly, Irene replied, "We can't say who it is, but we know that only you can answer why."

"Me?"

"Yes, you. You shared a secret with Linda. Poor Gunnela Hägg saw something that she shouldn't have seen. Now both Linda and Gunnela are dead."

Irene paused dramatically to let her words sink in before she continued. "A few evenings ago, Siv Persson received a visit from someone who knocked on her door and peered through her mail slot. Siv was home, and the killer could see her feet next to the door. Otherwise a fire might have broken out there as well. Who knows?"

"Why . . . why Siv?"

"She saw the murderer dressed as a ghost on the night of the murder. The only other witness was Gunnela Hägg, and now she's dead."

"How is Siv?"

"We've sent her away to a safe place. Now the killer has turned to you. Why?"

Although she cleared her throat a few times, Anna-Karin's voice wavered. "I . . . I don't know."

"Yes, you do. You know. Or you suspect. Your loyalty to

Linda is admirable but misguided. Remember, she's dead and you're next in line."

Anna-Karin began to shake. "That's . . . impossible. There can't be a connection."

With great care Tommy edged his way into the conversation. "Let us make that decision. Maybe what you know is just a tiny piece of the whole puzzle. But it might be the most important one, so much so that the killer is willing to murder you because of it." He placed his hand lightly over hers again. "You're protecting someone. Not Linda. Someone who is still alive. I have an idea who it might be, but you need to tell us his name."

Anna-Karin pulled her hand back and stared at Tommy wildly. He returned her look with calm, sympathetic brown eyes.

She opened and closed her mouth a few times, as if she were trying to catch her breath, her lips pale in her white face. Irene was afraid that she was going to pass out. Instead she exhaled slowly, and tears began to slide down her face again. Her voice sounded half suffocated, but she managed to say, "Sverker. Sverker Löwander." She received a fresh tissue and blew her nose again. It seemed that just pronouncing the doctor's name out loud broke a dam. "Sverker and Linda were . . . together. They were very much in love. Linda told me that they were going to get married as soon as his divorce from Carina was final."

Irene had had her suspicions but was surprised to have them confirmed. Sverker and Linda! He was twice her age! She gathered her scattered thoughts and remembered the effect he had even on herself. He had "it," as people used to say. The twins would say that he was "hot." Some have it, some don't. And some are monogamous by nature and some are not. Sverker Löwander had proved that he certainly wasn't monogamous when he left Barbro for Carina. This time he was having an affair with an even younger woman. Why hadn't he admitted to it?

"Do you know how long this has been going on?" she asked.

Anna-Karin nodded and swallowed. "Since the Christmas dinner. They were together after that."

"You know this for sure?"

"Yes. Linda told me how it happened. I promised never to tell anyone, but . . . I don't know. . . . It must be what you're talking about. . . . This must be the secret. Though I really don't understand why. Sverker loved Linda. He never would have hurt her. He's a gentle man." Anna-Karin fell silent and wiped her nose on a dry corner of the tissue.

"What else did Linda tell you? Did she say how it came about?"

"As I said, it was after the Christmas dinner for the employees. We always have a dinner before we close the hospital for Christmas vacation. We went to a restaurant. I guess they used to have the dinner at the hospital, but I wasn't there back then. Anyway, we had a Christmas smorgasbord, and there was dancing later. The older nurses went home early, but we younger ones stayed. Sverker Löwander stayed, too, and danced with all of us. He knows a bunch of different dances."

He's certainly old enough to have lived through all those dance styles when they were brand-new, Irene thought.

Anna-Karin paused for a moment to think. "We were all really loaded, too. We'd been drinking mulled wine, beer, and schnapps. Linda told me later that lightning seemed to strike them when they were out on the dance floor together. They probably slipped away in a taxi when we weren't looking."

"Where?"

"The hospital. They couldn't go to his place or hers. Pontus was still living with her, and Sverker had Carina. So they went to the on-call apartment."

Irene had the unpleasant thought that history certainly had a tendency to repeat itself. "Did they meet there often after that?"

Anna-Karin nodded. "Yes, that's the only place they could be together. On the weekends, when the hospital was empty. Then Linda broke up with Pontus. They probably could have gone to her place after that, but the neighbors. . . ."

"Linda told you that they were planning to get married?"

"Yes."

"When did she tell you that?"

Anna-Karin swallowed a few times before she replied in a whisper, "The weekend before she . . . died. She'd come to my place because I was alone. My guy was at work. We shared a bottle of wine. That's when she told me everything. Nobody else knew anything about it. But I guess she felt she had to confide in someone."

"Please excuse this personal question, but what is your boyfriend's name and why was he working on the weekend? We've heard he worked at a school, and they don't work on weekends, do they?"

A tiny smile appeared on Anna-Karin's otherwise troubled face.

"His name is Ola Pettersson, and he is the principal of Varberg's high school. He was one of the chaperones for a school dance Saturday evening, so we weren't together that weekend."

Irene returned to her main line of questioning. "So in that short space of time, Sverker had already proposed?"

"Yes, that's what she said."

"Did she say anything else? Did she feel threatened by anyone?"

"No, not at all. She was out of her mind with happiness."

Irene thought over what she'd just heard. Now she understood why Linda was at Löwander Hospital in the middle of the night. She asked carefully, "Do you believe that Linda was meeting Sverker the night she and Marianne were killed?"

Anna-Karin nodded and said with a shaking voice, "Yes, and I just can't figure it out. I've been beating my brains out over this. I was the only person who knew that they were together and meeting at the hospital. Why were Marianne and Linda killed? It can't have been Sverker. I know that. He loved Linda."

"How do you know that?"

"Because of what Linda said. And you police, too, must see that he's sick with sorrow! I can tell you he's aged ten years in just the few weeks since Linda disappeared—and was found."

Anna-Karin had turned her tissue into a hard ball by this point, and she started nervously plucking tufts from it. Irene sighed and reached for the wastebasket under her desk. She held it toward Anna-Karin as she said in a friendly manner, "You can throw it here."

For the first time that day, the nurse's pale face flushed again to the well-known bright red. It looked much healthier. Irene continued, "Have you thought of where you're going to live now that your apartment is gone?"

Anna-Karin started. "I haven't thought about that yet. I guess I'll have to stay with Mama for a while. She lives in Kungälv. I can take the bus to work from there."

"Good. We will need your telephone number and address there. However, do not go back to work until these murders have been cleared up. And under no circumstances are you to give your new address and phone number to anyone at Löwander Hospital. It's much too dangerous. Lie low for a while in Kungälv."

"Can I leave Kungälv to visit Ola in Varberg?" Anna-Karin asked meekly.

"Just keep in contact with him by phone for a few days. We have the feeling that we're going to solve this case and put the killer behind bars fairly soon."

Irene's voice sounded more certain than she felt, but Anna-Karin seemed to gather courage from her words.

Anna-Karin was given the opportunity to call her mother

and make arrangements. As she told her mother about the fire, the flood of tears returned, and the officers could hear that her mother was crying just as hard. Once she hung up, she seemed in a much better mood. Tommy arranged a police escort to Kungälv.

As soon as Anna-Karin left the room, Irene reached for the phone and called Löwander Hospital.

"YES, LINDA AND I have—had a relationship."

If Sverker Löwander had seemed hassled and worn out before, he was a total mess now. His eyes were sunken into their sockets. His hair was unwashed, and it appeared he'd lost twenty pounds during the past two weeks. His hands shook noticeably. He looks like he isn't eating or sleeping much at all, Irene thought.

"How long did your relationship go on?" Tommy asked.

"Right before Christmas. That's when we. . . ."

Sverker's voice trailed off and he stared dully at Tommy and Irene's messy bookshelf. Irene had placed herself on a chair by the door. Without discussing it beforehand, they had agreed that Tommy would lead the interrogation.

"Where did you usually meet?"

"The on-call apartment."

"Can you tell me what happened the night she disappeared?"

Löwander kept staring at the bookshelf, but he began to talk hesitantly. "We didn't see each other during the weekend."

He fell silent again. Patiently, Tommy asked, "Why not?"

"My daughter Emma left to go on a skiing vacation with friends. Carina and I were invited to an important party on Saturday. On Sunday, Linda was busy. She was helping Pontus pack up the last of his things."

"So you decided to meet at the hospital."

"Yes."

"Why did she come so late at night?"

Sverker held his head in his hands. "The ghost hour. No one on the night shift ventures out then. So there's little risk we'd be seen. We'd have a whole hour. . . ."

"Did she arrive on time?"

With his face still hidden in his hands, Sverker mumbled, "No. She never came. I never saw her alive again."

"Did you love her?" Tommy asked.

At first it seemed that Sverker didn't hear the question, but after a few moments he took his hands from his face and nodded slowly. "Yes, I did. Very much."

"So much that you were already discussing marriage?"

The doctor startled at this. For the first time, he looked directly at Tommy. "Discussing marriage? Who told you that?"

"So you weren't?"

Sverker seemed troubled and kept running his trembling hands through his dirty hair. Finally he replied, "Well . . . I did tell Linda that my marriage to Carina was in bad shape and that I was considering asking her for a divorce."

"Did you?"

"No."

"Why not?"

"I didn't have time before . . . it . . . happened."

"But Linda seemed to be very clear that you promised to marry her."

"She did? Well, we probably would have . . . eventually."

"Let's go back to the night of the murder. Tell us what happened while you were waiting for Linda."

"I was up in the apartment at eleven-thirty. I got undressed and got into bed. I tried to read for a while. Midnight came, and then it was a few minutes past."

"Were you worried?"

"Not really. I thought she might have been held up and was running late. The minutes kept ticking away, and she didn't come." He looked at his shaking hands and took a deep breath. "At exactly twelve-fifteen, the power went out. I had just looked at the clock. At first I was irritated, but then I heard the respirator alarm go off. I leaped out of bed, threw on some clothes, and you know the rest. During everything that happened, I kept wondering where Linda was. It was as if I had a premonition."

"Nurse Siv said that you took her flashlight and went to the operating rooms through the ICU's back door. You saw no trace of Linda or Marianne?"

"No. Of course I was looking for both of them. I didn't see anything. But I did feel as if I were being watched. Down in the entrance foyer . . . while I was waiting for the police. I know it sounds crazy, but I had the strong feeling of being observed. And I'm not superstitious."

"You don't believe it was the hospital ghost?"

"No. Every decent hospital that's been around for a while has a ghost, and ours is called Tekla. If that old nurse hadn't hanged herself in the attic, there would have been another ghost story about someone else."

"So if it wasn't a ghost watching, it must have been a human being."

"Yes."

"But you have no idea who it might have been?"

For a moment Irene felt that Sverker was hesitating; the expression in his eyes was difficult to interpret. He looked down before he answered, "No."

"Then . . . let's move on to something else that happened here. What were you doing last night at twelve?"

"Last night? I slept. I actually slept for the first time since . . . it happened. Six hours in a row. I think I fell asleep at eleven-thirty. Probably had something to do with the wine."

"Wine?"

"Carina had opened a bottle the night before last, and there was half a bottle left. She was making beef stew for dinner and put the bottle on the table. Red wine went with the food, so I had two glasses. It was just enough to knock me out."

"Were Carina and Emma at home?"

"Emma was already asleep when I went to bed. Carina finishes work late on Tuesdays. She teaches aerobics all evening and usually isn't home until eleven-thirty at the earliest."

"Did you hear her when she came home?"

"Yes, she arrived around the usual time, and I heard her come in before I drifted off. Why are you asking?"

"But you didn't see or speak with each other after that?"

"No, I was asleep by the time she came upstairs."

Tommy told the doctor about the arson at Anna-Karin Arvidsson's apartment. He also said that Anna-Karin would not be returning to work until the threat to her life was eliminated. In other words, when the killer was caught.

As Tommy was telling the story, Irene saw how Sverker had quietly withdrawn into his head. He had fastened his gaze back onto their bookshelf, and it was doubtful that he'd heard what Tommy was saying.

"HE SUSPECTS SOMETHING — OR knows something," Irene said.

"Why do you think so?" Tommy asked.

"When you were telling him about the arson at Anna-Karin's, I had the feeling he only half heard your words. He was thinking about something else."

"Yes, but he's at the end of his rope. Maybe he couldn't listen to any more bad news."

"Maybe not." Irene wasn't convinced, but there wasn't any evidence to back up her feeling. For now it would just have to wait. She changed the subject. "So this story comes back to fire again."

"Fire? Are you thinking about the garden shed and Mama Bird?"

"Yes, and also the fire ten years ago when the doctor's mansion burned down. So there are three fires. Let's think about the fire at the mansion. Who was involved in that story?"

"Barbro, Carina, and Sverker."

"And which of these three would have reason to set the other two?"

Tommy thought about it. "In principle, all three."

"That's right. Barbro lives alone and can come and go as she pleases now that her children are living in the United States."

"But what would be her motive?"

"Revenge. Hate."

"Maybe. As for Sverker and Carina, it would be much harder. They live together and know where each other should be."

"Do they? I think they live fairly separate lives. As far as the garden shed goes, either one of them could have set that fire. They didn't meet up until it was time to go to that party. Before then anyone could have arranged the candle and the rags. Neither of them has an alibi. Their daughter, Emma, was away on winter break. They didn't have to worry about her. Sverker says he was at the hospital looking through construction bids. Notice that he was at the scene. Two hours after he leaves the building, the fire breaks out. Carina said she was exercising in her private gym and then went jogging. She came home a few minutes after Sverker. It's strange, too, that they were able to pull themselves together for a party after everything that had been going on at the hospital."

"Neither Linda nor Gunnela had been found yet when the garden shed burned."

"Right. But Linda had gone missing."

"Sverker had to keep a calm façade and not let Carina know how worried he was."

"Exactly. And Carina hasn't seemed all that affected by any of this. She is one cool lady."

"Yes, goal-oriented. She's decided to turn the hospital into a fitness center, and so it will be."

Silence spread through the room until Irene finally asked, "So which of the three do you think is behind it?"

"Not Barbro. She has nothing to gain by killing Linda, Marianne, or Gunnela. If she were guilty, she would have aimed at hurting Carina directly. Or killed her."

"My thoughts exactly. Barbro as a suspect is too far-fetched. It's been too long since they divorced."

"Either Sverker or Carina, then."

"Yes, but I can't see a motive for either of them."

"What are we missing? Which questions haven't been answered?"

Irene thought. "Why did Marianne have Linda's day planner in her pocket? And where is Marianne's flashlight?"

"Yep. We know that the killer needed the flashlight to light the way up the stairs to the attic. Also for hanging Linda up. Probably the killer used it to walk through the operating rooms, since there are no windows there. Going down the stairs would be easier. The street lamps and the moon would have lit the way. According to Siv Persson, it was almost as light as day."

"So where did the murderer put the flashlight?"

"Where do people put flashlights?"

Tommy stared at Irene. "Where? Well, I have one in the garage. And one in the closet, though that one's broken. And one in the car."

Irene nodded. The gears in her head began to turn. "I also have one in the car. As well as a towrope and a jack. But I don't keep a toolbox in my car. Do you?"

"Not in my car, no. I keep mine in the garage. I have a set of wrenches instead and a jack. I don't have a towrope."

"So you don't have a toolbox with a hammer and a screwdriver and the like either?"

"No. What's this toolbox idea?"

"Carina Löwander said they keep a toolbox in their car. She said she'd taken the screwdriver from the toolbox in order to break open the suitcases in the attic. I would like to take a good look at that toolbox."

"Why?"

"Because if there isn't one, Carina got a screwdriver from somewhere else, and I'm going to put my money on the security guard's room. And as you well know, someone also took a large pair of wire cutters and a few yards of flag rope."

BY PHONE IRENE was able to reach Sverker Löwander at home around six that evening.

"Why do you need to look at our garage and our cars?" Sverker asked her suspiciously.

Irene always had difficulty skirting around the truth, so she explained calmly, "We're looking for an instrument that matches some break marks we found. Perhaps a dull knife or a screwdriver. We have not found anything that fits at the hospital or in the security guard's room. So now we are going to go through all the homes of everyone involved. Even those of the victims." Irene added the last sentence to make it appear more like a routine search.

"Where did you find these break marks?"

"I can't tell you. It's part of the investigation. "

This usually stopped further questions, and it worked on Sverker Löwander.

"I'm driving Emma to her riding lesson. We're already late. I'm staying there until she's done at eight-thirty. We're seldom home before nine."

"Is Carina at home?"

"No, she won't be home until eleven-thirty."

This family certainly kept late hours, and the cars wouldn't be in the garage. Irene thought quickly. "Could you just leave your car in the garage tomorrow morning?"

Silence on the other end of the line. Finally, "Sure. Anything to get this over with. But we don't keep a lot of tools in our cars, so I imagine your search won't take long. There are not many tools in the garage either. I'm not fond of home improvement or woodworking or that kind of thing."

"It's good we can do this as efficiently as possible. It's just routine. Everyone must be checked systematically, and we can't leave anything to chance, as you probably know," Irene chirped. She was surprised that he swallowed her weak story but relieved he didn't question their right to search his cars and his garage. It would have been much more difficult if he'd asked for a search warrant and demanded to know what his legal rights were. Irene knew that her suspicions weren't enough to authorize a search warrant, and in any event it just would take too long.

Chapter 21

COLD RAIN POURED from the black skies and trickled down Irene's neck as she crossed the short stretch from her police car to the Löwanders' front porch. She felt it run in little streams from her hair onto her neck as she rang the doorbell and heard it echo within the house. After the third ring, she heard footsteps on the other side. The brickred door was opened slightly, and through the gap, Irene heard an angry, snakelike hiss: "Who's there?"

"Inspector Irene Huss. I spoke to your husband and—"

The door opened wide. Irene saw the white robe covering a disheveled figure in the dark hallway.

"Well, hello. Come on in. What time is it?"

The voice was now warm and inviting, not at all snakelike, as Carina Löwander let Irene inside.

"It's almost eight."

"Good grief! I've overslept! Excuse me for a minute. I have to check and make sure that Emma has gotten off to school."

"This won't take long. I talked to Sverker yesterday. Didn't he mention it?"

Carina stopped in the middle of her run up the stairs to the second floor. "No, he was already sleeping when I came home last night, and I was asleep when he left. We haven't talked since yesterday morning."

Irene wasn't surprised. She said easily, "It's about a routine check, you see. Every vehicle that was near Löwander Hospital needs to be checked both inside and out."

"Inside and out? Why?"

"So they can be eliminated from the investigation. There are marks from a tool we're trying to track down. I can't say anything else about it. For investigative reasons."

Carina appeared doubtful. On the other hand, to Irene's great relief, she didn't demand to see a search warrant either.

"I see. Well. . . ."

Irene said quickly, "You don't have to accompany me. If you could just give me the garage and car keys for a moment, I'll take care of it myself."

Still obviously doubtful, Carina walked over to a tall, narrow dresser near the hat rack. The white-lacquered front seemed covered with tiny drawers. Carina pulled open one of the top ones and took out two key rings. She cast a brief, suspicious glance into the narrow pewter-framed mirror over the dresser. Their eyes met in the mirror. Irene had been prepared for this and gave the appearance of calm friendliness. Carina pressed her lips together and turned back to Irene as she said, "Here. The garage key is on both these key chains. You can tell which one belongs to the BMW and which one belongs to the Mazda."

"Thanks. This will just take a few minutes. I'll be right back with the keys."

Irene went out into the downpour again. As she passed the police car, she motioned to Tommy to stay there. It would be just as well that someone kept an eye on the house and its mistress.

Irene lifted the heavy garage door and pulled it shut behind her. After a few seconds of searching, she found the light switch. The two-car garage was lit by a single weak bulb attached to the ceiling. The blue Mazda and the silver BMW stood next to each other. Irene decided to look through the BMW first.

The car's inside was meticulously clean. It was almost new, certainly not more than a few months old. The glove compartment held a pair of sunglasses and a package of gum. The trunk was just as empty. A spare tire, a jack, and a first-aid kit from the Red Cross were the only items in it.

The Mazda seemed more promising. It was a few years old and was not nearly as clean. There was an empty pop can and piles of candy wrappers on the floor by the backseats. The glove compartment was filled, but nothing in it interested Irene.

The trunk contained the usual mess of stuff found in old cars. There really was a bag of tools, but it had no screwdriver. It did have various wrenches, an oilcan, a small jack, and a lug wrench in the shape of a cross. She lifted the bag of tools out of the way so that she could look behind it.

The weak light suddenly flashed on a reflection—something made of steel—deep inside the truck. Irene reached forward to fish it out. When her hand, enclosed in its glove, cautiously wrapped itself around the cold metal, her heart skipped a beat.

She lifted her discovery in pinched fingers and stretched to hold it closer to the dim light to see it better.

A very familiar scent slammed open a subconscious alarm, and she reacted with lightning speed. Instantly, she threw the object back into the trunk, grasped the molded edge of the car, and leaped up to kick back as hard as she could with both feet. A thud told her she'd hit the person coming up behind her. A loud "Ooofff" and another thud against the garage door confirmed that her kick had been hard and well placed. Unfortunately, the attacker had also managed a hard hit. But instead of landing on Irene's head, where the blow had been aimed, it hit her high on her calf. She felt how the blow connected and heard a dry crack on her right leg. A second later her lower leg went numb and no longer supported her weight. Irene swung around, using her left leg, and saw Carina pulling herself up, using the garage door as support, her left hand pressed against her chest. Not for nothing did Irene think of a ninja warrior as she saw Carina dressed in black leggings and a tight-fitting black T-shirt, her well-trained muscles rippling under the thin fabric of the shirt.

Where was Tommy? Why hadn't he followed Carina inside? He should have seen her sneak into the garage! From the corner of her eye, Irene noticed a half-open door next to the garage. She realized that someone could go straight from the house into the garage. Tommy had no idea that Carina was in here and had just whacked Irene's lower leg with a large, heavy crescent wrench.

Carina had managed to stand and was searching for the wrench again. She groaned in pain as she moved, which Irene was happy to hear. Perhaps Carina's breastbone and a few ribs were broken. They were close to even strength, then, although Carina had found a weapon while Irene's hands were empty. Still, Irene was a highest-level jujitsu practitioner. On the other hand, Carina was unusually strong and buff—not to mention murderously insane.

As fast as she could, Irene shuffled deeper into the garage to get the car between herself and Carina. It was difficult maneuvering. Her numb leg hindered her. She exaggerated the difficulties in her movements to make her opponent overconfident. Triumph lit Carina's crazy eyes. She was grinning as she started toward Irene, who was now on the other side of the Mazda's hood. Carina stopped on her side of the car and fixed Irene in her gaze. For a long time, they stood silently facing each other. Finally Irene spoke.

"Carina, don't make your situation worse than it already is. My colleagues know that I am here in your house. You're already a suspect and won't be able to get away with this. There's no reason to attack me—"

Carina made a sound somewhere between a howl and a hiss. Then she leaped onto the hood of the car, brandishing the wrench, and swung her arm to give Irene a backhanded blow to the head.

This fit Irene's strategy. She took two steps back to find support against the wall. Now Carina would have to jump off the hood and cover that distance to reach her. She did so, pouncing like a cat, the wrench still in a backhand swing. She was totally unprepared when Irene stepped forward and blocked her blow with her lower arms. Before Carina had the chance to react, Irene turned to the right, keeping her grip on Carina's arm, and took her down in a shiho-nage. The adrenaline rush made her use more force in her control grip than she needed. Carina screamed and dropped the wrench without resistance. Irene snatched it up.

Luckily, her muscles remembered her old handball moves. She targeted the window next to the garage door, which was two meters above the cement floor and just beneath the ceiling. The pane broke with a loud crashing sound, and the wrench, with a metallic bang, fell to the ground outside. The sound of the glass breaking seemed to bring Carina back to life. She began to wriggle beneath Irene, her strong, sinuous body tensed. Carina was the stronger, but Irene was a master of fighting techniques. Sweat poured down Irene's back as she parried each of Carina's attempts to free herself. The woman seemed to feel no pain. Irene's only chance was to grip Carina's hand even harder. Finally Carina's wrist broke, and she began to howl uncontrollably. Beneath the sound of her yowling, Irene heard Tommy pounding on the locked garage door and yelling something she couldn't understand. Then she heard running steps. A second later she heard the sound of a car screeching to a stop and Tommy's head and shoulders popped up on the other side of the broken window. She realized he'd parked the squad car under the window and had climbed onto its hood. He used the wrench to knock away the rest of the glass in the window frame. He was able to reach his hand in and unlock the window, which was wide enough for him to wiggle through and then slide down feet first. Irene felt her leg pound and throb. Her strength was ebbing, and she was relieved to have backup.

Tommy took out the handcuffs, and between the two of them they were able to cuff Carina, who yelled and writhed and somehow even managed to roll onto her back with her handcuffed wrists beneath her. Her broken wrist should have been unbelievably painful, but she kicked with undiminished power. Tommy managed to catch her legs and sit on them.

"As far as you're concerned, it's all over," he told her in a hard voice. "It's all over."

The result was immediate. Carina stopped still and stared at Tommy. If looks could kill, Tommy would have been her fourth victim. Fifth, if you included Nils Peterzén.

Chapter 22

"SHE REFUSES TO talk. Honestly, I don't think she even hears what I'm saying." The prosecutor, Inez Collin, looked concerned. She crossed her legs, one foot swinging impatiently. Irene admired her shoes, a deep burgundy made of kid leather, very expensive. They were the same color as her outfit, and Irene inwardly complimented her on her color sense. Inez wore a long jacket and a knee-length skirt. Her nails were impeccably manicured in deep wine red, and her blouse was a shimmering light gray silk. The same gray tinted the prosecutor's nylons and, incredibly, matched her eyes. How did she do it? Did she wear colored contact lenses? Probably not. Inez had always had the same gray eyes and platinum-blond hair in a severe ponytail. Irene couldn't help admiring her because she was good-looking and well-dressed, but Inez still didn't hold a candle to Carina Löwander.

Carina remained as silent as a nun. Three times a day, she did her workout in her cell. She played her gym routine on a tiny cassette player, the only item she was allowed. Her arm, in a cast, and her broken ribs didn't seem to trouble her in the least. When the investigators tried to question her, she sat with a faraway smile on her face, her eyes focused on the wall. A psychological evaluation had already been requested. It would take some time before her mental state could be assessed. Before then the investigative team wanted to clear up the last remaining questions.

"Our difficulty with finding proof is that only Carina herself can answer how the murders actually took place—and why. We really don't have much. Our main evidence is the flashlight, of course, which was found in the trunk of her car. Can you believe she kept that?! Especially since it was engraved with the letters ICU and M.S. The hair and fingerprints in the suitcases were hers. Still, none of this proves that she was the killer. All we really have is the attack on Inspector Huss," Inez Collin concluded.

"She's been pretty damn good at eliminating any witnesses," muttered Superintendent Andersson.

"She missed one," Birgitta Moberg said, then pausing for dramatic effect. "Siv Persson. I called her in London last night. She's returning home this afternoon with her son."

Jonny snorted. "She'll never admit that it wasn't a ghost."

"But she already has. I think it was her initial shock that made her believe she'd seen a ghost. On the phone she told me, 'That image is turning around in my head. I'll figure out who it was soon.' Maybe she recognized Carina as the ghost nurse after all," Birgitta concluded.

"That lady is completely nuts," Jonny said.

Irene carefully shifted her leg, which was in a cast. It was itching terribly. The operation on her muscles and tendons had gone well, but she'd have to wear the cast for several weeks more. Thankfully, no bone had been broken. At least osteoporosis wasn't showing up yet.

Inez Collin looked at Irene's leg thoughtfully. She cocked her head and finally said, "A cast on a leg looks more dramatic than one on a wrist."

The assembled group of investigators raised their eyebrows. The prosecutor said pensively, "I'm thinking about Carina's personality. My impression is that she believes she is above other people. Smarter. Stronger. More beautiful. She seems to believe she's entitled to use whatever methods she wants to reach her goals. Sociopathic. I believe she's as vain as other sociopaths. Extremely vain, in fact. Perhaps we should use that."

Inez quickly sketched her strategy. Irene protested at first, but then let herself be convinced. It was worth a try.

THEY BORROWED A wheelchair from Central. Irene sat down in the chair, and her colleagues helped unfold the footrest. With her leg sticking straight out, she definitely appeared pathetic, defenseless, and vulnerable.

Fredrik Stridh was playing her caretaker. The chair's wheels burned rubber as he cleared the corner to catch the elevator. He punched the top button, and soon they started their journey up to the prison floors.

CARINA HAD JUST had a shower and was drying her hair with a towel. The cold cell smelled like expensive perfume with an undertone of coconut, the same aroma that had alerted Irene's subconscious that day in the garage. So far Carina's prison stay had not even made her tan fade. *Hard to believe that this woman is a serial killer*, Irene thought.

Fredrik went in first and said, "You have a visitor." Without waiting for an answer, he went back to the hallway and returned pushing Irene in her wheelchair. Carina stopped in the middle of drying her hair and stared straight at Irene, still not saying a word.

Fredrik said, "It's crazy what you did to poor old Irene Her leg practically fell off. She's on months of sick leave."

Irene fumed inwardly. Fredrik was taking his role a little too seriously; he was overstepping the script as well. Carina did not appear to react, but there was a touch of curiosity in her eyes as she regarded Irene's cast.

Irene hurried to take over from Fredrik. "You're really strong. This was the worst fight I've ever been in. I told everyone you were the strongest and smartest person I've ever come up against. You are in fantastic shape."

She stopped talking, wondering if she'd spread it on too thick. Perhaps not, because Carina was starting to show the hint of a smile. At least she appeared to be listening. Encouraged, Irene continued. "The cleverest bit was when you decided to dress up in Nurse Tekla's old uniform from the suitcase. If anyone saw you, they'd think they'd seen the hospital ghost. Very clever."

To Irene's surprise, Carina answered. "It went just as I planned. Those superstitious old broads really believed I was the ghost." There she stopped, but her expression was no longer vague. She looked downright smug.

"What I don't understand is why Linda had to die, even though she tried to get her claws into your husband. . . ." Irene started.

Carina's eyes were bottomless pits of hate as she replied, "I don't give a damn what she and Sverker were up to in the on-call apartment! It was my hospital and my plan to make it into Göteborg's best-ever fitness center. All that work I put into the drawings and plans. And then that little piece of shit tries to convince Sverker to get a divorce."

"Did he say he wanted a divorce?" Irene said, pretending to be outraged.

"I heard them!" Carina stopped and gave Irene a suspicious look, but Irene was ready and made a sympathetic face. Carina was encouraged. She continued, "I was at the door to the on-call apartment and heard them. It was the first weekend after we returned from Thailand. Sverker suddenly had to go to the hospital. I knew what was going on, but I pretended not to. I've been through it before. And twelve years ago I was the one doing the same thing. Ha! So I followed them. . . . I opened the door—and I heard them. . . ."

Carina pressed her lips together. Her eyes thinned to slits.

Softly, she hissed, "I couldn't allow that. My plans . . . my hospital . . . It was her own fault she had to die. She could have kept on with the affair as long as she pleased, but she wanted to get married. That whore! No way could she marry him. I had no money to get the building on my own, so I could only keep it through Sverker. And we are married, after all." Carina lifted her chin defiantly and looked right at Irene, who nodded her agreement.

Irene phrased her next question carefully. "How did you get into the building? You'd given Sverker the main key, hadn't you?"

Carina nodded slyly and said in a confidential tone, "I didn't just find the drawings in Hilding's suitcase. There was a key chain as well, with the mansion key and the hospital key. They hadn't ever bothered to change the locks. Of course Hilding had a master key. Sverker had missed that fact completely!"

Carina beamed in triumph, very pleased with herself.

"When Sverker called and said that he had to stay late that night, I knew right away that she was going to be there, and I knew what time, too. Sverker has no imagination. I had hidden the uniform at home already, so I just took it with me in the car and changed in the grove. You should have seen me slipping across the lawn. If anyone had seen me, they'd have had a heart attack." She broke out in scornful laughter that made the hair on the back of Irene's neck stand on end.

Suppressing a shudder, Irene said, "God, you were clever. Though someone did see you. The homeless woman who was staying in the garden shed. Did you know she was there?"

Carina looked cross. "I noticed her during Christmas break when I was searching for the drawings. What a disgusting woman! I knew she was living in the shed. I'd forgotten her that night, but I knew who it was when I read the newspaper the next day. Since she'd seen me . . . I thought it'd be better if she disappeared."

"She'd seen you enter the hospital. Did you sneak in before or after Linda arrived?" Irene asked cautiously.

"Before. I was waiting for her. She sure looked surprised that last minute of her life." Again that horrible laugh filled the cell.

Irene let her finish before she asked, "But what had Marianne done to you? How did she threaten your plans?"

A wrinkle appeared between Carina's brows. "She heard me and Linda. That bitch Linda was carrying a little backpack, and she threw it down the stairs when I . . . grabbed her."

"So you were at the top of the stairway right outside the surgical ward?"

"Yes, right against the elevator. I only had to take one step to get to her as soon as she got off."

Irene shivered. "So unbelievably well thought out. But then Linda threw her backpack down the stairs, and Marianne heard it?"

"Yes, I went down to get that backpack, and I heard Marianne's key in the ICU door. I'd just made it back up the stairs, but there was no way to get rid of Linda. So when that incredibly stupid night nurse began walking up the stairs and yelling 'Hello? Linda, is that you?' I knew that I had to shut her up, too. And so I did."

"With the rope you used to hang Linda later?"

"It was the only thing I had."

"And then you carried Linda up inside the door to the attic, then rode the elevator with Marianne's body down to the basement. How did you get the idea to cut the electricity in the hospital?"

"I needed time. The business with that night nurse took more time than I'd planned. I didn't want Sverker to go all through the hospital looking for her. Not before I'd . . . finished."

"So everything went according to plan in the end." Irene tried to sound admiring.

Without warning, Carina leaned forward and whacked Irene's cast. Irene's cry of pain was not an act.

"Hurts, doesn't it?" Carina said contentedly.

Irene decided to whimper a bit before she asked another question. "Why did you go down the main staircase? There was the risk that Siv Persson would see you. And she did."

A new wrinkle appeared on Carina's brow when she heard the night nurse's name. She sat quietly for a while before she said, "As I was about to come down from the attic, I heard Sverker opening the ICU door. I realized he was looking for Marianne, and probably Linda, too, so I walked quickly through the surgical ward and then down the main staircase. And that idiot night nurse did see me, but she looked about to faint from fright. I had counted on that."

A self-satisfied smile played on the edges of Carina's mouth. An unnatural gleam came into her eyes as she bent close to Irene, who steeled herself for another blow to her leg. Instead, to her surprise, Carina began to whisper. "I heard Sverker following me. He took care of that confused nurse and left his flashlight with her. Then he walked down the stairs. I was so close to jumping out just to scare him, but I stood in the shadows and watched him as he opened the front door for the police. Then I went down the stairs, through the basement, and then up the back stairs and out the back door."

Carina's triumph surrounded her like an aura.

Irene felt a creeping feeling of sheer horror down her back.

Without showing her feelings, she said ingratiatingly, "Just think how you managed to get rid of Linda's bicycle. Because you did that, we were fooled into thinking she wasn't still in the hospital."

"It was easy to ride a bike on the frozen lawn. Still, it was so dark in the park and down by the stream that mostly I had to push it. I shoved the bike under the bridge and took off the nurse's clothes."

"Were you wearing different clothes underneath?" Irene made her eyes wide. She was laying it on thick.

"Of course. Tights and a black wool sweater. Though it was cold in the attic, I got pretty sweaty when I was . . . busy with Linda."

A short moment of silence.

"So did you park the car behind the grove of spruce trees?" Irene asked.

"Yes. It was just a few meters from the grove to the bridge. No one saw me."

"You could have frozen to death. It was fifteen below."

"I had my coat in the trunk."

Irene realized that that was the moment Carina had made her mistake. She must have thrown Marianne's flashlight into the trunk without thinking. She was under a lot of stress, after all. Irene decided not to bring up the flashlight. Carina probably didn't want to hear about any mistakes.

"You were unbelievably thorough at getting rid of all the evidence. I can understand how you saw Siv Persson as a threat. She could have recognized you, of course. But why Anna-Karin Andersson?"

Carina appeared reluctant to answer. Irene realized why. The arson attempt had gone wrong—Anna-Karin hadn't died. And plans gone wrong were the last thing Carina would want to discuss. Nevertheless, to Irene's surprise, Carina suddenly started to talk.

"I knew that Anna-Karin and Linda were best friends. Linda said to Sverker that she didn't even tell her best friend about their relationship, and Sverker had asked who that was. Linda said, 'Anna-Karin.'"

"So you heard all that by listening outside the door?"

"I couldn't take it for granted that Linda told the truth. She still could have said something to Anna-Karin."

It was uncanny how intuitive Carina was. Linda actually

had told her best friend everything, just a week after that conversation.

"I don't know how you found your way after you'd sabotaged the electricity," Irene said.

Carina appeared surprised as she answered. "You got that, didn't you? You found the flashlight. I'd only remembered it . . . when you went to our garage."

"So that was Marianne's?"

"Yes, indeed."

"And we found a day planner in her pocket. Did you see it?"

"No, but I don't care about that."

Marianne had Linda's day planner in her pocket when she was murdered. Only one thing could have happened—it had fallen from her backpack on its tumble down the stairs, and Carina hadn't found it when she ran to grab the backpack. But Marianne had found it, opened it, seen that it was Linda's, and therefore was calling Linda's name when she walked up the stairs into the hands of her killer.

"You set fire to the garden shed to get rid of the uniform, but also to send us chasing after red herrings. And you wanted to eliminate all traces of Gunnela Hägg."

Carina looked at Irene with empty eyes. "Her name was Gunnela Hägg?"

"That's right."

Carina didn't answer. She stared at the wall with that cold, scornful smile on her lips. She had sunk back into her own thoughts and didn't pay any more attention to Irene.

Irene nodded at Fredrik. He stood up from his place by the door and pushed the wheelchair out of the cell.

Once they'd reached the hallway, Fredrik snapped off the tape recorder hidden behind Irene's back. They wouldn't be able to use the tape in the courtroom, but it would certainly help the prosecutor prepare her case.

• • •

"ANYBODY WANT TO go to the pub and have a beer with me?"

Kurt Höök stuck his red-haired head through the doorway to Irene and Tommy's office.

"How about an hour from now? We're just about through wrapping up our reports on the Löwander Hospital murders," Tommy said.

Kurt nodded and looked at Irene. "You know where you'll find me."

He disappeared down the hallway. Tommy grinned at Irene. "That Höök guy—what a charmer!"

"You got that right!"

Tommy became serious and regarded Irene thoughtfully. "Talking about charmers, have you told Sverker Löwander the truth about his background?"

"No. Have you?"

"No."

Irene reached for her crutches and stood up. "Well, now I believe it's time for us to go have that beer."

"Yep."

Epilogue

IT WAS A starry night. The party at Tommy and Agneta's place had been pleasant, but Irene had had a bit too much wine. Luckily, Krister was the chauffeur for the evening. He had to work on Sunday, another reason they were on their way home already, just past the stroke of midnight.

They were practically the only ones on Delsjövägen. Suddenly Sammie began to whine in the backseat. They'd had to bring him because neither of the twins was at home that evening.

"Darn it all, we forgot to let the dog out before we started home," Krister said.

Irene awoke from her wine-induced slumber and looked around. When she realized where they were, she said, "Pull over there. You can park just past the bridge. Lots of people take their dogs for walks there. I know that for sure. It's been just four weeks since I was tramping through the poo."

Krister turned, drove over the bridge, and parked the car. Irene got out and stood on her somewhat unsteady legs. "You stay in the car," she said. "I'll take Sammie."

She drew the chilly night air deep into her lungs. In spite of the wine, she felt energized; after walking the dog, she'd be almost sober.

Sammie was eager and excited as he started sniffing around the spruce grove. Lots of new contacts! A veritable *People* magazine for dogs. I'm a tiny dachshund who'll have puppies in a week! German shepherd warns once and for all—this is my spot! No one knows now, but a female poodle and a male Doberman had a tryst here! Sammie sniffed to his heart's content with his nose to the ground.

Irene hung on to the leash.

It took her a while to realize that they were heading to the hospital park. Sammie wandered toward the lilac arbor. It was dark, and Irene stumbled a few times. Sammie made his mark and pulled at the leash. There was something interesting in the bushes.

Irene held tightly to Sammie, but both dog and mistress jumped high into the air when a deer leaped out.

Irene looked up at the quiet, dark building. The black windows seemed to glare back at her. Involuntarily, her gaze wandered to the tiny attic window. Beyond that glass two nurses had been found dead, fifty years apart. Irene shivered at the thought. A moment later she froze in terror.

Behind the windowpane, Irene believed she saw the outline of a person standing close to the glass. A slightly silver-glowing palm pressed against the pane. It did not disappear until the rest of the figure began to dissolve into the darkness.

Turn the page for a sneak preview of the next
Inspector Irene Huss investigation

THE GOLDEN CALF

Prologue

February 2000

FUZZY IMAGES FROM the bank's security cameras flickered across the TV screen. Three masked men were aiming weapons at customers and employees inside the building. The robbers wore dark overalls, black ski masks, and black gloves. Only their eyes were visible. Behind the counter, one of the men threw a large nylon bag at a cashier. A customer lay prone on the floor in the middle of the room while the second robber aimed a rifle directly at his head. The third armed man was posted near the entrance, his back to the camera. He kept glancing nervously in all directions. Then, in the upper corner of the picture, the glass door opened, emitting two spindly legs in calf-high leather boots. The robber at the entrance stepped forward and pulled an elderly woman into the frame. He spun her around by her arm, and she lost her balance and fell.

The movements of all three robbers were jerky, since the camera recorded footage in short sections in order to save film. Nevertheless, it was obvious that the robbers were becoming increasingly nervous. The man behind the counter was making threatening gestures at the cashier, who filled the bag with bills as fast as she could with shaking hands. The masked man seemed to become irritated as something shifted near him, and he hit the cashier across the mouth with the rifle barrel. She fell to the floor, out of sight.

• • •

". . .THESE BRUTAL PICTURES from inside the bank building." The female newscaster's well-modulated voice issued from the speakers of the wide-screen television. "A fourth man was waiting outside in a getaway car, a red Saab 9000, according to one witness. A similar car was reported stolen in Arvika a few hours earlier, which the police suspect was the same vehicle. A nationwide alert has been issued. The elderly woman seen in the video suffered a broken hip, and the cashier lost several teeth; both women have been admitted to the hospital. The hostage and remaining bank staff have received help from a crisis team. It is believed that the robbers got away with more than a million kroner. This is the fourth-largest bank robbery in northern Värmland this year, and so far there have been no arrests. The low police presence in the area may be why the criminals targeted this bank. Often, the only police car in the area may be more than twenty miles away, which delays response time."

"SUCH ANIMALS," THE man sitting on the sofa growled as he clicked off the television. There was a moment of silence after the picture faded.

"How horrible!" The man's young female companion laughed nervously. "Can you believe he was pointing that rifle right at her head? She must have been terrified!" She paused as the man filled her wine glass, then she continued, "But honestly, Philip, one million kroner. That's not bad at all. It's probably the easiest way to get hold of a lot of money fast." She giggled as she sipped.

"Too dangerous. You could be shot and killed."

The man lifted his glass to his nose and inhaled slowly, enjoying the aroma.

"Mmm. Sun-ripened blackberries with a hint of vanilla. Hope they catch those guys and throw them in the slammer. And let them rot there, I say," said the man who had embezzled a hundred million dollars.

Chapter 1

Detective Inspectors Irene Huss and Tommy Persson parked on the street between a blue-and-white patrol car and the anonymous car of the forensic technicians. The garage entrance had been blocked off by a sloppily parked silver Mercedes Cabriolet, its top raised.

The detectives hunched their shoulders against the harsh sea wind as they walked toward the front door. The house was brand new, but the surrounding grounds were nothing but clay and mud. One step off the stone pathway and a shoe would be sucked off by the muck. Despite the lack of landscaping, Irene saw that the location of the house was fantastic, high on a hill with a magnificent, wide-open view of Askim Bay. How could anyone afford property like this? The villa itself was all terracotta brick and huge panes of glass. Obviously the architect had spared no expense.

Tommy stopped to take a good look at the Cabriolet. He gave a silent whistle and sent Irene a meaningful glance. They continued to the front door and rang the bell. A female officer opened the door immediately. She looked young and serious.

"Hi. I'm Tommy Persson, and this is Irene Huss from Violent Crime."

"I'm Stina Lindberg," the uniformed woman replied. "The technicians have just arrived."

A baby was crying inside the house. Stina glanced nervously in that direction. "It's the baby," she explained. "Their baby. . . .

His wife found him . . . her husband . . . when she got home."
Stina's cheeks were pale, and she was obviously struggling to
control her discomfort. A murder would rattle anyone, but
everything was much worse when children were part of the
picture.

A tall policeman in complete protective gear appeared in
the spacious hallway. Both Irene and Tommy knew Criminal
Inspector Magnus Larsson well and were happy to see him. As
Irene and Tommy pulled on their own protective overalls, hats,
plastic gloves, and booties, Magnus gave them the rundown.

"A woman called 112 and said she'd found her husband
shot. We arrived within fifteen minutes of the alarm. She was
calm at first, but she broke down after a few minutes. She had
her mother's telephone number programmed into her cell
phone, so I've called her. Someone has to take care of the
child. Her mother is on the way, but she was in Borås when I
reached her."

"Who lives here?" asked Irene.

"Sanna Kaegler-Ceder and Kjell B:son Ceder."

The names felt vaguely familiar to Irene, but she couldn't
place them. She noticed that Tommy also reacted to the
names, but before Irene could ask, loud shrieks from an
unhappy baby echoed through the house. All three police
officers hurried toward the noise.

The living room was large, with a huge glass wall facing the
sea. Irene had been right—the view was fantastic. A young
woman sat hunched in a round swivel chair covered in leather
the color of eggshells. Eight identical chairs ringed an elliptical
glass table, which sat on a matching shag carpet, which popped
against the dark terra-cotta tile floor. Oversized modern oil
paintings stood out against almost-pure-white walls.

Irene and Tommy nodded at two uniformed officers
standing beside the woman, before taking a closer look at the
unmoving figure curled in the chair. Irene realized she had

seen the woman's face before. Again, she had no idea where or when.

Sanna Kaegler-Ceder stared into space with empty eyes. Her pale complexion and stiff expression made her face seem mask-like. At her feet was an infant in a blue corduroy baby bouncer. Irene guessed the baby was, at most, six months old. He was screaming, his face bright red from the exertion.

The glass wall continued to another doorway leading to an octagonal room enclosed in glass. In the center was a spiral steel staircase to the second floor. Sanna Kaegler-Ceder's husband lay on his back at the foot of the stairs. The two technicians near him were setting up their camera equipment. They nodded to Irene and Tommy.

"We need fifteen minutes," the older of the two said.

"That's fine," Tommy replied.

Irene walked to Sanna and lightly touched her shoulder. Sanna didn't appear to notice.

"Hello," Irene said softly. "My name is Irene Huss. Do you think your baby might want something to eat?"

The woman's only reaction was a slight flutter of her eyelashes.

Irene sighed and picked up the wailing bundle of a baby. A noticeable odor cried out for a diaper change.

"Come on, Tommy. Help me find the changing table and some baby food," Irene said with determination.

"What? Me?"

"It hasn't been that long since you changed your own baby's diapers."

"You're right. OK, off to find a dry diaper." Tommy made a raspberry sound and tickled the baby's tummy. The baby interrupted his crying to peer up at him.

After a few minutes of opening and shutting doors, they found a large bathroom with rose marble walls. There was an enormous changing table, complete with every possible item for baby care. The baby wore a soft denim romper suit and a light blue sweater with MADE IN NEW YORK written in flashy silver across the chest. As Irene lifted him from the table, his bottom dry, he began to fuss again. His hunger was making itself known.

Tommy had already gone to find the kitchen. When Irene, carrying the baby in her arms, followed, Tommy held up a bottle he'd found in the refrigerator in triumph.

"Hey, buddy! Now you'll get some grub!" Tommy said as he began to heat the bottle in the microwave.

On the counter was a plastic bottle top, which Tommy screwed in place with a practiced motion. He instinctively checked the milk's temperature against the inside of his wrist, then handed the bottle to Irene. Even though it had been years since his youngest child's last bottle, the preparation routine came back quickly.

Irene looked down at the baby, who was greedily sucking down the milk. The ultra-modern kitchen glistened in glass and brushed steel. Irene looked for somewhere to sit down, but there were only tall stools next to a bar counter. Irene leaned against one of the stools as the little boy noisily slurped the last drops. Then she lifted him to her shoulder and patted him on his diapered bottom. A huge burp was her reward.

"Huss, now your jacket will look like a seagull pooped on it." Tommy grinned. He found a roll of paper towels on a steel cylinder and helped Irene rub off the milk stain.

As they walked back to the living room, the baby fell asleep. Irene set him back into the baby bouncer and spread a soft, yellow blanket from a nearby chair over him.

Sanna hadn't moved. She appeared catatonic. She wore light-brown pants and a cobalt-blue top with a deep décolletage. Between her breasts glittered a large cross with closely set white and blue gemstones. Their crystal clear sparkle could hardly have come from anything other than authentic sapphires and diamonds. Sanna Kaegler-Ceder walks around with a fortune around her neck, thought Irene. And her reserve capital is on her left ring finger.

One of the force's crime scene technicians, Åhlén, stuck his bald head through the doorway to the octagonal room. He motioned to the officers, and Irene and Tommy walked over. As was his habit, Åhlén pushed his thick bottle-bottom glasses up his stubby nose with his left forefinger before he spoke.

"I've already secured the wife's prints and taken her jacket. No apparent spatter, but we'll have to wait for analysis. This is the scene of the crime. We haven't found the murder weapon yet."

"Are you absolutely sure this is the crime scene?" asked Irene.

"No doubt about it. See for yourself," replied Åhlén, gesturing toward where the body lay stretched out.

Kjell B:son Ceder was well-dressed in a dark suit. Two bullet holes marked his forehead, and his head lay in a pool of blood. A broken glass lay on the floor nearby, and the unmistakable scent of whiskey hovered.

"He's been dead for hours. Rigor mortis has set in completely," the technician continued.

"Looks like an execution. Two shots right into the brain," Tommy stated.

Irene was surprised at how much older than his wife Kjell B:son Ceder was. Even in death he was a good-looking man. His hair, though thickly matted with blood, was steel gray and full. All of a sudden, Irene realized where she'd seen him before: for the past few years, he had been the restaurant king of Göteborg. Irene's husband was a head chef at a competing restaurant, so she'd often heard Ceder's name. Krister worked at Glady's Corner, one of the finest restaurants in Göteborg, with a star in the international restaurant guide. The other two starred restaurants in Göteborg were owned by Kjell B:son

Ceder. One was located in the twenty-eight story Hotel Göte-borg, one of Göteborg's tallest buildings, which Ceder also owned. Whenever Irene was in her boss's office, she would see the mighty silhouette of the hotel rising above the rest of the city from Superintendent Sven Andersson's window. Slightly to the southwest, she could see the two Gothia Towers next to Svenska Mässan, the Swedish Conference Center. Gothia Towers also had a hotel and restaurant and was the main com-petitor of Hotel Göteborg.

"Stridner has promised to show up in all her imperial maj-esty," Åhlén said. "If I'm not mistaken, here she is now."

Irene and Tommy had also heard the energetic clack of high heels hitting the stone floor. No other person burst into a crime scene with quite the same tempo as Professor of Forensic Medicine Yvonne Stridner.

She swept through the entrance of the octagonal room, placed her bag on the floor, and took in the crime scene in one glance. Without greeting any of the officers, she got right to the point:

"Is this actually a murder?"

Irene, Tommy, and Åhlén all started in surprise. The pro-fessor rarely asked questions. Usually, she imparted certainties and issued commands.

"He's been shot. Two shots," said Åhlén dryly.

Without further commentary, the professor put on her pro-tective gown, gloves, and plastic booties. Just like her not to bother with protective clothing before entering a crime scene, thought Irene.

Stridner tossed her cape over a chair with a black oxidized steel frame and white leather cushions. Perhaps it was more comfortable than it appeared. There were five more chairs like it in the room as well as a matching table and chandelier.

Stridner walked over to the body and began her investiga-tion. Tommy nudged Irene with his elbow. "Let's go and try to talk to Sanna Kaegler-Ceder again."

Irene nodded. They could do nothing here until the body was removed, not even go up the spiral staircase to check the second floor.

Sanna Kaegler-Ceder was in the same chair, but she'd swiveled it toward the rain-streaked glass and was staring into the rapidly gathering twilight. The baby was fast asleep in his baby bouncer, blissfully unaware that he'd just become fatherless.

"Please forgive us for disturbing you at this sad time. My name is Tommy Persson, and I'm a detective. Are you able to answer a few questions?"

The woman did not move, just kept staring out at the autumn weather. When they were about to give up hope of response, she ducked her head slightly. Tommy interpreted this as a slight nod and asked a question quickly before she changed her mind.

"What time did you arrive home and find your husband's body?"

The woman swallowed a few times, then managed an answer. "I called . . . right away."

"The alarm came at four twenty-three P.M.," Magnus Larsson interjected.

"And the first patrol car arrived no more than fifteen minutes later?" asked Tommy.

"Correct," said the other detective.

Tommy turned back to Sanna and continued in a gentle voice, "Did you go to your husband before the police arrived?"

She shook her head slowly. "I saw that he was dead. All the blood. . . ."

"Where were you standing when you saw him?"

"At the entrance. . . ." Her voice failed her, and she swallowed hard.

"So you were standing at the entrance to this room?"

"Yes," she whispered.

It didn't seem possible, but the woman became even paler.

Her lips turned blue-gray, and Irene saw that she was about to faint.

"Come, let's have you lie down on the rug," Irene said as she helped Sanna to the floor. She lifted Sanna's lower legs a few centimeters, and the color slowly began to return to the woman's face. After a few minutes, Sanna said, "I'd like to sit up again." Irene helped her back into the chair. The young woman was still so pale that her face appeared to blend into the white leather. There was no question that she'd received a shock, though there was always the possibility she was reacting to committing a murder.

"When did you leave the house today?" asked Tommy.

"I didn't leave it today. The last time was yesterday afternoon."

"At what time?"

"Around four. We went to my sister's place to spend the night."

"Did you take your son with you?"

"Yes."

"So you spent the night with your sister?"

"Her husband was on call. We were both going to be alone that night anyway."

"Do you know who your husband planned to meet yesterday evening?"

"No idea." Her voice seemed tired and uninterested.

"When was the last time you spoke to your husband?"

"Yesterday at nine in the morning."

"Did he say that he had to meet someone that evening?"

"Not that I remember."

"Had you already made arrangements to spend the night at your sister's, or did you just decide to yesterday?"

"I called her yesterday around lunch. We'd been talking about doing this—having a nice evening with some good food and wine. She's also on maternity leave."

"Did you call up your husband and let him know that you were going to your sister's?"

"No."

"Why didn't you?"

"I'd told him that I might go when I talked to him on the phone that morning."

"So you didn't try to call him today?"

"No. He knew that Ludwig and I were at Tove's and not at home."

"Tove is your sister's name?"

"Yes. Tove Fenton. Her husband is a doctor. He was on call. . . ." Her voice sank to a whisper, and she didn't finish her sentence. Before any of the other police officers could ask another question, a young policewoman came in. Up until then, she hadn't moved from her post at the door. Irene remembered her first name was Stina, but she'd already forgotten her last name.

"The mother is here. That is, her mother." Stina motioned toward Sanna. They could hear an agitated female voice at the outer door.

"I have to know what's going on . . . my daughter! And Ludwig. . . ."

There was jostling at the doorway to the living room. Sanna's mother was trying to push inside, but two officers were holding her back. She was not as tall as her daughter, but she had the same pale coloring. Sanna shakily got up and walked toward her mother on unsteady feet.

"My dearest Sanna! What has been going on? The police called. . . ." Sanna's mother stopped talking the moment she saw the expression on her daughter's face. She stopped trying to force her way past the police. "Is it . . . Ludwig?" she asked in despair.

"Why are you wearing that ugly jacket?" asked Sanna—then she fainted.

About the author

HELENE TURSTEN WAS born in Göteborg on the Swedish west coast, where she lives today. As you have probably read on the back cover, she is in fact trained as a nurse and a dentist. After working as a nurse for three years, she decided to go to dental school. It was when she returned to school for her dental degree that Helene met her husband, who had been a policeman. They are still married more than 30 years later, with a daughter who is now an adult. The dog in the Irene Huss books, Sammie, is based on their real-life dog, who lived to the ripe old age of fifteen.

Helene spent ten years practicing dentistry before her career was curtailed due to rheumatic illness. That was when she turned to writing. Today she has written ten novels about Irene Huss and her colleagues at the police headquarters in Göteborg. The books have been translated into 18 languages.

There are also twelve 90-minute TV films that have been made featuring Detective Inspector Irene Huss. The films have been shown in many European countries. Helene wrote the story synopses and edited all the film scripts in collaboration with professional script writers. Working on the films has been a real kick for her, and she thinks, has also been good for her books. "There's a big difference between writing a book and writing a script for a film," Helene says. "When I am working with a film plot I have to think in pictures and within the limitations of a budget. It is very inspiring for me as a writer to think and work in a different way."

OTHER TITLES IN THE SOHO CRIME SERIES

Quentin Bates
(Iceland)
Frozen Assets
Cold Comfort

Cheryl Benard
(Pakistan)
Moghul Buffet

James R. Benn
(World War II Europe)
Billy Boyle
The First Wave
Blood Alone
Evil for Evil
Rag & Bone
A Mortal Terror
Death's Door

Cara Black
(Paris, France)
Murder in the Marais
Murder in Belleville
Murder in the Sentier
Murder in the Bastille
Murder in Clichy
Murder in Montmartre
Murder on the Ile Saint-Louis
Murder in the Rue de Paradis
Murder in the Latin Quarter
Murder in the Palais Royal
Murder in Passy
Murder at the Lanterne Rouge
Murder Below Montparnasse

Grace Brophy
(Italy)
The Last Enemy
A Deadly Paradise

Henry Chang
(Chinatown)
Chinatown Beat
Year of the Dog
Red Jade

Colin Cotterill
(Laos)
The Coroner's Lunch
Thirty-Three Teeth
Disco for the Departed
Anarchy and Old Dogs
Curse of the Pogo Stick
The Merry Misogynist
Love Songs from a Shallow Grave
Slash and Burn
The Woman Who Wouldn't Die

Garry Disher
(Australia)
The Dragon Man
Kittyhawk Down
Snapshot
Chain of Evidence
Blood Moon
Wyatt
Whispering Death
Port Vila Blues

David Downing
(World War II Germany)
Zoo Station
Silesian Station
Stettin Station
Potsdam Station
Lehrter Station
Masaryk Station

Leighton Gage
(Brazil)
Blood of the Wicked
Buried Strangers
Dying Gasp
Every Bitter Thing
A Vine in the Blood
Perfect Hatred

Michael Genelin
(Slovakia)
Siren of the Waters
Dark Dreams
The Magician's Accomplice
Requiem for a Gypsy

Adrian Hyland
(Australia)
Moonlight Downs
Gunshot Road

Stan Jones
(Alaska)
White Sky, Black Ice
Shaman Pass
Village of the Ghost Bears

Lene Kaaberbøl & Agnete Friis
(Denmark)
The Boy in the Suitcase
Invisible Murder

Graeme Kent
(Solomon Islands)
Devil-Devil
One Blood

Martin Limón
(South Korea)
Jade Lady Burning
Slicky Boys
Buddha's Money
The Door to Bitterness
The Wandering Ghost
G.I. Bones
Mr. Kill
The Joy Brigade

Peter Lovesey
(Bath, England)
The Last Detective
The Vault
On the Edge
The Reaper
Rough Cider
The False Inspector Dew
Diamond Dust
Diamond Solitaire
The House Sitter